A MAP OF DAYS

A MAP OF DAYS

THE FOURTH NOVEL OF

MISS PEREGRINE'S

PECULIAR CHILDREN

BY RANSOM RIGGS

DUTTON BOOKS

DUTTON BOOKS
An imprint of Penguin Random House LLC
375 Hudson Street
New York, NY 10014

CIP Data is available.

Printed in the United States of America
ISBN 9780525555636

10 9 8 7 6 5 4 3 2 1

Edited by Julie Strauss-Gabel
Design by Anna Booth
Text set in Sabon LT Pro

*N*ever have I doubted my soundness of mind as often as I did on that first night, when the bird-woman and her wards came to save me from the madhouse. That's where I was going, pinned between beefy uncles in the back seat of my parents' car, when a wall of peculiar children seemed to leap directly from my imagination into the driveway before us, aglow in our high beams like a formation of angels.

We skidded to a stop. A wave of dust erased everything beyond our windshield. Had I conjured their echo, some flickering hologram projected from deep within my brain? Anything seemed more believable than my friends being here, now. Peculiars had a way of making anything seem possible, but a visit from them was one of the few impossibilities of which I could still be certain.

It had been my choice to leave Devil's Acre. To go home again, where my friends couldn't follow. I had hoped that in returning I might sew together the disparate threads of my life: the normal and the peculiar, the ordinary and the extraordinary.

Another impossibility. My grandfather had tried to sew his lives together too and failed, estranged in the end from both his peculiar family and his normal one. In refusing to choose one kind of life over the other, he had doomed himself to lose both—just as I was about to.

I looked up to see a figure moving toward us through the clearing dust.

"Who the hell are you?" my dad said.

"Alma LeFay Peregrine," she replied, "Ymbryne Council leader pro tem and headmistress to these peculiar children. We've met before, though I don't expect you'd remember. Children, say hello."

CHAPTER ONE

*I*t's strange, what the mind can digest and what it resists. I had just survived the most surreal summer imaginable— skipping back to bygone centuries, taming invisible monsters, falling in love with my grandfather's time-arrested ex-girlfriend—but only now, in the unexceptional present, in suburban Florida, in the house I'd grown up in, was I finding it hard to believe my eyes.

Here was Enoch, splayed upon our beige sectional, sipping Coke from my dad's Tampa Bay Buccaneers tumbler; here was Olive, unstrapping her lead shoes to float ceilingward and ride circles on our fan; here were Horace and Hugh in our kitchen, Horace studying the photos on the fridge door while Hugh rustled for a snack; here was Claire, both mouths slack as she gazed at the great black monolith of our wall-mounted television; here was Millard, my mother's decor magazines rising from the coffee table and splitting in midair as he skimmed them, the shape of his bare feet imprinted into our carpet. It was a mingling of worlds I'd imagined a thousand times but never dreamed possible. But here it was: my Before and After, colliding with the force of planets.

Millard had already tried to explain to me how it was possible they could be here, apparently safe and unafraid. The loop collapse that had nearly killed us all in Devil's Acre had reset their internal clocks. He didn't quite understand why, only that they were no longer in danger of sudden catastrophic aging if they stayed too long in the present. They would get older one day at a time, just like I did, their debt of years seemingly forgiven, as if they hadn't spent most of the twentieth century reliving the same sunny day. It was undoubtedly a miracle—a breakthrough unprecedented in peculiar history—and yet how it had come to be was not half as amazing to me as the fact that they were here at all: that beside me stood Emma, lovely, strong Emma, her hand entwined with mine, her green eyes shining as they scanned the room in wonder. Emma, whom I'd so often dreamed about in the long, lonely weeks since my return home. She wore a sensible gray dress that fell below the knee, hard flat shoes she could run in if she had to, her sandy hair pulled back into a ponytail. Decades of being depended on had made her practical to the core, but neither the responsibility nor the weight of years she carried had managed to snuff the girlish spark that lit her so brightly from the inside. She was both hard and soft, sour and sweet, old and young. That she could contain so much was what I loved most about her. Her soul was bottomless.

"Jacob?"

She was talking to me. I tried to reply, but my head was mired in dreamy quicksand.

She waved at me, then snapped her fingers, her thumb sparking like struck flint. I startled and came back to myself.

"Hey," I said. "Sorry."

"Where'd you go?"

"I'm just—" I waved as if raking cobwebs from the air. "It's good to see you, that's all." Completing a sentence felt like trying to gather a dozen balloons in my arms.

Her smile couldn't mask a look of mild concern. "I know it must be awfully strange for you, all of us dropping in like this. I hope we didn't shock you too badly."

"No, no. Well, maybe a little." I nodded at the room and everyone in it. Happy chaos accompanied our friends wherever they went. "You sure I'm not dreaming?"

"Are you sure *I'm* not?" She took my other hand and squeezed it, and her warmth and solidness seemed to lend the world some weight. "I can't tell you how many times, over the years, I've pictured myself visiting this little town."

For a moment I was confused, but then . . . of course. My grandfather. Abe had lived here since before my dad was born; I'd seen his Florida address on letters Emma had kept. Her gaze drifted as if she were lost in a memory, and I felt an unwelcome twinge of jealousy—then was embarrassed for it. She was entitled to her past, and had every right to feel as unmoored by the collision of our worlds as I did.

Miss Peregrine blew in like a tornado. She had taken off her traveling coat to reveal a striking jacket of green tweed and riding pants, as if she'd just arrived on horseback. She crossed the room tossing out orders. "Olive, come down from there! Enoch, remove your feet from the sofa!" She hooked a finger at me and nodded toward the kitchen. "Mr. Portman, there are matters which require your attention."

Emma took my arm and accompanied me, for which I was grateful; the room had not quite stopped spinning.

"Off to snog each other already?" said Enoch. "We only just arrived!"

Emma's free hand darted out to singe the top of his hair. Enoch recoiled and slapped at his smoking head, and the laugh that burst out of me seemed to clear some of the cobwebs from my head.

Yes, my friends were real and they were here. Not only that, Miss Peregrine had said they were going to stay awhile. Learn about the modern world a bit. Have a holiday, a well-earned respite from the squalor of Devil's Acre—which, with their proud old house on Cairnholm gone, had become their temporary home. Of course they were welcome, and I was inexpressibly grateful to have them here. But how would this work, exactly? What about my parents and uncles, who at this very moment Bronwyn was guarding in the garage? It was too much to grapple with all at once, so for the moment I shoved it aside.

Miss Peregrine was talking to Hugh by the open fridge. They looked jarringly out of place amid the stainless steel and hard edges of my parents' modern kitchen, like actors who had wandered onto the wrong movie set. Hugh was waving a package of plastic-wrapped string cheese.

"But there's only strange food here, and I haven't eaten for centuries!"

"Don't exaggerate, Hugh."

"I'm not. It's 1886 in Devil's Acre, and that's where we had breakfast."

Horace burst from our walk-in pantry. "I have completed my inventory and am frankly shocked. One sack of baking soda, one tin of sardines in salt, and one box of weevil-infested biscuit mix. Is the government rationing his food? Is there a war on?"

"We eat a lot of takeout," I said, walking up beside him. "My parents don't really cook."

"Then why do they have this whomping great kitchen?" said Horace. "I may be an accomplished chef de cuisine, but I can't make something from nothing."

The truth was that my father had seen the kitchen in a design magazine and decided he had to have it. He tried to justify the cost by promising he would learn to cook and then throw legendary dinner parties for the family—but, like a lot of his plans, it fizzled after a few cooking lessons. So now they had this hugely expensive kitchen that was used mostly to cook frozen dinners and heat up day-old takeout. But rather than say any of that, I shrugged.

"Surely you won't perish of hunger in the next five minutes," Miss Peregrine said, and shooed both Horace and Hugh from the kitchen. "Now, then. You were looking a bit wobbly earlier, Mr. Portman. Are you feeling all right?"

"Better every minute," I said, a bit embarrassed.

"You may be suffering from a touch of loop lag," said Miss Peregrine. "Somewhat delayed in your case. It's absolutely normal among time travelers, especially those who are new to it." She was speaking to me over her shoulder as she moved through the kitchen, peeking inside each cabinet. "The symptoms are usually inconsequential, though not always. How long have you been feeling dizzy?"

"Only since you all got here. But really, I'm fine—"

"What about leaking ulcers, bunion clusters, or migraine headaches?"

"Nope."

"Sudden mental derangement?"

"Uh . . . not that I can remember?"

"Untreated loop lag is no laughing matter, Mr. Portman. People have died. Hey—biscuits!" She grabbed a box of cookies from a cabinet, shook one into her hand, and popped it into her mouth. "Snails in your feces?" she asked, chewing.

I choked back a snicker. "No."

"Spontaneous pregnancy?"

Emma recoiled. "You're not serious!"

"It's only happened once, that we know of," said Miss Peregrine. She set the cookies down and fixed me with a stare. "The subject was male."

"I'm not pregnant!" I said a little too loudly.

"And thank goodness for that!" someone shouted from the living room.

Miss Peregrine patted my shoulder. "It sounds as if you're in the clear. Though I should have warned you."

"It's probably better you didn't," I said. It would have made me paranoid, not to mention that if I'd spent the last month sneaking pregnancy tests and checking my feces for snails, my parents would have long before banished me to an asylum.

"Fair enough," said Miss Peregrine. "Now, before we can all relax and enjoy one another's company, some business." She began pacing a tight circle between the double ovens and the prep sink. "Item one: safety and security. I've scouted the perimeter of the house. All seems quiet, but appearances can be deceiving. Is there anything I should know about your neighbors?"

"Like what?"

"Criminal histories? Violent tendencies? Firearm collections?"

We had only two neighbors: ancient Mrs. Melloroos, a wheelchair-bound octogenarian who only left her house with the help of a live-in nurse, and a German couple who spent most of the year elsewhere, leaving their Cape Cod–style McMansion empty except during the winter.

"Mrs. Melloroos can be kind of nosy," I said. "But as long as no one's being flagrantly peculiar in her front yard, I don't think she'll give us any trouble."

"Noted," said Miss Peregrine. "Item two: Have you felt the presence of any hollowgast since you returned home?"

I felt my blood pressure spike at her mention of the word, which had crossed neither my mind nor my lips in several weeks. "No," I said quickly. "Why? Have there been more attacks?"

"No more attacks. No sign of them whatsoever. But that's what worries me. Now, about your family—"

"Didn't we kill or capture them all in Devil's Acre?" I said, not ready to change the subject away from hollowgast so quickly.

"Not quite *all*. A small cadre escaped with some wights after our victory, and we believe they absconded to America. And while I doubt they'll come anywhere near *you*—I daresay they've learned their lesson—I can only assume they're planning something. An abundance of caution couldn't hurt."

"They're *terrified* of you, Jacob," Emma said proudly.

"They are?" I said.

"After the thrashing you gave them, they'd be stupid not to be," said Millard, his voice ringing out from the edge of the kitchen.

"Polite persons do not spy on private conversations," Miss Peregrine huffed.

"I wasn't spying, I was *hungry*. Also, I've been sent to ask you not to hog Jacob. We came an awfully long way to see him, you know."

"They missed Jacob a lot," Emma said to Miss Peregrine. "Nearly as much as I did."

"Perhaps it's time you addressed everyone," Miss Peregrine said to me. "Make a welcome speech. Lay out some ground rules."

"Ground rules?" I said. "Like what?"

"They're my wards, Mr. Portman, but this is your town and your time. I'll need your help keeping everyone out of trouble."

"Just be sure to feed them," said Emma.

I turned to Miss Peregrine. "What were you saying before, about my family?"

They couldn't stay prisoners in the garage forever, and I was getting anxious about how we were going to deal with them.

"You needn't worry," Miss Peregrine said. "Bronwyn has the situation well in hand."

The words had hardly left her lips when a percussive, wall-rattling crash sounded from the direction of the garage. The vibrations sent glasses toppling from a nearby shelf to the floor, where they shattered.

"That sounds like a distinctly *out*-of-hand situation," said Millard.

We were already running.

◆　　◆　　◆

"Stay where you are!" Miss Peregrine shouted toward the living room.

I dashed out of the kitchen and down the back hall, Emma just behind, adrenaline sharpening me. I wasn't sure what to expect when we burst into the garage. Smoke? Blood? It had sounded like an explosion, but I definitely did not anticipate finding my parents and uncles passed out in our car, peaceful as babes. The car's rear end was wedged into a major dent in the rolled-down garage door, and the concrete around it sparkled with bits of broken taillight. The engine was on and idling.

Bronwyn stood at the front end of the car with the bumper dangling from her hands. "Oh, I'm so sorry, I don't know what happened," she said, and dropped the bumper with an echoing *clang*.

Realizing I had to kill the engine before we all suffocated, I peeled away from the others and ran to the driver's-side door. The handle was locked. Of course it was: My family had been trying to keep Bronwyn out. I'm sure they'd been terrified.

"I can open it," Bronwyn said. "Stand back!"

She planted her feet and grabbed the door handle with both hands.

"What are you—" I started to say, and then with a mighty heave, she pulled the door open and straight off its hinges. Weight and momentum being what they were, the door kept going, flying out of her hands and across the room before burying itself in the back wall. The noise was like a physical force pushing me backward.

"Oh, fiddlywinks," Bronwyn said into the ringing silence that followed.

The garage was beginning to resemble some of the bombed houses I'd seen in wartime London.

"Bronwyn!" Emma shouted, uncovering her head. "You might have decapitated someone!"

I ducked into the hole where the driver's-side door had been, reached across my sleeping father, and snatched the keys from the ignition. My mother was slumped against my father, who was snoring. In the back, my uncles slept in each other's arms. Despite all the noise, none of them had stirred. I knew of only one substance that could put people into such a deep sleep: a powdered piece of Mother Dust. When I stood up out of the car again, I saw Bronwyn holding a little pouch of the stuff as she attempted to explain what had happened.

"The man in the back," she was saying, pointing at my uncle Bobby, "I seen him using his, his little—" She pulled Bobby's phone from her pocket.

"Cell phone," I said.

"Right—that," she continued. "So I took it away, which made all of them as mad as a bag of ferrets, and then I did like Miss P showed me—"

"You used the powder?" said Miss Peregrine.

"I blew it right at 'em, but they didn't fall asleep straight off. Jacob's dad started up the car, but instead of going forward, he—he—" Bronwyn gestured to the dented garage door, words failing her.

Miss Peregrine patted her on the arm. "Yes, dear, I can see. You handled things just right."

"Yeah," said Enoch. "Right through the *wall*."

We turned to see the other kids peeping at us from a tight cluster in the hallway.

"I told you to stay where you were," said Miss Peregrine.

"After *that* noise?" said Enoch.

"I'm sorry, Jacob," Bronwyn said. "They got so upset, and I didn't know what to do. I didn't hurt 'em, did I?"

"I don't think so." I had experienced the velvety sleep induced by Mother Dust's powder, and it wasn't a bad place to spend a few hours. "Can I see my uncle's phone?"

Bronwyn handed it to me. The screen was spider-cracked but readable. When it lit up, I saw a string of texts from my aunt:

What's happening?

When will u be home?

Everything ok??

In reply, Uncle Bobby had started to type CALL THE COPS and then probably realized that he could just as easily call them himself. But Bronwyn had taken his phone before he was able to. If she'd been a few seconds slower, we might've had a visit from the SWAT team. My chest tightened as I realized how fast our situation could have become dangerous and complicated. *Hell*, I thought, looking from the ruined car to the ruined wall to the ruined garage door. *It already has.*

"Don't worry, Jacob. I've handled much stickier situations." Miss Peregrine was walking around the car, examining the damage. "Your family will sleep soundly until morning, and I daresay we should try to do the same."

"And then what?" I said, anxious and starting to sweat. The unair-conditioned garage was sweltering.

"When they wake, I'll wipe their recent memories and send your uncles home."

"But what will they—"

"I'll explain that we're distant relatives from your father's side of the family, here from Europe to pay our respects at Abe's grave. And as for your appointment at the asylum, you're feeling much better now and no longer require psychiatric care."

"And what about—"

"Oh, they'll believe it; normals are highly suggestible following a memory wipe. I could probably convince them we're visitors from a moon colony."

"Miss Peregrine, please stop doing that."

She smiled. "My apologies. A century of headmistressing trains you to anticipate questions for the sake of expediency. Now come along, children, we need to discuss protocol for the next several days. There's much to learn about the present, and no time like the present to start learning."

She began herding everyone out of the garage while they peppered her with questions and complaints:

"How long can we stay?" said Olive.

"May we go exploring in the morning?" said Claire.

"I would like to eat something before I perish from the earth," said Millard.

Soon, I was alone in the garage, lingering partly because

I felt bad about leaving my family there overnight, but also because I was anxious about their impending memory wipe. Miss
Peregrine seemed confident, but this would be a bigger wipe than
the one she had performed on them in London, which had only
deleted about ten minutes of their memories. What if she didn't
erase enough, or erased too much? What if my dad forgot all he
knew about birds, or my mom forgot all the French she learned
in college?

I watched them sleep for a minute, this new weight settling
upon me. I felt suddenly, uncomfortably adult, while my family—
vulnerable, peaceful, drooling a bit—looked almost like babies.

Maybe there was another way.

Emma leaned in through the open door. "Everything okay? I
think the boys are going to riot if dinner doesn't appear soon."

"I wasn't sure I should leave them," I said, nodding toward my
family.

"They aren't going anywhere, and they shouldn't need watching. With the dose they got, they'll sleep like rocks into the middle
of tomorrow."

"I know. I just . . . I feel a little bad."

"You shouldn't." She came and stood next to me. "It's not
your fault. At all."

I nodded. "It seems a little tragic, is all."

"What does?"

"That Abe Portman's son will never know how special a man
his father was."

Emma took my arm and draped it over her shoulders. "I think
it's a hundred times more tragic that he'll never know how special a
man his son is."

I was just leaning down to kiss her when my uncle's phone
buzzed in my pocket. It made us both startle, and I pulled it out to
find a new text from my aunt.

Is crazy J in the loony bin yet?

"What is it?" Emma asked.

"Nothing important." I returned the phone to my pocket and turned toward the door. Suddenly, leaving my family in the garage overnight didn't seem like such a bad idea. "Come on, let's figure out dinner."

"Are you sure?" Emma said.

"Very."

I flipped off the lights as we left.

                          ◆   ◆   ◆

I suggested we order pizza from a place that delivered late. Only a few of the kids even knew what pizza was, and delivery was a totally foreign concept.

"They prepare it remotely and bring it to your *home*?" said Horace, as if the idea were vaguely scandalous.

"Pizza—is that Floridian cuisine?" asked Bronwyn.

"Not really," I said. "But trust me, you'll like it."

I called in a massive order and we settled onto couches and chairs in the living room to wait for it to arrive. Miss Peregrine whispered in my ear, "*I think it's time to make that speech.*" Without waiting for a reply, she cleared her throat and announced to the room that I had something to say. So I stood up and began, somewhat awkwardly, to improvise.

"I'm so glad you're all here. I'm not sure if you know where my family was taking me tonight, but it wasn't a good place. I mean—" I hesitated. "I mean, it might be good for *some* people, you know, with real mental problems, but . . . long story short, you guys saved my ass."

Miss Peregrine frowned.

"It was you that saved *our* . . . bums," said Bronwyn, glancing at the headmistress. "We were only returning the favor."

"Well, thanks. When you all first arrived, I thought you were a dream. I've been dreaming about you visiting me here ever since we met. So it was pretty hard to believe it was really happening. Anyway, the point is, you *are* here, and I hope I can make you feel as welcome as you made me feel when I came to stay in your loop." I nodded and looked to the floor, suddenly self-conscious. "So, basically, thrilled you're here, love you guys, speech over."

"We love you, too!" Claire said, and she leapt out of her seat and ran to hug me. Then Olive and Bronwyn joined her, and soon almost everyone was bear-hugging the breath out of me.

"We're *so* happy to be here," said Claire.

"And not in Devil's Acre," added Horace.

"We'll have ever so much fun!" sang Olive.

"Sorry we broke part of your house," said Bronwyn.

"What do you mean, *we*?" said Enoch.

"Can't breathe," I gasped. "Squeezing too hard—"

The pack expanded enough for me to inhale. Then Hugh inserted himself into the gap and poked me in the chest.

"You know it's not *all* of us who are here, right?" A solitary bee zipped around him in agitated circles. The others moved back, giving Hugh and his angry bee some space. "When you said you were glad we were *all* here. Well, we're not."

It took me a moment to realize what he meant, and then I felt ashamed. "I'm sorry, Hugh. I didn't mean to leave out Fiona."

He looked down at his fuzzy striped socks. "Sometimes I feel like everyone but me has forgotten her." His bottom lip trembled, and then he clenched his fists to make it stop. "She's not dead, you know."

"I hope you're right."

He met my eyes, defiant. "She's *not*."

"Okay. She's not."

"I really miss her, Jacob."

"We all do," I said. "I didn't mean to leave her out, and I haven't forgotten her."

"Apology accepted," Hugh said, and then he wiped his face, turned on his heel, and walked out of the room.

"If you can believe it," Millard said after a moment, "that was progress."

"He'll barely even talk to any of us," said Emma. "He's angry, and he won't face the truth."

"You don't think it's possible Fiona could be alive somewhere?" I asked.

"I'd rate it unlikely," said Millard.

Miss Peregrine winced and put a finger to her lips—she'd been gliding toward us across the room—and with a hand on our backs, she pushed us into a private huddle. "We put out word to every loop and peculiar community we're in contact with," she said quietly. "We've distributed communiques, bulletins, photographs, detailed descriptions—I even sent Miss Wren's pigeon scouts to search the forests for Fiona. Thus far, nothing."

Millard sighed. "If she was alive, poor thing, wouldn't she have reached out to us by now? We aren't difficult to find."

"I guess so," I said. "But has anyone tried looking for her . . . um . . ."

"Her body?" Millard said.

"Millard, please," said the headmistress.

"Was that indelicate? Should I have chosen a less exact term?"

"Just be *quiet*," Miss Peregrine hissed.

Millard didn't lack feeling; he just wasn't good at minding the feelings of others.

"The fall that likely killed Fiona," Millard said, "occurred in Miss Wren's menagerie loop, which has since collapsed. If her body was there, it is no longer recoverable."

"I've been weighing whether to hold a memorial service," Miss Peregrine said. "But I can't even raise the topic without sending Hugh into a spiral of depression. I fear if we push him too hard—"

"He won't even adopt new bees," said Millard. "He says he wouldn't love them the same if they'd never met Fiona, so he only keeps the one, who's of a rather advanced age at this point."

"Sounds like this change of scenery might do him good," I said.

Just then the doorbell rang. And not a moment too soon, as the mood in the room was growing heavier by the second.

Claire and Bronwyn tried to follow me down the hall, but Miss Peregrine snapped at them. "I don't think so! You're not ready to talk to normals yet."

I didn't think there was much risk in them meeting the pizza delivery guy—until I opened the door to see a kid I knew from school, balancing a stack of pizza boxes in his hands.

"Ninety-four sixty," he mumbled, then jerked his head in recognition. "Oh, snap. Portman?"

"Justin. Hey."

His name was Justin Pamperton, though everyone called him Pampers. He was one of the pothead skaters who haunted the outer parking lots of our school.

"You look good," he said. "Are you, like, better now?"

"What do you mean?" I said, not actually wanting to know what he meant, counting out his money as quickly as I could. (I had earlier raided my parents' sock drawer, where they always kept a couple hundred bucks stashed.)

"Word is you went, like, *off the deep end*. No offense."

"Uh, nope," I said. "I'm fine."

"Righteous," he said, nodding like a bobblehead figurine. "'Cause what *I* heard was—"

He stopped mid-sentence. Someone inside was laughing.

"Dude, are you having a party right now?"

I took the pizzas from him, shoved the bills into his hand. "Something like that. Keep the change."

"With *girls*?" He tried to peek into the house, but I shifted to block his view. "I'm off in an hour. I can pick up some beers . . ."

I had never wanted anyone off my porch so badly.

"Sorry, it's kind of a private thing."

He looked impressed. "You handle that, dogg." He raised a hand to high-five me, realized I couldn't because of the pizzas, then made a fist and shook it. "See you in a week, Portman."

"In a week?"

"*School*, bro! What planet have you been living on?" He jogged off toward his idling hatchback, shaking his head and laughing to himself.

❖   ❖   ❖

Conversation ground to a halt as the pizza was distributed, and for a full three minutes there was only the sound of lips smacking and the occasional satisfied grunt. In the lull I kept replaying Justin's words. School started in a week, and somehow I had forgotten all about it. Before my parents decided I was certifiable and tried to have me committed, I'd made up my mind to go back to school. My plan had been to stick it out at home long enough to graduate, then escape to London so I could be with Emma and my friends. But now the friends I had thought so distant, and the world I had thought so inaccessible, had landed on my doorstep, and in the space of one night everything changed. My friends were now free to roam anywhere (and anytime) they liked. Could I really imagine sitting through interminable classes and lunch periods and mandatory assemblies every day while all that was waiting for me?

Maybe not, but it was too much to figure out right at that moment, pizza in my lap, still dizzy with the idea that any of this was possible. School didn't start for a week. There was time. Right now all I needed to do was eat and enjoy the company of my friends.

"This is the best food in the world!" Claire announced through a mouthful of gooey cheese. "I'll be having this every night."

"Not if you want to live out the week," said Horace, plucking the olives off his slice with fastidious precision. "There's more sodium in this than in the whole Dead Sea."

"Worried you'll get fat?" Enoch laughed. "Fat Horace. That I'd like to see."

"That I'll *bloat*," said Horace. "My clothes are tailored just so, unlike the flour sacks you wear."

Enoch glanced down at his clothes—a collarless gray shirt under a black vest, fraying black pants, and patent leather shoes that had long ago lost their shine. "I got these in *Pah-ree*," he said in an exaggerated French accent, "from a fashionable fellow who was no longer in need of them."

"From a *dead* fellow," said Claire, her lips curling in disgust.

"Funeral parlors are the best secondhand boutiques in the world," said Enoch, taking a massive chomp of pizza. "You've just got to get the clothes before their occupant begins to leak."

"Well, there goes my appetite," said Horace, tossing his plate down on the coffee table.

"Pick that up and finish it," Miss Peregrine scolded him. "We don't waste food."

Horace sighed and picked up his plate again. "Sometimes I envy Nullings. He could gain a hundred pounds and no one would notice."

"I'm quite svelte, for your information," said Millard, and made a sound that could only have been his hand smacking his bare stomach. "Come have a feel if you don't believe me."

"I'll pass, thanks."

"For bird's sake, *clothe* yourself, Millard," said Miss Peregrine. "What have I said about unnecessary nudity?"

"What does it matter if no one can see me?" Millard replied.

"It's in bad taste."

"But it's so hot here!"

"*Now*, Mr. Nullings."

Millard stood up from the couch and grumbled something about *prudes* as he breezed past, then came back a minute later with a bath towel tied loosely around his waist. But Miss Peregrine disapproved of this, too, and sent him away again. When he returned the second time, he was overdressed in clothes he'd ransacked from my closet: hiking boots, wool pants, a coat, a scarf, a hat, and gloves.

"Millard, you'll perish of heatstroke!" said Bronwyn.

"At least no one will have to imagine me in a state of nature!" he said, which had the desired effect of annoying Miss Peregrine. She announced that it was time for another security check and left the room.

The laughs many of us had been holding in burst out.

"Did you see her face?" said Enoch. "She was ready to kill you, Nullings!"

The dynamic between the kids and Miss Peregrine had shifted a bit. They seemed more like teenagers now—real ones, beginning to chafe against her authority.

"You're all being rude!" said Claire. "Stop it right now!"

Well, not *all* of them were chafing.

"Don't you find it wearying, being lectured about every little thing?" said Millard.

"*Little thing!*" Enoch said, then burst out laughing all over again. "Millard has a—*oww!*"

Claire had bit him on the shoulder with her backmouth, and while Enoch was rubbing the spot, she said, "No, I *don't* find it wearying. And it *is* strange for you to be nude in mixed company for no good reason."

"Ahh, balderclap," said Millard. "Does it bother anyone else?"

All the girls raised their hands.

Millard sighed. "Well, then. I shall endeavor to be fully dressed at all times, lest anyone be made uncomfortable by basic facts of biology."

◆   ◆   ◆

We talked and talked. There was so much to catch up on. We slipped back into easy familiarity so quickly that it felt like we'd only been apart a few days, but it had been almost six weeks. A lot had happened in that time—to them, anyway—though I'd gotten only occasional updates in the letters Emma sent. They took turns describing adventures they'd had exploring peculiar places via the Panloopticon—though only loops that had been pre-scouted and deemed safe by the ymbrynes, since it was not well-known what lay waiting behind all of the Panloopticon's doors.

They had visited a loop in ancient Mongolia and watched a peculiar shepherd speak the language of sheep, tending his flock without a stick or a dog, just the sound of his own voice. Olive's favorite had been a trip to a loop in the Atlas Mountains of North Africa, where in a certain little town every peculiar could float just like she did. They had strung nets everywhere above the town so the people could go about their days without weighing themselves down, and they bounced from place to place like acrobats in zero gravity. There was a loop in Amazonia, too, that had become a popular place to visit: a fantastic city in the jungle made from trees, the roots and branches all knotted together to form roads and bridges and houses. The peculiars there could manipulate plants much the way Fiona did—which Hugh had found so distressing and overwhelming that he had scurried out of the loop and back to Devil's Acre almost immediately.

"It was hot and the insects were terrible," said Millard, "but the locals were exceedingly nice, and they showed us how they make fantastic medicines from plants."

"And they go fishing with a special poison that stuns the fish, but doesn't kill them," said Emma, "so they can just scoop the ones they want out of the water. Absolutely brilliant."

"We did some other trips, too," Bronwyn said. "Em, show Jacob your snaps!"

Emma hopped up from the couch beside me and ran to retrieve them from her luggage. She returned a minute later with the photos in her hand, and we gathered around a floor lamp's glow to look at them.

"I only recently started taking pictures, and I still don't really know what I'm doing . . ."

"Don't be so modest," I said. "You sent some of your photos along with your letters, and they were great."

"Eek, I forgot about that."

Emma was anything but boastful, but neither was she afraid to trumpet her achievements when it came to things she did well. So the fact that she was shy about her photos meant she had high standards and aspired to live up to them. Lucky for both of us—since I have a hard time faking enthusiasm—she was a natural talent. But while the composition and exposure and all that were nice (not that I'm an expert), it was the subject matter that really made them interesting— and terrible.

The first photo showed a dozen or so Victorians posing, casual as picnic-goers, on the crazily slanted roofs of houses that looked like they'd been smashed by an angry giant.

"An earthquake in Chile," Emma explained. "Printed on non-archival paper that aged badly after we left Devil's Acre, unfortunately."

She flipped to the next picture: a train that had jumped its tracks and tipped over sideways. There were children—peculiar ones, presumably—sitting and standing all around it, smiling like they were having a grand old time.

"A train disaster," said Millard. "It was carrying some sort of volatile chemical, and a few minutes after this picture was taken, we retreated to a safe distance and watched it catch fire and explode in the most terrific way."

"What was the point of these trips?" I asked. "Seems a lot less fun than visiting some cool loop in the Amazon."

"We were helping Sharon," said Millard. "You remember him—tall, cloaked boatman from Devil's Acre? Rats for friends?"

"How could I forget?"

"He's developing a new and improved version of his Famine 'n' Flames Disaster Tour using the Panloopticon's loops, and he asked us to test out an early version. Besides the Chilean earthquake and the train wreck, there was a town in Portugal where it rained blood."

"Seriously?" I said.

"I didn't go along for that one," Emma said.

"Good thing, too," said Horace. "Our clothes were irreparably stained."

"Well, it sounds like you've all had a much more exciting time than I have," I said. "I think I've left my house about six times since I last saw you."

"I hope that's about to change," said Bronwyn. "I've always wanted to see America—and the present day, especially. Is New York City very far?"

"I'm afraid it is," I said.

"Oh," she said, sinking down into the couch cushions.

"I'd like to visit Muncie, Indiana," said Olive. "The guidebook says you haven't lived until you've seen Muncie."

"What guidebook?"

"*Peculiar Planet: North America*," Olive said, and held up a book with a tattered green cover. "It's a travel guide for peculiars. It named Muncie America's Most Normal Town six years running. Totally average in every way."

"That book is horribly out-of-date," said Millard. "In all likelihood useless."

Olive ignored him. "Apparently, nothing unusual or out of the ordinary has ever happened there. Ever!"

"Not all of us find normal people as interesting as you do," Horace said. "And anyway, I'm sure it's crawling with peculiar tourists."

Olive, who wasn't wearing her leaded shoes, floated over the coffee table, to the couch, and dropped the book in my lap. It was open to a page describing the only peculiar-friendly accommodations near Muncie—a place called Clownmouth House in a loop on the outskirts of town. True to its name, it appeared to be a room inside a giant plaster clown's head.

I shuddered a little and let the book fall closed.

"We don't have to go all the way to Indiana to find unextraordinary places," I said. "We've got plenty right here in Englewood, trust me."

"The rest of you can do what you like," said Enoch. "My only plan for the next few weeks is to sleep until noon and bury my toes in warm sand."

"That *does* sound nice," said Emma. "Is there a beach near here?"

"Across the street," I said.

Emma's eyes lit up.

"I *hate* beaches," Olive said. "I can never take my stupid metal boots off, which ruins all the fun."

"We could tie you to a rock near the water's edge," said Claire.

"Sounds magical," Olive grumbled, then snatched *Peculiar Planet* out of my lap and floated into a corner. "I'll just take a train to Muncie and fiddlywinks to the rest of you."

"You'll do no such thing." Miss Peregrine came into the room. I wondered whether she'd been eavesdropping on us from the hall, rather than doing an extra security round. "You children have earned a bit of a rest, certainly, but our responsibilities are such that we cannot simply while away the next several weeks in idleness."

"What!" said Enoch. "I distinctly remember you saying we were here on holiday."

"A *working* holiday. We can't afford to waste the educational opportunities presented us by being here."

At the word *educational*, groans went up around the room.

"Don't we do enough lessons as it is?" Olive whined. "My brain may split open."

Miss Peregrine shot Olive a warning look and stepped smartly to the center of the room. "I don't want to hear another word of complaint," she said. "With the extraordinary new freedom of movement you've been given, you'll be invaluable to the reconstruction effort. With the right preparation, you could be ambassadors to other peculiar peoples one day. Explorers of new loops and territories. Planners and cartographers and leaders and builders—as crucial to the work of remaking our world as you were to the wights' defeat. Don't you want that?"

"Of course," said Emma. "But what does that have to do with taking a holiday?"

"Before you become any of those things, you must first learn to navigate this world. The present day. *America.* You must familiarize yourselves with its idioms and customs and ultimately be able to pass as normal. If you cannot, you'll be a danger to yourselves and all of us."

"So you want us to . . . what?" said Horace. "Take normalling lessons?"

"Yes. I want you to learn what you can while you're here, not just bake your brains in the sun. And I happen to know a very capable teacher." Miss Peregrine turned to me and smiled. "Mr. Portman, would you accept the job?"

"Me?" I said. "I'm not exactly an expert on what's normal. There's a reason I feel so at home with you guys."

"Miss P's right," said Emma. "You're perfect for it. You've lived here all your life. You grew up thinking you were normal, but you're one of us."

"Well, I *had* planned on spending the next few weeks in a padded room," I said, "but now that that's not happening, I guess I could teach you guys a thing or two."

"Normalling lessons!" said Olive. "Oh, how fun!"

"There's so much to cover," I said. "Where do we start?"

"In the morning," Miss Peregrine said. "It's getting late, and we should all find beds."

She was right—it was nearly midnight, and my friends had begun their day in Devil's Acre twenty-three hours (and one hundred thirty–odd years) ago. We were all exhausted. I found places for everyone to sleep—in our guest bedrooms, stretched out on couches, in a tangle of blankets in a broom closet for Enoch, who preferred his sleeping arrangements dark and nest-like. I offered my parents' bed to Miss Peregrine, since they wouldn't be using it, but she demurred. "I appreciate the offer, but let Bronwyn and Miss Bloom share it. I'll be keeping watch tonight." She flashed me a knowing look that said, *And not just over the house*, and it took a lot of effort not to roll my eyes at her. *You don't have to worry*, I almost said, *Emma and I are taking things slow*. But what business was that of hers? I was so irritated that the minute she left to tuck Olive and Claire into bed I found Emma and said, "Want to see my room?"

"Abso*lute*ly," she replied, and we snuck into the hall and up the stairs.

◆　　◆　　◆

I could hear Miss Peregrine's voice drifting up from one of the guest bedrooms, where she was singing a soft and sad lullaby. Like all peculiar lullabies it was mournful and long—this one a saga about a girl whose only friends were ghosts—which meant we had several minutes, at least, before Miss P came looking for Emma.

"My room's kind of a mess," I warned her.

"I've been sleeping in a dormitory with two dozen girls," she said. "I am unshockable."

We darted up the stairs and into my bedroom. I flipped on the lights. Emma's mouth fell open.

"What *is* all this stuff?"

"Ah," I said. "Right." I wondered if I'd made a mistake. Explaining my room was going to eat up time we otherwise might have spent making out.

I didn't have *stuff*. I had *collections*. And I had a lot of them, spread across bookshelves that lined my room. I wouldn't have called myself a pack rat—and I wasn't a hoarder—but collecting things was one of the ways I had dealt with loneliness as a kid. When your best friend is your seventy-five-year-old grandpa, you spend a lot of time doing what grandpas do, and for us that meant hitting garage sales every Saturday morning. (Grandpa Portman might have been a peculiar war hero and a badass hollowgast hunter, but few things thrilled him more than a bargain.)

At each sale I was allowed to pick out one thing that cost less than fifty cents. Multiply that by several garage sales per weekend and that's how I amassed, over the course of a decade, a huge number of old records, dime-store detective novels with silly covers, *MAD* magazines, and other things that were objectively junk but nevertheless arranged like treasures along the shelves around my room. My parents often begged me to cull the herd and throw most of it away, and while I had made a few halfhearted attempts, I never got far—the rest of the house was so big and modern and *blank* that I had developed a sort of horror of empty space, so when it came to the only room in the house over which I had some control, I preferred it full. Which is why, in addition to all the overflowing bookshelves, I had plastered one wall floor to ceiling with maps, and another with old record album covers.

"Oh, wow. You really like music!" Emma broke away from me and went to the wall—the one with album covers growing over it like scales. I was starting to resent my distracting decor.

"Doesn't everyone?" I said.

"Not everyone papers their walls with it."

"I'm mostly into the older stuff," I said.

"Oh, me too," she said. "I don't like these new groups, with their loud guitars and long hair." She picked up a copy of *Meet the Beatles!* and wrinkled her nose.

"That record came out, what . . . fifty years ago?"

"Like I said. But you never mentioned liking music so much." She walked along the wall, trailing her hand over my records, looking at everything. "There are lots of things I don't know about you, but I want to."

"I know what you mean," I said. "I feel like we know each other so well in some ways, but in others it's like we just met."

"In our defense, we were both quite busy, what with trying not to die and rescuing all those ymbrynes and such. But now we have time."

We have time. Whenever I heard those words, an electric feeling of possibility uncoiled in my chest.

"Play me one," said Emma, nodding at the wall. "Whichever is your favorite."

"I don't know if I have a favorite," I said. "There are so many."

"I want to dance with you. Pick a good one for dancing."

She smiled and went back to looking at things. I thought for a moment, then found *Harvest Moon* by Neil Young. I slid the album from its sleeve, placed it on the turntable, and dropped the needle carefully into the gap between the third and fourth song. There was a warm crackle and then the title track began to play, wistful and sweet. I was hoping she'd join me in the middle of the room, where I'd cleared a little space for us to dance, but she had come upon my wall of maps. There were layers upon layers of them—maps of the world, city maps, subway maps, tri-fold maps torn from old *National Geographic* magazines.

"These are *amazing*, Jacob."

"I used to spend a lot of time imagining I was somewhere else," I said.

"Me too."

She came to my bed, which was shoved against the wall and surrounded by maps. She climbed up onto the comforter to examine them.

"Sometimes I remember you're only sixteen," she said. "*Actually* sixteen. And it kind of breaks my head open."

She turned to look down at me in wonder.

"What made you say that?" I asked.

"I don't know. It's just strange. You don't *seem* only sixteen."

"And you don't seem ninety-eight."

"I'm only *eighty*-eight."

"Oh, well, you definitely seem eighty-eight."

She laughed and shook her head, then looked back at the wall.

"Come back here," I said. "Dance with me."

She hadn't seemed to hear. She had come to the oldest part of my map wall—the ones I had made with my grandfather when I was eight or nine, drawn on everything from graph paper to construction paper. We'd spent many a long summer day making them, inventing cartographical symbols, drawing strange creatures in the margins, sometimes overwriting real places on the maps with our own invented ones. When I realized what she was staring at, my heart sank a bit.

"Is this Abe's handwriting?" she asked.

"We used to do all kinds of projects together. He was basically my best friend."

Emma nodded. "Mine too." Her finger traced some words he had written—*Lake Okeechobee*—and then she turned away from it and climbed down from the bed. "But that was a long time ago."

She came over to where I stood, took my hands, and rested her head on my shoulder. We began to sway with the music.

"I'm sorry," she said. "That caught me by surprise."

"It's okay. You were together for so long. And now you're here . . ."

I felt her shake her head. *Let's not ruin it.* Her hands slipped out of mine and wrapped around my waist. I lowered my cheek to her forehead.

"Do you ever still imagine you're somewhere else?" she asked me.

"Not anymore," I said. "For the first time in a long time, I'm happy where I am."

"Me too," she said, and she lifted her head from my shoulder, and I kissed her.

We danced and kissed until the song ended. Eventually, a soft hiss filled the room, and we kept dancing awhile longer because we weren't ready for the moment to end. I tried to forget the strange turn things had taken, and how I'd felt when she'd mentioned my grandfather. She was going through something and that was okay. Even if I couldn't understand it.

For now, I told myself, all that mattered was that we were together and we were safe. For now, that was enough. It was more than we'd ever had. There was no clock counting down to the moment she would wither and turn to dust. There were no bombers turning the world to fire around us. There were no hollowgast lurking outside the door. I didn't know what our future held, but in that moment it was enough just to believe we had one.

I heard Miss Peregrine talking downstairs. That was our cue.

"*Until tomorrow*," she whispered in my ear. "*Good night, Jacob.*"

We kissed one more time. It felt like an electric pulse, and left every part of me tingling. Then she slipped out the door, and for the first time since my friends had arrived, I was alone.

◆ ◆ ◆

That night, I could hardly sleep. It wasn't so much the snores of Hugh as he dozed in a pile of blankets on my floor as it was a buzzing in my head, filled now with uncertainty and exciting new prospects. When I left Devil's Acre to come back home, it was because I had decided that finishing high school and keeping my parents in my life were important enough goals that they were worth enduring Englewood for a couple more years. The time between now and graduation had promised to be a special kind of torment, though, especially with Emma and my friends stuck in loops on the other side of the Atlantic.

But so much had changed in one night. Now, maybe, I didn't have to wait. Maybe now I wouldn't have to choose one or the other: peculiar or normal, this life or that. I wanted, and needed, both—though not in equal measure. I had no interest in a normal career. In settling down with someone who didn't understand who I was, or in having kids from whom I had to keep half my life a secret, like my grandfather had.

That said, I didn't want to go through life a high school dropout—you can't exactly put *hollowgast tamer* on a résumé—and though my mom and dad were never going to win Parents of the Year, I didn't want to cut them out of my life, either. I also didn't want to become so alienated from the normal world that I forgot how to navigate it. The peculiar world was wonderful and I knew I would never be whole without it, but it could also be extraordinarily stressful and overwhelming. For the sake of my long-term sanity, I needed to maintain a connection to my normal life. I needed that balance.

So: Maybe the next year or two didn't have to feel like a prison sentence as I waited for it all. Maybe I could be with my friends and with Emma *and* have my home and my family. Emma could even go to school with me. Maybe all my friends could! We could take classes together, eat lunch together, go to stupid school dances. Of course—what more perfect place to learn about the lives and habits of normal teenagers than high school? After a semester of that, they'd be able to impersonate normals with no problem (even I had learned to do it, eventually), and to blend in when we ventured out into the larger world of peculiar America. Whenever time permitted we would travel back to Devil's Acre to help the cause, rebuild the loops, and hopefully make peculiardom impervious to future threats.

Unfortunately, the key to it all was my parents. They could make this easy or they could make it impossible. If only there was a way for my friends to be here without my mom and dad losing it, so that we wouldn't have to tiptoe around them, afraid that an accidental display of peculiarness would send them screaming into the streets and bring hell down upon our heads.

There had to be something I could tell my parents that they would believe. Some way to explain my friends. Their presence, their strangeness—maybe even their abilities. I racked my brain for the perfect story. They were exchange students I had met while in London. They had saved my life, taken me in, and I wanted to repay them. (That this wasn't far from the truth appealed to me.) They also happened to be expert magicians who were always practicing their act. Masters of illusion. Their tricks so refined you can never tell how they achieve them.

Maybe. Maybe there was a way. And then things could be so *good*.

My brain was a hope-making machine.

CHAPTER TWO

I woke the next morning with a sour pit in my stomach, certain it had all been a dream. Steeling myself for disappointment, I ventured downstairs, half expecting to find my bags packed and my uncles once more guarding the doors against escape. Instead, I was greeted by a scene of peculiar domestic bliss.

The whole downstairs was full of cheerful conversation and the warm smells of cooking food. Horace was banging around in the kitchen while Emma and Millard set the table. Miss Peregrine was whistling to herself and opening windows to let in a morning breeze. Outside I could see Olive and Bronwyn and Claire chasing one another around the yard—Bronwyn catching Olive and tossing her twenty feet into the air, Olive laughing like mad as she fluttered down again at half speed, the weight of her shoes just enough to overcome her natural buoyancy. In the living room, Hugh and Enoch were glued to the television, watching a commercial for laundry detergent in rapt wonderment. It was as welcome a sight as I could have imagined, and for a long moment I stood unnoticed at the bottom of the stairs, taking it in. In the space of a single night, my friends had managed to make my house a happier, cozier place than it had been in all years I lived here with my parents.

"Nice of you to join us!" Miss Peregrine sang out, jolting me from my daydream.

Emma rushed over to me. "What's wrong?" she said. "Feeling dizzy again?"

"Just appreciating the scenery," I said, and then I drew her close and kissed her. She slid her arms around me and kissed me back, and I was overwhelmed by a tingling warmth that flooded my brain and a sudden sensation of being out of my body, like I had floated up to the ceiling and was looking down on the soft, beautiful face of this amazing girl and my friends and the whole sweet scene, and I wondered how it was that such an exquisite moment had appeared in my life.

The kiss ended too soon—but before anyone else in the room noticed it had happened—and we linked arms and walked toward the kitchen.

"How long has everyone been awake?" I asked.

"Oh, for hours," Millard said, carrying a pan of biscuits toward the dining room. "We're loop lagged rather terribly."

He was wearing a full outfit, I noticed. Plum-colored pants, a light sweater, and a scarf around his neck.

"I dressed him this morning," Horace said, popping his head out of the kitchen. "He's quite the blank slate, sartorially speaking." Horace himself was wearing an apron over a white collared shirt, a tie, and pressed pants—which almost certainly meant he'd gotten up extra early just to iron his clothes.

I excused myself and slipped away to check on my family in the garage. They were still asleep, right where I'd left them. They'd hardly even shifted positions in the night. Then something unpleasant occurred to me, and I ran to the car and held my hand in front of each of their noses. When I was satisfied they were still alive, I went back to join my friends.

Everyone was gathered around what my parents called the "good table," a long slab of black glass in our rarely used formal dining room. It was a space I associated with stiff manners and unpleasant conversations because it was only used either when family came over on holidays or when my parents had "something important" to discuss with me, which usually meant a lecture about my grades, bad attitude, friendships or lack thereof, etc. So it was sweet to find the room filled with food and friends and laughter.

I wedged myself into the seat next to Emma. Horace made a big show of unveiling the platters of food he'd prepared.

"This morning we've got *pain perdu*, potatoes à la royal, a *viennoiserie* of French pastries, and porridge with caramelized fruits!"

"Horace, you've outdone yourself," said Bronwyn, her mouth already full.

Plates were filled and thanks were given. I was so eager to eat that it was several minutes before I thought to ask where the groceries had come from.

"They may or may not have floated off the shelves of a market down the road," said Millard.

I stopped mid-chew. "You *stole* all this?"

"Millard!" said Miss Peregrine. "What if you had gotten caught?"

"Impossible, I'm a master thief," he said. "It's my third-most impressive skill, after my extreme intelligence and near-perfect memory."

"But they have cameras in stores now," I said. "If they get you on video, it could be a big problem."

"Oh," said Millard. He seemed suddenly fascinated by the caramelized peach slice at the end of his fork.

"*Very* impressive thieving," said Enoch. "What was your first-most impressive skill again?"

Miss Peregrine put down her silverware and snapped her fingers. "All right, children. We're adding stealing from normals to the mustn't-ever list."

Everyone groaned.

"I'm quite serious!" Miss Peregrine said. "If the police were to pay us a visit, it would be no small inconvenience."

Enoch slumped dramatically in his chair. "The present is so *tiresome*. Remember how easy these things were to sort out in the loop?" He drew a line across his throat: "*Ckkkkk!* Goodbye, troublesome normal!"

"We're not on Cairnholm anymore," Miss Peregrine said, "and this isn't a game of Raid the Village. The actions you take here have real and permanent consequences."

"I was only kidding," Enoch grumbled.

"No, you *weren't*," Bronwyn hissed.

Miss Peregrine held up her hand for silence. "What's the new rule?"

"Mustn't steal," the kids chorused unenthusiastically.

"And?"

A few seconds passed. The headmistress frowned.

"Mustn't kill normals?" Olive ventured.

"That's right. There will be no killing of *anyone* in the present."

"What if they're really annoying?" asked Hugh.

"No matter. You may not kill them."

"Without permission from *you*," said Claire.

"No, Claire," said Miss Peregrine sharply. "No killing at *all*."

"Oh, all right," said Claire.

It might have been chilling talk had I not known them so well. Still, it was a stark reminder of how much they had to learn about life in the present. Which reminded me—

"When should we start these normalling lessons?" I asked.

"How about today?" Emma said eagerly.

"Right now!" said Bronwyn.

"What should I start with? What do you want to know?"

"Why don't you fill in our knowledge of the past seventy-five years or so," said Millard. "History, politics, music, popular culture, recent breakthroughs in science and technology . . ."

"I was thinking more along the lines of learning to talk like you're not from 1940 and crossing the street without being killed."

"I suppose that's important, too," said Millard.

"I just want to go *outside*," said Bronwyn. "We've been here since yesterday and all we've done so far is muck through a stinky swamp and ride a bus at night."

"Yeah!" said Olive. "I want to see an American city. And a municipal airport. And a pencil factory! I read a fascinating book about pencil factories—"

"Now, now," said Miss Peregrine. "We're not going on any grand expeditions today, so just get that out of your minds. We've got to walk before we can run, and given our limited transportation options, a walk sounds just about right. Mr. Portman, is there an underpopulated place we can perambulate that's proximate to here? I don't want the children interacting with normals unnecessarily before they've had more practice."

"There's the beach," I said. "It's pretty dead in the summertime."

"Perfect," said Miss Peregrine. She sent the kids off to change— "I want to see sun protection!" she called after them. "Hats! Parasols!"—and I was about to go and change, too, when I felt the dread return.

"What do we do about my family?" I asked her.

"They were dosed with enough dust to keep them sleeping into the afternoon," she said. "But just in case, we'll post someone here to keep watch over them."

"Okay, but then what?"

"You mean, after they wake?"

"Yeah. How am I supposed to explain . . . *you*?"

She smiled. "That, Mr. Portman, is entirely your decision. But if you like, we can talk strategy as we walk."

◆   ◆   ◆

I gave my friends permission to raid the closets for beach-appropriate clothing, since they had none, and it was truly strange to see them return a few minutes later dressed in something like modern outfits. Nothing fit Olive or Claire, so they added floppy sun hats and dark glasses to what they were already wearing, which made them look like celebrities trying to dodge paparazzi. Millard wore nothing at all save a slather of sunscreen across his face and shoulders, which turned him into a sort of walking blur. Bronwyn had on a floral top and slouchy linen pants, Enoch had snagged some swim shorts and an old T-shirt, and Horace looked downright preppy in a blue polo and a pair of khaki chinos, cuffs neatly rolled. The only one who hadn't changed was Hugh; still moody and moping, he had volunteered to stay behind and watch over my parents. I gave him my uncle's phone, pulled up my own cell number on the screen, and showed him how to call me in case they started waking up.

Then Miss Peregrine came into the room, and everyone *oohed* and *ahhed*. She wore a fringed top with scooped-out shoulders, tropical-print capri pants, aviator sunglasses, and her perpetually upswept hair towered through the middle of a pink plastic sun visor. It was slightly disconcerting to see her dressed in my mom's clothes, but she looked absolutely normal, which was, I suppose, the point.

"You look so modern!" Olive cooed.

"And *strange*," said Enoch, wrinkling his nose.

"We must be masters of disguise, if we're to pass in different worlds," Miss Peregrine said.

"Careful, Miss P, all the bachelors will be after you!" Emma said as she walked in.

"*You're* one to talk," Bronwyn said. "Woo-woo, look out, boys!"

I turned to her, and the breath caught in my throat. She wore a one-piece swim dress with a skirt bottom that stopped mid-thigh. It was far from scandalous, but easily the most revealing thing I'd ever seen her wear. (She had *legs*!) I'd known it since the moment I met her, but Emma Bloom was achingly pretty, and I had to make a conscious effort not to stare.

"Oh, hush," Emma said, and then she caught me looking and smiled. That smile—my God—it lit me up from the inside.

"Mr. Portman."

I turned to face Miss Peregrine, my dopey grin melting.

"Uh, yeah?"

"Are you ready? Or have you been entirely incapacitated?"

"No, I'm good."

"I'll bet you are," Enoch said with a snicker.

I knocked him with my shoulder as I parted the crowd, and then I threw open the front door and led my peculiar friends out into the world.

◆   ◆   ◆

I lived on a skinny barrier island called Needle Key: five miles of touristy bars and waterfront houses with a bridge at each end, bisected by a winding lane overhung with banyan trees. It only qualified as an island thanks to a long ditch of water that separated us from the mainland by about a thousand feet, which at low tide you could cross without getting your shirt wet. Rich people's houses fronted the Gulf; the rest of us looked out on Lemon Bay, which on quiet mornings was really very nice, with sailboats drifting by and herons fishing for their breakfast along the banks. It was a safe and sweet place to grow up, and I probably should have been more grateful, but I had spent my youth fighting the sensation—creeping at first, then overwhelming—that I belonged elsewhere, that my brain had begun to melt, and that if I stayed here a day past graduation it would liquify entirely and run out of my ears.

I kept us hidden behind a thicket of hedge at the end of my driveway until all the cars within hearing range had passed, and then we darted across the street to a footpath, intentionally neglected and overgrown with mangroves so tourists couldn't find it. After a minute or two of bushwhacking, the path broke open onto Needle Key's main attraction: a long white-sand beach and the gulf, emerald-green and spreading out endlessly.

I heard a few gasps escape my friends. They had seen beaches before—had lived on an island for most of their unnaturally long lives—but they'd rarely seen one so pretty, with water as flat and calm as a lake, an apron of powdery white sand that curved away gently, fringed palms waving. This pristine view was the entire reason some twenty thousand souls lived in an otherwise nowhere town, and in moments like this, with the sun high in the sky and an easy breeze chasing away the heat, you couldn't fault them their choice.

"Goodness, Jacob," said Miss Peregrine, taking in a lungful of air. "What a little paradise you have here."

"Is that the Pacific?" asked Claire.

Enoch snorted. "It's the Gulf of Mexico. The Pacific's on the opposite end of the continent."

We strolled along the beach, the smaller kids circling us as they ran to collect shells, the rest just enjoying the view and the sunshine. I slowed to match Emma's stride and took her hand. She glanced at me and smiled, and we both sighed at the same time, then laughed. We talked for a while about the beach and how pretty it all was, a topic that was quickly exhausted—and then I asked the group about how life in Devil's Acre had been for them. I had only heard about their trips outside the Acre via the Panloopticon, but surely they had done more than travel.

"Travel is crucial to one's development," said Miss Peregrine, her tone strangely defensive. "Until they have traveled, even the most educated person is ignorant. It's important the children learn that our society is not the center of the peculiar universe."

Aside from these occasional field trips, Miss Peregrine explained that she and the other ymbrynes had made a mighty effort to create a stable environment for their wards. Like my friends, most had been torn away from the loops where they'd lived much of their lives. In some cases those loops were now collapsed, gone forever. Many had lost friends in the hollowgast raids, been injured, or endured other traumas. And though Devil's Acre, with its filth and chaos and its history as the center of Caul's evil empire, was not an ideal place to recover from trauma, the ymbrynes had done their best to make it a sanctuary. The refugee children, along with many peculiar adults who had fled the wights' campaign of terror, found new homes there. They had founded a new academy, where daily lectures and discussions were held, taught by ymbrynes when they were available, and by peculiar adults with areas of special expertise when they were not.

"It can be a bit dull, sometimes," said Millard. "But it's nice to be among scholars."

"It's only dull because you think you know more than the teachers," said Bronwyn.

"When they aren't ymbrynes, I usually do," he replied. "And the ymbrynes are nearly always busy these days."

They were busy, Miss Peregrine said, with "a hundred thousand unpleasant tasks," most of which had to do with cleaning up after the wights.

"They left a frightful mess," she said. There was the literal mess—the wights' battle-scarred compound, the loops they had damaged but not quite destroyed. More troublesome was the tide of damaged and compromised people they had left behind, like the ambrosia-addicted peculiars of Devil's Acre. They needed treatment for their addictions, but not all would accept it voluntarily. Then there was the thorny question of who among them could be trusted. Many had collaborated with the wights, some under duress, others willingly and to a degree that seemed clearly malicious, even treasonous. Trials were required. The peculiar justice system, which had been designed to handle at most a few cases per year, was being rapidly expanded to deal with dozens, most of which had not yet begun. Until they did, the accused sat cooling their heels in the prison Caul built for the victims of his cruel experiments.

"And when we aren't dealing with all of that unpleasantness," Miss Peregrine said, "the Ymbryne Council is holding meetings. Meetings all day, meetings into the night."

"About what?" I asked.

"The future," she replied stiffly.

"The council is having its authority challenged," said Millard. Miss Peregrine's expression curdled. Millard went on, oblivious. "Some people are saying it's time for a change in the way we govern ourselves. That the ymbryne system is outmoded, better suited to an earlier era. That the world has changed, and we must change with it."

"Ungrateful sods," Enoch said. "Throw them in jail with the traitors, I say."

"Now, that's exactly wrong," said Miss Peregrine. "Ymbrynes govern by popular consent. Everyone must be allowed to air their ideas, even if they are misguided."

"What do they disagree with you about?" I asked.

"Whether to go on living in loops, for one thing," Emma said.

"Don't most peculiars *have* to?" I said.

"Yes—unless we were to attempt a large-scale loop collapse event," said Millard, "like the one that reset our internal clocks. *That* certainly raised some eyebrows."

"Made people *jealous*, is what it did," said Emma. "The things people said to me when they heard we were coming here for a long visit! *Green* with envy."

"But we could have died in that loop collapse," I said. "It's too dangerous."

"That's true," said Millard, "at least, until we can understand the loop collapse phenomenon more completely. If we can make a proper science out of it, it might be possible to re-create what happened to us safely."

"But that could take a long time," said Miss Peregrine, "and some peculiars are not willing to wait. They're so tired of living in loops, they would risk dying."

"Absolute madness," said Horace. "I had no idea how many muddle-brained peculiars there were until we were all thrust into the Acre together, cheek by jowl."

"They're not half as crazy as the New World crowd," said Emma, and just the mention of their name made Miss Peregrine sigh. "They want to engage with normal society."

"Don't get me started on those lunatics!" said Enoch. "They think the world has become such an open and tolerant place that we could simply come out of hiding—*Hello, world! We're peculiar and proud of it!*—as if we wouldn't all be burned at the stake, just like old times."

"They're young, that's all," said Miss Peregrine. "They've never lived through a witch hunt or an anti-peculiar panic."

"Dangerous is what they are," said Horace, picking at his hands anxiously. "What if they do something reckless?"

"We ought to jail them, too," said Enoch. "That's what I think."

"And that's why you're not on the council, dear," said Miss Peregrine. "Now, that's quite enough. Politics is the last thing I want to discuss on a such a fine day."

"Hear, hear," said Emma. "What am I wearing this swimming costume for if we're not going in the blasted water?"

"Last one in's a rotten egg!" Bronwyn shouted, then took off running, which sparked a race for the water's edge.

Miss Peregrine and I stood and watched—I had my mind on other things and didn't feel much like swimming. But Miss Peregrine, despite all our talk of trouble and complication, didn't seem weighed down at all. She had a lot on her plate, but her problems—what I knew of them, anyway—had to do with growth and healing and freedom. And that was something to be grateful for.

◆　　◆　　◆

"Jacob, come and join us!"

Emma was shouting to me from the water's edge, holding up a starfish she'd plucked from the surf. Some of my friends were splashing around in the shallows, but others had dived right in and were swimming. The gulf in summer was warm as bathwater, nothing like the stormy Atlantic that lashed Cairnholm's cliffs. "It's magnificent!" Millard cried, his body a person-shaped vacuum in the sea. Even Olive was having fun, despite sinking three inches into the sand with every step.

"Jacob!" Emma called, waving me over as she bobbed through a wave.

"I'm wearing jeans!" I called back, which was true, but really I was happy just observing; there was something so sweet about watching my friends enjoy themselves here. I could feel it melting a patch of ice that had formed over my idea of home. I wanted them to have this whenever they wanted it—this uncomplicated peace—and maybe there was a way they could.

I had just figured out how to deal with my parents. It was so simple, I don't know why I hadn't thought of it before. I didn't have to concoct some airtight lie. I didn't need an expertly crafted cover story. Stories could be contradicted and lies could be found out, and even if they weren't, we would constantly have to tiptoe around my parents, always nervous they might see something peculiar, freak out, and blow our uncomplicated peace to bits. What's more, the idea of indefinitely hiding who I was from them sounded exhausting, especially now that my normal and peculiar lives were colliding. But the heart of it was this: My parents weren't bad people. I hadn't been abused or neglected. They just didn't understand me, and I thought they deserved a chance to.

So I would tell them the truth. If I revealed it gradually and gently enough, maybe it wouldn't be too traumatic for them. If they met my friends in a calm setting, one by one, and my friends' peculiarities were introduced only after my parents had gotten to know them a bit, maybe it would work. Why not? My dad was a father, and son, of peculiars. If any normal should be able to understand, it was him. And if my mom was slow to warm up, Dad would pull her along.

Maybe then—finally—they would believe me, and accept me for who I was. Maybe then we would feel like a real family.

I felt a little nervous about suggesting it, so I tried to bring it up to Miss Peregrine without the others hearing. Most were still swimming or beachcombing in the shallows. She was being followed by a flock of tiny sandpipers, pecking at her ankles with their long beaks.

"Shoo!" she said, sweeping her foot at them as she walked. "I'm not your mother."

They fluttered off in a wave, but kept following.

"Birds love you, don't they?" I said.

"In Britain they respect me—and my personal space. Here they seem downright needy." She swept her foot again. "Go on, shoo!" They skittered into the water.

"We were due for a chat, yes?"

"I was thinking. What if I just explained everything to my parents?"

"Enoch, Millard, stop that roughhousing!" she shouted through cupped hands, then turned to me. "And we don't wipe their memories?"

"Before I give up on them completely, I'd like to give it one good try," I said. "I know it might not work, but if it did, things would be so much easier."

I was afraid she would shut me down right away, but she didn't—not exactly.

"That would be making a big exception to a long-established rule," she said. "There are very few normals who are privy to our secrets. The Ymbryne Council would have to grant special approval. There's an initiation process. An oath-taking ceremony. A long probationary period . . ."

"So you're saying it's not worth it."

"I'm not saying that at all."

"Really?"

"I'm only saying it's complex. But in the case of your parents, it could be worth the trouble."

"What could?"

Horace had come up behind us. So much for keeping this between me and Miss Peregrine.

"I was thinking about telling my parents the truth about us," I said. "To see if they can handle it."

"What? *Why?*"

That was more the reaction I'd been expecting.

"I think they deserve to know."

"They tried to have you committed!" Enoch said. Now the others were coming out of the water and starting to gather around.

"I know what they did," I said, "but they only did it because they were worried about me. If they had known the truth—and were *okay* with it—they never would have done that. And it would make things so much simpler any time you guys wanted to come visit, or when I want to visit you."

"You mean you aren't coming back with us?" said Olive.

Emma had just arrived, dripping seawater, and when she heard this she narrowed her eyes at me. We hadn't talked about this privately yet, but here I was discussing it with everyone.

"I'm going to finish high school first," I said. "But if I handle this right, we can see one another all the time over the next couple of years."

"That's a very big *if*," said Millard.

"Just imagine," I said, "I could come help with the reconstruction efforts—on weekends, maybe—and you guys could come here whenever you like, and learn about the normal world. You could even go to school with me, if you wanted."

I glanced at Emma. Her arms were crossed, her face unreadable.

"Go to school with *normals*?" said Olive.

"We don't even answer the door when the pizza arrives," said Claire.

"I'm going to teach you how to deal with them. You'll be experts in no time."

"This is sounding more far-fetched by the second," said Horace.

"I just want to give my parents a chance," I said. "If it doesn't work . . ."

"If it doesn't work, Miss P can wipe their memories," said Emma. She walked over to me and threaded her arm through mine. "Doesn't it seem tragic that Abe Portman's own son doesn't know who his father was?"

She was on board. I squeezed her arm, grateful for the backup.

"Tragic, but necessary," said Horace. "His parents can't be trusted. No normal can. It makes me nervous just thinking about what they might do. They could expose us all!"

"They wouldn't," I said, though a little voice in my head added, *Would they?*

"Why don't we just pretend we're normal when they're around?" asked Bronwyn. "Then they won't be upset."

"I really don't think that would work," I said.

"Some of us don't have the privilege of pretending we're normal," said Millard.

"I hate pretending anyway," said Horace. "How about we just be ourselves and Miss Peregrine can wipe their memories at the end of every day?"

"Too many wipes and people go soft in the head," said Millard. "Moaning, drooling, the whole bit."

I looked to Miss Peregrine, who verified this with a quick nod.

"What if they were to go on holiday somewhere far away?" Claire suggested. "Miss P could plant the idea in their heads after the wipe, when they're suggestible."

"And what about after they come back?" I said.

"Then we lock them in the basement," Enoch replied.

"We should lock *you* in the basement," said Emma.

I was causing everyone stress and anxiety they didn't need. They would worry. *I* would worry. And all for the sake of my parents, who had caused me nothing but grief for the last six months.

I turned to Miss Peregrine. "It's too complicated," I said. "You should just wipe their memories."

"If you want to try telling them the truth, I think you should," she replied. "I find it's nearly always worth the effort."

"Really?" I said. "Are you sure?"

"If it looks like it could work, I'll seek council approval retroactively. If it doesn't, I have a feeling we'll know rather quickly."

"Fantastic!" said Emma. "And now that we've got that sorted . . ." She pulled me by the arm toward the water—"It's time to swim!"—and I was caught so off guard that I couldn't stop her.

"Wait—no—my phone!"

I rescued it from my jeans pocket just before I fell chest-high into the water, then tossed it to Horace back on the shore.

◆   ◆   ◆

Emma splashed me and swam away, and I paddled after her, laughing. I was suddenly wildly happy. Happy to be among friends, my eyes dazzled by the sun, paddling after a beautiful girl who liked me. *Loved* me, she'd said once.

Bliss.

Up ahead, Emma had found a sandbar. She stood in waist-high water despite being far from shore. It was a trick of these friendly tides that I had always loved.

"Why, hello!" I said, slightly out of breath as I planted my feet on the sandbar.

"Do you always go swimming in blue jeans?" she said, grinning.

"Oh yeah. Everyone does. It's the latest thing."

"It is not," she said.

"Seriously. It's called nano-denim, and it dries five seconds after you get out of the water."

"Really. That's astounding."

"It folds itself, too."

She squinted at me. "You're serious?"

"And it makes you breakfast."

She splashed me. "It's not nice, playing tricks on girls from past centuries!"

"You make it too easy!" I said, ducking and then splashing her back.

"Actually, I was expecting more in the way of flying cars and robot assistants and such. Robot pants at the *very* least."

"Sorry about that. We made the internet instead."

"Very disappointing."

"I know. I'd rather have flying cars."

"I mean it's disappointing that you've turned out to be such a liar. I really had high hopes for us. Ah, well."

"I just had to get it out of my system. No more tricking, I promise!"

"You *promise* promise?"

"Ask me something else. I *promise* promise to tell you the truth."

"Okay." She grinned, raked wet bangs away from her eyes, and crossed her arms. "Tell me about your first kiss."

I felt myself blush and tried sinking into the water to hide it— but of course I couldn't really because I had to breathe.

"I walked right into that, didn't I?"

"You know practically every nook and cranny of *my* romantic history. How is it fair that I don't know anything about yours?"

"Because there's nothing worth knowing."

"Oh, bunkum. Not even a kiss?"

I glanced around, hoping for some distraction that might interrupt her line of questioning.

"Um . . ." I let my mouth sink below the waterline and mumbled something that came out as bubbles.

She lay her palms on the surface of the water. After a moment it began to hiss and steam. "Tell me or I'll boil you!"

I bobbed upward. "Okay, okay, I confess! I dated a supermodel rocket scientist. And a pair of twins who won a grant for their humanitarian work and exotic lovemaking skills. But you're better than any of them!"

The steam had briefly obscured her, and when it cleared, she was no longer there.

"Emma?" I panicked, searching the water. "Emma!"

Then a splash came from behind me, and I spun around and got a face full of water. There she was, laughing at me.

"I said no tricks!"

"You freaked me out!" I said, wiping my eyes.

"You can't expect me to believe that such a handsome young lad never had a *single* kiss before I came along."

"Okay, one," I admitted, "but it's hardly worth mentioning. I think the girl was, like, experimenting on me."

"Oh my. Now, that *does* sound interesting."

"Her name was Janine Wilkins. She kissed me behind the bleachers during Mehlanie Shah's birthday party at the Stardust Skate Center. She said she was tired of being a 'kiss virgin' and wanted to see what it felt like. Then she swore me to secrecy, and said if I told anyone about it she'd spread a rumor that I still wet the bed."

"Goodness. What a trollop."

"And that's my whole exciting history."

Her eyes got wide, then she lay back in the water and let herself float. The happy chatter of our friends rose and fell beneath the gentle crash of surf. "Jacob Portman, pure as the driven snow."

"I, uh—yeah," I said, feeling awkward. "That's a weird way to put it."

"It's nothing to be ashamed of, you know."

"I know," I said, though I'm not sure I did, then. Every movie and TV show aimed at teenage guys made it seem like not having lost your virginity by the time you had your driver's license was some kind of personal failure. Which I knew was idiotic—but it's hard not to internalize that stuff when you hear it so often.

"It means you're careful with your heart," she said. "I appreciate that." She cocked an eye at me. "And I wouldn't worry, in any case. I'm certain it's not . . ." She dragged a finger across the water, a trail of steam chasing it ". . . a permanent condition."

"Oh yeah?" I said, a little thrill shooting through me.

"Time will tell," she said, letting her legs sink, then righting herself. She was focused on me in this intense way, studying me as we drifted closer, our hands linking and feet entangling underwater. Before anything else could entangle, we heard shouts, and I saw Miss Peregrine and Horace waving us in from the shore.

◆　　◆　　◆

"It's Hugh," said Horace, handing me my phone as I slogged out of the surf.

I held it away from my dripping head. "Hello?"

"Jacob! Your uncles are waking up. Your parents, too, I think."

"I'll be there in five minutes," I said. "Just keep them where they are."

"I'll try, but hurry," said Hugh. "I don't have any more of that dust stuff, and your uncles are *mean*."

And then all of us who could run, ran.

Bronwyn carried Olive. Miss Peregrine, who could walk and fly but could not run, told us to go on ahead, and over my shoulder I watched as she dove into the sea and disappeared beneath the waves. A moment later her clothes floated to the surface without her, and then she burst out of the water in bird form and flapped over our heads toward my house. Seeing her shape-shift always made me want to clap my hands and shout, but I restrained myself in case any normals were watching, and ran on.

We arrived at my front door sweaty, sandy, and panting, but there was no time to clean up. I could hear my uncles' angry voices through the garage door. We had to take care of them first, before old Mrs. Melloroos heard and called the cops.

As soon as we got inside, I went to the garage and began apologizing to my uncles. They were angry and confused and starting to get belligerent, and after a minute they barged past me into the house. Miss Peregrine was waiting in the hall with her feather and her penetrating stare, and soon both uncles were calm, quiet, and as pliable as Play-Doh. Their minds were so easy to wipe it was almost disappointing. In the dopey, highly suggestible state that followed, Miss Peregrine let me do the talking. I sat them on counter stools in the kitchen and explained that the last twenty-four hours had been totally uneventful, that my mental health was beyond reproach, and that all the recent family drama was the result of a misdiagnosis on the part of my new psychiatrist. Just to be on the safe side, I told them that any strange British people they might run into over the next few weeks—or speak to on the phone if they called the house—were distant relatives on my dad's side, and they had come to pay respects to my dear departed grandfather. Uncle Bobby replied with hypnotized nods. Uncle Les kept muttering "Mm-hmm," while filling his pockets with scrambled eggs from the leftover scraps of breakfast. I told them to go get some sleep, called them taxis, and sent them home.

Then it was time to deal with my parents. I asked Bronwyn to carry them upstairs to their bedroom before the sleep dust wore off, so they wouldn't wake up in a wrecked car, surrounded by reminders of the previous night's trauma. She left them in their bed and closed the door, and for a minute I paced the hall outside, leaving sandy footprints on the carpet, nervously trying to figure out what to say.

Emma came up the stairs. "*Hey,*" she whispered. "Before you go in, I wanted you to know something."

I went to her and she clasped my hand. "Yeah?"

"She fancied you."

"Who?"

"Janine Wilkins. A girl doesn't lose her kiss virginity to just anyone, you know."

"I, uh—" My brain was trying and failing to be in two very different places at once. "You're messing with me, right?"

She laughed and looked down. "I mean, she *did,* but yes. I just came to wish you good luck. Not that you need it. You've got this."

"Thanks."

"We're right downstairs, should you need anything."

I nodded. And then I kissed her. She smiled and slipped back down the stairs.

◆　　◆　　◆

They woke up gently in their own bed, sun laddering through the shutters. I watched them from a chair in the corner, nibbling my fingernails and trying to stay calm.

My mom opened her eyes first. She blinked, rubbed them. Sat up and groaned and massaged her neck. She had no idea she'd been sleeping in a car for eighteen hours. It would make anybody sore.

Then she saw me, and her brow furrowed.

"Honey? What are you doing here?"

"I, uh—I just wanted to explain some things."

Then she looked down at herself, noticed that the clothes she was wearing were the same she'd been wearing last night. A confused look stole over her face.

"What time is it?"

"About three," I said. "Everything's okay."

"No," she said, looking around the room, confusion turning to panic.

I stood up. She pointed at me. "Stay there."

"Mom, don't freak out. Let me explain."

She looked away—ignored me, as if maybe I weren't really there. "Frank." She shook my father awake. "Frank!"

"Mmm." He rolled over.

She shook harder. "*Franklin.*"

This was it: my last opportunity. The moment I'd been ready-ing myself for. I had run through a few different approaches in my mind, but they all sounded ridiculous to me now—too blunt, too dumb. Just as my dad sat up and began to rub the sleep from his eyes, I all but lost my nerve, suddenly convinced I didn't have the right words.

It didn't matter. Ready or not, it was showtime.

"Mom, Dad, there's something I need to talk to you about."

I walked to the foot of their bed and started talking. I can hardly remember what it was I said, only that I felt like a door-to-door salesman whose pitch was bombing. I tried to explain how my grandfather's last words and his strange snapshots and the postcard from Miss Peregrine had led me to discover the pe-culiars' house, and in it all of Abe's old friends, who were not only still alive, they weren't even old. But I found myself dancing around terms like *time loop* and *powers* because it just seemed like it was too soon, too much. My clumsily censored version of the truth combined with jitters seemed only to confirm to them that I was out of my mind, and the more I talked, the more they inched away from me, my mom drawing the comforter up around her shoulders and my dad scooting back against the headboard, that vein that popped out from his forehead when he was stressed dancing a jig. As if whatever mania was in me might be conta-gious.

"Just stop!" my mom shouted, finally interrupting me. "I can't listen to any more of this."

"But it's *true*, and if you'd only hear me out—"

She threw the covers back and leapt out of bed. "We've heard enough! And we already know what happened. You were torn up about your grandpa. You secretly quit taking your medication." She was pacing, angry. "We sent you halfway around the world at the worst possible time on the advice of a quack, and you had a breakdown! It's nothing for you to be ashamed of, but we have to deal with this honestly. Okay? You can't keep hiding behind these . . . *stories*."

I felt like I'd been slapped. "You won't even give me a chance."

"We've given you a *hundred*," my dad said.

"No. You never believe me."

"Well, of course we don't," my mom said. "You're a lonely boy who lost someone important. And then you meet these kids, who are 'special' just like your grandpa was, and only *you* can see them? It doesn't take a PhD to diagnose. You've been making up imaginary friends since you were two."

"I didn't say I was the only one who could see them," I said. "You met them last night in the driveway."

Both my parents looked, for an instant, like they'd seen a ghost. Maybe they had blocked what happened last night from their minds. That can happen sometimes, when an isolated event so thoroughly disagrees with a person's concept of reality.

"What are you talking about?" my mom said, her voice quavering.

It seemed there was nothing left to do but introduce them to my friends.

"Do you want to meet them?" I said. "Again?"

"*Jacob*," said my father, his tone a warning.

"They're here," I said. "I promise they aren't dangerous. Just . . . be cool, okay?"

I opened the door and brought Emma into the room. She had gotten as far as "Hi, Mr. and Mrs. Portman," when my mom screamed.

Miss Peregrine and Bronwyn ran in.

"What's the matter?" Miss Peregrine said.

My mom shoved her—actually *shoved* Miss Peregrine—"Get out. Get OUT!" I saw Bronwyn restrain herself from grabbing my mom and throwing her into a wall.

"Maryann, calm down!" my dad shouted.

"They're not going to hurt you!" I said.

I tried to grab her by the shoulders, but she wrenched out of my grip and sprinted from the room.

"Maryann!" my dad shouted again, but when he tried to run after her, Bronwyn grabbed him by the arms. He was too groggy from the dust to fight her.

I chased my mom down the stairs. She ran into the kitchen and grabbed a carving knife. The other peculiars came out of hiding, and as she stood with her back against the refrigerator, waving the knife, they ringed around her, just out of stabbing range.

"Calm down, Mrs. Portman!" Emma said. "We don't mean you any harm!"

"Get away from me!" my mom screamed. "Oh God. Oh *God*!"

Maybe it was Olive crawling toward her along the ceiling—she'd grabbed a fishing net from the garage and meant to drop it on my mom—or Millard's voice shouting from what seemed a floating bathrobe, but finally my mom just fainted. The knife clattered to the tile floor, and she slumped down next to it—a sight so pathetic I had to look away.

I could hear my dad shouting from upstairs. He was calling my mom's name. It must have sounded like we'd killed her.

"We've got her," Emma said to me. "Go to your father."

I stepped on the dropped knife and slid it under a cabinet, just in case my mom came to. Emma, Horace, Hugh, and Millard lifted her and carried her toward the couch. There was nothing more I could do, so I ran upstairs.

My dad was crouched in the corner of the bedroom, clutching a pillow. Bronwyn stood guard in the doorway with her arms spread, ready to catch him if he tried to run.

When my dad saw me, his expression turned to ice.

"Where is she?" he said. "What did they do to her?"

"Mom's okay," I said. "She's sleeping now."

He was shaking his head. "She'll never get over this."

"She will. Miss Peregrine has the power to take away certain memories. She won't remember."

"And your uncles?"

I nodded. "Same for them."

Miss Peregrine came in. "Mr. Portman. How do you do?"

My dad ignored her. Kept his eyes locked on me. "How could you?" He spat the words. "How could you bring *these people* into our house?"

"They came to help me," I said. "To convince you I wasn't insane."

"You can't do this to people." He was talking to Miss P now. "Blaze into their lives. Scare the hell out of everyone. Erase whatever you want. It isn't *right*."

"It seems the truth is more than your wife can handle—for the time being, anyway," Miss Peregrine said. "But Jacob was very much hoping that wouldn't be the case for you."

He stood up slowly. Let his hands drop to his sides. He looked resigned, resentful.

"Well, then. I guess you'd better lay it on me."

I turned to look at Miss Peregrine.

"You'll be okay?"

I nodded.

"We'll be right outside," she said, and she and Bronwyn went out, closing the door behind them.

❖   ❖   ❖

I talked for a long time. I sat on the edge of the bed, and my dad sat in the chair in the corner, his eyes low and shoulders slumped, like a child enduring a lecture. I didn't let his manner bother me. I told my story from the beginning, and this time I was calm.

I told him what I'd found on the island. How I had met the children and who they turned out to be. How I discovered I was one of them. I even told him about the hollowgast, though I didn't go into the complexities of what came after, the battles we fought or the Library of Souls or Miss Peregrine's evil brothers. It was enough, for now, that he know who his father was, and who I was.

When I finished, he hadn't spoken in several minutes. He didn't look afraid anymore. He just looked sad.

"Well?" I said.

"I should have known," he said. "The way you and your grandpa got along. Like you had a secret language." He was nodding gently to himself. "I should have known. I think part of me *did* know."

"What do you mean? You knew about Grandpa, but not about me?"

"Yes. No. Hell, I don't know." He was staring past me, hard, like he was trying to see through fog. "I guess deep down I knew, but I never wanted to believe it."

I inched toward the edge of the bed. "He told you?"

"I think he tried to, once. But I must have blocked it out—or someone stole the memory from me. But last night—" He tapped his forehead. "Seeing those people jogged something loose in my brain."

Now it was his turn to talk and mine to listen.

"I was around ten when it happened. Your grandfather would go on these long business trips. He'd be away for weeks at a time. I always wanted to go with him, and I used to beg and plead, but he always, always said no. Until one day. One day he said yes."

My father stood up and began pacing, as if just remembering this was giving him nervous energy to burn.

"We drove up to, I don't remember exactly, North Florida or Georgia. We picked up an associate of his along the way. I knew him; he'd been by the house a time or two. Black guy. Always had a cigar in his mouth. Abe called him H. Just H. Anyway, he'd been real friendly the other times I'd met him, but this time he had a weird energy and he kept *looking* at me, and a couple of times I heard him say to my dad, *You sure about this?*

"Anyway, it got dark and we stopped for the night. Some ratty old motel. And in the middle of the night my dad wakes me up, and he's scared. He says, *Frank, get your things*, and he rushes me out to the car. I'm still in my pajamas, and now *I'm* scared. Because nothing frightened my dad. *Nothing.* Well, we tear out of that parking lot like zombies are chasing us, but we don't get more than a couple of blocks before the car goes *whoom*—it just lurches, like something hit us from the side, only there were no other cars around. And then Dad hits the brakes and throws it in park and jumps out. He says, *Get down, Frank, stay outta sight*, but I can't look away, and the next thing I know he gets yanked up into the air by something I can't see. And he starts making these awful noises in his throat, and he drops back down to Earth, and he's still making those god-awful sounds like an animal, and his eyes—I can see him in the headlights of the car—his eyes are rolled back in his head, all white, and his clothes are all stained with this black crud, and I get out of the car and start running, right into this cornfield. And I don't look back. I think I must have passed out at some point, because the next thing I remember is I'm back in a motel room bed, and there's my dad and H and two or three other people. And they're so *strange*-looking. They're all covered in dirt and blood, and the smell . . . God, the *smell*. And one of them—I'll never forget—he's got no face at all. Just a mask of skin. I'm so scared. Too scared to even scream. And Dad's saying, *It's okay, Frankie, don't be scared, this lady's gonna talk to you now, don't be scared.* And this woman, she looked kind of like *her*—" At some point Miss Peregrine had cracked the door and leaned into the room, and my dad gestured at her. "She did something to me, so that the next day the memories were barely there anymore. Like it was just a bad dream. And my dad never ever spoke about it after that."

"She was supposed to wipe your memories," Miss Peregrine said. "It seems she didn't quite finish the job."

"I wish to God she had," my dad said. "I had nightmares for years. For a while I thought I was really losing it. My dad told her not to get rid of my memories completely. Kind of a sadistic thing to do to a kid, don't you think? But part of him *wanted* me to know. It was like a . . . a blackboard that had been wiped, but if you squinted hard enough you could still read it a little? But I didn't want to see it. I didn't want to know. Because I really, really did not want that to be true about my father. That he was . . . *like that.*"

"You just wanted a normal father," I said.

"Right," said my dad, as if, finally, I had understood.

"Well, he wasn't," I said. "And neither am I."

"So it would seem." He stopped pacing and sat on the edge of the bed, his body angled away from mine.

"Your son is a brave and gifted young man," Miss Peregrine said icily. "You should be very proud of him."

My father muttered something. I asked him what he'd said.

He looked up, and there was a look in his eyes now that hadn't been there a moment ago. It was something like loathing.

"You made a choice."

"It wasn't a choice," I said. "It's who I am."

"No. You chose them. You chose these . . . *people* . . . over us."

"It doesn't have to be like that. Either-or. We can coexist."

"Tell that to your mother, screaming like a lunatic! Tell that to your uncles, who are—where? What did you do to them?"

"They're fine, Dad."

"Nothing is FINE," he bellowed, jumping to his feet again. "You've destroyed everything!"

Miss Peregrine had been lingering at the door but now stormed into the room, Bronwyn close behind her. "Sit *down*, Mr. Portman—"

"No! I will not live in a madhouse! I will not subject my family to this insanity!"

"This could *work*," I said, "I'm telling you—"

He came at me in a rush, and I thought for a moment he might hit me. But he stopped short. "I made my choice, Jacob. A *long* time ago. And now it looks like you've made yours." We were chest to chest, my father red-cheeked and breathing hard.

"*I'm still your son,*" I whispered.

His jaw was set, but I saw his lip tremble, as if he were about to speak. Then he turned away and went to the chair and sat again, his head in his hands. It was silent in the room for a moment, the only sounds his uneven, hitching breaths.

Finally, I said, "Tell me what you want."

He raised his head without looking at me. Pressed a finger to his temple. "Go ahead," he said hoarsely. "Wipe it. That's what you were going to do anyway."

I felt a sudden desperation.

"Not if you don't want us to. Not if you think—"

"It's what I want," he said, looking to Miss Peregrine. "Only this time, finish the job."

He sat back in the chair, limp, and the light seemed to go out of his eyes.

Miss Peregrine looked at me.

I could feel myself going numb, head to toe.

I nodded at her. And then I left the room.

◆   ◆   ◆

Emma stopped me as I was rushing down the stairs.

"Are you okay? I didn't hear what happened—"

"I'm fine," I said.

I was not, but I did not yet know how to talk about it.

"Jacob, please talk to me."

"Not now," I said.

I needed, very badly, to be alone. More specifically, I needed to scream out the window of a fast-moving car until my breath gave out.

She let me go. I didn't look back; I didn't want to see the look on her face. I ran past my mother crumpled on the couch and my friends in a nervous, whispering cluster. I snatched the car keys from the wooden bowl on the kitchen counter, went into the garage, and slapped the door button. The garage door made a painful grinding whine as it tried to open, but the car's rear bumper was so badly wedged into it that it would not, and a moment later it gave up and went silent. I swore and kicked the closest thing to me as hard as I could. It happened to be a boxy old TV stashed under the garage workbench. My shoeless foot went through the back of it and shards of plastic went flying, my foot now numb and probably cut. I extracted it roughly and limped out the side door into the yard and screamed at the trees.

The knot of boiling anger in my chest shrank a little.

I rounded into the backyard, crossed the grass, and walked down our little sun-warped dock that jutted into the bay. My parents didn't own a boat. Not even a canoe. I only ever used the dock for one thing: sitting on the end with my feet dangled into the brown water, thinking about unpleasant things. Which is what I did now.

After a minute or two, I heard footsteps coming down the planks. I was ready to turn and bark at whoever it was to please go to hell, but then the slightly uneven gait gave her away, and I couldn't bring myself to be rude to Miss Peregrine.

"Watch out for nails," I said without turning.

"Thank you," she replied. "May I sit?"

I kept my eyes on the water. Shrugged. A boat puttered by in the distance.

"It's done," she said. "Your parents are in a suggestible state now, ready for input. I need to know what you'd like me to tell them."

"I don't care."

A few seconds passed. She sat down on the dock beside me.

"When I was your age," she said, "I tried something similar with my parents."

"Miss Peregrine, I really don't feel like talking right now."

"So, listen."

Sometimes Miss Peregrine couldn't be argued with.

"I had been away at Miss Avocet's ymbryne academy for a few years," she began, "when it occurred to me that I still had a mother and father, and it would please me to see them again. Because some considerable time had passed since I'd gotten my wings and been rather unceremoniously driven from my home, I thought they might see me in a different light—as a person, and a daughter—rather than some loathsome aberration. I found them living in a hovel on the outskirts of our village. They had been shunned because of me. Even our relations refused to associate with them. Everyone believed they were consorts of the devil. I tried to win them over. They still loved me, but they feared me even more. It ended with my mother cursing the day I was born and my father chasing me from the house with an iron from the fire. Years later, I heard they had died—sewed stones into their pockets and walked into the sea."

She sighed. A breeze whisked up, carrying away the stagnant summer heat for a moment. It hardly seemed possible that the world she was describing could exist alongside this one.

"I'm sorry that happened to you," I said.

"Our blood relationships often don't survive the truth," she replied.

I thought about that for a moment, and then I got annoyed. "That's not what you said an hour ago. You said the truth is worth the trouble, or something."

She shifted uncomfortably, brushing sand from the hem of her dress. "I thought I should let you try."

"Why?" I said, my voice starting to rise.

"It's not my place to tell you how to be a son to your parents."

"As far as I'm concerned, I don't have parents."

"Don't say that," she said. "I know they said terrible things to you, but you can't—"

I stood up suddenly and jumped into the water. I held my breath and stayed down, hoping the blackness and the sudden chill would blot out my thoughts:

He doesn't want to know you.

He chose oblivion rather than knowing you.

And then I screamed into the muddy depths until I ran out of breath. When I surfaced again, maybe twenty feet from the dock, Miss Peregrine was on her feet, about to dive in after me.

"Jacob! Are you—"

"I'm fine, I'm fine," I said. The water was so shallow that I could easily touch bottom. "I told you I didn't feel like talking."

"That you did," she said.

She stood on the dock and I stood in the bay up to my waist, my feet sinking into the mud while little fish nibbled at my legs.

"I'm going to say something," she said, "and you aren't allowed to throw a tantrum in response."

"Fine."

"I know you don't like it much right now, but I promise you will regret throwing this normal life away."

"What life? I've got no friends here. My parents are afraid and ashamed of me."

"They are alive, which is more than most of us can say. And, as of five minutes ago, they don't remember any of what just happened."

"Well, I do. And I'm not interested in pretending I'm someone I'm not for the rest of my life. If that's the price of being their son, it's not worth it."

She looked as if she wanted to shout something at me, but then swallowed it back. "I never claimed being peculiar was easy," she said after a moment. "There are many unpleasant and difficult things about being one of us. Learning how to negotiate a world of people who can't understand you and don't want to—that's probably the hardest bit. Many find it impossible and retreat into loops. But I never saw that for you. You've got a very special talent, and I don't mean your facility with hollowgast. You're a shape-shifter of sorts, Jacob, able to move easily between worlds. You were never meant to be tied to just one home, or one family. You'll have many, like your grandfather did."

I looked up as a pelican sailed overhead, each wingbeat a little sigh, and imagined my grandfather's life. He had lived most of it in a crappy little house on the edge of a swamp. His wife and kids hardly knew him. He risked his life, year after year, fighting for the peculiar cause, and his reward in the end was to be treated like a senile old crank.

"I don't want to be like my grandfather. I don't want his life."

"You won't, you'll have your own. What about school?"

"I don't think you're listening to me. I don't want"—I turned around, flung my arms wide, screamed it across the water—"ANY! OF THIS! SHIT!"

I turned back to her, face flushing.

"Are you quite finished?" she said.

"Yes," I said quietly.

"Good. Now that I'm fully briefed on all the things you don't want . . . what *do* you want?"

"I want to do something to help the only people in the world who ever truly gave a damn about me. Peculiars. And I want to do something important. Something *big*."

"All right, then." She crouched down and extended her hand. "You can start right now."

I waded over and she hoisted me up onto the dock.

"I have a job that's absolutely crucial and that no one in peculiardom can do but you," Miss Peregrine was saying as we walked.

"Okay. What is it?"

"The children need contemporary outfits. I need you to take them shopping."

"*Shopping?*" I stopped walking. "You've got to be kidding."

She turned to face me. Her expression was flat.

"I am not."

"I said I want to do something important. In the *peculiar* world!"

She moved in close, her voice low and intense. "I've said it before, but it bears repeating. It is imperative to the future of *that* world that these children understand how to navigate *this* one. And there is no one but you to teach them, Jacob. Who else? The ones who've been living in loops for decades know nothing of it—they couldn't manage a modern-day street crossing! And the ones who haven't lived in loops are either very old or so young and new to our peculiar world that they're but neophytes themselves." She grabbed my shoulders in her hands and squeezed them. "I *know*. I know you're angry and you want to leave. But I beg you. Stay just a little longer. I think I know a way for you to exist here—only sometimes, whenever you like—while also doing important work with us in the loops."

"Yeah?" I said skeptically. "What is it?"

"Give me until—" She fished her pocket watch from her pants and glanced at it. "Until nightfall. Then you'll see. Satisfactory?"

My first thought was that it had something to do with the Panloopticon in Devil's Acre, but the closest loop, the one they'd used to get here last night, was hours away in the middle of a swamp. And, anyway, I didn't want to come and go like a commuter.

I wanted to leave all this behind, to go and *stay* gone. But Miss Peregrine was hard to say no to, and I had agreed to help my friends learn something about the present. I didn't feel right reneging on that promise outright.

"Fine," I said. "Tonight."

"Excellent." She was about to go when she said, "Oh, before I forget," and pulled an envelope out of her other pocket and handed it to me. "To cover the shopping."

I peeked inside. It was stuffed with fifty-dollar bills.

"Will that be sufficient?"

"Uh. I think so."

She nodded smartly and started toward the house, leaving me stunned with the envelope in my hand. "Much to do, much to do," she was muttering, and then she called over her shoulder, jabbing a finger into the air: "Tonight!"

CHAPTER THREE

*B*ecause my parents' now-three-doored sedan could only accommodate half our group, we'd have to go shopping in two shifts. Shift one would include Emma, because I always gave her preferential treatment and made no secret of it; Olive, because she was a cheerful presence and I wanted some cheering; Millard, because he wouldn't stop pestering me; and Bronwyn, because her muscles were the only way to force open the stuck garage door. I promised Hugh, Horace, Enoch, and Claire that I'd be back for them in a couple of hours. Horace said he wasn't interested in buying new clothes, anyway.

"The day denim became acceptable as daily wear," he said, side-eyeing me, "contemporary fashion lost all credibility. The modern runway looks like a hobo camp."

"You *have* to have new clothes," said Claire. "Miss Peregrine says."

Enoch scowled. "Miss Peregrine says, *Miss Peregrine says!* You sound like a windup toy."

We left them squabbling and went to the garage. With some duct tape, baling wire, and a little spot-welding by Emma, we managed to reattach the driver's-side door; it didn't open or close, but we were a lot less likely to get pulled over by curious police officers with four doors than with just three. When we were finished we all piled in. A minute later we were winding down the banyan-shaded road that traced the spine of Needle Key.

Big houses loomed on either side of us, glimpses of beach in the gaps between. It was the first time my friends had seen so much of this world by day, and they were quiet as they drank it in, the girls glued to the windows in back, Millard's breath fogging the glass on the passenger's side. I tried to imagine what it looked like to them, these sights that had long ago faded into near invisibility for me.

The key narrowed as we drove south, the big houses giving way to smaller ones, then to colonies of squat condos from the seventies, gaudy signs announcing their names: POLYNESIAN ISLES, PARADISE SHORES, FANTASY ISLAND. As we hit the commercial zone, more blasts of color: pink-roofed knickknack shops that sold sunscreen and beer cozies; bright yellow bait stores; striped-awning real estate offices. And bars, of course, their rows of tiki torches dancing and doors flung open to let the sea breeze in and the creaky warble of Jimmy Buffett karaoke covers out, echoing all the way down to the water's edge. The speed limit was so glacial, and the road so clogged with sun-drunk beachgoers, that there was time to sing along as you passed by. None of it had changed in my lifetime. Like a long-running play, you could set your watch to the movements of the actors and the timing of the set pieces, the same every day: the European tourists red as lobsters, wilting in the pencil-thin shade of cabbage palms; the leathery fishermen standing sentry along the bridge, hats and bellies drooping, casting lines into the shallows beside their Igloo coolers.

Leaving the key, we rose above the shimmering bay, tires humming over the bridge's metal grates. Then we descended to the mainland side, an archipelago of mini-malls and shopping plazas encircled by oceanic parking lots.

"What a strange landscape," said Bronwyn, breaking the silence. "Why did Abe move here, of all places in America?"

"Florida used to be one of the best areas for peculiars to hide," said Millard. "Before the hollow wars, anyway. It was the winter home of all the circuses, and the whole middle of the state is a great trackless swamp. They said anybody, no matter how peculiar, could find a place to blend in here—or to vanish."

We left behind the beige heart of town and headed out toward the boonies. Past the shuttered outlet mall, past the half-built housing development being slowly reclaimed by underbrush, loomed the biggest of the big-box stores. That's where we were headed. I turned down Piney Woods Road, the mile-long corridor along which all the town's nursing homes, over-fifty-five trailer parks, and retirement communities had been built. The road was lined with unsubtle billboards for hospitals, urgent care clinics, and mortuary parks. Everyone in town called Piney Woods Road the Highway to Heaven.

I started to brake as we approached a large sign depicting a circle of pine trees, and it wasn't until I'd actually made the turn that I caught myself. There were several routes to the shopping center we were going to, but by force of habit I'd chosen this one, and because I'd let my mind wander, my subconscious had made the turn for me. It was the entrance to Circle Village, my grandfather's subdivision.

"Oops, wrong way," I said, stopping the car and putting it into reverse.

But before I could turn around and get back onto the road, Emma said, "Wait a minute. Jacob—wait."

My hand lingered on the gearshift as a little wave of dread passed through me.

"Yeah?"

Emma was looking around, craning her neck to see out the back window.

"Isn't this where Abe used to live?" asked Emma.

"It is, yeah."

"Really?" said Olive, leaning up between the passenger's and driver's seats. "It *is*?"

"I turned in by accident," I said. "I've driven here so many times, it was just, like, muscle memory."

"I want to see," said Olive. "Can we look around?"

"Sorry, there's no time today," I said, stealing a glance at Emma in my mirror. I could see only the back of her head; she was turned all the way around, staring out the rear window at the guard station that marked the beginning of the neighborhood.

"But we're here *now*," Olive said. "Remember how we always used to talk about visiting? Didn't you always wonder what his house looked like?"

"Olive, *no*," said Millard. "It's a bad idea."

"Yeah," said Bronwyn, poking Olive and then jerking her head toward Emma. "Maybe another day."

Olive finally got the hint. "Oh. Okay. You know, actually, I don't feel like it, either . . ."

I hit the turn signal. I was just about to pull onto the road when Emma faced forward in her seat.

"I want to go," she said. "I want to see his house."

"You do?" I said.

"Are you sure?" asked Millard.

"Yes." She frowned. "Don't *look* at me like that."

"Like what?" I said.

"Like I won't be able to handle it."

"Nobody said that," said Millard.

"You were thinking it."

"What about the clothes shopping?" I said, still hoping to get out of this.

"I think we should pay our respects," said Emma. "That's more important than clothes."

The idea of touring them around Abe's half-empty house sounded downright morbid, but at this point it seemed cruel to deny them.

"All right," I said reluctantly. "Just for a minute."

For the others, I think, it was simple curiosity, to learn more about who Abe had become after he left their loop. For Emma, it was more than that. Since she had arrived in Florida, I knew she had been thinking about my grandfather. She had spent years trying to imagine how and where he lived, piecing together an incomplete picture of his life in America from occasional letters. For years she had dreamed of coming to visit him and now that she was actually here, she couldn't put it out of her mind. I felt her trying to, and failing. She'd spent too long dreaming about it—about him, about this place. In a way that felt entirely new and unsettling, I had started to feel his ghost looming between us in private moments. Maybe seeing where he had lived—and died—would help lay it to rest.

◆   ◆   ◆

I hadn't been to my grandfather's house in months, not since before my dad and I left for Wales—back when I knew nothing. Of all the surreal moments I had experienced since my friends came to stay, none felt more like a dream than driving through my grandfather's lazy, looping neighborhood with the very people he'd sent me abroad to find.

How little it had changed: Here was the same guard waving us through the gate, his face ghostly white with sunblock. Here were the yard gnomes and plastic flamingoes and rusting fish-shaped mailboxes, the houses they fronted all alike, a paint box of fading pastels. Here were the same craggy wraiths, slow-pedaling their orthopedic tricycles between the shuffleboard court and the community center. As if this place, too, were stuck in a time loop. Maybe that's what my grandfather had liked about it.

"Certainly is a humble place," said Millard. "No one would think a famous hollow-hunter lived here, that's certain."

"I'm sure that was intentional," said Emma. "Abe had to keep a low profile."

"Even so, I was expecting something a *bit* grander."

"I think it's sweet," said Olive. "Little houses all in a row. I'm just sorry that after all these years wishing we could pay Abe a visit, he isn't here to greet us."

"Olive!" Bronwyn hissed.

Olive glanced at Emma and winced.

"It's fine," Emma said breezily. But then I met her eyes in the rearview mirror, and she quickly looked away.

I wondered if the real reason she'd wanted to come here was to prove something to me—that she was over him, that the old wounds didn't ache anymore.

Then I turned a corner, and there it was, finally, humble as a shoebox, at the end of a weedy cul-de-sac. All along Morning-bird Lane the houses looked a bit abandoned—most of the neighbors were still up north for the summer—but Abe's looked worse, its lawn gone to seed, the yellow trim along the roofline beginning to flake and peel. Abe, as his neighbors would return to find come autumn, was gone forever.

"Well, this it," I said, pulling into the driveway. "Just a regular house."

"How long did he live here?" Bronwyn asked.

I was about to answer, but I was distracted by something unfamiliar that had escaped my notice until just then: a FOR SALE sign staked into the grass. I got out and marched through the yard, pulled it out of the ground, and threw it into the ditch.

No one had told me. Of course they hadn't: I would have thrown a fit, and my parents didn't want to deal with it. My feelings were too much trouble.

Emma came up behind me. "Are you okay?"

"I should be asking you that," I said.

"I'm okay," she said. "It's just a house. Right?"

"Right," I said. "So why does it bother me so much that my parents are selling it?"

She hugged me from behind. "You don't have to explain. I understand."

"Thanks. And I totally get it if you need to leave, whenever. Just say the word."

"I'll be fine," she said. Then, quieter, "But thank you."

There was a sudden commotion behind us, and we turned to see Bronwyn and Olive standing by the trunk of the car.

"There's someone in the boot!" Bronwyn cried.

We ran over. I could hear a muffled voice shouting. I pushed a button on the key fob and the trunk opened. Enoch popped up.

"Enoch!" cried Emma.

"What the hell are you doing here?" I said.

"You really thought I was going to let you leave me behind?" He blinked in the sudden sunlight. "Think again!"

"Your brain," said Millard, shaking his head. "Sometimes it just defies belief."

"Yes, my brilliance catches a lot of people off guard." Enoch clambered out onto the driveway, then looked around, confused. "Wait. This isn't a clothing shop."

"Goodness, he *is* brilliant," said Millard.

"It's Abe's house," said Bronwyn.

Enoch mouth fell open. "What!" He raised an eyebrow at Emma. "Whose idea was this?"

"Mine," I said, hoping to shut down an awkward conversation before it began.

"We're here to pay our respects," said Bronwyn.

"If you say so," said Enoch.

I hadn't brought the keys to the house, but it didn't matter. There was a spare hidden beneath a conch shell in the vegetable garden, one only Grandpa Portman and I knew about. There was something sweet about finding it just where it was supposed to be. Moments later I was unlocking the front door and we were stepping inside.

The air-conditioning had probably been off for most of the summer, and the house was hot and stale. Worse than the stifling temperature was the state of the place. Clothes and papers were stacked in unsteady piles on the floor, household items were littered across countertops, trash spilled from a pyramid of garbage bags in the corner. My father and my aunt had never finished sorting through Grandpa Portman's things. Dad abandoned the project (and the house, it seemed) when we left for Wales and planted a FOR SALE sign out front in the hope someone else might do the work instead. It looked like a ransacked Salvation Army store, not the home of a respected elder, and I was overcome by a wave of shame. I found myself trying to apologize and explain and tidy up all at the same time, as if I could hide what my friends had already seen.

"Gosh," said Enoch, clicking his tongue as he looked around, "he must have really been bad off at the end."

"No—it was—it was never like this," I stammered, scooping old magazines from the seat of Abe's armchair. "At least, not while he was alive—"

"Jacob, wait," said Emma.

"Can you guys go outside for a minute while I do this?"

"Jacob!" Emma caught me by the shoulders. "*Stop.*"

"I'll be quick," I said. "He didn't live like this. I swear."

"I know," said Emma. "Abe wouldn't even have breakfast without a clean collared shirt on."

"Exactly," I said. "So—"

"We want to help."

Enoch pulled a face. "We do?"

"Yes!" said Olive. "We'll all pitch in."

"I agree," said Bronwyn. "It shouldn't be left like this."

"Why not?" said Enoch. "Abe's dead. Who cares if his house is clean?"

"*We* do," said Millard, and Enoch stumbled as if Millard had shoved him. "And if you're not going to help, go lock yourself in the boot of the car again!"

"Yeah!" cried Olive.

"No need to get violent, mates." Enoch grabbed a broom from the corner and twirled it around. "See, I'm game. Sweepy-sweep!"

Emma clapped her hands. "Then let's get this place shipshape."

We dove in and started working. Emma took charge, giving orders like a drill sergeant, which I think helped keep her mind from wandering into painful territory. "Books on shelves. Clothes in closets. Trash in cans!"

With one hand, Bronwyn lifted Abe's easy chair over her head. "Where does this go?"

We dusted and swept. We threw open windows to let in fresh air. Bronwyn took room-sized carpets into the yard and beat the dust out of them—by herself. Even Enoch didn't seem to mind the work once we settled into a rhythm. Everything was coated with dust and grime, and it got onto our hands and clothes and in our hair. But nobody minded.

As we worked, I saw ghostly images of my grandfather everywhere. In his plaid chair, reading one of his spy novels. At the living room window, silhouetted against a bright afternoon, just watching—*for the postman*, he would say, and chuckle. Stooped over a pot of Polish stew in the kitchen, tending it while telling me stories. At the big drawing table he kept in the garage, pushpins and yarn spread out everywhere, making maps with me on a summer afternoon. "Where should the river go?" he would say, handing me a blue marker. "What about the town?" White hair rising like tendrils of smoke from his scalp. "Here maybe is better?" he'd say, urging my hand a little this way or that.

When my friends and I were finished, we went out to the lanai, seeking refuge in the slight breeze and mopping our brows. Enoch had been right, of course—no one would care that the work had been done. It was a gesture, useless but meaningful. Abe's friends had not been able to attend his funeral. Somehow, cleaning his house had become their goodbye.

"You guys didn't have to do that," I said.

"We know," said Bronwyn. "But it felt good."

She popped the top on a soda we'd found in the fridge, then took a long drink, burped, and passed it to Emma.

"I'm only sorry the others couldn't be here," said Emma, taking a small sip. "We should bring them later, so they can see it, too."

"We're not finished, are we?" said Enoch. He actually sounded let down.

"That's the whole house," I replied. "Unless you want to clean the yard, too."

"What about the war room?" asked Millard.

"The what?"

"You know, where Abe planned attacks on hollowgast, received encoded communications from other hollow-hunters, et cetera . . . he must have had one."

"He, uh—No, he didn't."

"Maybe he didn't tell you about it," said Enoch. "It was probably full of top secret stuff, and you were just too small and dumb to understand."

"I'm sure if Abe had had a war room, Jacob would have known," said Emma.

"Yeah," I said. Though I wasn't so sure. I was the same kid who, after my grandfather had told me the truth about the peculiars, had let bullies at school convince me it was a fairy tale. I'd basically called him a liar to his face, which I know had hurt his feelings. So maybe he wouldn't have trusted me with a secret like that, because I hadn't trusted him. And anyway, how could you hide something like a war room in a little house like this?

"What about a basement?" asked Bronwyn. "Abe must have had a fortified basement to protect against hollowgast attacks."

"If he'd had a place like that," I said, getting frustrated, "then he wouldn't have gotten killed by a hollowgast, would he?"

Bronwyn looked hurt. There was a brief, awkward silence.

"Jacob?" ventured Olive. "Is this what I think it is?"

She was standing by the screen door that opened to the backyard, running her hand down a long, flapping gash in the netting.

I felt a new flare of anger toward my father. Why hadn't he fixed it, or torn it out entirely? Why was it still hanging there, like evidence at a crime scene?

"Yeah. That's where the hollow came in," I said. "But it didn't happen here. I found him . . ." I pointed at the woods. "Way out."

Olive and Bronwyn exchanged a loaded glance. Emma looked at the floor, the color draining from her cheeks. Maybe this, finally, was too much for her.

"There's nothing to see, really, it's just bushes and stuff," I said. "I'm not sure I could find the exact spot again, anyway."

A lie. I could have found it blindfolded.

"If you could bring yourself to try," Emma said, looking up at me. Her jaw was set, her brow furrowed. "I need to see the place where it happened."

◆　　◆　　◆

I led them through knee-high grass to the edge of the woods, then plunged into the gloomy pine forest. I showed them how to navigate the spiny underbrush so they didn't get cut on saw-toothed palmettoes or tangled in thickets of vine, and how to identify and avoid the patches where snakes made their nests. As we made our way, I retold the story of what happened that fateful evening—the night that had split my life into Before and After. The panicked call I'd gotten from Abe while I was at work. My delay in getting here because I'd had to wait to catch a ride with a friend—a delay that may have either cost my grandfather his life, or saved mine. How I'd found the house a wreck, then noticed my grandfather's still-lit flashlight in the grass, shining into the woods. Fording into the black trees, just like we were doing now, and then—

A rustle in the brush sent everyone leaping into the air.

"It's just a raccoon!" I said. "Don't worry, if there were any hollows around right now, I'd feel it."

We circled a patch of brush that seemed familiar, but I couldn't be sure I'd found the exact spot where my grandfather died. The woods in Florida grew quickly, and since I'd been here last it had squirmed and shifted into an unfamiliar new configuration. I guess I couldn't have found it blindfolded, after all. It had been too many months.

I stepped into a sunny clearing where the vines were low and the brush seemed to have been tamped down. "It was around here. I think."

We gathered in a loose circle and observed a spontaneous moment of silence. Then, one by one, my friends took turns saying goodbye to him.

"You were a great man, Abraham Portman," said Millard. "Peculiarkind could use more like you. We miss you dearly."

"It isn't fair, what happened to you," said Bronwyn. "I wish we could have protected you like you used to protect us."

"Thank you for sending Jacob," said Olive. "We would all be dead without him."

"Let's not go overboard," said Enoch, and then because he had spoken, it was his turn. He twisted his shoe in the dirt for a long moment, then said, "Why'd you have to do something stupid, like get yourself killed?" He laughed dryly. "I'm sorry if I was ever an ass to you. If it changes anything, I wish you weren't dead." And then he turned his face away and said quietly, "Goodbye, old friend."

Olive touched her heart. "Enoch, that was nice."

"Okay, settle down." Enoch shook his head, embarrassed, and started walking back. "I'll be at the house."

Bronwyn and Olive looked to Emma, who hadn't spoken yet.

"I'd like a moment alone, please," she said.

The girls looked a little disappointed, and then everyone but me went after Enoch.

Emma glanced at me. I raised my eyebrows.

Me too?

She looked a bit sheepish.

"If you don't mind."

"Of course. I'll just be over here. In case you need anything."

She nodded. I walked about thirty paces, leaned against a tree, and waited. Emma stood at the spot for several minutes. I tried not to stare at her, but the more time passed, the more I caught myself watching the back of her head to see if it was bobbing, and her shoulders to see if they were shaking.

My eyes drifted to a vulture circling overhead. I looked down a moment later when I heard a noise in the brush.

Bronwyn was racing toward me. I startled so badly that I almost fell over.

"Jacob! Emma! You have to come quick!"

Emma saw and ran over to us.

"What happened?" I said.

"We found something," said Bronwyn. "In the house."

The look on her face made me think it was something awful. A dead body. But her voice was full of excitement.

◆　　　◆　　　◆

They were standing in the room Abe had used as his office. The old Persian carpet that stretched nearly wall to wall had been rolled up and pushed to one side, revealing pale, worn floorboards beneath.

Emma and I were panting from running.

"Bronwyn says . . . you found something," Emma said.

"I wanted to test a theory," said Millard. "So while you two were dallying in the woods, I asked Olive to take a walk around the house."

Olive took a couple of steps, her lead shoes making a heavy thud with each footfall.

"Imagine my surprise when I had her walk through this room. Olive, would you demonstrate?"

Olive started at the wall and stomped across the room. When she reached the very center of the floor, the sound her lead shoes made changed from a solid *thwump* to something more hollow—and slightly metallic.

"There's something under there," I said.

"A void. A concavity," said Millard.

I heard Millard's knee connect with the floor, and then a letter opener floated over the floor, point down. It was thrust between two boards, and with a grunt Millard pried up a section of floor about three feet square. It swung back on a hinge, revealing a metal door that looked just large enough for a grown man to fit through.

"Holy *shit*."

Olive looked aghast. I rarely swore in front of them, but this was just . . . well, *holy shit*.

"It's a door," I said.

"More of a hatch, really," said Bronwyn.

"I hate to say I told you so," said Millard. "But—I told you so."

The metal door was made of dull gray steel. It had a recessed handle and a number pad. I knelt down and rapped the metal with my knuckle. It sounded thick and strong. Then I tried the handle, but it wouldn't budge.

"It's locked," said Olive. "We already tried to open it."

"What's the combination?" Bronwyn asked me.

"How should I know?"

"Told you he wouldn't," said Enoch. "You don't know much, do you?"

I sighed. "Let me think for a second."

"Could the code be someone's birthday?" asked Olive.

I tried a few—mine, Abe's, my dad's, my grandmother's, even Emma's—but none worked.

"It's not a birthday," said Millard. "Abe would never have made the combination something so obvious."

"We don't even know how many numbers are *in* the combination," said Emma.

Bronwyn squeezed my shoulder. "Come on, Jacob. *Think.*"

I tried to focus, but I was letting hurt feelings distract me. I had always thought of myself as closer to Abe than anybody. So how was it that he never mentioned the secret door in the floor of his study? He lived more than half his life in the shadows, and never made a real attempt to share it with me. Sure, he told me stories that sounded like fairy tales and shared a few old photos, but he never *showed* me anything. I never would have doubted his stories if he'd made more of an effort to prove them—like showing me the secret door to his secret room.

Unlike my father, I *wanted* to believe.

Had he really been so injured by my skepticism that it made him abandon some plan to tell me everything? I couldn't believe that anymore. If he had told me the truth plainly, I would've guarded his secrets with my life. I think, in the end, he just didn't want me to know because he didn't trust me. And now here I was trying to guess the combination to a door he had never told me about, behind which were secrets he had never meant for me to uncover.

So why was I bothering?

"I'm out of ideas," I said, and stood up.

"You're giving up?" said Emma.

"Who knows," I said. "Maybe it's just a root cellar."

"You know it's not."

I shrugged. "My grandmother took fruit preservation very seriously."

Enoch let out a frustrated sigh. "Maybe you're holding out on us."

"What?" I said, turning toward him.

"I think you know the code but you want to keep Abe's secrets for yourself. Even though *we* found the door."

I took an angry step toward him. Bronwyn put herself between us.

"Jacob, settle down! Enoch, shut up. You're not helping."

I gave him the finger.

"Ahh, who cares what's in Abe's dusty old hole in the ground," said Enoch, and then he laughed. "It's probably just a thousand old love letters from Emma."

Now Emma gave him the finger, too.

"Or maybe a shrine with a big photo of her and candles all around . . ." He clapped his hands gleefully. "Oh, that would be *so* awkward for you two!"

"Come here so I can burn your eyebrows off," said Emma.

"Ignore him," I said.

She and I retreated to the doorway with our hands in our pockets. He'd gotten to both of us.

"I'm not hiding anything," I said quietly. "I really don't know what the code is."

"I know," she said, and touched my arm. "I was thinking. Maybe it's not a number."

"But it's a number *pad*."

"Maybe it's a word. Look, the keys have letters and numbers."

I went over to the door and looked. She was right: Every number key had three letters below it, like the buttons on a telephone.

"Was there a word that would have meant something to the both of you?" she said.

"*E-m-m-a?*" Enoch said.

I turned toward him. "I swear to God, Enoch . . ."

Bronwyn picked him up and threw him over her shoulder.

"Hey! Put me down!"

"You're getting a time-out," said Bronwyn, and she walked him out of the room while he wriggled and complained.

"As I was saying," said Emma. "Some secret you had between the two of you. Something only you would know."

I considered it for a moment, then knelt down by the hatch. First, I tried names—mine, Abe's, Emma's—but no dice. Then, just for the hell of it, I keyed in the word *p-e-c-u-l-i-a-r*.

Nope. Way too obvious.

"You know, it might not even be in English," said Millard. "Abe spoke Polish, too."

"Maybe you should take the night to think it over," Emma said.

But now my mind was whirring. Polish. Yes, he spoke it now and then, mostly to himself. He'd never taught me any, except for one word. *Tygrysku*—a pet name he'd given me. It meant "little tiger."

I punched it in.

The tumblers inside the lock opened with a *clunk*.

Holy shit.

◆　　◆　　◆

The door opened to reveal a ladder descending into darkness. I swung my foot onto the first rung.

"Wish me luck," I said.

"Let me go first," Emma said. She held out her palm and made a flame.

"It should be me," I said. "If there's anything nasty waiting down there, I want to get eaten first."

"How very chivalrous," said Millard.

I climbed down ten steps onto a concrete floor. It was cooler than the house above by ten or fifteen degrees. Before me was total darkness. I took out my phone and shone its light around, which was only bright enough to show me the walls—curved, gray concrete. It was a tunnel: claustrophobically tight, so low I had to hunch. My phone light was too puny to see what lay ahead, or how far the tunnel went.

"Well?" Emma called down.

"No monsters!" I shouted. "But I could use more light."

So much for chivalry.

"Be right there!" said Emma.

"Us too!" I heard Olive say.

It was only then, as I was waiting for my friends to climb down, that it hit me—my grandfather *had* meant for me to find this place.

Tygrysku. It was a bread crumb in the forest. Just like the postcard from Miss Peregrine that he'd tucked into that volume of Emerson.

Emma reached the bottom and lit a flame in her hand. "Well," she said, looking at the tunnel ahead. "It's definitely not a root cellar."

She winked at me and I grinned back. She seemed cool and collected, but I'm pretty sure it was an act; every nerve in me was jangling.

"May I come down?" Enoch called down from the room above. "Or am I to be punished for having a sense of humor?"

Bronwyn had just reached the bottom of the ladder. "You stay where you are," she said. "In case anyone comes, we don't want to be caught down here unawares."

"In case who comes?" he said.

"Whoever," said Bronwyn.

We gathered in a cluster with Emma at the front, her flame held out to make a light.

"Move slowly, listen out for anything strange, and keep your wits about you," she said. "We don't know what's down here, and it's possible Abe could have booby-trapped the place."

We began to move forward, hunched and shuffling. I tried to imagine where we were in relation to the house above us, based on the direction the tunnel was facing. After twenty or thirty feet, we were most likely beneath the living room. After forty, we were leaving the house altogether, and after fifty, I was fairly certain we were under the front yard.

Finally, the tunnel ended at a door. It was heavy-looking, like the hatch behind us, but it was hanging slightly ajar.

"Hello?" I called. At the sound of my voice Bronwyn startled badly.

"Sorry," I said to her.

"Are you expecting someone?" Millard asked.

"No. But you never know."

Though I tried not to show it, I was so nervous I was vibrating.

Emma stepped through the door, then stood shining her flame around for a moment. "Looks safe enough," she said. "But this might be useful . . ."

She reached for the wall, flicked a switch, and a bank of fluorescent lights clinked on inside the room.

"Hey now!" Olive said. "That's more like it."

Emma closed her hand to extinguish her flame, and we piled in after her. And then I turned a slow circle, taking everything in. The room was small, maybe twenty feet by fifteen, but I could finally stand up to full height. In the way of my grandfather, it was meticulously organized. Along one wall were four metal beds arranged bunk-style in two stacks, a tight roll of sheets and blankets sealed in plastic at the foot of each. There was a big locker bolted to the wall, which Emma opened to find all kinds of supplies: flashlights, batteries, basic tools, and enough canned and dried food to last several weeks. Beside that was a big blue drum filled with drinking water, and next to that, a strange-looking plastic box, which I recognized from the survivalist magazines I sometimes found in Abe's garage as a chemical toilet.

"Wow, look at this!" said Bronwyn. She was standing in a corner, her eye pressed against a metal cylinder that protruded down from the ceiling. "I can see outside!"

The cylinder had handles attached at the base and a viewing lens. Bronwyn stepped aside so I could look through it, and I saw a slightly blurred image of the cul-de-sac outside. I grabbed the handles and turned it, and the view rotated until I could see the house, partly obscured by a field of high grass.

"It's a periscope," I said. "It must be hidden at the edge of the yard."

"So he could see them coming," said Emma.

"What *is* this place?" said Olive.

"It must be a shelter," said Bronwyn. "In case of hollowgast attack. See the four beds? So his family could hide, too."

"It was for more than just waiting out attacks," said Millard. "It was a receiving station."

His voice came from the opposite wall, next to a big wooden desk. Its surface was almost entirely taken up by an odd-looking machine made of chrome and green-plated metal—like a cross between an archaic printer and a fax machine, with a keyboard stuck awkwardly to the front.

"This must be how he communicated."

"With who?" said Bronwyn.

"The other hollow-hunters. See, this is a pneumatic teleprinter."

"Oh, wow," said Emma, crossing the small room to look at it. "I remember these. Miss Peregrine used to have one. Whatever happened to it?"

"It was part of a scheme for ymbrynes to communicate with one another without having to leave the safety of their loops," Millard explained. "It didn't work, in the end. Too complex, and too vulnerable to interception."

But I was in a daze, only half listening. I'd been trying to wrap my mind around the fact that all this had been so close to me—quite literally under my feet—for *years*, and I hadn't known it. That I had spent afternoons playing in the grass just twenty feet above where I was standing now. It boggled the mind, and it made me wonder: How much more peculiarness had I been exposed to without realizing it? I thought about my grandfather's friends—the old fellows who would come around to visit now and then, whiling away a few hours chatting with Abe out on the back porch, or in his study.

I knew him back in Poland, my grandfather had said about one such visitor.

A friend from the war, was how he'd described another.

But who were they, really?

"You say this thing was for communicating with other hollow-hunters," I said. "What do you know about them?"

"About the hunters?" said Emma. "We don't know much, but that was by design. They were extremely secretive."

"Do you know how many there were?"

"Not more than a dozen, I suppose," said Millard. "But that's just an educated guess."

"And could they all control hollows?" I asked.

Maybe there were other peculiars like me out there. Maybe I could find them.

"Oh, I don't think so," said Emma. "That's why Abe was so special."

"And you, Mr. Jacob," said Bronwyn.

"There's one thing that doesn't make sense," said Millard. "Why didn't Abe seek shelter down here the night the hollowgast came for him?"

"Maybe he didn't have time," said Olive.

"No," I said. "He knew it was coming for him. He called me in a panic, hours earlier."

"Maybe he forgot the combination code," said Olive.

"He wasn't senile," Emma said.

There was only one explanation, but I could hardly say it; even thinking it made the breath lock in my throat.

"He didn't come down here," I said, "because he knew I'd come to the house looking for him. Even though he begged me to stay away."

Bronwyn looked pained and raised her hand over her mouth. "And if he was down here . . . while you were up *there* . . ."

"He was protecting you," Emma said. "Trying to draw the hollow away, off into the woods."

My body felt too heavy for my legs, and I sat down on one of the cots.

"You couldn't have known," Emma said, perching herself next to me.

"No." I let out a breath. "He told me monsters were coming, but I didn't believe him. He might still be alive today—but I didn't believe him. Again."

"No. Don't do this to yourself." She sounded angry. "He didn't tell you enough—not nearly enough. If he had, you would've believed him. Right?"

"Yeah . . ."

"But Abe loved his secrets."

"Did he ever," said Millard.

"I think he loved them more than people sometimes," said Emma. "And in the end, that's what got him killed. His secrets—not you."

"Maybe," I said.

"Definitely."

I knew she was right—mostly. I was angry at him for not sharing more with me, but it was hard to let go of the idea that he might have told me everything, if only I hadn't pushed him away. So I felt angry and guilty at the same time, but I couldn't talk to Emma about it. So I just nodded and said, "Well . . . at least we found this place. One less secret for Abe to take with him to the grave."

"Maybe more than one," Millard said, and he slid open a drawer in the desk. "Something here you might be interested in, Jacob."

I was off the cot and across the room in a second. In the drawer was a big metal-ringed binder stuffed with pages. A label on the front read OPERATIONS LOG.

"Whoa," I said. "Is this . . . ?"

"Just what it says," Millard said.

The others crowded around as I slid my fingers under it and lifted it out of the drawer. It was several inches thick and weighed at least five pounds.

"Go on, then," said Bronwyn.

"Don't rush me," I said.

I opened to a random page in the middle—a typewritten mission report with two photos stapled to it, one of costumed child on a sofa and one of a man and woman dressed as clowns.

I read the report aloud. It was written in the terse and emotionless language of law enforcement. It outlined a mission to rescue a peculiar child from a wight and a hollowgast who were hunting him, then deliver the child to a safe loop.

I flipped a few pages in the binder, which was full of similar reports stretching all the way back to the 1950s, then closed it.

"You know what this means, don't you?" said Millard.

"Abe did more than just find and kill hollows," said Bronwyn.

"Right," said Millard. "He was saving peculiar children, too."

I looked at Emma. "Did you know?"

She looked down. "He never discussed his work."

"But rescuing peculiar children is an ymbryne's job," said Olive.

"Yeah," said Emma, "but if the wights were using the kids as bait, like in that entry, maybe they couldn't."

I was hung up on another detail, but for now I kept it to myself.

"HEY!" a voice shouted from the doorway, and we all jumped and turned to see Enoch standing there.

"I told you not to come down here!" said Bronwyn.

"What did you expect? You left me alone for ages." He stepped into the room and looked around. "So, this is what all the fuss and bother was about? Looks like a prison cell."

Emma looked at her watch. "It's almost six. We'd better be getting back."

October 31, 1967 — HOUSTON, TEXAS

    Rec'd report of previously uncontacted
peculiar male, approx. 13 yrs of age,
manifesting moderate ability, runaway
given up for adoption. Operatives A and
H discovered 2 wights posing as adoption
officials, using subject as bait for
ymbrynes. They had 1 hollowgast in tow.
Contact was made during local Halloween
parade. Enemies separated from crowd and
engaged. Hollowgast silently killed using
compact bow and arrow. Wights escaped.
Male injured in leg, female unhurt. Wights
believed to be traveling under aliases Joe
and Jane Johnson. Never seen unmasked.
    Result: subject extracted, delivered
safely to loop A-57 near Marfa, Tex. into
the care of a Miss Apfel, November 10,
1967.

"The others are going to kill us," said Olive. "We've been gone all afternoon, and we still haven't got new clothes!"

Then I remembered Miss Peregrine's promise. She'd have something to show me at nightfall, she said, which was in just an hour or two. Truth be told, I didn't much care about whatever it was she had to show me anymore. All I could think about was getting home to my bedroom, closing the door, and reading my grandfather's logbook from cover to cover.

◆　　◆　　◆

When we got home, the sun was just starting to dip below the trees. The friends we'd left behind complained loudly about our having been gone so long, but when we told them why—and what we'd found—they forgot their anger and hung on Millard's every word as he recounted the story.

My parents were gone. They had packed their bags and left for a trip to Asia. I found a note in my mom's handwriting on the kitchen counter. They would miss me lots, the note read, were available by phone or email anytime, and would I please remember to pay the gardeners. I could tell from the breezy and casual tone of the note—*Love you, Jakey!*—that Miss Peregrine had done a great job erasing the last few months of worrying about me from their minds. They didn't seem concerned that I might have a breakdown or run away again while they were gone. In fact, they didn't seem to care very much at all. And that was fine. *Good riddance*, I thought. At least we had the place to ourselves.

Miss Peregrine wasn't around, either. She'd left the house just after we had and had been gone all day, Horace reported.

"Did she say where she was going?" I asked.

"She only said that we were to meet her at precisely seven fifteen at the potting shed in your backyard."

"The potting shed."

"At seven fifteen, precisely."

That gave me just over an hour of free time.

I snuck up to my room. I put *IV* by Led Zeppelin on the record player, which is what I listened to whenever I was doing something that required serious concentration. I climbed onto my bed with my grandfather's logbook, laid it out in front of me, and began to read.

I hadn't read more than a page when Emma poked her head into the room. I invited her to join me.

"No, thanks," she said. "I've had quite enough of Abe Portman for one day." And she went out.

There were many hundreds of pages in the logbook, spanning a period of decades. Most of the entries followed the format of the one I'd read down in the bunker: light on detail, free from emotion, and often accompanied by a photo or some other piece of visual evidence. It would've taken me a week to read every word, so even with an hour on my hands, I could only skim. But it was enough to form a sketchy outline of Abe's work in America.

He usually worked alone, but not always. Some entries referenced other "operatives," named only with single letters—F, P, V. But most often, H.

H was the man my father had met, if his partially wiped memory could be trusted. If Abe had trusted H enough to introduce his son to him, he must've been important. So who was he? What was the structure of their organization? Who assigned their missions? Every new piece of information spawned a dozen more questions.

In the early days, their work was focused almost exclusively on hunting and killing hollows. But as the years progressed, more and more of the missions involved finding and rescuing peculiar children. Which was admirable, no doubt, but Bronwyn's question stayed with me: Wasn't that the ymbrynes' job? Was there something stopping American ymbrynes from doing it?

Was something *wrong* with them?

The entries began in 1953 and stopped abruptly in 1985. Why

did they stop? Was there another logbook I hadn't found yet? Had Abe retired in 1985? Or had something changed?

After an hour of reading, I had a few more answers and a lot more new questions. First among them: Was there more work like this to be done? Was there still a group of hollow-hunters out there somewhere, fighting monsters and rescuing peculiars? If so, I wanted very much to find them. I wanted to be part of it, to use my gift to carry on my grandfather's work here in America. After all, maybe that's what he wanted! Yes, he'd locked away his secrets, but he'd done it using the name he'd given me as the key. But he'd died too soon to tell me.

First things first. To get answers to my questions, I'd have to find the only person in the world likely to know Abe's secrets.

I had to find H.

CHAPTER FOUR

e milled around my backyard, waiting for Miss Peregrine. It was seven twelve, and the light had mostly gone out of the sky. I glanced at the potting shed, a neglected shack made from latticed wood that stood against the oleander hedges. My mother had gone through a gardening phase a few years back, but these days the shed was just a shelter for weeds and spiders.

Then, at precisely seven fifteen, there was a snap of static electricity in the air that we all felt—it made Horace go "Ooooh!" and Claire's long hair rose and stood on end—and then the shed lit up from the inside. It was a brief, bright flash, the hundreds of holes in its latticed walls turning white before fading to shadow. Then we heard Miss Peregrine's voice from inside the shed.

"Here we are!" She strode out onto the grass. "Ahh," she said, taking in a lungful of air. "Yes, I much prefer this weather." She looked around at all of us. "Sorry I'm late."

"Only by thirty seconds," said Horace.

"Mr. Portman, you look a bit confused."

"I'm not super clear on what just happened," I said. "Or where you were. Or . . . anything?"

"That," she said, pointing to the shed, "is a loop."

I looked from her to the shed. "There was a loop in my backyard?"

"There is now. I made it this afternoon."

"It's a pocket loop," said Millard. "Miss P, that's brilliant! I didn't think the council had approved any yet."

"Only this one, and just today," she said, grinning with pride.

"Why would you want a loop of this afternoon?" I asked.

"The time you loop isn't the point of a pocket loop. The advantage is their extremely small size, which makes them a snap to maintain. Unlike a normal loop, these only need to be reset once or twice a month, as opposed to daily."

The others were grinning and trading excited looks, but I was still baffled.

"But what good is a loop the size of a potting shed?"

"None as a place of refuge, but they are extraordinarily useful as a portal." She reached into her dress pocket and pulled out a slim brass object that looked like an oversized bullet with vents cut into it. "With the shuttle—another of my brother Bentham's ingenious inventions—I can stitch this loop back into his Panloopticon. And *voilà*! We have a door to Devil's Acre."

"Right here," I said. "In the backyard."

"You don't have to take my word for it," she said, holding her hand out toward the potting shed. "Go and see for yourself."

I took a step toward it. "Really?"

"It's a brave new world, Mr. Portman. And we'll be right behind you."

◆   ◆   ◆

Forty seconds: That's all the time it took for me to travel from my backyard to a nineteenth-century time loop in London. Forty seconds from reaching the back of the potting shed to stepping out of a broom closet in Devil's Acre. The sensation left me dizzy, my head and stomach no longer accustomed to the sudden lurch of loop travel.

I stepped out of the broom closet and into a familiar hallway: long, lushly carpeted, and lined with identical doors, each bearing a small plaque. The one across the hall read:

DEN HAAG, NETHERLANDS, APRIL 8, 1937

I turned to look at the door behind me. There was a piece of paper fixed to the wall:

JACOB PORTMAN HOME, FLORIDA, PRESENT DAY.
A. PEREGRINE AND WARDS ONLY

I was in the heart of Bentham's reality-bending Panloopticon machine, to which my house was now connected. I was still trying to wrap my mind around that when the door opened and Emma walked out. "Hello, stranger!" she said, and kissed me on the face. She was followed by Miss Peregrine and the rest of my peculiar friends. They were chattering excitedly, unfazed by their instantaneous journey across an ocean and a century.

"This means we don't have to sleep in Devil's Acre ever again, if we don't want to," Horace was saying.

"Or make that long drive to the swamp just to reach Jacob's house," said Claire. "I get carsick."

"The best part is the food," Olive said, shoving her way through the pack. "Just think, we can have a proper English breakfast, pizza at Jacob's house for lunch, and mutton chops fresh from Smithfield Market for supper!"

"Who knew such a little person could eat so much," said Horace.

"Eat enough and maybe you won't need those lead shoes!" said Enoch.

"Isn't it wonderful?" Miss Peregrine said, taking me aside. "Now you see what I meant about a solution. With this pocket loop, you can live in one world without cutting yourself off from the other. With your help, we can continue to expand our knowledge of present-day America without shirking our duties here in Devil's Acre. There are loops to be rebuilt, traumatized peculiars to be rehabilitated, captured wights to be dealt with . . . and I haven't forgotten my promise to you. You shall have very engaging work to do here. How does that sound?"

"What kind of work did you have in mind?" I said, my head spinning with the possibilities that had just opened up before me.

"The Ymbryne Council gives out the assignments, so I don't know just yet. But they've told me they have something very interesting for you."

"What about the rest of us?" said Enoch.

"We want assignments of consequence," said Millard. "Not just busywork."

"Or cleaning up," added Bronwyn.

"You'll have important work to do, I promise," said Miss Peregrine.

"I thought learning to pass as normals in the present *was* the important work," said Enoch. "So why are we wasting our time in this dump?"

The headmistress pursed her lips. "While you build your knowledge and skills in the present, you can simultaneously aid the reconstruction effort here in the Acre. We'll commute back and forth, just like modern people. Isn't that fun?"

Enoch shook his head and looked away. "It's politics. That's what you won't admit."

Miss Peregrine's eyes flared.

"You're being rude," said Claire.

"No, go on, Enoch," said Miss Peregrine. "I want to hear this."

"Someone high up on the food chain decided it doesn't look good, us hanging around Jacob's house in the present while everyone else is stuck here, living like refugees and cleaning up the wights' mess. But I don't care what anybody thinks about it. We *deserve* a holiday, damn it!"

"Everyone here deserves a holiday!" Miss Peregrine snapped. She shut her eyes and pinched the bridge of her nose, as if battling a sudden headache. "Think of it this way. It will be inspiring to the other children to see you, the heroes of the Battle for Devil's Acre, working alongside them for the common good."

"Bah," Enoch said, and started cleaning his fingernails.

"Well, *I'm* excited," said Bronwyn. "I always wanted a real job with real responsibilities, even if it means cutting into our normalling lessons a bit."

"Cutting into?" said Horace. "We haven't had a single one yet!"

"Not even one?" Miss Peregrine looked at me. "What about the shopping trip?"

"We, uh . . . got a little sidetracked," I said.

"Oh," she said with a frown. "No matter, there's plenty of time. Just not today!" And then she was tromping down the hall, waving at us to catch up.

◆　　◆　　◆

As we followed Miss Peregrine down the long hall, people came and went through the Panloopticon's many doors. They were all very serious-looking and busy, and they wore vastly different outfits suited to very different purposes. There was a lady in a blue bustle dress that ballooned around her so widely that we had to fall into single file and squeeze against the wall to get by her. There was a man in a heavy white snowsuit and a round fur hat, and another man in seven-league boots that reached his mid-thigh and a naval coat that shone with gold buckles. I was so distracted by all the wardrobe that when we rounded a corner I nearly smacked into a wall—or what I thought was a wall until it began speaking to me.

"Young Portman!" a voice boomed, and I looked up, craning my neck to take in the man's full height. Seven feet tall, in a heavy black robe, he was both a vision of death incarnate and an old friend I'd found myself missing from time to time.

"Sharon!"

He bowed and greeted Miss Peregrine, then reached out and shook my hand, his long, icy fingers wrapping so far around mine that they met his thumb on the other side.

"Finally come to greet your fans, have you?"

"Ha-ha," I said. "Right."

"He isn't joking," Millard said. "You're a celebrity now. When we go outside, watch out."

"What? Seriously?"

"Oh yeah," said Emma. "Don't be surprised if you get asked for autographs."

"Don't get a big head about it," said Enoch. "We're all a bit famous now, after what we did in the Library of Souls."

"Oh, really!" Emma said. "*You're* famous?"

"A little," Enoch said. "I get fan letters."

"You got one. Singular."

Enoch shuffled his feet. "That you know of."

Miss Peregrine cleared her throat. "In any case! The children are to receive their reconstruction assignments from the council today. Sharon, if you wouldn't mind escorting us to the ministries building?"

"Of course." Sharon bowed to her, and the scent that wafted from his cloak was one of mildew and wet earth. "For esteemed guests like yourselves, I'm happy to carve some time out of my busy schedule."

As he walked us down the hall, he turned to me and said, "You see, I'm the majordome of this house, as well as the general overseer of the Panloopticon and its many portals."

"I still can't believe they put *him* in charge," muttered Enoch.

Sharon turned to look straight at him, and a demented smile gleamed out of his dark hood.

Enoch shrank behind Emma and tried to disappear.

"We have a saying around here," said Sharon. "'The pope is busy and Mother Teresa is dead.' No one knows this place better than me—except perhaps old Bentham, who is, thanks to young

Portman, permanently indisposed." His tone was carefully neutral; it was impossible to tell whether or not he regretted the death of his former employer. "So I'm afraid you're stuck with me."

We turned another corner and came into a wide hallway. It was as busy as an airline terminal at the holidays: Travelers laden with heavy bags came and went through doors that lined both walls. Long lines trailed away from podiums where uniformed clerks checked documents. Gruff border guards kept watch over everyone.

Sharon barked at a nearby clerk. "Keep that door shut! You're letting in half of Helsinki, Christmas of 1911!"

The clerk snapped up from his chair and slammed a door that had been open a crack, out from which snowflakes had been drifting.

"We're making sure people travel only to loops they've been approved to visit," Sharon explained. "There are over a hundred loop doors in these halls, and the Ministry of Temporal Affairs has declared fewer than half of them safe. Many have not been sufficiently explored; some haven't been opened in years. So, until further notice, all Panloopticon trips must be cleared by the ministry—and yours truly."

Sharon snatched a ticket from the hand of a mousy fellow in a brown trench coat. "Who are you and where are you going?" He was clearly delighted to have been given some authority, and couldn't help showing it off.

"My name's Wellington Weebus," the man lisped. "Destination Pennsylvania Station, New York City, June 8, 1929. Sir."

"What's your business there?"

"Sir, I'm a linguistical outreach officer assigned to the American colonies. I'm a translator."

"Why would we need a translator in New York City? Don't they speak the King's English?"

"Not exactly, sir. They have a rather odd way of speaking, actually, sir."

"Why the umbrella?"

"It's raining there, sir."

"Have your clothes been vetted for anachronisms by the Costumers?"

"They have, sir."

"I thought all New Yorkers of that era wore hats."

The man pulled a small cap from his trench coat. "I have one here, sir."

Miss Peregrine, who had been tapping her foot for some time now, reached the end of her fuse. "If you're needed here, Sharon, I'm sure we can find our own way to the ministries building."

"I won't hear of it!" he said, then handed back the man's ticket. "Look sharp, Weebus, I'm watching you."

The man scurried off.

"This way, children. It isn't far."

He cleared a path for us through the crowded hall, then led us down a flight of stairs. On the ground floor we passed Bentham's grand library, where the furniture had been cleared away to make room for a hundred or more cots.

"That's where we used to sleep, until we came to live with you," Emma said to me. "Ladies in that room, men in this one."

We passed what had formerly been a dining room, now crowded with even more cots. The whole bottom floor of Bentham's house had been turned into a shelter for displaced peculiars.

"Were you comfortable there?" I asked.

A dumb question.

Emma shrugged; she didn't like to complain. "It's certainly better than sleeping in a wightish prison," she said.

"Not *much* better," said Horace—who loved to complain and had sidled up to me the moment he sensed an opportunity. "Let me tell you, Jacob, it was awful. Not everyone takes their personal hygiene as seriously as we do. Some nights I had to plug my nose with camphor sticks! And there isn't any privacy, nor any wardrobes nor dressing rooms nor proper washing-rooms, even, and not an *ounce* of creativity coming out of the kitchen"—we were passing it now, and through the door I could see a battalion of cooks chopping things and stirring pots—"and so many of these poor devils from other loops have nightmares that you can hardly sleep at night for all the moaning and screaming!"

"*You're* one to talk," said Emma. "You wake up screaming twice a week!"

"Yes, but at least my dreams mean something," he said.

"You know, there's a girl in America who can remove nightmares," I heard Millard say. "Perhaps she could be of assistance."

"There is no one in the world qualified to manipulate my dreams," Horace said testily.

Emma's letters to me had been so breezy and cheerful, always focused on the happy times and the little adventures they were having. She had never mentioned the living conditions here or their daily struggles, and I felt a surge of new respect for her resilience.

Sharon threw open the huge oaken door at the end of the hallway. Street noise and daylight flooded in.

"Stay together!" Miss Peregrine shouted, and then we were outside, plunging into the flow of bodies on the sidewalk.

◆   ◆   ◆

If Emma hadn't grabbed my hand and pulled me along, I might've stayed frozen where I stood. I hardly recognized the place. When I had last seen Devil's Acre, Caul's tower was a pile of still-smoking bricks, and wights were fleeing through the streets pursued by angry mobs. There were riots as addicts looted stashes of unguarded ambrosia and the wights' collaborators burned buildings filled with evidence of their crimes. But that was a while ago, and it looked like the place had made great progress since then. It was still a hellhole at heart—the buildings were caked with grime and the sky was the same poisonous yellow it had always been—but the fires had been put out, the debris cleared away, and there were uniformed peculiars directing horse-and-buggy traffic in the crowded street.

More than the place, though, it was the people who had changed. Gone were the prowling, hollow-eyed addicts, the dealers in peculiar flesh displaying their wares in shop windows, the ambrosia-enhanced gladiators with light beaming from their eyes. Judging from their eclectic and era-spanning costumes, these peculiars hailed from loops across Europe, Asia, Africa, the Middle East—and from many different time periods, as well.

In their hunt for peculiar souls the wights had not discriminated, and their reach had extended much farther than I had realized.

What struck me more than their costumes was the dignity with which they carried themselves, in spite of their circumstances. They had come seeking refuge from damaged and destroyed loops. They had lost their homes, seen friends and loved ones killed before their eyes, suffered unimaginable traumas. But there were no shocked and vacant stares. No one dressed in rags. Each one of them had had a giant hole blown through their lives, but the street pulsed with determined energy.

Perhaps they simply did not have time to mourn. But I preferred to believe that, for the first time in nearly a century, peculiars could do more than just hide in their loops and hope. The worst had come to pass. Having survived it, there was much to do: They had a world to remake. And they could make it *better*.

For a block or two, I was so absorbed in staring at all of them that I didn't notice how many of them were staring back. But then someone did a double take, and someone else pointed at me, and I could have sworn I saw my name form on their lips.

They knew who I was.

We passed a young boy hawking newspapers, and he was shouting: "Jacob Portman to visit the Acre today! Hero returns to Devil's Acre for first time since his victory over the wights!"

I felt my face go hot.

"Why does Jacob get all the credit?" I heard Enoch say. "We were there, too!"

"Jacob! Jacob Portman!" Two teenage girls were following me, waving a piece of paper. "Would you sign this for us?"

"He's late for an important meeting!" Emma said, pulling me on through the crowd.

We hadn't gone even ten feet when a sturdy pair of hands stopped me. They belonged to a fast-talking man with a single eye in the middle of his forehead and a hat that read PRESS.

"Farish Obwelo from the *Evening Muckraker*. How about a quick photo?"

Before I could answer, he had turned me to face a camera—a giant antique that must have weighed a ton. A photographer ducked behind it and held up a flash. "So, Jake," Farish said, "what was it like to command an army of hollowgast? How did it feel to win a battle against so many wights? What were Caul's last words before you struck the blow that killed him?"

"Uh, that's not exactly how it—"

The camera flashed, and for an instant I was blind. Then another pair of hands were on me—this time Miss Peregrine's, dragging me away. "Don't speak to the press," she hissed in my ear, "about anything, but *especially* not about what happened in the Library of Souls!"

"Why?" I said. "What do they think happened?"

She didn't answer. Couldn't, because suddenly I was being hoisted up over Bronwyn's head, where she carried me like a platter, out of reach of the crowd. We made our way like that, Sharon forming a wedge with his arms to part the human sea and pointing up ahead—*yes, there, we're nearly there*—to a gate in a tall iron fence. Beyond it rose a building of hulking black stone.

A guard waved us through the gate into a courtyard, and we left the crowd behind us. Bronwyn set me down and everyone crowded around as I brushed myself off.

"I thought someone was going to take a bite out of you!" Emma said.

"I told him he was famous!" said Millard, his tone both teasing and a little jealous.

"Yeah, but I didn't think you meant—"

"*Famous* famous?" said Emma.

"Flavor of the month," said Enoch, waving his hand. "Watch, they'll have forgotten all about him by Christmas."

"God, I hope so," I said.

"Why?" said Bronwyn. "You don't want to be famous?"

"No!" I said. "That was"—I wanted to say *terrifying*—"a bit much."

"You handled yourself splendidly," said Miss Peregrine. "And it will get easier. Once people become accustomed to seeing you, they won't make such a fuss. You've been gone for some time, Jacob, and your legend has grown quite a bit in your absence."

"I'll say it's grown. But what was that about me killing Caul?"

She leaned toward me and lowered her voice. "A necessary fiction. The ymbrynes decided it was best that everyone believe him dead."

"Well, isn't he?"

"Very likely," she said, in a tone too casual to be completely believable. "But the truth is, we don't know what happens inside a collapsed loop. No one's ever escaped one to tell. Caul and Bentham may be dead, or they may just be . . . *elsewhere*."

"Extra-dimensionally inaccessible," Millard said.

"Permanently, of course," Miss Peregrine hastened to add. "But we don't want the public—or the few wights who have managed to evade us—to have any doubt. Or to get any strange ideas about rescuing him."

"So, congratulations, you killed Caul, too," Enoch said, his voice dripping with sarcasm.

"Couldn't it have been one of *us* who killed him?" Horace whined.

"You mean, *you*?" Enoch sneered. "Who'd believe that?"

"Keep your voices down!" snapped Miss Peregrine.

I was still grappling with the idea that Caul was only *very likely* dead, or that anyone, even the super-monster he had become at the end, could survive something as violent as a loop collapse, when a slap on the back from Sharon almost knocked me down.

"My boy, I should be getting back. Please don't hesitate to call for me if you need another escort."

Miss Peregrine thanked him. He bowed deeply, then turned and left, his cloak swishing behind him dramatically.

We turned to face the dour building that loomed before us.

"So, what is this place?" I asked.

"It's the heart of peculiar government, for the time being," said Miss Peregrine. "Where the Ymbryne Council now holds its meetings and where the various ministries conduct their business."

"It's where we get our work assignments," said Bronwyn. "We turn up here in the mornings, and they tell us what needs doing."

"St. Barnabus' Asylum for Lunatics," I said, reading words carved into stone above the building's iron doors.

"There wasn't a lot of vacant real estate to choose from," Miss Peregrine said.

"Once more into the breach, dear friends," said Millard, and he laughed and nudged me forward.

◆   ◆   ◆

The institution's full name was St. Barnabas' Asylum for Lunatics, Mountebanks, and the Criminally Mischievous, and all the inmates—most of which had been there on a voluntary basis, anyway—had run away in the chaos that followed the wights' defeat. The asylum had sat empty until the Ymbryne Council, whose building had been encased in ice during a hollowgast raid and rendered uninhabitable, requisitioned it as their temporary headquarters. It was now home to most of European Peculiardom's government ministries, and its miserable dungeons, padded cells, and dank corridors had been stocked with desks and meeting tables and filing cabinets. They looked no less like torture chambers despite the change in furnishings.

We strode through a gloomy entrance hall buzzing with bureaucrats and office workers, most wearing formal waistcoats and loaded down with papers and books. Built into the walls were an array of windows, each manned by a receptionist and marked with a department name: Temporal Affairs, Anachronisms, Normal Relations, Phono- and Photographic Records, Micro-management and Pedantry, Reconstruction Dept. Miss Peregrine marched us to the last window and announced herself.

"What-ho, Bartleby," she said, rapping on the desk. "Alma Peregrine to see Isabel Cuckoo."

A man looked up and blinked at her. Squeezed between his temples were five eyes, and pinched in the central one was a monocle. "She's been expecting you," he said.

Miss Peregrine thanked him and started back.

"What are you staring at?" he said to me, blinking with four of his eyes.

I hurried after the others.

There were several doorways leading off the entrance hall, and we passed through one into a smaller room. Inside were several rows of chairs and half a dozen peculiars sitting in them, filling out forms.

"Aptitude tests," Emma said to me. "To see what sort of work you're best suited for."

A woman came striding toward Miss Peregrine, arms outstretched.

"Alma, you're back!"

They traded kisses on the cheek.

"Children, this is Miss Isabel Cuckoo. She's an old, dear friend of mine, and she also happens to be the ymbryne in charge of high-level reconstruction assignments."

The woman had shining dark skin and a smooth French accent. She wore a dazzling suit of blue velvet with wide, winglike shoulders that narrowed to a fitted waist and was trimmed with bright gold buttons. Her hair was short, parted, and metallic silver. She looked like a rock star from the future, not a Victorian lady from the past.

"I've so looked forward to meeting you all," she said warmly. "Alma has been telling me about you for so long, I feel like I already know you. You must be Emma, the spark. And Hugh, the auto-apiarist?"

"Pleased to meet you," said Hugh.

She knew most everyone, and went around shaking their hands. Then she came to me.

"And you're Jacob Portman. Your reputation precedes you!"

"So I've heard," I said.

"He does not sound thrilled?" Miss Cuckoo said, turning to Miss Peregrine.

"He was caught off guard by all the attention," Miss Peregrine replied. "He's just come off a rather quiet time in the present."

Miss Cuckoo laughed. "Well, his days of quiet are over now! If you're willing to do a bit of work for a good cause, that is."

"I want to help however I can," I said. "What have you got for me?"

"Ah-ah!" She wagged her finger. "All good things in time."

"I'd like to request something more than just day labor," said Millard. "I think my voluminous talents are better suited elsewhere."

"You're all in luck. There are no unimportant assignments here, and there is no peculiar talent, however unusual, that cannot be made useful to the cause. Just last week I assigned a boy with adhesive saliva to a job fashioning unbreakable leg restraints. Whatever your talent, I've got the task for you. Yes?"

Enoch had his hand raised. "My talent is hypnotizing ladies with my good looks. What have you got for me?"

Miss Cuckoo flashed him a sharp smile. "Enoch O'Connor,

dead-riser, born to a family of undertakers." She smiled. "And has a cheeky sense of humor. I'll remember that."

Enoch grinned at the floor, his cheeks going red. "She *does* know me," I heard him say.

Miss Peregrine looked like she was going to murder him. "I'm so sorry, Isabel—"

She waved it off. "He's silly, but he's brave. That could be useful." She looked around at the rest of us. "Anyone else got a joke for me?"

No one said a word.

"Then let's put you to work."

She linked arms with Miss Peregrine and they strode together toward the exit, looking like sisters from different centuries. We followed them up a flight of stairs.

"Enoch, what's gotten into you?" I heard Millard say. "She's a hundred years your senior, and an *ymbryne*!"

"She said I was brave," Enoch said, a dopey look on his face.

Suddenly he didn't seem to mind having a job in the Acre.

"I thought I'd never understand boys," said Bronwyn, shaking her head. "But now I think I've got it. They're all idiots!"

◆　　◆　　◆

We followed the ymbrynes down a gloomy corridor flickering with gaslights. "This is where the sausage gets made," Miss Cuckoo was saying, walking backward to face us as she spoke. "The ministry offices."

Every few yards there was a door, and each was labeled two ways: Signs original to the asylum were carved into the wood in bold block letters, and above those the ministries had tacked signs of their own, stenciled on paper. Through an open door that read both MIS-CREANTS and MINISTRY OF TEMPORAL AFFAIRS, I saw a man clacking away at a typewriter with one hand while holding an umbrella in the other, the ceiling dripping so badly I thought for a moment it was raining inside the room. Through the next door (PERVERTS/DEPT. OF INHUMAN AFFAIRS) a woman was using a broom to defend her lunch from a small horde of rats. Emma, who was unterrified of most things but despised rodents, grabbed my arm.

"I'm surprised you chose this particular building for the ministry offices," Emma said to Miss Cuckoo. "Are you comfortable here?"

Miss Cuckoo laughed. "Not at all, but that is intentional. None of our displaced wards are comfortable in Devil's Acre, so neither should we be. This way, everyone is motivated to keep the reconstruction effort moving along efficiently, so we can get out of here and back to our loops as quickly as possible."

I wasn't sure how efficient a workforce could be if it had to spend half its time battling rats and dripping ceilings, but it was a noble sentiment. If the ymbrynes and officials had set themselves up in some golden palace, it would have looked bad. There was a certain honor in the rat battles.

"Now, as you can imagine, there is plenty of reconstruction work right here in London," Miss Cuckoo was saying, "and in this peculiar labor market of ours, you are all very hot commodities. We need cooks, guards, people who can lift heavy things." She pointed to Bronwyn. "There are several departments clamoring for Miss Bruntley's help. Salvage and Demolition, the Wardening and Guardening force . . ."

I glanced quickly at Bronwyn, and I could see her smile fading.

"Come now, Bronwyn," said Miss Peregrine. "That's certainly better than clearing rubble!"

"I was hoping to be assigned to the expeditionary force in America," Bronwyn said.

"There is no expeditionary force in America."

"Not yet. But I could help create one."

"With ambition like that, I don't doubt you will," said Miss

Cuckoo. "But we must season you a bit before we send you to the front lines."

Bronwyn looked as if she wanted to say more, and she might have if it were only Miss Peregrine she was talking to. But in front of Miss Cuckoo, she held her tongue.

Miss Cuckoo pointed to the space beside me, where Millard's coat and pants bobbed along in the air. "Mr. Nullings, you have a plum job offer from Peculiar Intelligence—invisibles always make top field agents."

"Wouldn't the Ministry of Mapping be a better fit?" Millard replied. "Any invisible can sneak around and overhear secrets, but I'd wager my cartographic expertise is equal to anyone's."

"It may be, but Intelligence is understaffed and Mapping is full up. I'm sorry. Now, please go report to Mr. Kimble in Intelligence, room three-oh-one."

"Yes, ma'am," Millard said, the excitement in his voice gone. He turned and walked the other way down the hall.

Miss Cuckoo indicated a large, high-ceilinged office we were passing where half a dozen men and women were combing through stacks of mail. "Mr. O'Connor, I'm sure the Dead Letters Office would appreciate your help."

Enoch looked crestfallen. "Sorting undeliverable mail? What about my talent?"

"Our Dead Letters Office doesn't handle undeliverable mail. It deals with correspondence to and from the dead."

One of the workers held up an envelope smudged with grave mud. "Their handwriting is rubbish," the man said. "And their grammar is even worse. It takes a regular scientist to sort out who these letters are meant for." He tipped the envelope, and a small pile of worms and bugs poured out of it. "Now and then we'd like to go back to the source and ask them, but none of us can dead-rise."

"The dead write letters to one another?" Emma said.

"They're always asking after people and wanting to send news to old friends," Enoch said. "They're right gossips, half of them. If I have time, sometimes I'll let 'em write a postcard before they go back in the ground."

"Think about it!" the man said. "We're always shorthanded."

"I'm not!" said a worker in the back, and he raised one freakishly long arm, brushed the ceiling with his fingers, then began to cackle as we walked away.

Miss Cuckoo was waving at us to hurry up.

"Miss Bloom, I could easily place you in the Warden's office. You would make an excellent prison guard for our most dangerous wights. But Miss Peregrine tells me you've developed another interest of late?"

"Yes, miss. Photography. I've already got a handheld flash . . ."

She held up her palm and sparked a flame. Miss Cuckoo laughed.

"That's very good. We will surely want qualified photographists to document things as we reestablish contact with the American colonies. For the moment, though, your pyrogenic skills are still most useful to us as a weapon, so I'd like to keep you on call for security emergencies."

"Oh," she said, clearly disappointed but trying to hide it.

Emma gave me a resigned look, like she'd been foolish to expect more. Her abilities with fire were so powerful that it put her in a box, peculiarly speaking, and I could see the limits of it beginning to gnaw at her.

After a few minutes, everyone had been given a task that sounded, if not always super cool or vital to the cause, at least relevant to their peculiar skills. Except me. One by one, my friends peeled off to consult with whichever ministry official they'd been assigned to, and I was alone with Miss Cuckoo and Miss Peregrine. We came into a large conservatory, the walls a puzzle of windows suffocated from the outside by vines. The room was dominated by a huge black conference table embossed with the ymbrynes' official seal—a bird with a watch dangling from its mouth, one talon pinning down a snake. This was the chamber of the Council of Ymbrynes, where they held their meetings and decided our futures, and I felt a strange sort of reverence, being there, even if it was only a temporary space. The only bit of decoration in the room was a series of maps tacked onto the lower windows.

"Please," Miss Cuckoo said, gesturing to the chairs arranged around the big table. "Sit."

I pulled back a chair—modest, upholstered in simple gray fabric—and sat. There was no gold anywhere in the room, nor any thrones, scepters, robes, or other such trappings. Even the ymbrynes' decor choices were humble, meant to demonstrate that they didn't think of themselves as better than the rest, and that the leadership roles entrusted to them were a responsibility, not an entitlement.

"Please give us a moment, Jacob," said Miss Peregrine, and she and Miss Cuckoo walked together to the other side of the room, each step of Miss Cuckoo's heels a hammer blow on the stone floor. They spoke in hushed tones, glancing back at me now and then. Miss Peregrine seemed to be explaining something, and Miss Cuckoo was listening, brow furrowed.

She must have something really big for me, I thought. Something so important, so dangerous, that she's got to persuade Miss Cuckoo to let me do it first. *Someone so young, so inexperienced— it's unprecedented*, I imagined Miss Cuckoo saying. But Miss Peregrine knew me, knew what I was capable of, and she would have no doubt that I could do it.

I tried not to get too excited. I didn't want to get ahead of myself. But my eyes began wandering the room, and when they landed once again on the maps, an idea began to form about what Miss Peregrine had in mind for me.

They were maps of America.

There was a modern one, several older ones from before Alaska and Hawaii were states, and even one so old that the country's border traced the Mississippi River. That one was divided into several big swaths of color: The Southeast was purple, the Northeast green, most of the West orange, and Texas was gray. There were fascinating symbols and legends inscribed here and there—reminiscent of the ones I'd seen on Miss Peregrine's Map of Days, and I started to lean out of my seat to get a better look.

"A thorny problem!" said Miss Cuckoo.

"What is?" I said, spinning to look at her.

"America," she replied, crossing the room toward me. "It has for years now been a terra incognita. A Wild West, if you will, its temporal geography no longer well understood. Many of its loops have been lost, and many more are simply unknown."

"Oh?" I said. "Why is that?"

I was getting excited now. America—of course. I was the perfect peculiar to tackle a dangerous mission in America. It was *my turf*.

"The biggest problem is that America has no centralized peculiar authority, no governing body. It is fractured and split between a number of clans—only the largest of which we maintain diplomatic relations with. But they are locked in a long-simmering conflict over resources and territory. For years the hollowgast menace acted as a lid on that pot, but now that it's been lifted, we are concerned that old grudges could boil over into armed physical conflict."

I straightened my back and looked Miss Cuckoo in the eye. "And you want me to help put a stop to it."

When I looked up, Miss Cuckoo had the funniest look on her face, like she was trying not to laugh, and Miss Peregrine looked pained.

Miss Cuckoo put a hand on my shoulder. Sat down next to me. "We had . . . another idea."

Miss Peregrine sat down on my other side. "We want you to share your story."

My head swiveled from one to the other. "I don't understand."

"Life in Devil's Acre can be hard," said Miss Cuckoo.

"Draining, demoralizing. The peculiars here need inspiration, and they love to hear the story of how you bested Caul."

"The Battle for Devil's Acre is what the little ones all want to hear at bedtime," said Miss Peregrine. "It's even being adapted for the stage by Miss Grackle's troupe of thespians—and set to music!"

"Oh my God," I said, mortified.

"You'll start here, in the Acre," said Miss Peregrine, "and then travel to some of the outer loops, the ones hit hard by the wights but still occupied—"

"But . . . what about America?" I said. "Your thorny problem?"

"At the moment, we're primarily focused on rebuilding our own society," said Miss Cuckoo.

"Then why did you tell me all that?" I asked her.

Miss Cuckoo shrugged. "You were staring at the maps with such longing."

I shook my head. "You said America was full of unknown loops. And there was fighting and trouble."

"Yes, but—"

"I'm an American. I can help. So can my friends."

"Jacob—"

"We could all help, once I teach them how to pass as normal. Hell, Emma's ready now, and with most of them I'd only need a few days, maybe a week of focused lessons—"

"Mr. Portman," said Miss Peregrine, "you're getting ahead of yourself."

"Isn't that why you want them to learn about the present? Isn't that why you brought them to live with me?"

Miss Peregrine sighed sharply. "Jacob, I admire your ambition very much. But the council doesn't think you're ready yet."

"You only just learned you were peculiar a few months ago," said Miss Cuckoo.

"And you only decided you needed to help the cause this morning!" Miss Peregrine added.

It almost sounded like she was poking fun at me.

"I'm ready," I insisted. "So are the others. I want us to work for you in America, like my grandfather used to."

"Abe's group didn't take orders from us," said Miss Peregrine. "They were entirely self-directed."

"They were?"

"Abe did things his own way," Miss Peregrine said. "Our world has changed a lot since then, and we can no longer function in such a manner. In any case, the way Abe conducted business does not affect this conversation. All that matters is that the situation in America is still developing. Right now that's all we can tell you. When we need your help there—and when the council thinks you and your friends are ready—we will ask for it."

"Yes," said Miss Cuckoo. "But until then—"

"You want me to be a motivational speaker."

Miss Peregrine sighed. She was starting to get exasperated with me, and I was starting to get angry. "You've had a hard day, Mr. Portman."

"You don't know the half of it," I said. "Look, I just want to do something that *matters*."

"He wants maybe to be an ymbryne?" Miss Cuckoo said, smirking.

I pushed my chair back and stood up.

"Where are you going?" asked Miss Peregrine.

"To find my friends," I said, and started toward the door.

"One step at a time, Jacob!" Miss Peregrine called after me. "You have the rest of your life to be a hero."

◆　　◆　　◆

My friends were still elsewhere in the building, discussing the details of their work assignments, so I sat on a bench in the busy lobby and waited, and while I was waiting, I decided something.

My grandfather had never asked the ymbrynes' permission to do his work, and I didn't need their permission to continue it. That Abe had left his logbook for me to find was permission enough. I needed a mission. And to get one of those—

"*Omigod.*"

"Uhhhhhh. Are you Jacob Portman?"

Two girls had sat down next to me. I tore myself away from my train of thought to look over at them, and was surprised to see only one girl. She was Asian, a bit younger than me, dressed in seventies-era flannel and bell-bottoms—and most definitely by herself.

"I'm him," I said.

"Would you sign my arm?" she said, holding out one arm. Then she held out the other and said, in a deeper voice, "And mine, too?"

She saw my confusion. "We're a binary," she explained. "Sometimes we're confused for a dual-personality person, but we actually have two hearts, souls, brains—"

"And voice boxes!" said her other voice.

"Wow, that's cool," I said, genuinely impressed. "It's great to meet you. But . . . I don't think I should be signing body parts."

"Oh," they said together.

"Are you excited about Miss Grackle's production?" said the deeper voice. "I can't wait. She did one about Miss Wren and her animals last season. *The Grass Menagerie.*"

"It was far out. Very groovy."

"Who do you think they'll get to play you?"

"Uh, wow, I really don't know. Hey, would you guys excuse me?"

I stood up, apologized again, and started quickly across the room. Not because I wanted to get away from them—well, not entirely—but because I had spotted someone who looked familiar in a way that made my brain itch, and I had to go and find out who he was.

He was a clerk behind one of the lobby windows. A young man with close-cropped hair, deep brown skin, and soft features. I knew his face from somewhere but couldn't quite place it. I thought if I spoke to him it might jog my memory. He saw me coming, snatched a quill pen from his ink stand, and pretended to be writing as I arrived at his window.

"Do I know you from somewhere?" I asked him.

He didn't look up. "No," the man said.

"I'm Jacob Portman."

He glanced up at me. Unimpressed. "Yes."

"We haven't met before?"

"No."

I was getting nowhere. Engraved on the window was INFORMATION.

"I need some information."

"About?"

"An associate of my grandfather's. I'm trying to get in contact with him. If he's still alive."

"We're not a directory service, sir."

"Then what sort of information do you give out?"

"We don't give it. We collect it."

He reached across his desk, then handed me a long form. "Here, fill this out."

"You've got to be kidding," I said, and dropped it back on his desk.

He scowled at me.

"Jacob!"

Miss Peregrine was walking toward me across the lobby, my friends trailing behind. In a moment I would be surrounded.

I leaned through the window and said, "I *do* know you from somewhere."

"If you insist," said the man.

"Ready to go?" said Horace.

"I'm starving," said Olive. "Can we have American food again?"

"So, what's your assignment?" Emma asked me.

As they buoyed me away toward the exit, I looked back at the man. He was sitting very still, watching me go, brow furrowed with worry.

Miss Peregrine took me aside. "We'll have a talk very soon, just you and me," she said. "I'm very sorry if your feelings were stepped on in our meeting. It's very important to me, and all the ymbrynes, that you feel fulfilled. But the American situation is, as we mentioned, a sticky one."

"I just want you guys to have faith in me. I'm not asking to be the captain of an army, or something." *I'm not asking for anything anymore*, I thought, but did not say.

"I know," she said. "But please be patient. And please believe that if we seem overly cautious, it's for your own safety. If anything was to happen to you—or any of you—it would be a disaster."

I had an uncharitable thought: that what she really meant was it would *look* bad if something happened to me, just like it would look bad if we didn't help the reconstruction effort in a way that was visible to everyone in Devil's Acre. I knew that wasn't her whole rationale. Of course she cared about us. But she also cared about the opinions of people who were strangers to me, and what they thought about how I lived my life—and I did not.

But instead of saying any of that, I said, "Okay, no problem, I understand," because I knew there was no changing her mind about this.

She smiled and thanked me, and I felt a little bad for lying to her—but not too bad—and then she bid us goodbye.

The clock had just ticked past noon in Devil's Acre. Miss Peregrine had some business left to take care of here, but ours was done for the day, so we were to meet her at my house later on.

"Go directly there," she warned us. "Do not loiter, linger, dally, or dawdle."

"Yes, Miss Peregrine," we chorused.

CHAPTER FIVE

*W*e didn't go directly. I asked the others if we could find a route that avoided some of the thickest crowds, and in the spirit of exploration and mild disobedience, they agreed. Enoch claimed to know a fast way that was almost sure to be deserted, and a minute later we were tracing the banks of the river, Fever Ditch.

This part of the Acre had not been cleaned up like the center had been. Perhaps it was not cleanable. Devil's Acre was a loop, so the basic environmental facts of the place would reset themselves daily. The Ditch would always be a brown and polluted ribbon of filth. What sun was able to filter down through the pall of factory smoke that hung above us would always be the color of weak tea. The normals who were stuck here, part of the endlessly repeating scenery, would always be the same miserable, half-starved wretches who peered suspiciously at us from the alleys and tenement windows we were now passing. Millard said that somewhere there must have been a map of all the murders, assaults, and robberies that took place the day Devil's Acre was looped, so those dangerous places could be avoided, but none of us had ever seen it. Everyone knew to be careful when passing through the normal regions. For as long as we could stand the smell, we hugged the edge of the Ditch to avoid passing too close to the dark buildings.

When they were not glancing nervously around them, my friends discussed their new assignments. Most of them sounded disappointed. A few sounded bitter.

"I should be charting maps of America!" Millard grumbled. "Perplexus Anomalous is head of the blasted Mapping Department now. If the ymbrynes don't think they owe us anything for all we did, he surely does."

"Then you should appeal directly to him," said Hugh.

"I'll do that," Millard said.

Enoch, once his initial excitement had worn off, had realized that his job in the Dead Letters Office was about 5 percent dead-rising, 95 percent filing. "How can they stick us with grunt work, after what we pulled off in the Library of Souls?" he said. "We saved the ymbrynes' hides. They should either let us have a nice long holiday, or give us shiny jobs with loads of underlings beneath us."

"I wouldn't say it precisely that way," said Horace. "But I agree. Assistant to the anachronist in the Costumes Department? I should be advising the Ymbryne Council on strategy, at the very least. I can see the future, for birds' sake!"

"I thought Miss Peregrine believed in us," said Olive.

"She does," said Bronwyn. "It's the other ymbrynes. They don't know us as well."

"They're threatened by us," said Enoch. "These assignments? They're meant to send a message. You're still just peculiar children."

Emma sidled up to me, and we trudged side by side. I asked her how her assignment meeting had gone.

"Look at this," Emma said, pulling a slim rectangular box from her bag. "It's a folding camera." She flipped a switch and a lens accordioned out of the body.

"So they gave you the job you wanted, after all? Documenting things?"

"Nah," she said. "I nicked it from the equipment room. They gave me three shifts a week guarding ymbrynes during wight interrogations."

"That could be interesting, though. You might hear some crazy things."

"I don't *want* to hear all that. Going over all their crimes and what they did to us for years and years . . . I'm tired of rehashing ancient history. I want to see new places, meet new people. What about you?"

"Me too," I said.

"I mean, what about your assignment? I'm dying to know what they gave you. Something amazing, I'm sure."

"Motivational speaker," I said.

"What the devil is that?"

"I'm supposed to go around to different loops telling people about myself."

She screwed up her face. "For what?"

"To . . . inspire them?"

She laughed so hard it actually hurt my feelings a little.

"Hey. It's not *that* weird," I said.

"Don't take this the wrong way: I think you're *very* inspiring. But I just . . . I can't see it."

"Me, neither. That's why I'm not going to do it."

"Really?" she said, impressed. "So what are you going to do?"

"Something else."

"Oh. I see. Very mysterious."

"Yep."

"You'll let me know?"

I smiled. "You'll be the first."

I didn't want to keep Emma in the dark about my plans. I just didn't exactly *have* plans yet, only a certainty that something would bubble up.

And then something did. There was a noise from the river—a splash followed by a loud drawing of breath.

Claire shouted, *"Fish monster!"*

We all turned to look, but what seemed like a sea creature at first glance turned out to be a heavyset man with pale fishy skin. He was swimming quickly alongside us, submerged but for his

head and shoulders, propelled beneath the surface by something we couldn't see.

"Ho there!" the man called out. "Young people, halt!"

We walked faster, but somehow the man was able to match our speed.

"I just want to ask you a question."

"Everyone stop," said Millard. "This man won't hurt us. You're peculiar, aren't you?"

The man rose up and a pair of gills on his neck gasped open and spat out black water.

"My name is Itch," the man answered, and whether he was peculiar was no longer in question. "I only want to know one thing. You are the wards of Alma Peregrine, correct?"

"That's right," said Olive, standing right at the edge of the Ditch to show she wasn't afraid.

"And is it true you go where you like and will never age forward? That your internal clocks have reset?"

"That was two questions," said Enoch.

"Yes, it's true," said Emma.

"I see," Itch said. "And when can we have our clocks reset?"

"Who's we?" asked Horace.

Four more heads popped up from of the water around him—two young boys with fins on their backs, an older woman with scaled skin, and a very old man with wide, fishy eyes, one on each side of his head. "My adoptive family," Itch said. "We've been living in this cursed Ditch and breathing its polluted water for far too long."

"Time for a change of scenery," the fish-eyed man croaked.

"We want to go somewhere clean," said the scaly woman.

"It's not that easy," said Emma. "What happened to us was accidental, and it could have killed us."

"We don't care," said Itch.

"They just don't want to share their secret!" said one of the finned boys.

"That's not true," said Millard. "We aren't even sure if the reset could be re-created. The ymbrynes are still studying it."

"The ymbrynes!" The woman spat black water from her gills. "Even if they knew, they'd never tell. Then we'd all leave their loops and they'd have nobody left to lord over."

"Hey!" Claire shouted. "That's a terrible thing to say!"

"Downright treasonous," said Bronwyn.

"Treason!" shouted Itch, and he swam to the edge and pulled himself up onto the pavement. We edged away from him as the water ran off his body, revealing a coat of long green algae that covered him from chest to feet. "That's a dangerous word to bandy about."

The boys pulled themselves up out of the Ditch and so did the woman—she was similarly clothed in algae—leaving only the old man in the water, swimming agitated circles.

"Look," I said—I hadn't spoken yet, and thought maybe I could calm things down. "We're all peculiar here. There's no reason to fight."

"What do you know about it, newcomer?" said the woman.

"He thinks he's our savior!" said Itch. "You're nothing but a phony who got lucky."

"False prophet!" shouted one of the boys, and then the other boy shouted it, too, and then they all were—"False prophet! False prophet!"—while closing in on us from three sides.

"I never claimed I was a prophet," I tried to say. "I never claimed I was *anything*."

Dozens of normal tenement-dwellers had leaned out of the windows of the building behind us, and now they were shouting, too, and raining garbage down on our heads.

"You people have been in that Ditch for too long!" Enoch shouted back. "Your brains are polluted!"

Emma started to light a flame and Bronwyn looked ready to take a swing at Itch, but the others pulled them back. We were watched closely in Devil's Acre, and hurting another peculiar, even in self-defense, would have looked very bad.

The dripping Ditch dwellers had backed us into an alley, their cries of "false prophet" turning into demands that we give up our secret. Finally, we had no choice but to turn and run, their shouts echoing after us as we turned a corner.

Somehow we found our way out of the dangerous part of town and back to the center, though everything after was a bit of a blur; we were shaken, and the friendly hellos and handshakes that came at us as we parted the crowd near Bentham's house felt unreal.

What was behind all those smiles?

How many of them secretly resented us?

Then we were in the Panloopticon, getting waved through peculiar customs, plodding quietly up the stairs and down the long hall, everyone silent, in their own heads.

◆   ◆   ◆

We packed into the broom closet, then stumbled, after a lurching rush, out into a hot Florida night. Faint steam rose from the shed's peaked roof, accompanied by a light hissing sound, like a hot engine cooling down.

"Ozone," said Millard.

"Twenty-two minutes forty seconds." Miss Peregrine was standing in the yard, arms crossed. "Is how late you are."

"But, miss," said Claire, "we didn't mean to—"

"No one say *anything*," Emma hissed. Then, louder, "We tried a shortcut but got lost."

We stood there in the yard, exhausted, still freaked out from our encounter at the Ditch, and endured a lecture about punctuality and responsibility. I could hear my friends' teeth gritting. Once she'd made it overabundantly clear that she was disappointed in us, Miss Peregrine assumed bird form, flew to the top of my roof, and perched there.

"What just happened?" I said in a low voice.

"That's what she does when she needs to be alone," said Emma. "She must be really upset."

"Because we were twenty-two minutes late?"

"She's under a lot of pressure," said Bronwyn.

"And she's taking it out on us," said Hugh. "It isn't fair."

"I think there are a lot of peculiars who don't want to listen to the ymbrynes right now," said Olive, "but Miss P has always been able to count on *us* listening. So when we muck something up, even a wee little bit . . ."

"Well, she can stuff it up her hindfeathers!" said Enoch a little too loudly.

Bronwyn clapped her hand over his mouth, and the two of them fell to the ground, scuffling.

"Stop it, stop it!" said Olive, and she and Emma and I pulled them apart and in the process were thrown to the ground ourselves, and then we were lying on the grass panting and beginning to sweat in the humid night air.

"This is so stupid," said Emma. "No more fighting amongst ourselves."

"Truce?" said Bronwyn.

Enoch nodded and they shook on it.

Everyone wanted a break and a reset from the events of the day, so we went inside the house, where Horace made something amazing from what remained of the stolen groceries, and then I introduced them to the time-honored American tradition of eating in front of the television. I channel surfed while my friends stared at the screen, some so absorbed in it that they forgot all about the plates of food growing cold in their laps. The Home Shopping Network, commercials for dog food and ladies' hair products, a preacher on the religious network, a talent competition show, snippets of news about conflicts in foreign lands: It was all equally alien to them. Once they got over the shock of having a screen like this *right in the house*, with a full-color picture and surround sound and a hundred different channels to choose from, they started asking questions. Some took me by surprise.

While lingering on an old episode of *Star Trek*, Hugh asked, "Do a lot of people own spaceships now?"

Bronwyn, while watching *The Real Housewives of Orange County*: "Are there no poor people in America anymore?"

And Olive: "Why are they so rude to one another?"

During a car ad, Horace asked, "Is that noise meant to be music?"

Flipping past a news show, Claire winced and said, "Why are they shouting like that?"

I could see it was starting to upset them. Emma was tense, Hugh was pacing, and Horace was squeezing the arm of the sofa in a death grip.

"It's too *much*," Emma said, pressing the heels of her hands into her eyes. "Too loud, too fast!"

"It never settles on anything for more than an instant," said Horace. "The effect is dizzying."

"No wonder normals rarely notice peculiars out in the world anymore," said Enoch. "Their brains have melted!"

"If modern people watch, then we shall, too," said Millard.

"But I don't *want* a melted brain," said Bronwyn.

"Nothing's going to melt," Millard reassured her. "Think of it as a vaccine. Just a bit will be enough to inoculate you against the bigger shocks of this world."

We flipped channels for a while longer, but its numbing effect began to wear off and my mind drifted toward unpleasant things. It occurred to me, as we lingered on an episode of *The Bachelor*, how little I understood the world I'd grown up in. All my life, normal people had mostly baffled me—the ridiculous ways they strove to impress one another, the mediocre goals that seemed to drive them, the banality of their dreams. The way people rejected anything that didn't fit their narrow paradigm of acceptability, as if those who thought or acted or dressed or dreamed differently from them were a threat to their very existence. That, more than anything, was why I had felt so alone growing up. Things that normal people thought were important, I thought were dumb. And there was never any-one I could talk to about it, so I kept my thoughts to myself. I had returned to that normal world with the assurance that I now had a home waiting for me in the peculiar world. But today in Devil's Acre left me feeling like I was a stranger there, too—a hero to some, a phony to others. Misunderstood by everybody, just like at home.

I was trying to explain *The Simpsons* and succumbing to a deep sleepiness (it had been a long day) when something in my brain un-locked, and I remembered where I had seen that clerk's face before. I handed the remote to Enoch, excused myself to the bathroom, and ran upstairs.

Closing the door to my room, I pulled out Abe's operations log from under my bed, and began flipping through it, searching for the clerk's face. It took a few minutes to find it—there were so many pages and so many faces—but I finally did, in an entry from 1983. The photo was old, from the 1930s or 40s, I guessed, but the clerk looked the same today as he did in the photo, which meant he had been living in loops for a long time. His name was noted as Lester Noble, Jr. In the picture he wore a big round hat and gazed placidly at the camera, no trace in his expression of the fear I'd seen on his face earlier in the day. I read my grandfather's notes on the mission, then pried loose the staples that attached the photo to the log page and tucked the photo into my pocket.

I ran into Emma in the hallway.

"I was just coming to find you," she said.

"And I was coming to find you. I need your help."

She leaned in. "Sure, anything."

"Cover for me. Just for an hour or two. I need to go back to the Acre."

"Why? For what?"

"There's no time to explain," I said. "When I get back."

"I'm coming, too."

"I need to do this alone."

She crossed her arms. "This better be good."

"It will be. I think."

I kissed her, then slipped down the stairs, outside through the garage, and into the potting shed.

❖   ❖   ❖

When I got back to the lobby of the ministry building, he was gone. His window was shut and there was no one behind it. I slid over to the next window and asked the woman working there if she knew where the clerk was.

She squinted at me through thick glasses. "Who?"

"The man who works right there. Lester Noble."

"I don't know any Lester Noble," she said, tapping her fountain pen on her desk, "but the chap who works next to me just left for the day. You might still catch him if you—oh, *there* he is."

She pointed across the lobby. I turned to see the clerk hurrying toward the exit. I muttered a quick thanks and ran across the room, catching him just before he made it through the door.

"Lester Noble," I said.

He turned a bit pale. "My name is Stevenson. And you're blocking my way."

He tried to push past me, but I stood my ground, and he clearly didn't want to make a scene. "Your name is Lester Noble, Jr., and you're faking that British accent."

I pulled his photo from my pocket and held it up for him to see. He froze, then snatched it from my hand. When he looked up and met my eyes again, he seemed afraid.

"*What do you want?*" he whispered.

"To get in contact with someone."

His gaze flicked across the lobby, then back at me. "Walk down that hall. Meet me at room one thirty-seven in two minutes. We can't be seen walking together."

I snatched the photo back. "I'm keeping this. For now."

Two minutes later, I met him outside a plain wooden door that was only marked 137. He fumbled with the keys. His hands were shaking. We went inside and he closed and locked the door behind us. The room was small and filled with manila file folders, wall to wall, floor to ceiling.

"Look, kid," he said, turning to me with his hands pressed together. "I'm not a criminal, okay?" His British accent had vanished, replaced by a slight southern twang. "There are some bad people in America, and I couldn't let them find me. I changed my name when I got here. I never thought I'd hear the old one again."

"Were the hollows over there really that much worse than the ones here?" I asked him.

"They were bad, but that's not why I left. It was the peculiars. They're crazy."

"Oh? How?"

Lester shook his head. "I'm breaking about a hundred rules, taking you back here. If you want a file, okay, but there's no time for stories."

"Fine," I said. "What do you have on the hollow-hunters?"

Lester hesitated. "Who?"

"I know you know who I'm talking about," I said, and I told him what I knew from Abe's mission report.

The report said Lester had been living in a loop of January 5, 1935, in Anniston, Alabama, until the loop had been raided and its ymbryne killed. Abe and H had found Lester holed up in a motel in the present—then 1983—where he'd been in bad danger of aging forward. They'd managed to ferry him to safety in another loop. He must have found his way to England at some point afterward, which was no doubt a harrowing story all its own. But it was one I didn't have time to hear, and one that Lester, after I'd finished telling him about himself, seemed in no mood to share, anyway.

"How do you know all that?" Lester said. His whole body had gone rigid, like he was steadying himself for bad news.

"Abe was my grandfather," I said.

"He told you about me?" His voice was rising steadily. It seemed I'd really spooked him.

"Not as such," I said. "Look, there's nothing to worry about and there's no need to go into too many details. I'm not here to dig up bodies from your past. I just need to get in touch with the one called H. You spent time with him. You work here, in the inner sanctum . . ." I tumbled my hands, a gesture meant to imply the connection. "You're my best bet."

He sighed, and I saw him relax a little. He folded his arms across his chest and leaned against one of the shelves. "They didn't leave me their business card, or anything," he said, "and even if they had, that was a long time ago."

"I was hoping there might be something in your files," I said. "The ymbrynes must have had some way to get in touch with them."

"So why don't you ask the ymbrynes?"

Now he was getting a little *too* comfortable. "I'm trying to be discreet. But if I have to, I'll be sure and let them know it was Lester Noble, Jr., who referred me to them."

He frowned. "Okay, then," he said tersely. "Let me see what I have." He turned and walked down a wall, running his index finger along the folders as he went. He pulled a file folder from a shelf. Flipped through its contents, mumbling to himself. Then crossed to another wall and another shelf, and pulled two more folders. Shook his head, tucked them under his arm, and moved on. After a few minutes, he came to me with his hand held out. In his palm was an old matchbook.

"What's this?" I said.

"That's all there is."

I took the matchbook. It was wrinkled at the edges, like it had spent a lot of time in someone's pocket. The outside cover was blank. On the inside was an advertisement for a Chinese restaurant, an address, some random-looking numbers and letters, and a penciled note that read, *Burn after reading.* Clearly, someone had ignored those instructions.

"Now, then." Lester snatched his photo from me. "I'd say that's an even trade, seeing as I could get fired for just letting you into this room, much less letting you walk out with that."

"It's just an old matchbook," I said. "What am I supposed to do with this?"

"That's for you to figure out." He went to the door, opened it, and waited for me to leave. "Now, do me a favor, mate," he said, his British accent returning, "and forget we ever met."

◆   ◆   ◆

I crossed the Acre in such a rush, and with such focused intensity, that even those people who recognized me didn't have the nerve to stop me. I came to Bentham's house, ran up the stairs and down the long Panloopticon hall to the door marked A. PEREGRINE AND WARDS ONLY, dove in, and a moment later was spat onto the grass of my backyard. I stood dazed for a moment in the warm night, listening to the crickets and frogs harmonize, as TV light flickered from the windows of my living room.

Miss Peregrine wasn't perched on the roof anymore. No one had seen me return. I still had some time to myself. I crossed the yard to the dock, walked to the end of it, and sat. It was the only place I could think of where I'd be assured some privacy, and if anyone came to check on me, I'd hear their approach.

I took out my phone and the matchbook, and set to figuring

Hong's

17 MOTT ST
NEW YORK CITY
RES: LT1-6730

• *Chinese Food At Its Best*
• *Party Facilities*

BURN AFTER READING

out how it could be used to reach H. A few minutes of thumb-typed research yielded this: The odd-looking string of letters and numbers below the address was a phone number, albeit an un-dialable one, in an alphanumeric style that had fallen out of use in the 1960s.

I did a search for the name of the restaurant advertised on the matchbook. A lucky break: It was still in business. I looked up its modern phone number, and called it.

I heard a series of clicks, like the call was being routed through some foreign exchange. Then it began to ring, maybe ten, twelve times, until a gruff male voice finally answered.

"Yeah."

"I'm calling for H. This is—"

The line went dead. He'd hung up on me!

I called back. This time he picked up after two rings.

"You got the wrong number."

"This is Jacob Portman."

There was a pause. He didn't hang up.

"I'm Abe Portman's grandson."

"So you say."

My heart sped up. The number was still good. I was talking to someone who knew my grandfather. Maybe H himself.

"I can prove it."

"Let's say I believe you," the man said. "Which maybe I do, maybe I don't. What does Jacob Portman want?"

"A job."

"Try the want ads."

"A job doing what you do."

"Crossword puzzles?"

"What?"

"I'm retired, son."

"What you used to do, then. You and Abe and the others."

"And what do you know about that?" His tone was suddenly defensive.

"I know a lot. I read Abe's mission logs."

There was a metallic squeak and then a grunt, like H had just risen from a chair.

"And?"

"And I want to help. I know there are still hollowgast out there. Maybe not a lot of them, but even one could cause serious trouble. And there's plenty to do besides that."

"That's charitable of you, son. But we're not in business anymore."

"Why not? Because Abe died?"

"Because we got old."

"Well, then," I said, feeling a surge of confidence, "I'll start it up again. I have friends who can help, too. A new generation."

I heard a cupboard slap shut, a spoon tinkle in a cup. "You ever see a hollow in person?" he asked.

"I have. And I've killed them."

"Is that right?"

"You didn't hear about the Library of Souls? The Battle for Devil's Acre?"

"I'm not exactly up on the latest current events."

"I can do what Abe did. I can see them. Control them, too."

"You know . . ." He sipped a drink loudly. "Maybe I did hear something about you."

"You did?"

"Yeah. You're raw, untested. Impulsive. And in our line of work, that gets you killed real fast."

I gritted my teeth, but managed to keep my voice even and calm. "I know I have a lot to learn. But I think I have a lot to offer, too."

"You're serious, huh." He sounded both amused and impressed.

"I am."

"All right. You talked yourself into a job interview."

"This wasn't it?"

He laughed. "Not even close."

"Okay, well, what do I—"

"Don't call again. I'll call you."

The line went dead.

◆　　◆　　◆

I dashed into the house, waved to my friends as I darted past them in the living room—they were watching some zombie movie—and Emma jumped up and followed me into an empty bedroom.

She hugged me hard, then poked me in the chest. "Start talking, Portman."

"I made contact with one of Abe's old partners. I just talked to him on the phone."

She let me go and took a step back, eyes wide.

"Pull the other one."

"I'm serious. This guy, H, worked with my grandfather for decades. They ran tons of missions together. But now he's old, and he needs our help."

I was reaching a little there, maybe. But only a little. H *did* need our help, he just needed to be convinced of it first.

"With what?"

"A mission. Here in America."

"He should call the ymbrynes if he needs help."

"Our ymbrynes don't have authority in America. And apparently America doesn't have ymbrynes of its own."

"Why not?"

"I don't know, Em. There are a hundred thousand things I don't know. But I do know that Abe locked that door in his floor with a passcode only *I* would know. And he left that mission log for me to find. And if he'd had any idea there was a chance *you* would be here, he would've meant for you to find it, too."

She looked away, wrestling with something.

"We can't just run off on some mission. Miss Peregrine would never allow it."

"I know that."

She fixed me with a stare. "A mission doing what?"

"I don't know yet. H said he'll be in touch."

"You really hate the assignment the ymbrynes gave you, huh?"

"Yeah. A lot."

"I think you'd be good at it. That was a pretty motivational speech."

"So you're in?"

A grin spread across her face.

"Hell, yes."

CHAPTER SIX

*T*hat night I had a terrible dream. I was in a wasteland of burning fields, the horizon all soot and flame, black ooze puddled across the earth. I was frozen in the air, suspended above a deep pit. From its depths glowed two blue lights. They belonged to Caul—Caul in his monstrous form, a hundred feet tall, his arms like tree trunks and his fingers long, grasping roots reaching up toward me.

He was calling my name. *Jacob, Jacob*, his voice a high and taunting singsong. *I see you. I see you there. I seeeeee youuuuuuuuu . . .*

Waves of putrid air funneled up around me, the smell like burning flesh. I wanted to gag, to escape, but I was paralyzed. I tried to speak, to shout down at him. But no words would come.

There was a skittering sound, like rats were climbing the walls of the pit.

"You're not real," I finally managed to say. "I killed you."

Yes, he said. *And now I am everywhere.*

The skittering grew louder, until Caul's fingers crawled over the lip of the pit—ten long and gnarled roots, coming at me, wrapping around my throat.

I've got big plans for you, Jacob . . . Big, big plans . . .

I thought my lungs would explode, then felt a sharp pain in my stomach.

I bolted upright, gasping for breath, and clutched my gut. I was awake, at home, on the floor of my bedroom, my sleeping bag twisted around me.

A slash of moonlight divided the room. Enoch and Hugh lay snoring in my bed. The hurt in my stomach was an old and familiar one. It was both pain and a compass needle.

The needle pointed downstairs and outside.

I disentangled myself from the sleeping bag and dashed out of the room and down the stairs. I moved silently, running on my toes. If this was what I thought it was, there wasn't much my friends could do to help me. They would only get in the way, and I didn't want to wake them up and cause a panic before I had assessed the situation. Fear only fueled a hollowgast.

Fear made them hungry.

I pulled a knife from the block on my way through the kitchen— not much good against a hollow, but better than nothing—then exited through the garage and outside, nearly tripping over a coiled garden hose as I rounded into the backyard. A hazy trail of ozone rose from the potting shed's roof. The pocket loop had been used very recently.

And then, as suddenly as the feeling had come upon me, it vanished. The compass needle moved toward the bay, then flipped around completely toward the gulf, then went slack. That had never happened before, and I couldn't understand it. Could the whole thing have been a false alarm? Could nightmares trigger my peculiar reflex?

Feeling the wet grass between my toes, I glanced down at what I was wearing: ripped sweatpants, an old T-shirt, no shoes, and I thought, *This is how Abe died. This, almost exactly.* Lured into the dark in his bedclothes, gripping an improvised weapon.

I lowered the knife. Slowly, my hand stopped shaking. I walked the perimeter of my house, back and forth, waiting. No feeling came. Eventually I went back to my room and slipped into the sleeping bag on my floor, but I did not sleep.

◆　　◆　　◆

The next morning I was checking my phone every minute, hoping for a call from H. He hadn't said when he would be in touch. Emma and I debated telling the others, but decided to wait until we had a mission—and maybe we wouldn't say anything even then. Maybe the mission would only involve the two of us. Maybe some of our friends wouldn't want to go, or would be against the whole idea. What if one of them spilled the beans and told Miss Peregrine what we were planning before we had a chance to leave?

After breakfast, I was obligated to take the peculiars out clothes shopping. It seemed like a good way to kill time while I waited, so I tried to throw myself into it and forget about H's call.

The first batch were Hugh, Claire, Olive, and Horace. I drove them to the mall. Not the mall by my house, where I worried we might encounter someone from my school. I picked the Shaker Pines mall, out by the Interstate. On the way, I pointed out the basic components of modern suburbia—*that's a bank, that's a hospital, those are condos*—because they kept asking what everything was. What seemed utterly banal to me was wondrous to them.

In her loop, Miss Peregrine had worked miracles protecting her wards from physical harm, but in her zeal to keep them safe, she had banned anyone who visited from talking to them about the modern world, and that had put them at a disadvantage. They had been too sheltered, and now they were like little Rip van Winkles, waking after a long sleep to a world they didn't understand. They knew about modern things up to a point—electricity, telephones, cars, airplanes, old movies, old music, and other things that were generally known and popular prior to September 3, 1940. After that, their knowledge was spotty and inconsistent. They had spent no more than a few sporadic hours in the present, and those were mostly on Cairnholm, where time had practically stood still even as the calendar changed. Compared to their island, even my small town seemed to move at a million miles per hour, and it occasionally paralyzed them with anxiety.

In the mall's colossal parking lot, Horace became overwhelmed and refused to get out of the car. "The past is so much less terrifying than the future," he explained after some coaxing. "Even the most terrible era of the past is at least knowable. It can be studied. The world survived it. But in the present, one never knows when the whole world could come to a terrible, crashing end."

I tried to reason with him. "The world's not going to end today. And even if it does, it'll happen whether or not you go into this mall with us."

"I know that. But it *feels* like it will. But perhaps if I just sit here and don't move, everything will stop moving with me, and nothing bad will happen."

Just then a car playing loud, bass-heavy music rolled by with its windows down. Horace tensed and squeezed his eyes shut.

"See?" said Claire. "The world goes banging on, even if you just sit. So come inside with us."

"Oh, bollocks," he said, and threw the car door open.

As the others applauded his bravery, I made a mental note that Horace might not be the best companion to bring along on our first mission, whatever it was.

Shaker Pines was a classic, as malls went—noisy, antiseptically bright, and layered in baffling cultural references (you try explaining the Bubba Gump Shrimp Co. or the As Seen on TV store to someone from the first half of the last century). It was also crowded with teenagers, which was half the point. We weren't here just to outfit them in modern clothes. I wanted to expose them to normal kids, kids they would be expected to imitate. It was more than a shopping trip; it was an anthropological expedition.

We walked and browsed, the peculiars bunched in a knot around me like explorers in a jungle infamous for tiger attacks. We ate greasy things at the food court and sat watching other teenagers, my friends quietly studying their behavior: their whispers and jokes; their startling bursts of laughter; the way they grouped themselves, tight and clannish, rarely mixing; how they did everything, even ate, without ever letting go of their phones.

"Do they come from very rich families?" Claire asked, leaning into our group over her plastic tray, voice lowered.

"I think they're just normal teenagers," I said.

"They don't work?"

"They might have summer jobs part-time. I don't know."

"When I was growing up," said Hugh, "if you were old enough to lift something heavy, you were old enough to work. There was no sitting around all day, eating and talking."

"We were old enough to work even before we could lift heavy things," said Olive. "My father sent me to work at a boot-blacking factory when I was five. It was awful."

"Mine sent me to a workhouse," said Hugh. "I spent all day making rope."

"Good God," I muttered.

They came from a time before the concept of teenager-hood even existed. That was an invention of the postwar years, before which you had been either a child or an adult. I wondered how they would be able to impersonate modern teenagers if the very concept was foreign to them.

What if this whole thing was a bad idea?

Nervously, I checked my phone.

Nothing from H. Nothing at all.

We went to buy clothes, but along the way we lost Horace, who veered off into a grocery store that occupied one whole wing of the mall. We found him standing awestruck before a massive wall of cheese in the refrigerated foods section.

"Feta, mozzarella, Camembert, Gouda, cheddar!" he said, rapturous. "A gourmand's fantasyland."

It was just cheese to me, but to Horace it was a miracle: thirty feet of the stuff, sliced, whipped, in blocks and chunks, separately packaged, available in skim, whole, and 2 percent fat. He stood reading the labels as if in a trance, and I had to keep shushing him, lest his amazement draw attention.

"It's everything," he muttered. "It's *everything*."

"Look at this!" he said, turning to an old man who happened to be pushing a cart nearby. "*Look at it!*"

The old man hurried away.

"Horace, you're scaring people," I said, drawing him close. "It's only cheese."

"Only *cheese*!" he said.

"Okay, it's a *lot* of cheese."

"It's the pinnacle of human achievement," he declared seriously. "I thought Britain was an empire. But this—*this*—is world domination!"

"My stomach hurts just looking at it," said Claire.

"How dare you," Horace replied.

When we finally managed to drag him out of the grocery store and into a shop that sold clothes, Horace was less impressed by the selection. I had purposely chosen the blandest store and steered them toward the blandest choices—simple colors, standard combinations; whatever the mannequins were wearing.

His mood darkened as we filled the basket.

"I'd rather go naked," he said, holding a pair of jeans I'd handed him like it was a poisonous snake. "This is how you want me to dress? In denim, like a farmer?"

"Everybody wears jeans now," I said. "Not just farmers."

In fact, a pair of nice jeans was pretty fancy compared to what most people in the store were wearing that day. I saw Horace's face pale as he took stock of the gym shorts, cargo pants, sweats, and pajamas nearby shoppers were sporting.

He let the jeans drop to the floor.

"*Oh no,*" he whispered. "*Oh no, no.*"

"What's the matter?" said Enoch. "Their fashion not up to your high standards?"

"Forget standards. What of decency? What of self-respect?"

A man walked by wearing camouflage pants, orange flip-flops, and a SpongeBob sweater with the sleeves scissored off.

I thought Horace might cry.

While he mourned the end of civilization, we picked out clothes for everyone else. Because the lead shoes Olive usually wore looked like they belonged to Frankenstein's monster, we let her choose a new pair—something a size or two too large, so we could fill the extra space with weights.

At my insistence the kids kept quiet as the cashier ran the items through the checkout. They stayed quiet even as they trailed me out of the mall and back across the parking lot to the car, their arms loaded with bags and their brains overloaded with stimuli.

◆　　◆　　◆

We returned home to find everyone else gone to the Acre for the afternoon—something about reconstruction assignment orientation meetings, according to the note Miss Peregrine had left. Emma had stayed behind, said the note, but for the longest time I couldn't find her. Finally I heard her whistling inside the upstairs guest bathroom.

I knocked. "It's Jacob. Everything okay in there?"

A faint red light glowed beneath the door.

"Just a moment!" she called.

I could hear her fumbling around. A moment later the light clicked on and the door swung open.

"Did he call?" she said eagerly.

"Not yet. What's going on?"

I peeked past her into the small bathroom. There was photo-developing equipment everywhere—metal canisters lining the toilet tank, plastic trays surrounding the sink, a bulky enlarger on the floor. I wrinkled my nose against the sharp smell of developing chemicals.

"You don't mind if I convert the loo into a darkroom, do you?" Emma said with a sheepish grin. "Because I kind of already did."

We had two other bathrooms. I told her I didn't mind. She invited me inside to watch her work. There wasn't much space, so I had to press myself into a corner. She was efficient but unhurried, talking as she went. Though she claimed to be new at this, her actions looked like muscle memory.

"I know, it's such a cliché." She squatted, her back to me, twiddling dials on the enlarger. "The peculiar photophile."

"Is it a cliché?"

"Ha, very funny. I take it you've noticed how every ymbryne has her big album of snaps, and there's an entire government ministry devoted to cataloging us photographically, and every third peculiar fancies themselves some kind of genius with a camera . . . though most of them couldn't take a photo of their own feet. Here, give me a hand with this." She slid her hands under one side of the enlarger, and I lifted the other—it was surprisingly heavy—and we set it on a plank she'd laid across the bathtub.

"Any theories about why?" I hadn't given it much thought until then, but it did seem odd that people who lived the same day over and over would need to remember them with photographs.

"Normals have been trying to erase us for centuries. I think photography is a way to fix ourselves in place. To prove we were here, and we weren't the monsters they made us out to be."

"Yeah." I nodded. "That makes sense."

An egg timer buzzed. She picked up one of the metal canisters from the toilet, uncapped it, and poured a stream of chemicals into the sink. Then she slid a plastic spool out of it, unreeled from the spool a roll of negatives as long as her arm, squeegeed it dry with two fingers, and hung it from a wire she'd stretched across the shower.

"But now that we're in the present, it's different," she said. "I'm getting older, and for the first time since I can remember, every day I live is one I'll never live again. So I'm going take at least one picture every day to remember it by. Even if it's not very good."

"I think your pictures are great," I said. "That photo of people walking down steps toward the beach that you sent me over the summer? That was so beautiful."

"Really? Thanks."

She was rarely shy about anything. I found her modesty immensely charming.

"Okay, then, if you're interested . . . I've just been developing some rolls of film I was shooting over the past few weeks." She reached up and unclipped a photo from the wire. "These are members of the peculiar home guard." She handed it to me. The print was still slightly wet. "They're filling in the hole where Caul's tower used to be. They've been working in twelve-hour shifts for ages. It was a huge mess."

The photo showed a line of uniformed men standing at the top of a deep crater, shoveling rubble down into it.

"And here's one I took of Miss P," she said, handing me another print. "She doesn't like having her picture made, so I had to catch her from the back."

In the photo, Miss P was wearing a black dress and a black hat and walking toward a black gate. "It looks like she's going to a funeral," I said.

"Yes, we all were. There were funerals almost every day in the weeks after you left, for all the peculiars who were killed in the hollowgast raids."

"I can't imagine going to a funeral every day. That must have been terrible."

"Yes. It was."

Emma said she had some more photos to develop.

"Mind if I watch?" I asked.

"If you don't mind the smell of the chemicals. It gives some people headaches."

She went back to fiddling with the enlarger.

"I'm curious why you don't use a digital camera," I said. "It'd be a lot easier."

"Is it like your computer telephone?"

"Sort of," I said, and having been reminded of it, I checked my phone again, but there were no missed calls.

"Then it wouldn't work inside most loops," she said. "Just like your computer telephone doesn't. But this old mare"—she held up her folding camera—"she can go anywhere. Okay, close the door."

I pushed it shut. She turned on the red light and turned off the white one overhead. We were plunged into near darkness, and the space was so tight with the two of us in there that it was hard not to bump her while she worked.

Photo developing involves a lot of carefully timed waiting. Every forty-five seconds, she would have to agitate one of the canisters, or pour out a batch of chemicals and pour in another, or hang the negatives up to dry. In between, there was nothing to do but wait. Wait, and kiss, in the corner of the cramped and red-lit bathroom. Our first forty-five-second kiss was tentative and gentle, just warming up. The second was less so. During the third we kicked over a tray of chemicals, and after that we started ignoring the egg timer altogether. I'm pretty sure a roll of Emma's film got ruined.

And then my phone began to ring.

I let go of Emma and snatched it from my pocket. The screen read *no caller ID*. I answered.

"Hello?"

"Pay attention." It was the same gruff voice on the other end. H. "Abe's spot, nine p.m. sharp. Sit at his booth. Order his usual."

"You want me to . . . meet you?"

"And come alone."

He hung up.

I lowered the phone.

"That was fast," said Emma. "And?"

"We've got a date."

◆   ◆   ◆

What do you wear to a job interview with a hollowgast hunter? I wasn't sure, so I played it safe—jeans, my nicest pair of sneakers, and the most professional shirt I owned, a powder-blue polo shirt from Smart Aid with my name embroidered above the pocket. Emma elected to stay in her 1930s wartime clothes: a simple blue dress tied at the waist with a gray ribbon and black flats. I didn't mention that H had told me to come alone. I didn't want to go on any mission without her, so it only made sense that she be there. Telling her she hadn't been invited would only make her feel awkward.

The friends I'd taken mall shopping earlier were trying on their clothes, and the rest of the peculiars were still in the Acre. It was easy to slip away unnoticed. By eight thirty, we were driving into town.

I hoped I had understood H's terse instructions. "Abe's spot" might've meant anything, but "his booth" and "his usual" put me in mind of one place in particular—the Mel-O-Dee Restaurant, an old-school diner out on US 41, that had been serving greasy burgers and blue plate specials since God was a child (or 1936, which was close enough). A happy fixture in my childhood memories, it had been my and Abe's go-to place. I loved it, but my parents would never go (it was "depressing" and served "old people food"), so it was mine and Abe's alone. We could be found in the same booth by the window nearly every Saturday afternoon, me with a gooey tuna melt and a strawberry milkshake and Abe with a plate of liver and onions. I hadn't been back since I was twelve or thirteen. I couldn't remember even driving by recently, and I found myself hoping it was still there. The town was changing fast, and most of the characterful old places had been torn down to make room for bland, modern shopping centers. I sped up, playing the radio and drumming the wheel to calm my nerves.

I rounded a curve and it appeared behind a cluster of live oaks. It looked like it was barely clinging to life, its parking lot nearly empty and its old neon sign partly burned out.

"This is where he wanted to meet us?" Emma asked, peering out the window as I pulled into the lot.

"I'm ninety-eight percent sure."

She looked at me skeptically. "Brilliant."

We walked inside. The place hadn't changed at all. Yellow plastic booths separated by fake plants, a long Formica counter, a soda fountain. I looked around for people who looked like they might be H, but there was just a decrepit old couple in the corner and a raggedy-looking middle-aged guy nursing a cup of coffee at the counter.

The waitress shouted to us across the dining room.

"Anywhere you like!"

I led Emma to the booth by the window where Abe and I always sat. We picked up menus.

"Why is it called the Mel-O-Dee?" she asked.

"I think it used to be one of those singing-waiter places, a long time ago."

The waitress shuffled over. She had a hunched back and a blond wig that didn't match her wrinkles and she hadn't put her makeup on quite straight. NORMA, her name tag read. I recognized her—she'd been working here a long time. She took off the reading glasses she'd been wearing and looked at me, then smiled.

"That you, junior?" she said. "My goodness, you got handsome." She winked at Emma. "Speaking of handsome, how's your grandpa?"

"He died. Earlier this year."

"Oh, I'm real sorry to hear that, honey."

She reached over the table and rested her spotted hand on mine.

"It happens," I said.

"You don't have to tell me. You know, I'll be *ninety* next year."

"Wow, that's amazing."

"It's sure something. Practically everyone I used to know is dead. Husband, friends, brother, and two sisters. Sometimes I think these good genes are a curse from God." She flashed her big dentures at us. "What're you kids having?"

"Coffee," said Emma.

"The, uh, liver and onions," I said.

Norma looked at me, like my order had sparked something in her memory. "No tuna melt for you?"

"I'm trying new things."

"Mm-hmm." She held up one finger, then walked away from the table, ducked behind the counter, and came back with something in her hand. She leaned in and whispered, "*He's waiting for you.*" She opened her palm and placed a small blue key before me, then turned and pointed toward the back of the restaurant. "Down the hall, last door past the bathrooms."

◆　　◆　　◆

The last door past the bathrooms was made of heavy insulated metal and had a sign that read NO ADMITTANCE. I turned the key in the lock and opened the door, and we were embraced by a shroud of frozen air. Hugging ourselves against the chill we walked inside.

Shelves stocked with frozen food lined the walls. Icicles like the spikes of an iron maiden were aimed down at us from the ceiling.

"There's no one in here," I said. "I think Norma's gone senile."

"Look at the floor," said Emma. There were arrows made with electrical tape leading to the back of the room, where a curtain of thick plastic flaps hung from ceiling to floor. Stencil-painted across them were the words MEATING ROOM.

"Is that a misspelling?" Emma said. "Or a strange joke?"

"Let's find out."

I shouldered through plastic curtains caked with frozen meat slime and led us into a smaller, even colder room that flickered under the light of a faulty fluorescent tube. There were cuts of meat everywhere, spilling from torn-open boxes, scattered across the floor, dusted with frost.

"What the hell happened?" I said.

I nudged a rack of lamb with my foot. The still-frozen meat had been bitten clean in half. I got a sudden, sinking feeling.

"I think we should get out of here," I said. "This might be a—"

The word *trap* was leaving my lips when three things happened in quick succession:

—I put my foot down on a big X made of tape on the floor.

—The flickering bulb above our heads shattered, and the room went black.

—I felt a roller-coastery lurch in my stomach and a sudden pressure change in my head.

Then the light came back on, only now it was a yellow incandescent bulb in a wire cage. The boxes of meat were gone, replaced by bags of frozen vegetables. And I felt a sharp, unmistakable pain bloom in my gut.

I touched Emma's hand and raised a finger to my lips. I mouthed the word *Hollow.*

Emma looked, for an instant, terrified—and then she swallowed hard and reined it in. She put her lips to my ear.

"*Can you control it?*" she whispered.

It felt like ages since I'd spoken hollowgast or even confronted a hollow in person. I was way out of practice, and even at the top of my game, my control over a hollow had never come instantly.

"*I need time to feel it out,*" I whispered. "*A minute or two.*"

Emma nodded. "Then we'll wait."

It was in the cold storage locker with us. My inner compass needle was warming up, even as my body was freezing, and it told me the beast was just beyond the plastic curtains. We could hear it chewing on something, grunting and slavering as it ate. We crouched by a wooden crate, trying to make ourselves invisible as the seconds ticked by.

The hollow tossed aside whatever it had been eating and let out a thunderous belch.

Emma shot me a questioning look—*Anything?*—and I shook

my head. Nothing yet. Before I could start to gain control over it, I needed to hear it speak.

It took a step toward us, its shadow falling crooked across the plastic curtains. I listened in vain for anything I could use to get a toehold in its brain—any little utterance would help—but the only sound it made was a ragged intake of breath. It was sniffing the air, gathering our scent. Working up a new appetite.

I tapped Emma and pointed upward. We rose slowly to standing. We were going to have fight.

Emma put out her hands, palms up, and I gritted my teeth, which were chattering either from cold or from fear. More likely the latter. I was surprised at how scared I was.

The hollow's shadow warped. One of its muscular tongues poked through the curtain flaps and curled experimentally in the air, like a periscope that was spying on us.

Emma took a half step forward and quietly lit her hand-flames. She kept them small, but I could tell from the way she tensed her forearms that she was building up to a burst. Now the hollow's second tongue pierced the curtains. Emma's flames climbed a little higher, then higher still. A drop of freezing water hit the back of my neck. The icicles on the ceiling were starting to melt.

It happened suddenly, as violence often does. The hollowgast screamed and punched its last tongue through the curtains, and then all three of them came at us. Emma shouted and released the blast of fire she'd been working up. Just as the tongues reached us, they got burned and reeled suddenly back again—but not before one of them wrapped around my foot, and dragged me along with it.

I slid across the floor on my back, through the curtains, out into the larger cold-storage room. The hollow had flung itself backward against the door to escape the fire, and it was pulling me toward its open mouth. I stuck out my hand as I slid, raking it along the shelves until I managed to hook my fingers into something. But it didn't stop me—it was just a wooden crate, and it yanked away from the shelf with me as I slid by.

I heard Emma shouting my name. Acting purely on reflex, I grabbed the crate with my other hand and held it out in front of me. When I reached the hollow, I jammed it right between the creature's jaws.

It let my ankle go for a moment, giving me enough time to scramble away into a corner. I'd heard it utter a few sounds now and I tried them in my own throat, summoning the strange guttural language of hollows from wherever it had been slumbering inside me.

Emma ran to where I was kneeling. "You okay?"

"Yeah," I said. "But we have to get out of this room. Never fight hollows in a confined space."

With her eyes she followed the crate in the air to the door. "It's blocking the exit," she said.

The hollow gave up trying to dislodge the crate using its tongues and clamped its jaws shut instead, crunching the wood to splinters like it was a mouthful of potato chips.

Move, I said, testing out a word of hollowspeak.

It took a step toward us, but it was still blocking our escape. I tried a slight modification. *Move aside.*

It took another step forward. Its tongues danced in the air like rattlesnakes ready to strike.

"It's not working," Emma said. Her flames were starting to melt everything around us, and drips of water from the ceiling were forming a puddle on the floor.

"Make it ever hotter," I said. "I have an idea."

Emma took a deep breath, tensed, and her flames burned a little higher.

"*When I say the word,*" I whispered, "*you run that way and I'll run this way.*"

The hollow let out a sharp cry and ran at us. I shouted, "NOW!" and Emma jumped right and I leapt left. The hollow's tongues shot over our heads, and I kept running to the corner. The hollow tried to spin and follow me, but it slipped in the puddle and fell, then cried out and sent its tongues after me, but one of them tangled in the rungs of a metal shelf against the wall. Trying to yank free, the hollow brought the heavy shelf, and all its crates of frozen food, down on top of itself.

I shouted, "GO!" met Emma at the door and pulled it open, and in a moment we were out in the hall and pulling the door closed behind us.

"Lock it!" Emma said. "Where's that key?"

But this door had a different handle and no lock at all, so we turned and ran down the hall and back into the restaurant's dining room. It was filled with morning sun and diners in crisp vintage clothes, all turning now to stare at the strangers in their midst, soggy and out of breath. Emma remembered the fire in her hand too late, then tucked it behind her back while three waiters, the only people in the room who hadn't yet noticed us, went on harmonizing:

"*Hello my baby, hello my honey, hello my ragtime gaaaaaa—*"

A huge crashing sound came from down the hall, and the waiters stopped mid-*gal*. The people who had been staring leapt up from their tables.

"Get out!" I shouted. "Everyone get out of here right now."

Emma brought the flames out in front of her again. "That's right! Get out, get out!"

It was the next crash that did it—the sound of the metal door flying from its hinges—and now almost everyone was on their feet, panicked and streaming toward the exits.

We spun to look behind us. The hollowgast stomped into the hallway, turned toward us, and howled, its three horrible tongues reeling down the hall like hard-cast fishing lines before snapping taut and vibrating with its scream.

The soda jerk shoved past me and ran for the nearest door. The sound alone was enough to terrify everyone. The nightmarish sight was mine alone to bear.

"Tell me you're close," Emma said.

"I've almost got him."

The hollow started toward us down the hall. I shouted at him—
Stop! Lie down! Shut your mouth!

He slowed a bit, as if my words had penetrated his skull but not quite entered his brain, then came at us twice as fast. I wished we could run outside and face him in the parking lot, but the exits were jammed with fleeing diners. We clambered behind the long counter and ran to the far end, by the cash register. I kept shouting at him, trying different variations of the same phrases. *Be still! Sleep! Sit down! Don't move!* But I could hear the hollow wrecking the place as it got closer to us. Tables and chairs were flying, people screaming bloody murder. I risked a peek over the counter and saw the hollow lasso a waiter around the waist and throw him through a plate-glass window.

Emma stood up quickly and grabbed a heavy bottle full of green liquid. She unscrewed the top, then began to tear her dress.

"What are you doing?" I asked her.

"Making a Molotov cocktail," she said, stuffing the torn cloth into the bottle.

The bottle said Bubble Up! "It won't work—that's soda!"

She swore, then lit the cloth and lobbed it over the counter anyway.

My compass needle shifted. The hollow was drawing near.

"*This way*," I hissed. We scrambled on hands and knees toward the other end of the counter. A moment later the hollow's tongues raked the wall above where we'd been crouched, and fifty glass bottles came crashing down at once.

I heard a woman scream. People were being hurt, maybe even killed. Looped people, who would never know what had happened to them and had no tomorrows to miss out on—but still. There was no escape, no better way. I had to face the beast, now or never.

I stood up from behind the counter and shouted at the thing. It had a lady in pink hair curlers by the neck, and she was screaming so hard the curlers were shaking loose. When it saw me it let her go. She fell on her side, then scurried off to hide under a booth. And then it came at me, muttering and gibbering. I stood my ground and began to imitate it, noise for noise, repeating what it said, though I didn't know what it meant.

It paused to knock a table out of its path. My tongue, which was beginning to pick up the tonalities of this hollow's speech, seemed to start on its own . . .

STOP! LIE DOWN!

It hesitated, then dropped to the ground.

SHUT YOUR MOUTH.

It reeled its three tongues back into its mouth. I picked up a steak knife from a pile of silverware on the floor. Emma approached with her flame high and hot.

DON'T MOVE.

I could see the thing squirming, trying to break free from my commands, but it was frozen now and all we had to do was—

"That's quite enough!"

The voice was loud and familiar. I spun around to see who it belonged to. It was an older man in a tan suit, seated calmly at a booth in the corner—Abe's booth—his body angled toward me, one elbow propped casually on the table. He was the only other person left in the restaurant, and he didn't seem the least bit afraid.

"My goodness," the man said. "You really do have your grand-father's gift."

He slid to the edge of the booth and stood. "Now, if you wouldn't mind letting go of Horatio . . ." He muttered under his breath in hollowspeak, and I felt my control over the beast vanish. "I promised him a hot meal if he was good today. Didn't I, fella?"

The hollow reeled in its tongues, scampered over to him, and sat down by his feet like a big puppy.

◆   ◆   ◆

The man plucked a steak off his table and tossed it to the hollow, who caught it in its jaws and swallowed it in a single gulp. The man began to slide out of the booth and stand up, but Emma took a step toward him with her flame high and shouted, "Stay where you are!"

He stayed seated. "I'm a friend, not a wight."

"Then why do you travel with a hollowgast?"

"I don't go anywhere without Horatio anymore. I'd rather not end up like this boy's grandfather, if I can help it."

I said, "You're H, aren't you?"

"The very same." He gestured to the empty seat across from him. "Would you join me?"

"You're completely mad!" said Emma. "Your hollowgast nearly killed us!"

"You were never in real danger, I assure you." He gestured again. "Please. We have five minutes until the police arrive and a lot of ground to cover before then."

I glanced at Emma. She looked annoyed, but closed her hand, extinguishing her flame, and let her arm fall. We crossed the dining room, picking our way through a tide of broken dishes and toppled furniture, to the booth where H sat. The hollow had finished its steak and curled itself on the floor by H's side, where it appeared to be napping. The compass-needle pain in my gut had dulled, but not disappeared, and I realized that its intensity changed depending on the mood of the hollowgast. Aggressive, hungry hollows were more painful than calm, sated ones.

We slid into the booth, Emma first so I would be closest to the hollow. H leaned forward on his elbows, sipping from a tall glass through a straw. He was calm and collected.

"I'm ready for the interview," I said.

H held up a finger, still drinking. I studied him while we waited. His face was crookedly handsome and deeply lined, his eyes deep-set and piercing, and he had a scraggly beard and a sweater vest that gave him a vaguely professorial air. I had seen a photo of him in Abe's logbook, I realized, in which he'd been wearing almost the exact same outfit.

When he'd drained the glass, he pushed it away and leaned back against his seat. "Root beer float," he said, and let out a satisfied sigh. "Food's got no taste anymore. That's why I try not to pass up a meal anytime I'm in a loop." He nodded at several plates of food on the table. "Got you a country-fried steak and a slice of key lime pie. I would've ordered for you, too, Miss Bloom"—he shot me a peevish look—"but I asked Jacob to come alone."

"You know who I am?" said Emma.

"Of course. Abe spoke of you often."

Emma looked down, but couldn't hide her smile.

"She and I are a team," I said. "We work together."

"I can see that," said H. "You passed, by the way."

"Passed what?" I said.

"Your job interview."

I laughed the way you do when something's more surprising than funny. "That was the interview? Being attacked?"

"First part, anyway. Had to see if you were the real deal."

"And?"

"Your command of the language could be better. You need to establish control faster—some of these casualties could've been avoided." He pointed to the broken window, the waiter outside, crumpled and groaning on the hood of a Chevrolet. "But you're the real deal. No doubt."

I felt a blush of pride.

"Don't get happy yet. There are some things you need to know."

I stifled my smile. "I want to know everything."

"What did your grandfather tell you about his work?"

"Nothing."

He looked surprised. "Nothing at all?"

"He said he used to be a traveling salesman. My dad told me

Abe used to go on these weeks-long business trips, and once or twice he came back with a broken leg or a bandage on his face. The family thought he'd gotten mixed up with some bad people, or he had a gambling problem."

H ran a hand over his bearded chin. "Then we'll only have time for the basics. Abe came to America after the war. He wanted to live as normal a life as he could, because he felt that his diminished powers were more of a danger than a help to his fellow peculiars—Miss Bloom and her loop-mates, specifically. At that time, America was a relatively peaceful place. Normals had persecuted us plenty over the years and sown a lot of mistrust between the different peculiar clans, but we'd never had the problems with hollows and wights that Europe did. Until the late fifties, that is. They came in hard, they went after the ymbrynes, and they did a lot of damage. That's when Abe decided he had to come out of his early retirement, and he started the organization."

I realized I was holding my breath. I had been waiting so long for someone to tell me about my grandfather's early years in America, I almost couldn't believe it was happening.

H went on, twisting the end of his short beard between his fingers as he spoke. "There were twelve of us. We led normal lives, to all appearances. None of us lived in loops—that was a rule. A few of us had families, regular jobs. We met in secret and communicated in code. At first we just went after hollows, but when the ymbrynes had to go underground because the wights were picking off so many of them, we started doing the jobs they couldn't do anymore."

"Reaching uncontacted peculiar children," said Emma. "Delivering them to safety."

"You read the logbook."

I nodded.

"It wasn't easy. And we weren't always successful. Now and then you get it wrong. One slips through the cracks." He glanced out the window, feeling some old pain. "I carry those failures with me still."

"Where are the others?" I asked. "The other ten members?"

"Some were killed in the line of duty. Some walked away. Couldn't live the life anymore. The eighties were rough on all of us."

"And Abe never replaced them?"

"It was hard to find people we could trust. The enemy was always trying to infiltrate us, crack open our secrets. We were a real thorn in their side, I'm proud to say. And the threat started to die down as the wights turned their focus back to Europe. They'd gotten pretty much what they wanted here, though thanks to us it cost them more than they'd bargained." He looked down for a moment. "But maybe now there's a new era dawning. I always hoped my phone would ring one day and it would be you."

"*You* could've called *me*," I said.

"I promised Abe I wouldn't make first contact. Your grandpa, he didn't want to push you into all this. He wanted it to be your choice. But I always had a feeling you'd come around, eventually."

I looked at him. "You talk like we've met before."

He winked at me. "Remember Mr. Anderson?"

"Oh my God. Yes! You gave me a big bag of saltwater taffy."

"I think you were about eight, nine years old." He grinned and shook his head. "Oh, that was a day. Abe never wanted any of us coming to his house—he was always so careful—but I wanted to meet this grandson he was so proud of. So I just showed up one afternoon, and you happened to be there. He was so mad you could've fried an egg on his forehead! It was worth it, though. And I could tell the minute I met you that you had the gift, too."

"I always thought my grandfather and I were the only ones."

"In our group, four of us could see hollows. It was only Abe and I who could control them to any degree. And you're the only one I've ever heard of who's been able to control more than one at a time."

In the faraway distance I could hear sirens.

"So, have you got a job for us?" I said.

"As a matter of fact, I do." He reached down beside him and placed two small packages on the table. They were each about the size of a paperback book, wrapped in plain brown paper. "I need you to deliver these. Unopened."

I almost laughed. "That's it?"

"Consider it part two of your job interview. Prove to me you can handle this, and I'll give you a real mission."

"We can handle it," Emma said. "Have you any idea of the things we've done?"

"That was Europe, little lady. America's a whole other kettle of fish."

"I am many years your elder. And what an odd saying."

"This is the way it's got to be."

"Fine," I said. "So where do we take them?"

"Says right on the packages."

Handwritten on one package were the words *Flaming Man*.

The other read *Portal*.

"I don't get it," I said.

"Here's a little clue to get you started." He lifted his glass and slid the paper place mat that was under it across the table. For as long as I'd been going there, the Mel-O-Dee's place mats were printed with a cartoony map of Florida that had tourist attractions marked on them—but little else. No roads or highways, no small or medium-sized towns. The state's capital was obscured completely by a drawing of an alligator sipping a cocktail. But the seriousness on H's face as he slid this across the table made it seem like he'd just given us a map to buried treasure. He tapped the center of it, where his glass had left a wet ring around a place called Mermaid Fantasyland.

"When the packages have been delivered, I'll be in touch. You have seventy-two hours."

Emma was peering at the place mat in disbelief. "This is absurd. Give us a real map."

"Nope," he said. "If it fell into enemy hands, the whole jig would be up. And part of the job is finding things that aren't easily found." He tapped the water ring on the cartoon map again. The sirens were getting close now, and looky-loos were starting to congregate around the edges of the parking lot. "You didn't touch your food."

"I'm not hungry," I said. "When a hollow's this close, my stomach goes into knots."

"Waste not, want not." He cut a bite from my uneaten pie with his fork, popped it into his mouth, and stood up. "Come on, I'll walk you out."

Two old-style police cars screamed into the parking lot. I scooped the two packages into my arms and folded the place mat map between them, then slid out of the booth. H did a two-finger whistle. His hollowgast uncurled itself from the floor and bounded after us toward the hallway, tame as an old hound.

"A few things to remember," H said, talking as we walked. "Peculiar places and people in America aren't like what you're used to. It's a mess over here. No ymbrynes to speak of. In some places, it's every peculiar for themselves, and you can't trust just anybody."

"And there's been fighting between some of the loops?" I said.

He shot me a look over his shoulder. "Let's hope not. And I don't want to get ahead of myself, but I will say this. You might have chased the wights out of Europe, but I have a feeling they're not done with us over here. I think they'd like a war between the peculiars. I think that would suit their ends just fine."

He opened the door to the cold-storage room and we filed in. "Another thing. Don't tell people who you're working with. The organization never reveals itself."

"What about Miss Peregrine?" Emma asked.

"Not even her."

We entered the curtained-off area and crowded into the corner where the X had been. As we were crossing over, something occurred to me. When the rushing sensation had abated and we were all back in the present, I asked, "If there are no ymbrynes anymore, how does this loop stay open?"

H parted the plastic curtains and his hollowgast ran out. "I didn't say there were none," H said. "But the ones we've got—the ones that are left, I should say—aren't exactly of the caliber you're used to."

Out in the hallway, our friendly old waitress was leaned against the wall, puffing from a cigarette and blowing the smoke out an exit door.

"We were just talking about you," said H, smiling wide. "Miss Abernathy, how are you doing?"

She tossed her cigarette out the door and gave H a spindly hug. "You don't come visit me anymore, you bad man."

"Been real busy, Norma."

"Sure, sure."

"Is she an *ymbryne*?" said Emma.

"Some people call us demi-ymbrynes," Norma said, "but I think *loop-keeper* rolls off the tongue better. I can't turn myself into a bird or make new loops or anything fancy like that, but I can keep open ones going a good long time. Pay's okay, too."

"The *pay*?"

"You think I'd do this out of the goodness of my heart?" She threw back her head and cackled.

"Norma here manages a small portfolio of loops around South Florida," said H. "The organization keeps her on retainer." H reached into his pocket and pulled out a wad of money in a rubber band. "Thanks for your help today."

"It's a strictly cash business," said Norma, winking as she stuffed the wad into her apron. "Gotta avoid the tax man!" She laughed again and waddled into the storage room. "I better close up shop, see what kind of mess you all made. Don't let the door hit ya where the good Lord split ya."

We went out to the parking lot together. The moon was high

and the night air cool. The hollowgast ran to chase a stray cat, and we walked toward my car, one of only two left in the lot.

"So," I said, "we deliver these packages, then we get the real mission?"

"That depends."

"On what?"

He grinned out of the side of his mouth. "On whether you make it."

"We'll make it," said Emma. "But no more surprise hollowgast attacks, okay?"

"If you see any more hollows, they won't be Horatio, so you better make sure you kill 'em."

We arrived at my car. When H saw the missing bumper and the wired-shut door, he winced. "You *can* drive, can't you, son?"

"It wasn't me," I said. "I'm a good driver."

"I hope so, because you need to be for this job. Good or not, you can't drive *that* thing—you'll get pulled over by the cops every ten miles. Take one of Abe's instead."

"Abe didn't drive. He doesn't have a car."

"Oh, he does. A beauty, too." He raised an eyebrow at me. "You mean to tell me you got all the way down to his underground bunker but you didn't find his . . ." He laughed and shook his head.

"His what?" Emma and I said at the same time.

"There's another door down there."

He turned to go.

"Can you tell us anything about the mission?" I said.

"You'll know when you need to know, and no sooner," he replied. "But I can tell you this: It involves an uncontacted peculiar child who's in trouble. In New York City."

"So why don't *you* go help them?" Emma said.

"I'm getting a bit long in the tooth, if you haven't noticed. I got sciatica, bad knees, high sugar . . . and anyhow, I'm not the right person for the job."

"We are," I said. "I promise you that."

"That's what I'm hoping. Good luck to you both."

He walked off toward the other car in the lot—a sleek old Cadillac with suicide doors—and whistled for his hollowgast. It came running and dove through an open window into the back seat. The car started with an uproarious noise. H gave us a little salute, then peeled out of the lot with a trail of tire-smoke.

◆　　◆　　◆

"So this is totally nuts, right?" I was driving but staring mostly at Emma in the passenger seat, my eyes flicking back to the road ahead every few seconds. "I mean, this is a certifiably terrible idea for all sorts of reasons. Right?"

She was nodding. "We barely know who this man is. We just met him."

"Right."

"We don't even know his real name. And he's trying to send us on some strange long-distance errand—"

"Right, right . . ."

"Running packages we're not even allowed to *look* inside—"

"Right! And this mission could be really dangerous. Whatever it is! We don't even know."

"And Miss Peregrine will be so mad at us."

I pulled into the oncoming lane to pass a car. I drive fast when I'm anxious.

"She'll be furious," I said. "She may never speak to us again."

"And not all of our friends will agree with this."

"I know, I know."

"It could split the group," she said.

"That would be so terrible."

"It would," she said.

"It really would."

I glanced at her. "And yet."

She sighed. Folded her hands in her lap and looked out the window.

"And yet."

Red light. I slowed to a stop. It was quiet for a moment, and now I could hear a song playing quietly on the classic rock station, which I had not quite turned all the way down. I took my hands off the wheel and turned my body to face her.

She looked at me. "We're doing this, aren't we?"

"Yeah. I think we are."

It began, gently, to rain. The lights of suburbia blurred around us. I flicked on the windshield wipers.

As we drove to my house, we talked specifics. We would tell our friends but not Miss Peregrine, in the hope she wouldn't find out what we were up to until we were too far away to be stopped. We would bring two friends with us—whoever seemed most capable and enthusiastic. And from this point on, we would entertain no second thoughts. My gut was telling me very loudly that this mission was something I needed. That this was the life I wanted to make for myself: One not completely of the normal world, not completely of the peculiar one, and not ruled by the whims and dictates of the ymbrynes.

Part of me wanted to go directly to Abe's house to satisfy my curiosity about what else was down in his bunker (a car? really?) but before we did anything else, we had to talk to the others.

When we walked through the front door of my house, the first thing I heard was Olive's voice above my head—"Where have *you* been?"—and I nearly fell over with a heart attack. She was glaring at us from the ceiling, seated upside down, arms crossed.

"How long have you been waiting there?" said Emma.

"Long enough." Olive pushed off the ceiling toward the floor, where she righted herself and tucked her feet into the leaden shoes that were waiting for her there in one deft move.

The others heard us and crowded into the front hall from various points around the house, eager to interrogate us.

"Where's Miss Peregrine?" I said, glancing past them toward the living room.

"Still in the Acre," said Horace. "Lucky for you all the ymbrynes are in a very long council meeting."

"Something big is going on," said Millard.

"Where were you two?" said Hugh.

"Bum-touching on the beach?" said Enoch.

"Off in Abe's secret bunker?" said Bronwyn.

"And what secret bunker would you be referring to?" asked Hugh.

He wasn't with us when we'd found it. He didn't know.

"We weren't sure if you wanted us to tell everyone," said Bronwyn.

I started to explain but things soon devolved into a chaos of shouted questions, everyone talking over one another, until finally Emma had to flap her arms and shout for quiet. "Everyone, come into the living room. Jacob and I have a story to tell."

We sat them down and proceeded to lay it all out—the discoveries we'd made the previous day at Abe's house, the meeting we'd had with H, and the miniature quest he'd given us, along with a promise of a much more important one.

"You're not actually considering this, are you?" said Horace.

"Damn right, we are," I said. "And we want a couple of you to come with us."

"We're a team," said Emma. "All of us."

Their reactions were divided. Claire got angry and Horace got quiet and nervous. Hugh and Bronwyn were cautious, but I thought they could be swayed. Enoch, Millard, and Olive, on the other hand, seemed ready to jump in the car with us right then.

"Miss P's been so good to us," Claire said dourly. "We owe her more than this."

"I agree," said Bronwyn. "I won't lie to her. I *hate* lying."

"In my opinion, we're much too concerned with what Miss Peregrine thinks," said Emma.

"I think missions like the ones my grandfather and his group used to do are what we're supposed to be doing," I said. "Not glorified office work for the reconstruction."

"I *like* my assignment," said Hugh.

"But we're wasted in the Acre," said Millard. "We can go fearlessly into the present. Who else with our level of experience can do that?"

"She didn't mean we should go *now*," said Hugh. "We've only had one day of normalling lessons!"

"You could be ready," I said.

"Half of us don't even have modern clothes yet!" said Horace.

"We'll figure it out!" I said. "Look, there are peculiar children in America who need our help, and I think that's more important than rebuilding some loops."

"Hear, hear," said Emma.

"There's *one* who needs help," said Hugh. "Maybe. *If* this H fellow isn't lying."

"Abe's logbook is filled with hundreds of missions," I said, trying not to show my rising frustration, "half of which involved helping young peculiars in danger. Peculiars didn't stop being born after Abe stopped working. They're still out there, and they still need help."

"They have no real ymbrynes of their own," said Emma.

"*This* is why you're here," I said. "*This* is what we're supposed to do. The hollow-hunters got old, the ymbrynes are too busy having meetings, and there's no one more equipped to help than us. This is our time!"

"If we can just prove it to some guy we don't even know!" Enoch said sarcastically.

"It's a test," I said. "And it's one I intend to pass. Anybody who feels the same, be downstairs with a bag packed at nine a.m. sharp."

CHAPTER SEVEN

I was packing a bag in my room later that night when my eyes stopped on something: the maps plastered on the wall above my bed. There were layers upon layers of them, taped and tacked over one another in a big mosaic that had become, over time, little more than wallpaper to me. But I noticed something now that grabbed my attention, and I stopped what I was doing to climb onto my bed. I stood on my pillows to study a little drawing that peeked out from under three intersecting *National Geographic* maps: a cartoon alligator sipping a cocktail.

I untacked the maps that were on top of it and peeled them away to find an old place mat from the Mel-O-Dee, the one with the map of Florida on it. The Mel-O-Dee used to give out crayons for kids to draw with while they ate, and my grandfather and I had used them to decorate this place mat. I had forgotten about that day, or that this map was even here. But now I saw what Abe had done—it was mostly his steady hand that had drawn on this map. Right in the center he had circled Mermaid Fantasyland, just as H's wet glass had. Abe had also drawn a little skull and crossbones beside it. Deep in the Everglades swamp, he had doodled a school of fish with legs. (Or were they people with fish heads?) He had also drawn spiral shapes in several places around the state, and if I remembered the legend from Miss Peregrine's now-lost Map of Days correctly, that meant LOOP HERE. There were a few other symbols I couldn't decipher, too.

We don't make maps, H had said. But if that was one of the hollow-hunters' laws, Abe had broken it by drawing me this one. And in doing it, he had taken a risk.

The question was, *why?*

I took the map down carefully, then I scoured the rest of the wall for anything Abe had drawn on. What other bread crumbs had he left for me, hiding in plain sight? I worked myself into a frenzy, taking down anything that had been annotated or added to. I found a few maps that had been drawn from scratch on blank construction paper, but they weren't labeled and there were no boundary lines around them with shapes I could recognize. There was a AAA map of Maryland and Delaware that had markings on it, so I folded it and stacked it with the Mel-O-Dee map. There were a couple of postcards pinned to the wall from places Abe had traveled through—motels, roadside tourist traps, towns I'd never heard of. Abe only stopped traveling when I was about eleven. Despite my parents' objections, he used to go on road trips by himself "to visit friends out of state," and while he never bothered to call my dad to check in, he would always send me postcards from the places he went. I didn't know if they had any relevance, but I stacked them with the maps, just in case, and slid them all inside a hardcover book. Then I put that in my duffel bag, on top of the changes of clothes I'd packed. Earlier in the day I had gathered up whatever cash I could find around the house, which wasn't a lot except for the wad my parents kept in a sock in one of their dresser drawers. I wrapped it in a rubber band and packed it into my old plastic Pokémon lunch box with some basic toiletries, including a package of Tums and a bottle of Pepto-Bismol, in case we spent any appreciable time near a hollowgast.

I was about to zip the whole thing shut when I thought of something. I knelt down and pulled Abe's operations log out from under the bed. I picked it up and weighed it in my hand, trying to decide whether to take it. It was fat and heavy and full of sensitive information that H would almost certainly not want me exposing to possible loss or theft. I knew I probably should have locked it in

Abe's bunker for safekeeping. But what if I needed it? It was packed with photos and clues about how Abe and H had done their work. It was a gold mine.

I pulled the clothes and toiletries from the duffel, then took the maps and postcards out of the hardback and tucked them into the back flap of the logbook instead. I shoved the logbook into the bottom of the duffel bag, stacked the clothes and toiletries on top, zipped the bag shut, and test-lifted it with one hand. It was like curling a thirty-pound dumbbell. I dropped it onto the bed. It bounced and rolled onto the floor and made a thud that shook the room.

◆　　◆　　◆

I hardly slept a wink that night. In the morning I rose at dawn and snuck out with Emma. We drove to Abe's house, threw open the hatch in the floor of his office, and descended into the bunker to see what undiscovered thing lay waiting for us there. I was hoping—as H had implied—that it would be a car with four working doors, but I could not fathom how a car would fit inside a tunnel too small for me to stand up in, or how I would drive it out again, even if one did.

We'd only been looking around my grandfather's subterranean workshop for a few minutes when we found the handle in the wall. It was partially hidden in a darkened gap between two metal shelves. I reached in and twisted the handle, and a door in the wall opened outward, moving the shelves with it and revealing a new section of tunnel. We ventured in—hunched over once again, as this tunnel was even more claustrophobically low-ceilinged than the other section. Emma lit a flame for light and I propped the door with a metal box filled with freeze-dried "breakfast entree" from one of Abe's shelves.

After a hundred feet or so, we came to a narrow concrete staircase. It led to a thick metal door, which slid to the side rather than swinging in or out. Beyond it was a closet. A carpeted household closet. I slid open its slatted door and we walked out into a suburban

MEL♂DEE

FAMILY RESTAURANT

Why not try one of our delicious
Homemade Desserts!

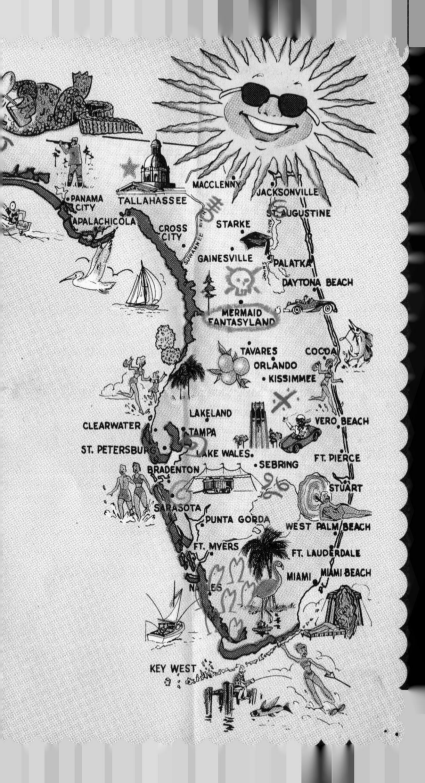

bedroom. There was a bed with a bare mattress, a nightstand, and a dresser. Nothing on the walls. The windows were shuttered, the only light in the room filtering through cracks between the nailed-on boards.

We were in another house in Abe's cul-de-sac.

"What is this place?" said Emma, tracing a finger-trail on the dusty dresser.

"It could be a safe house," I said, peeking into the attached bathroom, empty but for a single pink hand towel hung by the sink.

"Think anyone's here?" Emma whispered.

"Probably not. But keep your guard up anyway."

We crept down a short hallway, looking into other rooms as we passed them. It was sparsely furnished in the style of a model home or a chain motel—anonymous, but enough to create the illusion that someone actually lived here. I went to the end of the hall and took a left turn into what I knew would be the living room. The layout was identical to my grandfather's house, and it gave me a strange feeling of déjà vu to know every inch of a place I'd never set foot in. The living room windows were boarded, too, so I walked to the front door and put my eye to the peephole.

There was Abe's house, a few hundred feet away, across the street.

Then we came to the garage, and it was clear the moment we stepped inside that the house's only real purpose was this room. The walls were covered with pegs and shelves and all manner of tools and spare parts. In the center of it all, surrounded by floodlights, two cars were parked side by side.

"I'll be damned," I said. "He *did* have cars."

One was a white Caprice Classic. It looked like a bar of soap on wheels, and was unfailingly popular with Florida's elderly drivers. I recognized it as my grandfather's car, the one he used before my parents made him stop driving. (I thought he'd gotten rid of it, but here it was.) The other was a muscular black coupe that looked like a sixties-era Mustang, but with wider hips and swoopier lines. I wasn't sure what it was, exactly, because there was no badging on the car to identify it.

The Caprice was for traveling incognito, I guessed. The other was for traveling fast, and in a bit of style.

"You really didn't know he had these?" Emma said.

"None. I knew he used to drive, but my dad made him give it up when he failed a vision test at the DMV. He used to go on these solo trips. Days at time, sometimes weeks. Just like when my dad was a kid, only less frequent. To go from that to needing me and my parents to drive him to the grocery store and the doctor—that must have been hard."

Though it occurred to me, even as I was saying it, that Abe may never have stopped driving at all; he just started keeping it a secret.

"And yet he kept the cars," said Emma.

"And maintained them," I said. The cars, unlike everything else in the house, were a little dusty, but immaculately clean otherwise. "He must've snuck out here every so often to work on them. Shine them, change the oil. So they'd be easily accessible but hidden from my family."

"It makes you wonder why he bothered," Emma said.

"Fighting hollows?" I asked.

"Having a family," she replied.

I didn't know what to say to that, so I didn't say anything. I opened the Caprice and ducked inside, popped the glove box, and found the registration card. It was still current, renewed just a few weeks before Abe died. But it wasn't in his name.

"Ever heard of Andrew Gandy?" I said, handing the card to Emma through the open door.

"Must have been a false name he used." She handed the card back. "God."

I shut the glove box and got out of the car. Emma had a funny look on her face. "What?"

"I wonder if Abe was even his real name," she said.

It wasn't a crazy question, but for some reason it stung me.

"It *was*."

She looked at me. "You sure about that?"

In her eyes was an unasked question. If Abe was capable of such deceit, was I?

"I'm sure," I said, and turned away. "It's almost nine. Let's pick a car and go."

"You're driving. You choose."

It was an easy choice. The Caprice was more practical—it had four doors rather than two, more trunk space, and would attract less attention on the road. But the other car was much, much cooler and faster-looking, and after three whole seconds of deliberation, I pointed to it and said, "This one." I had never been on a road trip before (just across the fat belly of Florida to visit cousins in Miami, which hardly counted), and the idea of doing one in this car was too tempting to resist.

We got in. I opened the garage door and started the engine, which roared to life with a glorious, throaty growl that made Emma startle. As I backed it out of the driveway into the street, I saw her roll her eyes.

"Just like Abe!" she said, shouting over the engine.

"What is?"

"To have a car like this for *secret* missions."

I left the car idling in the street, parked my parents' car in Abe's garage, and closed the door. Then I got back into the mystery coupe, grinned at Emma, and stamped my foot down on the accelerator. The engine barked like an animal as we peeled out and were thrown back into our seats.

Sometimes you have to have a little fun. Even on a secret mission.

◆　　◆　　◆

While Emma and I were gone, Miss Peregrine had returned from her all-night meeting in the Acre and collapsed in her bed upstairs—one of the rare times I'd known her to actually sleep. We convened all the kids in a downstairs bedroom and shut the door, so our voices wouldn't wake her.

I asked for a show of hands.

"Who's in?"

Enoch, Olive, and Millard raised their hands. Claire, Hugh, Bronwyn, and Horace did not.

"Missions make me nervous," said Horace.

"Claire," Emma said, "why isn't your hand up?"

"We already *have* missions," she said. "I'm head of lunch and dessert distribution to all the loop reconstruction teams in Belgium."

"That's not a mission, Claire, that's a job."

"You're delivering packages!" Claire sneered. "How is *that* a mission?"

"The mission is helping a peculiar in danger," said Millard. "*After* the packages are delivered."

"Bronwyn, what about you?" I said. "In or out?"

"Lying to Miss P makes me uncomfortable. Shouldn't we tell her about this?"

"NO," everyone but Claire said in unison.

"Why not?" asked Bronwyn.

"It makes me uncomfortable, too," I said, "but she'll stop us from going, so we can't."

"If we really want to help peculiarkind, this is how," said Emma. "By becoming the next generation of fighters, not posing for photo opportunities in the Acre."

"Or asking permission every time we want to do anything," said Enoch.

"Exactly!" said Millard. "The headmistress still treats us like children. We're all nearly a century old, for bird's sake, and it's about time we started acting our age. Or half our age, anyway. We've got to start making decisions for ourselves."

"Just what I've been saying for years," said Enoch.

My peculiar friends had changed, I realized, but Miss Peregrine's way of parenting them had not. They had gotten a big dose of freedom after being chased from Cairnholm—as had I—and their time in the Acre, under the supervision of not just one, but more than a dozen ymbrynes, had left them feeling suffocated. They had grown up more in the past few months than they had in the past half century.

"What about you, Apiston?" Emma said to Hugh.

"I would come," he said, "but I've got my own mission to do."

We knew what he meant without having to say it. He would be searching the Panlooptricon for Fiona.

"We understand," I said. "We'll keep a lookout for her on our travels."

He nodded heavily. "Thanks, Jacob."

They were all in except for Horace, Claire, and Bronwyn—and then Bronwyn changed her mind.

"Okay, I'll come. I don't like lying, but if we're really out to help a peculiar child whose life in is danger, and lying is the only way to do that, then it would be immoral *not* to lie, wouldn't it?"

"That idea went past smart and back to dumb," said Claire.

"Welcome aboard," said Emma.

All that was left was to choose our crew. I said we could only take two, which elicited some groans of disappointment. Despite what I'd said the night before, I was a little worried about their one half of a normalling lesson and a potential lack of preparedness to face the modern world. And while I wanted and needed their help, I also needed to focus on our mission, not on explaining how crosswalks and elevator doors and simple interactions with modern normals worked. But instead of going into all that, which might have hurt their feelings, I claimed I didn't want to overload the car.

"Then pick me!" said Olive. "I'm small and weigh next to nothing."

I imagined Olive forgetting to put on her shoes and having to chase after her like a lost balloon. "For this one, we need people who look older." I didn't say why, and she didn't ask.

Emma and I talked in the corner for a minute, then announced our choices—Millard and Bronwyn. Bronwyn for her brute strength and reliability, and Millard for his mind, mapping abilities, and his ability to slip away when cornered, simply by taking off his clothes.

The others were disappointed, but we promised to take them on future missions.

"*If* there are future missions," said Enoch. "Provided you don't muck this one up."

"And what shall the rest of us do while you're gone?" asked Horace.

"Just do your assignments in the Acre and act like nothing's wrong. You don't know anything about us or what we're up to."

"Yes, we do," said Claire. "And if Miss Peregrine asks, I'm telling her."

Bronwyn picked up Claire by the armpits and held her at eye level. "Now, *that* is a dumb idea," she said, the threat in her voice both clear and surprising. Bronwyn always handled the two smallest peculiars with kid gloves.

Claire's backmouth growled at Bronwyn. "Put me down!" she shouted with her normal mouth.

Bronwyn did, but Claire looked chastened, anyway. Message received.

"When Miss Peregrine wakes up, she'll start asking where we are," said Emma. "She really just . . . went to sleep?"

It was very out of character for an ymbryne, even after an all-nighter.

"I may have blown just a *pinch* of dust into the room," said Millard.

"Millard!" Horace cried. "You scoundrel!"

"Well, that will certainly buy us some time," Emma said. "With any luck, she won't notice we're gone until tonight."

◆   ◆   ◆

"Now this," Millard said, slapping the hood of the black coupe as we stood around it in the driveway, "is a proper road journey car."

"It isn't," said Bronwyn. "It's too flash, and it's British."

It was cool-looking, certainly, but it wasn't what I thought of as super-attention-grabbing—it wasn't bright red and didn't have shiny rims or a big spoiler, like a lot of sports cars did.

"What's wrong with it being British?" asked Emma.

"It'll break down a lot. That's what they say about British cars, anyway."

"Would Abe really have used this for rescue missions if it was mechanically unsound?" said Millard.

"Abe knew lots about cars, including how to fix them," said Enoch.

He was leaning against the trunk with a bag over his shoulder and a smug smile on his face.

"You're not coming with us," I said. "There's no room."

"Did I say I wanted to come?" said Enoch.

"You *look* like you want to come," said Emma. "Now move."

I nudged him aside so we could open the trunk (sorry, the "boot") and load our bags—but after twenty seconds of fiddling around, I realized I didn't know how.

"Allow me," said Enoch, and he twisted a knob between the taillights that popped the trunk. "Aston Martin." He caressed the side panel as he walked the length of the car. "Abe always did have style."

"I thought it was some kind of Mustang," I said.

"How dare you," said Enoch. "This is a 1979 Aston Martin V8 Vantage. Three hundred ninety horsepower, zero to sixty in five seconds, top speed a hundred seventy miles per hour. A real beast—Britain's first true muscle car."

"Since when do you know so much about cars?" I said. "Especially ones made after 1940?"

"Magazines and manuals via mail order," said Millard. "Delivered to his post office box in present-day Cairnholm."

"Oh, he loves cars," said Emma, rolling her eyes. "Never actually drove one, mind you, but don't get him started on what's under the bonnet . . ."

"I'm fascinated by the mechanical as well as the biomedical," Enoch said. "Organs. Engines. Swap oil for blood and they aren't so different. And I can resurrect a dead engine without needing a jar of hearts. Which is a good thing because this car, being British and nearly forty years old, is notoriously unreliable unless religiously maintained. And with Abe being dead and all, I'm fairly certain that I'm the only person within a thousand miles of here qualified to work on this car. Which is why, even though I don't *want* to"—he tossed his bag into the boot alongside mine—"you *need* me to come with you."

"Oh, just get in so we can *go* already," said Emma.

"Shotgun!" Enoch cried, diving into the passenger seat.

"It's going to be a very long trip," said Millard.

I sighed. It seemed I had no choice.

Our friends gathered in the driveway to see us off. We exchanged hugs and they wished us good luck—all but Claire, who sulked in the doorway.

"When will you be back?" asked Hugh.

"Give us a week before you start worrying," I said.

"Way ahead of you," said Horace. "I'm worrying already."

CHAPTER EIGHT

*W*e drove down the key and over the bridge, then out toward the boonies and the far edge of town. That's where we would pick up Interstate 75 and head north. The first stop was Flaming Man, whatever that was, which H had indicated could be found inside the wet-glass ring he'd made on the Mel-O-Dee map. That narrowed down our destination to about thirty square miles in the swampy middle of the state, a few hundred miles to the north.

I was at the wheel, consumed with the task of mastering my grandfather's powerful but quirky old car. It had heavy steering and lurched around corners in a way that made my heart skip, and all its dials and gauges were located in odd places. Emma sat beside me in the passenger seat, a regular, non-peculiar road atlas of Florida spread across her lap. (Millard had also brought along *Peculiar Planet*, though its maps were very out-of-date.) I had insisted Emma be our navigator because it gave me an excuse to force Enoch into the back seat and to spend the next couple of days glancing over at her face instead of his. Enoch sulked out the window and periodically gave the back of my seat a kick. Millard sat beside him, squished against Bronwyn, who had to turn diagonally so her long legs would fit.

"From here to the ring on the map it's about three hundred miles," said Emma, looking from the cartoon map to the road atlas and back. "If we don't stop, we could be there in five hours."

"We've got to stop sometime," said Bronwyn. "You haven't bought us modern clothes yet."

She was right. Everyone I'd taken shopping had stayed behind; the ones who had come were still wearing the clothes they had arrived in. Their outfits would soon become a liability.

"We'll stop soon," I said. "I just want to put some distance between us and Miss Peregrine first."

"Where do you think Portal is?" asked Enoch. "Very far?"

"Could be," I said.

"Will you be able to stand that much driving?" asked Millard.

"I'll have to," I said. We couldn't drive in shifts because my friends didn't have licenses. And besides that, Millard was invisible, which would get us pulled over instantly, Bronwyn was too scared to drive, and Enoch had no experience. Only Emma was competent behind the wheel, but again, no license. So it was all me.

"Just keep me caffeinated," I said.

"I'll help," said Enoch. "I'll get us there a lot faster than you could, too."

"Forget it," I said. "You can take a driver's-ed class when we get back, but this is no time to learn."

"I don't need lessons," he said. "I already know everything about how cars work."

"It's not the same."

He kicked my seat again, hard.

"What was that for?"

"Driving like a granny."

We happened, just then, to arrive at the interstate on-ramp. I swung the car onto it and floored the accelerator. The engine wailed and I let out a giddy laugh, and by the time we'd merged onto the highway Enoch was screeching at me to slow down. I checked my mirrors for police cars, eased back on the gas, and pushed all the window buttons.

"Oooooh," Bronwyn cooed as her window slid down. "Fancy!"

"Music?" I said.

"Yes, please," said Emma.

Abe had a radio and some ancient kind of tape deck. There was already a cartridge inside, so I hit play. A moment later, a wailing guitar and a huge voice came crashing out of the speakers—Joe Cocker singing "With a Little Help from My Friends." After three minutes I was convinced no music had ever sounded as good, and my friends, who were all grinning and bopping in their seats, the wind in their hair, seemed to agree. There was something in the act of shouting along to that particular song with these particular people while driving that particular car that gave me a crazy, spine-tingling high like I'd never experienced before. It felt like we were claiming the world for ourselves and our lives as our own.

This is mine. Yes. I'll do with it what I like.

◆   ◆   ◆

It felt so strange and unnatural to think of Miss Peregrine as anything other than our protector and champion, but today she felt like an adversary. When she found out that we had left, it was inevitable she would come looking for us, and she'd do it the best way she knew how—from the air. Her speed, the heights she could fly to, her precise, long-distance vision, and her inbuilt radar for peculiar children meant that we wouldn't be hard to find if we were within a hundred miles and out in the open. That's why I didn't stop at all for the first three hours, not even to let Bronwyn use the bathroom. I wanted to put as much distance between the headmistress and us as possible. After two hundred miles, I finally relented to the rising chorus of complaints from the back seat, but even then I was wary, glancing at the clouds as we exited the highway into a shopping center parking lot. I saw Emma do the same thing.

I filled the Aston's tank while the others used the bathroom in the filling station's convenience store. Through its big windows, I could see the clerk and a few other customers checking out my friends as they waited their turn for the single restroom—craning their heads, whispering to one another, outright staring. One guy even took a picture of them with his phone.

"We've got to buy you modern outfits," I said when they came back outside. "Now."

No one objected. And anyway, I had chosen this highway exit with that in mind. Across the street from the filling station was the biggest of all big-box stores: a twenty-four-hour Super All-Mart. It was the retail mother ship. A city unto itself.

"My God, what *is* this place?" Millard said as we pulled into its endless parking lot.

"It's just a store," I said. "A big one."

We crossed the parking lot to the entrance, and a bank of automatic doors hissed open before us. Enoch leapt with fight-or-flight surprise.

"What, what, WHAT!" he shouted, raising his fists.

Now people were staring. We hadn't even made it inside.

I took my friends aside and explained about motion sensors and sliding doors.

"What's wrong with using a handle to open a door?" Enoch asked, irritated and embarrassed.

"It's hard if you have a lot of stuff," I said. "Like this guy." I pointed at a man pushing a full cart out through the whooshing doors.

"Why would anyone need so many things?" said Emma.

"Maybe he's stocking up for an air raid," said Enoch.

"I think you'll understand once we're inside," I said.

I'd grown up shopping at stores like All-Mart, so the essential strangeness of them had never fully occurred to me. But as my friends followed me inside and came to a dead stop at the checkout stands, shock and wonder on their faces, I began to understand.

Aisles stretched into a hazy distance. A kaleidoscopic array of items sang out for attention from every shelf. A small army of sullen stock clerks patrolled in uniforms emblazoned with giant yellow smiley faces. It was a thousand times larger than the corner store Millard had stolen groceries from. Of course my friends were overwhelmed.

"Just a store, he says," Emma said, craning her neck to take it all in. "This isn't like any store *I've* seen."

Enoch whistled. "More like a blimp hangar."

I grabbed a cart, and, with some cajoling, managed to get us moving again, if not quite in the right direction. Once they got over the sheer size of the place, they marveled at the huge and bizarre variety of things for sale. I was attempting to navigate us toward the clothing section, but my friends kept getting distracted, splitting off from the group, and plucking random things from shelves.

"What's this?" Enoch said, waggling a pair of slippers with microfiber knobbles on the bottom.

I took it from him and put it back. "It's so you can dust the floor with your feet? I think?"

"And this?" said Emma, pointing at a box labeled TALKING BIRD FEEDER—NOW WITH BLUETOOTH!

"I'm not really sure," I said, feeling like a harried mom herding toddlers, "but we only have seventy-two hours to complete these tasks, so we shouldn't—"

"Sixty-two now," said Emma. "Or maybe less."

A display of books came tumbling down at the end of the aisle, and I had to run and stop Millard—naked and thus invisible—from trying to right it again. I kept an especially watchful eye on Millard (or where I thought he might be) because I really didn't want to lose an invisible boy in All-Mart.

Our momentum never lasted long. We'd just moved past the Bluetooth bird feeders when Enoch got hung up in the sporting goods aisle. "Ooh, this little sweetheart would make quick work of a chicken's rib cage!" he cooed at some folding knives in a locked case.

Emma kept asking *why*. Why did we need so many varieties of everything? What was it all for? She found the women's beauty aisle especially vexing. "Who would need so many different kinds of skin cream?" she asked, plucking a box labeled EXTRA-FIRMING ANTI-AGING OVERNIGHT RENEWAL SERUM from a shelf. "Is everyone ill with skin diseases? Has there been a plague of skin-related deaths?"

"Not that I know of," I said.

"It's very strange!"

"Easy for you to say, honey," said a lady with voluminous hair and hoop earrings who'd been standing nearby. "You've got skin like a baby!"

Emma returned the box quickly to its shelf, and we slinked away.

Millard didn't say much (because I'd begged him not to), but I could tell he was taking mental notes from the little sighs and *hmms* he made. How many lifetimes of loop days would it take, I wondered, for Millard to make a history of everything that happened in this place in a twenty-four-hour period?

When we finally made it to the clothing section, I was feeling pressed for time—I worried about the ticking clock, about the normals who'd been staring since we walked in, about Miss Peregrine finding us if we stayed put too long, even though we were hundreds of miles from my house and she was hopefully still sleeping off the effects of Mother Dust's powder. I barely paid attention to the clothes my friends put into our cart. And I only realized that I was hungry as we were checking out. Everyone else was, too, but rather than diving back into the store itself for food, we grabbed what we could from the checkout lane: chocolate bars, Funyuns, candy.

"Immortal food," Emma said, noting the expiration date on the back of a bag of Wild Cherry Jim Jams. "How novel."

We cleared the checkouts and headed for the bathrooms, where everyone ducked inside to change into the clothes they'd bought. As they emerged one by one, it was clear there was more work to be done. They were wearing the most normal clothes from the most normal store there was, but they did not yet look convincingly normal. Maybe they weren't comfortable, or I was so used to seeing them in their old clothes that the sudden change in their appearance threw me off, but for some reason it looked like they were wearing costumes.

All except Emma. She came out wearing tight black jeans, white Reebok Classics, and a billowy top the color of root beer. She looked beautiful, I thought, as she turned to frown at a mirror.

"I look like a man."

"You look great. And modern."

She sighed and lifted the plastic bag into which her old dress had been rudely stuffed. "I miss this already."

"This fabric is so . . . *itchless*," said Bronwyn, pulling at the gray henley shirt we'd bought her. "I can't get used to it."

Enoch emerged from the bathroom in thick-soled creeper sneakers, pajama bottoms with flaming skulls emblazoned on each knee, and a T-shirt that read NORMAL PEOPLE SCARE ME.

Emma shook her head. "That's the last time you pick out your own clothes."

There was no time to return anything, so we walked out—somehow attracting even more stares than we did walking in. As we pushed our cart through the automatic doors, a loud, bleeping alarm sounded.

"What's that?" Emma yelped.

"We may not have, er, paid for everything," said Millard.

"What! Why?" I said.

Two guys in blue vests were speed-walking toward us.

"Old habits die hard," Millard said. "Never mind, run for it!" He grabbed the cart from me and sprinted toward the car with it—and now easily a hundred people were watching the cart apparently steer itself across the pavement, followed by a clutch of weird-looking kids and two loss-prevention agents.

We dove into the car with our bags. I jammed the key into the ignition and twisted it, and the car started with a loud bark that made me cringe. I floored the gas, tore down the aisle of cars and through the two blue-vested agents, who dove in opposite directions to avoid being run over.

"If you're going to break the law, at least do it with a little *panache*, Millard," said Emma. "You're not even trying!"

"I knew about the cameras," said Millard. "No one told me about the alarms!"

◆　◆　◆

After racing down the interstate for several miles and checking the rearview mirror constantly for police lights, I realized no one was chasing us. Eventually we exited onto a little state road and veered away from the coast toward the heart of Florida. On the Mel-O-Dee map, H's ring had circled an area in the middle of the state that was crossed by only one major road—the one we were on now. Within that zone was Mermaid Fantasyland. I wasn't sure if that's where we would find Flaming Man, but as it was the only thing marked on that section of the map it made sense to start looking there.

"Wait a minute," said Bronwyn from the back seat. "We're heading *away* from the ocean now. Why would mermaids live in a swamp?"

"They aren't real," I said. "It's just a cheesy old tourist trap."

"Perhaps," said Millard, "but Mermaid Fantasyland is also listed in *Peculiar Planet*." He raised the guide to show it to me, then read from it. "Brand-new syndrigast-friendly attraction features delightful aquatic performances. Time-looped accommodation nearby. Bring the kids!"

"That doesn't mean the mermaids are peculiar," said Emma. "It just means there's a loop in town."

"Or there used to be," said Millard. "Remember, this guide is nearly seventy years old. Everything in it should be treated with the highest skepticism."

We drove on, the sun sinking lower in the sky, the road narrowing from two lanes in each direction to just one. We were entering a part of Florida that felt like a different state altogether. Away from the moneyed coasts there were no chain stores, no shiny new developments. The woods closed in from both sides, and in the occasional gaps there were signs for U-pick strawberry farms, free dirt, and bail bonds.

Instead of cookie-cutter suburbs that spread out for miles, here there were small towns clustered around intersections of roads. The bigger towns had fast food on the outskirts and a few blocks of dying main street in the middle—a venerable old bank, a shuttered movie theater, a storefront church. In every single town that had a stoplight, we caught the light red and had to sit and wait while old people on benches and pedestrians with nothing better to do stared at us like we were the most interesting thing that had ever come through. We came to dread those stoplights. At the third or fourth one, a young guy with a mullet and an open beer yelled, "Halloween's not till next month!" at us and walked away cackling.

A few miles later, we passed a fading billboard for Mermaid Fantasyland, and a few miles after that, we finally came upon it: a dirt field occupied by a few sad-looking tents, and in the distance, cinder-block houses that might've been an office or staff quarters. The entrance was blocked by a closed gate, so I parked along the shoulder of the road, and we walked in. We crossed the field toward the tents. It didn't seem like anybody was around, but then we heard someone grunting and swearing from around the back of the nearest tent.

"*Hello?*" I said, leading my friends toward the sound.

Rounding the tent, we came upon two people in clown makeup. One had a frizz of blond hair and was dressed in a mermaid costume, and the other was awkwardly carrying her, toddling backward with his arms linked around her waist, since her legs and feet were encased inside the costume.

"Can't you read?" the mermaid said, glaring at us. "We're closed!"

The other clown didn't say a word or even look in our direction.

"We didn't see a sign," I said.

"If you're closed, why are you in costume?" asked Enoch.

"Costume? What costume?" She wiggled her obviously fake tail and laughed strangely. Then her smile vanished. "Get lost, okay? We're renovating." She elbowed the clown carrying her. "George, keep moving."

The other clown resumed lugging her toward the tent.

"Wait," said Emma, following them. "We read about you in the guide."

"We're not in any guide, honey."

"Yes, you are," Emma said. "*Peculiar Planet.*"

The mermaid's head snapped toward her. "George, stop." He stopped. She studied us for a moment, suspicious. "Where'd you get one of those old things?"

"We just . . . found it," Emma said. "It says there are some things to see here."

"You don't say. There *are* some things to see, for the right kind of people. What kind of people would you say you are?"

"That depends. What kind are you?"

"George, put me down." He did, and the mermaid balanced on the bend in her tail while leaning against George with one arm. The tail flexed muscularly rather than crinkling like a costume would have. "We're in show business. But it's been a while since we've had an audience worth performing for." She gestured to the tent flap. "Would you care to see the show?"

She seemed to have made up her mind that we were peculiar, which made me suspect that she was, too. Her tone had shifted from bitter and prickly to sickly sweet.

"We're only interested in the fire act," said Bronwyn.

The mermaid cocked her head. "We don't have a fire act. Do I look like a fire act?"

"Then who's the Flaming Man?" said Bronwyn.

"We have something to give him," I said. "That's why we're here."

A look of surprise flickered across her face, then was quickly suppressed. "Who sent you?" she said, her fake warmth gone. "Who do you work for?"

I remembered H's warning not to mention his name. "Nobody," I said. "We're here on private business."

George cupped his hand over the mermaid's ear and whispered something.

"You're not from around here, I can see that." Sweet again. "There's no flaming anything in our show, but why don't you stay awhile and enjoy the other parts?"

"We really can't," said Emma. "You're sure you don't know anything about a flaming man?"

"Sorry, kiddos. But we do have three mermaids, a dancing bear, and George here can juggle pickaxes . . ."

Just then, two people came around the corner of the tent— another man in clown makeup and someone in a bear costume.

"We'll throw in dinner," the mermaid was saying, not taking the hint as we backed away. "Dinner and a show, what could beat that?"

"A song!" answered the clown, and he began to grind a box organ that was strapped around his waist, which the bear—who was wearing the most horrible, handmade, skull-like bear mask— took as his cue to start singing. But the words he sang were in some strange language, and his cadence was so slow and his voice so deep that I began to feel immediately sleepy, and I could see from my friends' nodding heads that the song was having a similar effect on them.

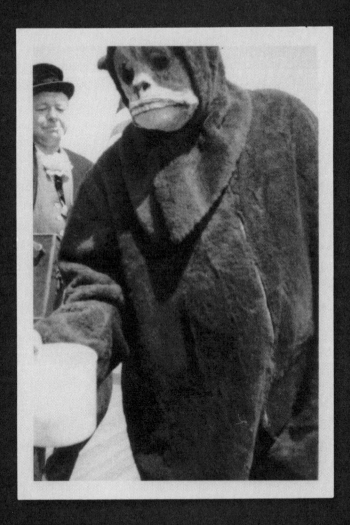

"*Sofur thu svid thitt*," he sang. "*Svartur i augum*."

We started to back away. "We can't," I said, the words coming slow and thick. "We . . . have to . . ."

"Best show in town!" the mermaid said, wobbling toward us on her tail.

"*Far i fulan pytt*," sang the bear-man. "*Fullan af draugum*."

"What's happening to me?" Bronwyn said dreamily. "My head feels like candy floss."

"Mine too," said Millard. And when his voice came suddenly out of the air, the mermaid and the bear and the two clowns all jumped, then looked at us with a new kind of hunger. If there had been any doubt as to our peculiarness before, Millard erased it.

Somehow, we made ourselves run—pushing and pulling one another, stumbling through the field—and though they didn't try to stop us physically, with their hands and their bodies, getting away felt like an almost impossible task, like breaking free from a hundred giant spiderwebs. Once we made it to the gate, those webs seemed to break, and our speech and our wits returned to us.

We fumbled the car doors open. I started the engine. We shot away, the tires spitting an arc of dirt.

◆   ◆   ◆

"Who were those awful peculiars?" asked Bronwyn. "And what were they doing to us?"

"It felt like they were trying to crawl inside my brain," said Enoch. "Ugh, I can't shake the feeling."

"They must have been why Abe marked the map with a skull and crossbones," Emma said. "See?" She held up the Mel-O-Dee map that Abe had annotated and showed the others.

"If this place is dangerous, why did H send us here?" Bronwyn asked.

"Maybe it's a test," said Millard.

"I'm sure it is," I said. "The question is, did we pass? Or was that just the beginning?"

As if on cue, I glanced at my rearview mirror to see a police car coming up fast behind us.

"Cops!" I said. "Everyone act normal."

"Do you think they know about Millard stealing from that store?" asked Bronwyn.

"No way," I said. "That was too far back."

Still, it was clear they were following us. They rode my bumper so hard I thought they might tap it. Then the road widened into a passing lane, and they poured on the speed and pulled up alongside us. But they didn't turn on their siren or their roller lights. They didn't shout over the loudspeaker for me to pull over. They just stayed even, the driver's elbow out his window, real casual, and stared.

"What do they want?" Bronwyn said.

"Nothing good," said Emma.

The other strange thing about these cops was their patrol car. It was old. Thirty, maybe forty years old. They didn't make them like that anymore, I pointed out. Hadn't for a long time.

"Maybe they can't afford new ones," Bronwyn said.

"Maybe," I replied.

The cops braked and fell back. I could see the driver speaking into a CB radio as he receded in my mirror. Then they made a sharp turn, off onto some dirt road, and were out of view.

"That was *so* strange," I said.

"Let's get out of here before they come back," said Enoch. "Portman, quit driving like my nan and stomp that rightmost pedal."

"Good idea," I said, and sped up. But a few miles later, the engine developed an alarming rattle and a red light flashed on the dashboard.

"Oh, what the *hell*," I muttered.

"Could be simple to fix," Enoch said. "But I won't know until I have a look."

We had just passed a sun-faded billboard that read WELCOME TO STARKE, POP. 502.

Beyond it was a handmade sign that read SNAKES 4 SALE—PETS OR MEAT.

The car's rattle grew steadily louder. I really did not want to stop in the town of Starke, pop. 502, but it seemed we had little choice. So I pulled into a truck wash with a mostly deserted parking lot and we all got out to watch Enoch poke around under the hood.

"It's the strangest thing," he said, emerging after a brief investigation. "I see which part failed, but I can't understand what happened to it. It should last a hundred thousand miles."

"Do you think someone tampered with it?" I said.

Enoch scratched his chin, transferring a smear of engine oil to his face. "I don't see how that's possible, but I'm not sure how else to explain it."

"We don't care *how* it broke," Emma said. "Only whether you can fix it."

"And how fast," Bronwyn said, glancing at the darkening sky.

It was getting toward evening, and thunderclouds were gathering in the distance. It was shaping up to be a nasty night.

"Of course I can *do* it," Enoch said, puffing his chest, "though I might need a bit of help from the human blowtorch here." He cocked his head toward Emma. "How long depends on a few things."

"Evening," said a new voice, and we turned to see a boy standing a little ways away, on a rise where the parking lot met a field of wild grass.

He looked about thirteen. He had brown skin and wore an old-style shirt and a flat cap. He spoke softly and walked more softly still—so much that none of us had heard him approach.

"Where'd you come from?" Bronwyn said. "You scared me!"

"Over yonder," the boy said. He pointed to the field behind him. "My name's Paul. You need some help?"

"Not unless you have a twin-choke downdraft carburetor for a 1979 Aston Martin Vantage," said Enoch.

"Nope," said Paul. "But we've got a place you can hide that thing while you tinker with it."

That got our attention. Enoch drew his head out from under the hood.

"And who are we supposed to be hiding from?"

Paul studied us for a moment. He was engulfed in shadow, silhouetted against the sky's last light, and I couldn't read his expression. He cut a strangely authoritative figure for a boy his age.

"Y'all ain't from here, are you?"

"We're from England," said Emma.

"Well," he said. "Around here, folks like us don't want to be out after dark unless they've got a damn good reason to be."

"What do you mean, *like us*?" said Emma.

"You're not the first out-of-town peculiars to have an automobile breakdown along this particular stretch of road."

"What did he—" said Millard, daring to speak for the first time. "Did you just say *peculiar*?"

The boy didn't seem at all surprised to hear words emanating from the empty air. "I know what you are. I'm one, too." He turned and began to walk into the field. "Come on. You don't want to be here when the people who sprung this trap come to see what they caught. And bring that car, too," he called over his shoulder. "I reckon the strong one can just push it."

We watched him go, amazed, but unsure of what to do. Our interactions with peculiars in this part of the world had left us wary. Then Emma leaned into me and said, "We should ask him about the—"

And at the very moment she said the words they flashed into view in the distance, beyond the field Paul was crossing, written in neon.

FLAMING MAN

It was a sign. A literal and actual one made of neon. It had once read FLAMINGO MANOR, but a few letters had burned out. The manor itself—or whatever it was—was mostly obscured by a stand of pine trees.

Emma and I looked at each other, thunderstruck and smiling.

"Well," she said. "You heard the young man."

"Peculiars have to stick together," I said.

And we all started after him.

We followed the boy through the field, down a dirt path that was grassed over and hidden from the road. Bronwyn was at the rear, grunting as she pushed the hobbled Aston over uneven terrain. Aside from the occasional car passing along the main road or the hiss of air brakes at the truck wash behind us, the evening was quiet.

We passed the old motel sign and cleared the trees, and there was the motel—or what was left of it. It had probably been the height of cool in about 1955, with its flying-V roof, kidney-shaped pool, and detached bungalows, but now it did a passable impression of an abandoned building. The roof was patched with tarps. The courtyard was a jungle of overgrown trees. Junk cars were rusting in the pitted parking lot. The pool was empty save a few inches of green water and a long, loaf-shaped thing that might have been—though it was hard to tell in the near-dark—an alligator.

"Don't mind the look of the place," said Paul. "It's nicer on the inside."

"There's no way I'm going in there," said Bronwyn.

"It's got to be a loop, dear," said Millard. "In which case, I'm *certain* it's nicer on the inside."

Loops were often downright frightening at their entrance points—it helped keep normal people away—and the *Peculiar Planet* guide had mentioned "looped accommodations" near Mermaid Fantasyland. The Flaming Man must've been it. And if that weren't a good enough reason to follow the boy, we also couldn't leave until Enoch fixed the car.

"*Look*," Bronwyn hissed, and we turned toward the truck wash. The old police car was back, driving slowly past it, its searchlight panning from side to side.

"I'm going in," said Paul, his voice edged with a new urgency. "I advise that you follow."

We took no convincing.

CHAPTER NINE

*P*aul led us into a long, covered porte cochere that led through the parking lot to the inner courtyard of the motel. We ventured inside, Bronwyn pushing the car behind us. At the halfway point I felt a quickening, and, in a flash, the dusk before us turned to daylight. We came out into a cool, bright morning and a neat, paved courtyard that was ringed by motel rooms, which were day-glo pink and almost new. Now there were no tarps on the roof, the pool sparkled with blue water, and the junk cars in the parking lot were gone, replaced with cars from the fifties and sixties in terrific shape. That's when we must've been—the late sixties or early seventies.

"A loop entrance built to accommodate cars," Millard said. "How modern!"

I ran ahead to catch up with Paul. "Okay, we're here. Now, will you answer our questions?"

"You'd better ask Miss Billie," he said. "She runs the place."

He led us across the courtyard toward a bungalow that was set apart from the rest and had a sign next to it that read OFFICE.

"Leave that," Paul said to Bronwyn. "No one will bother it."

She stopped pushing the Aston and jogged to catch up with the group. There were other people here, on this side of the loop. A couple of old men sat by the pool doing crossword puzzles and lowered their papers to stare as we passed by. A curtain in another bungalow moved, and a woman's face peered through the window at us.

"Miss Billie?" Paul said, knocking on the door to the office.

He opened it and gestured for us to go inside. "These people broke down."

We filed into a room with a registration desk and a few chairs. The woman Paul had addressed was sitting in one. She was an older white lady, and she wore a nice dress and lipstick and held three miniature poodles in her lap, her arms encircling them protectively.

"Oh Lord," the woman said in a thick southern accent. The poodles trembled. She made no move to get up. "Anyone see 'em come in?"

"I don't think so," said Paul.

"What about the highwaymen?"

"No sign of them."

If the highwaymen were those guys in the police car, Paul had just lied for us. I wasn't sure why, but I was grateful nonetheless.

"I don't like it," Miss Billie said, shaking her head firmly. "It's a risk. Every time, it's a risk. But so long as you're here . . ." She lowered her horn-rimmed glasses a bit and looked at us. "Don't reckon I can just throw you to the wolves, now can I?"

"If you'll excuse me," Paul said, "I've got some things to tend to."

Paul went out. Miss Billie kept her eyes locked on us. "You ain't gonna turn old on me, are you? I got enough old folks here as it is, and if you're fixin to die you can just go on and do it somewhere else."

"We're not going to die," I said. "We just have some questions."

"Such as, are you the headmistress here?" said Bronwyn.

Miss Billie frowned. "Head-what?"

"An ymbryne," said Bronwyn.

"Oh, Lordy!" Miss Billie said, rearing back in her chair. "Do I really look *that* old?"

"She's a *demi*-ymbryne," Emma said.

"It's like an ymbryne-lite," I explained to our friends.

"I'm the manager and that's enough," said Miss Billie. "I collect the money and try to keep the place from falling down. Rex stops in every few weeks to wind the clock." She pointed to a grandfather clock that stood against the opposite wall. Old, massive, and incongruously ornate, it looked out of place amid the gaudy motel decor.

"Rex?" I said.

"Rex Posthlewaite, loop-keeper extraordinare. He does plumbing and a little electrical, too, though he ain't licensed."

"Let me get this straight. You don't have an ymbryne here, and the fake one only stops by every few *weeks*?"

"Only he can wind it. Or another loop-keeper, I suppose. But Rex works the whole northern part of Florida, so the pickings are mighty slim."

"What if he gets sick?" asked Millard.

"Or dies?" said Enoch.

"He ain't allowed to."

"What is this thing, anyway?" said Enoch, stepping toward the clock. "I've never seen a—"

All three dogs began to yap loudly.

"Don't you go near that!" Miss Billie snapped.

Enoch spun away from it. "I was only looking!"

"Don't look at it, neither," said Miss Billie. "Can't have you messin' with my loop clock, boy. You could knock everything out of whack."

Enoch folded his arms and fumed. I figured it was time to get down to business, so once the dogs stopped barking, I said, "I've got something for you."

I held out the package from H, the one marked Flaming Man.

She peered at it over the rim of her glasses. "What is it?"

"I don't know, but if you're the manager, then I think it's for you."

She wrinkled her brow. "You open it."

I tore the paper open. I'd been dying to see what was inside ever since H had given it to me.

It was a pouch of dog treats. BIG FLAVOR! BIG FUN! read the label.

"You've got to be joking," muttered Emma.

Miss Billie's face lit up. "How nice! These are the girls' favorite!" The dogs saw the pouch and started squirming. Miss Billie snatched it from me and held it high above their heads. "Eh! Eh! Don't be greedy!"

"We went through all that to deliver some *dog food*?" said Enoch.

"Not just any old dog food," said Miss Billie, turning to drop the pouch into her purse as the dogs' noses followed it.

"You're not curious who it's from?" said Emma.

"I know who it's from. When you see him, thank him kindly for me, and tell him he's back on my Christmas list. Now—" She squeezed the dogs tight to her chest and stood up with them held against her. "I got to take the girls for a tinkle, so here's the rules of my place. Number one, don't touch my clock. Number two, we don't like noise or commotion here, so don't go making any. Number three, there's a filling station with a garage next door where you can work on your busted car. When you're done, I expect you to be gone. There's no vacancy."

She turned to go.

"Have you got anything for *us*?" I asked.

She frowned. "Like what?"

"A clue," I said. "We're looking for a . . . portal?" At the very least, I had hoped she might give me something useful in return for the package—a section of map, a postcard with an address on it—something that could help us find our next destination.

"Oh, honey. If you don't have a clue, I'm afraid I can't help you!" She laughed out loud. "Now go on, I've got to walk the girls."

◆　　◆　　◆

Out in the courtyard, the residents of Flamingo Manor watched us through their blinds as we talked by the deserted swimming pool.

"Dog food," Bronwyn said. "I can't believe it."

"The contents of the package hardly matter," said Enoch. "Only that we delivered it."

"He wants to know he can rely on us," I said.

Paul came over to where we were standing.

"I've talked to the garage next door," he said, pointing to a building beyond the Flamingo's bungalows. "They have some spare parts, though I don't know about any carburetors."

"Even a socket wrench would be better than nothing," Enoch replied. "Thanks."

Paul nodded and hurried off again, and we huddled up to plan our next move.

"What about the next place—this *portal*?" asked Bronwyn. "How do we find it?"

"We'll ask around," said Emma. "Somebody's bound to know."

"Unless H sent us here for no reason," said Enoch, "other than to test our patience."

"He wouldn't have," Emma said.

Enoch kicked a beach ball that was lying at his feet. It went flying into the pool. "Maybe you're not used to having tricks played on you, but it's just the sort of thing Abe would have done—to me, anyway—and this bloke worked for him."

"*With* him," said Emma, who still soured the moment anyone criticized my grandfather.

"Same thing!"

"Just go and fix the car!" she shouted. "That's the only reason you're here, isn't it?"

Enoch looked stung. "Come on, Bronwyn," he mumbled, "the queen's giving orders again."

He and Bronwyn went to the car. Enoch got in, pointed to the garage, and shouted, "MUSH!"

Bronwyn shook her head and sighed. "I'd better get a double helping of supper after all this," she said, then put her hands on the bumper and started pushing.

"Well, hello, young man. Hello, young lady!"

I turned to see a smiling man striding toward me. He wrapped a big, calloused hand around mine, and we shook. "Adelaide Pollard, very pleased to meet you." He was tall black man in a beautiful blue suit and a matching hat. He looked about seventy, but might've been older, this being a loop.

"Adelaide," said Emma, smiling like I'd never seen her smile at a stranger. "That's not a usual name!"

"Well, I'm not a usual man! What brings you all to our little neck of the swamp?"

"We stopped at a place called Mermaid Fantasyland," said Millard, and I saw Adelaide's face cloud. "I think they tried to put a spell on us, or some such thing."

"We got away," said Emma, "but then some policemen followed us, and pretty soon after that, our car broke down."

"I'm real sorry to hear that," he said. "It's just sad, people pulling this stuff on their own kind. Just sad."

"Who are they?" Emma said.

"Nothing but slimy reprobates," he said. "They try to lure out-of-town peculiars who don't know better into their little trap, and then they sell 'em to the highwaymen."

"You mean the cops?" I said.

"Pretend cops. They're like a gang, you could say. They go up and down the highway, harassing folks, stealing, playing like they own the whole county. Ain't nothing but thugs and shakedown artists."

"Used to be we only had those shadow monsters to worry about." An old white man in a wheelchair came up behind Adelaide. The left leg of his pants was rolled up and pinned, and he held an ashtray in his lap into which he tapped a lit cigar. "I swear, sometimes I miss 'em. Ever since the monsters disappeared, these highwaymen have been running wild. They think they can do whatever they like." He puffed his cigar through the gap in his missing front teeth. "Al Potts, by the way." He gave us a little salute. "Mr. Potts to you."

"I'm just sorry as hell about this, young people," said Adelaide. "You seem very nice."

"We are," said Millard. "But we'll be all right."

"'*We are*,' he says!" Adelaide laughed. "I like that."

Mr. Potts leaned over and spat through his teeth onto the ground. "You laugh too damn much, Adelaide."

Adelaide ignored him. "It's a shame," he said. "This was a nice place once. Nice peculiars like you used to come here to have a good time. Now people just wash up like flotsam and get stuck."

"I ain't stuck," said Mr. Potts. "I'm retired."

"Sure, Al. Tell yourself that."

"What happened to the ymbryne who made this loop?" Millard asked. "Why didn't she stay around to help protect it?"

Adelaide looked at me and whistled. "*Ymbryne.* When's the last time you heard that word, Al?"

"Long time ago," said Mr. Potts.

"I haven't seen one in . . . oh, forty years," said Adelaide, his voice softening with nostalgia. "A real one, I mean. Not one of these halfsies who can't even shape-shift."

"Where did they all go?" Emma asked.

"There weren't all that many to begin with," said Mr. Potts. "I remember back in the fifties, the loop up in Indiana where I lived shared an ymbryne with the next closest loop. Miss Pigeon Hawk. Then one day it seemed like the wights and their shadow creatures were everywhere all of a sudden, and they just hated ymbrynes worse than poison. They tried everything they could to get rid of 'em. Did a pretty good job of it, too."

"How?" said Emma. "We'd had hollows and wights in Europe since 1908 and they hated our ymbrynes just as much, but most of ours managed to survive."

"Can't say I'm an expert on how the wights operate," said

Adelaide. "But I'll say this: Our ymbrynes were every bit as tough and smart as anyone else's, if not more. I'd trust an American ymbryne with my life—if I could find one. So it's not that they lacked mettle."

"And instead you have a so-called loop-keeper," said Millard, sounding doubtful.

"Old Rex," said Potts. "Passable keeper. Terrible drunk."

"He drinks?" Millard said.

"Like a tent preacher," said Adelaide. "Rex comes every few weeks to fiddle with the loop clock, day turns to night, and so on—"

"And then he finishes off a bottle of Miss Billie's homemade rye," said Potts, "which I believe is how she pays him."

Emma turned to Millard and said, "Have you ever heard of such a thing?"

"Only apocryphally," he replied.

Adelaide clapped his hands. "Have you all eaten? I got a pot of coffee on in my room, and Al always has a few crullers stashed away."

"You leave my crullers alone," said Potts.

"These young people are having a bad day, Al. Get the crullers." Potts grumbled something under his breath.

Adelaide walked us across the courtyard to his room. We passed a bungalow where a woman was singing opera, loudly, behind a closed door.

"You're sounding fine this morning, Baroness!" Adelaide shouted.

"Thank *youuuuuuuuuuu*," the woman sang back.

"*Is it just me*," Emma whispered, "*or is everyone here a little—*"

"Nuts?" said Potts, and broke out cackling. "Yes, we are, honey. Yes, we are."

"Wow, his hearing's good," I said.

"Eyes are shot," said Potts, pushing past us in his wheelchair. "The ears still work."

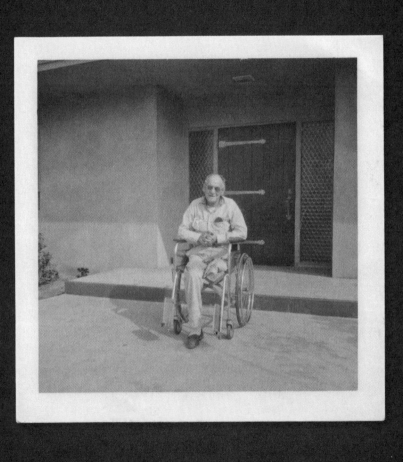

We had coffee and crullers around a little table in the living room of Adelaide's bungalow, a tiny space appointed with a floral-patterned sofa and chair, a knob-operated TV bolted to the wall, and flowers in vases. I noticed he had a suitcase packed by the door, and I asked about it.

"Oh, I'm leaving," Adelaide said.

Potts laughed. "So you keep saying."

"Any day now."

I glanced at Potts. Potts shook his head.

"Headed to Kansas City," said Adelaide. "To see an old girl-friend."

"You ain't goin' anywhere," said Potts. "You're stuck here just like the rest of us."

It reminded me of the nursing home where we used to visit my grandma on my mom's side, who had Alzheimer's. Leaving was all she talked about, but of course she never could.

"We're supposed to find a portal," I said. "Have you heard of one around here?"

Adelaide looked at Potts, who grunted and shook his head. "I sure haven't," said Adelaide.

"There's no such thing as portals," said Millard. "We're just going to keep getting the same answer. It's a dead end."

"You all should talk to the baroness," said Adelaide. "Or Weiss, our nonagenarian bodybuilder. Those two have been every-where."

"We will," I said. "Thanks."

We ate our crullers in silence for a minute or two. Then Bron-wyn set her coffee mug down loudly and said, "I hope I'm not being too forward, but what are you gentlemen's peculiarities?"

Adelaide coughed and looked down, and Potts pretended he hadn't heard the question. "What say we go outside and get some sun?" he said.

My friends and I looked at one another. It was an odd moment.

We went outside. Paul was walking by.

"Young man!" said Adelaide, raising an arm and waving.

Paul came over. He had a slim, knotted tree limb under one arm and a knife in his hand. "Yessir?"

"These people want to find a—what is it again?"

"Portal," said Emma.

"Oh," said Paul, nodding. "Sure."

He didn't seem confused at all. Totally normal thing to be looking for.

"Really?" I said.

"Well, we better get back to it," said Adelaide, and he grabbed the handles of Potts's wheelchair and began to push. "Good luck to you all."

"Thanks for the food," Bronwyn said. "Sorry if I made you uncomfortable."

I cringed. They pretended they hadn't heard that, either, and disappeared into Adelaide's bungalow. We turned back to Paul, trying to put the momentary awkwardness behind us.

"You say you know where the portal is," Emma said.

"Surely do," he replied. "That's where I'm from."

"You're from a portal?" said Millard. "There's no such thing as—"

"I'm *from* Portal," said Paul. "The town. Portal, Georgia?"

"There's a town called Portal?" I said.

"It's not famous or anything. But yeah."

"Where is it? Can you show us on a map?"

"Surely can. But is it the town you want? Or the loop that's nearby? There ain't much to the town."

I broke into a grin. "The loop. Definitely."

"Then that's a different story. You can't get to the loop without me."

"I'm a certified cartographer," said Millard. "I'm sure I can handle even the most complex directions."

"It's not a matter of directions. The location of the entrance changes."

Millard snorted. "It changes?"

"Only peculiars of my persuasion can find it. Diviners."

"Well, could you take us there?" I asked.

"Um. I don't know."

"Come on," said Emma. "We're good company."

"I don't much like to travel. Besides, it isn't a nice trip."

"What's so bad about it?" I asked.

He shrugged. "It's just . . . not so nice."

"Matchstick. I need you."

It was Enoch, his arms painted in grease to the elbows. He darted toward Emma like he was going to wipe filth on her new clothes, and she squealed and leapt out of range. He laughed, then started back toward the garage.

Emma's shirt had come partly untucked. She fixed it, glaring after him. "Idiot."

We followed Enoch toward the garage. So did Paul, whose curiosity about what we were up to apparently overwhelmed whatever awkwardness he felt about denying our request.

As we were making our way across the parking lot, Bronwyn said, "Did I cross a line back there, asking those old fellows about their peculiarities?"

"Peculiar abilities are like muscles," Millard replied. "If you don't use them for a long time, they can atrophy. Perhaps they've none left, and you hit a nerve."

"It wasn't that," said Paul. "They weren't allowed."

"What do you mean?" said Emma.

"The gang in charge made a law that nobody can use peculiarities but them. They even hire snitches to make sure nobody does."

"My God," said Millard. "What kind of country is this?"

"A cruel one," said Emma.

Paul sighed. "Is there another kind?"

◆　　◆　　◆

The sign said ED'S GARAGE, but it just looked like an old barn to me. There was nobody around; the loop must've been made on a Sunday or a holiday. Bronwyn had pushed the Aston into an empty bay lined with tools, and Enoch nearly had the car running now. There was some metal to be welded, he said, and for that he needed Emma's fire to finish the job.

It took several minutes of sustained effort, pacing and rubbing her hands together, for Emma to make her hands hot enough to weld metal. They were nearly white, and so dangerous she had to hold them well away from her body, lest her clothes catch fire. We stood back while she leaned under the hood and sparks flew. It was so noisy and fascinating that only when she'd finished, sweat pouring down her face and breathing hard, did we hear angry shouts coming from the motel.

We dashed out of the garage. The same vintage police car that had harassed us earlier was now parked in the Flamingo's forecourt with its doors flung open.

"Looks like the highwaymen tracked you down," said Paul. "You all better run. Take the back way out." He pointed to a road that led behind the garage and out of town.

"We can't leave all of them at the mercy of those thugs," said Millard.

"What?" said Enoch. "Of course we can."

Just then one of the fake cops dragged Miss Billie through the courtyard by her arm, her three poodles yapping crazily and nipping at his heels.

"If you can spare me for one moment," said Bronwyn, "I'm going to go and break that man's jaw."

"It's no use fighting them," said Paul. "It just makes them madder. They'll come back with more people and more guns and it'll be even worse."

"There's always use in fighting," said Emma. "Especially when it makes terrible people cry." She laced her fingers together and popped the knuckles, and sparks flew from her still-glowing hands. "Enoch, how's the car running?"

"Good as new," he said.

"Jolly. Keep it idling for us." She turned to me. "Back in two shakes." She turned to Bronwyn. "Coming?"

Bronwyn rolled her shoulders and shook her arms, limbering up, then nodded.

I secretly loved it when Emma got like this—so pissed off that she grew oddly calm, her anger a focused tool she could wield to great and destructive effect. She and Bronwyn started walking toward the motel. The rest of us weren't going to stay behind, of course, but since Emma and Bronwyn were the ones among us most capable of wreaking havoc, we kept a few paces behind them.

In the forecourt, one of the highwaymen had Miss Billie by the wrists and was shouting questions at her while the other one rampaged from bungalow to bungalow. "They was here, I know it!" he shouted, and burst out of Adelaide's place. "Every one of you who's lyin' is gonna wish to hell they hadn't! You know the punishment for disobeyin' orders!"

They didn't look much like cops, on closer inspection. They were wearing green fatigue pants and army boots, and they had the buzz-cut hair and dumb, overconfident swagger I'd come to know well growing up in Florida. The shorter of the two wore a gun holstered on his hip.

"Disobeyin' orders is even worse than not payin' your protection fees!" the taller one shouted. "Next time your clock needs windin', maybe old Rex don't turn up."

"You leave him alone!" cried Miss Billie.

He drew back his arm to slap her but stopped short when the smaller one said, "There they is, Darryl!" His mouth formed an O as he pointed to us.

"Well, well, well," said Darryl.

He let Miss Billie go. She scurried off behind the POOL RULES sign. We came into the forecourt and stopped where it met the pool. There were about twenty feet separating us. Emma and Bronwyn stood at the front of our little group, Enoch and I at the back. Millard was silent and, I hoped, sneaking around to flank the highwaymen. I kept Paul behind me.

"Y'all must be new in town," said Darryl. He cleared his throat loudly. "The road you was on is a toll road. What's the toll today, Jackson?"

"Gets a sight higher if you try an' skip out on it." Jackson joined the other highwayman at their squad car, leaned against the door, and hooked his thumbs into his holster belt. He'd been looking us up and down, and he didn't seem worried about what he saw. His lips broadened into a greasy smile. "How 'bout their cash and their wheels." He nodded toward the garage. "Why, I think I seen one of those babies in a magazine."

I could see the residents of Flamingo Manor peeking out through their blinds, like a scene in an old Western movie.

"You can go to hell," Emma said.

Now Darryl was smiling, too. "Bless her heart, ain't she got a mouth."

"I don't allow anybody to disrespect me," said Jackson. "Least of all a woman."

"*Least* of all," Darryl agreed. He snorted again, then took a handkerchief from his pocket and rubbed his nose with it. " 'Scuse me." He turned slightly, pressed a finger to one nostril, and with a sharp exhalation fired a little black snot rocket onto the ground, where it proceeded to steam, eating a small hole in the pavement.

I heard Emma gag.

"Wow," Enoch whispered beside me. He sounded jealous.

"That's one nasty habit, Darryl," Jackson said.

"It ain't a habit. It's an affliction."

Emma took a step toward the men. Bronwyn followed her lead.

"So he's got nuclear phlegm," said Emma to the short one. "What's your peculiarity—being the planet's biggest asshole?"

Darryl burst out laughing. Jackson's smile vanished. He unleaned himself from the patrol car and unbuttoned his holster.

Emma and Bronwyn took another step toward them.

"I think they wanna dance," said Darryl. "Which one you want?"

"The littler one," he said, staring at Emma. "I *like* her mouth."

The girls broke into a run toward the two men. Jackson went for his gun, and Emma, who had kept her hot, glowing hands hidden behind her back, whipped them around to her front and grabbed the man's gun as he raised it.

The gun instantly melted. As did Jackson's right hand. He fell to the ground, writhing and howling.

Darryl dove behind the squad car. Before he could begin firing, Bronwyn rammed the driver's-side door with her shoulder. The car skidded sideways, tires squealing, then tipped onto its side and fell over on its roof, pinning the man beneath it.

The whole encounter had lasted about fifteen seconds.

"Holy Mother of Moses!" I heard Adelaide shout, and I turned to see him watching from the doorway of his bungalow.

Potts was cheering and cackling in his wheelchair. A few doors down, a woman peeked out of her room—had to be the baroness, because she was wearing a sparkly dress and long white gloves—and she sang out, "Thank Goooooooooooood!" in a quivering vibrato.

"Uh-oh," Bronwyn said, peeking under the car. "Are they dead?"

"Close enough," Emma said, giving the short one a nudge with her foot.

Miss Billie emerged from behind the trash cans, trailed by her three shivering poodles. "There was a third one," she said. "Little skinny fella."

"Watch *ouuuuuuuut*!" sang the baroness.

She was pointing one of her gloved hands toward the loop exit. We heard feet pounding pavement. The third man had jumped from wherever he'd been hiding and was bombing toward the loop exit.

"STOP!" Emma shouted, and started after him.

The guy looked back once, terrified. Then he seemed to make a decision, and he pulled a gun from his waistband and turned to face us.

"Git on the ground!" he shouted at us. "Don't move a muscle!"

We put up our hands and did as he asked. From the corner of my eye, I saw Miss Billie dig something out of her purse. "Here you go, sweeties!" she said in the high-pitched voice she used with her dogs.

The man spun and pointed his gun at her, but when he saw her poodles, he laughed. "You gonna sic them little things on me? You done lost yer mind, lady. Now, git on the ground over there with the rest of 'em."

Miss Billie raised her hands and walked toward us. Her poodles yipped and scarfed the treats.

The man came toward us, cautious, his stiff arms shaking with adrenaline. He saw what we'd done to his friends, and he looked ready to do worse to us.

"I'll have the keys to that there automobile," he said. "Somebody toss 'em at me."

Enoch took the keys from his pocket and threw them. They landed on the pavement near the man's feet.

"Good. Now I'll take any money you got."

My mind was racing, trying to figure out how we could get out of this. Maybe if we could trick him somehow, lure him closer, then jump him. But, no. He'd seen what happened to his friends when they let the girls get near them, and he wasn't going to make the same mistake.

"Now!" he screamed, and fired his gun into the air. I flinched, my whole body tensing. I hadn't heard a gun fired in months, and I wasn't used to it.

I told him I had a few hundred dollars in the car.

"Go git it."

Slowly, keeping my hands raised, I got up. "I need the keys. The money's locked in the glove box."

"Yer a damned liar. I should shoot you right now." He was inching closer to me, closing the gap between us. "Fact, I think I will."

Miss Billie put two fingers in her mouth and whistled. The man spun and pointed his gun at her. "Hey, lady, what the hell you think yer—"

And then came a loud, low-pitched panting, and from behind one of the bungalows galloped one of Miss Billie's poodles—only it was twenty times larger than it had been three minutes earlier, the size of a full-grown hippopotamus.

The man turned, screamed, and aimed his gun at the giant dog. "Shoo! Go on now! Shoo!"

Then the other two dogs appeared, jumping out from between another pair of bungalows and growling like a pair of truck engines. He whirled toward them, and the second his back was turned, the first dog leapt, jaws wide and teeth gleaming, and bit his head off. What remained of him went limp and fell to the ground.

"Good girl! Good girl!" Miss Billie cried, clapping her hands.

Everyone in the Flamingo began to cheer. My friends got up off the ground.

"My bird," said Bronwyn. "What kind of dogs are those?"

"Colossus poodles," Miss Billie answered.

One of them trotted toward me with its mouth open, and I put my arms out and fell back a few steps. "Whoa, whoa, whoa, I think he's still hungry!"

"Don't run, he'll think it's a game!" said Miss Billie. "He's just bein' friendly."

The dog's tongue came at me like a huge pink surfboard and licked my head from neck to scalp. I think I squealed. I was left dripping and grossed out, but grateful to be alive.

Miss Billie laughed. "See? He likes you!"

"Your dogs saved us," said Emma. "Thank you."

"It was you ladies who gave them a chance," she said. "Thank you both for your bravery. And tell H thanks, too, when you see him."

Adelaide strode across the forecourt pushing Potts in his wheel-chair. "Young people, fine work today!"

"Yeah, but who's gonna clean up this mess?" Potts grumbled.

"I don't suppose they'll bother you again," Emma said, nodding toward the fallen highwaymen.

"I wouldn't count on it," said Miss Billie.

Emma and I took Paul aside.

"Last chance," Emma said. "Would you consider coming with us?"

He thought for a moment, looking from Emma to Bronwyn to me, then nodded. "I'm overdue for a visit home, anyhow."

"Yes!" Emma shouted. "Portal, here we come."

"But where's he going to sit?" said Enoch. "There's only room for five!"

"He can sit up front," said Emma. "And you can ride in the boot."

CHAPTER TEN

I drove slowly into the dark porte cochere, through which we'd had to push the lamed car a few hours earlier. The Aston purred happily now, thanks to Enoch's know-how and Emma's welding skills. The sudden gravitational rush came as we rolled through the middle of the short tunnel. I gripped the wheel a little tighter against the sensation that the car was falling off a cliff's edge, and then we emerged into the wee hours of the present-day night.

I reached to turn on the headlights.

"*Wait,*" Paul hissed, and I stalled my hand.

He pointed out the windshield, across the wide field. "There. Look."

At the truck wash, two pairs of headlights were crossed, and silhouetted in them were several men. They'd been waiting, covering the exit. One was holding something near his face that might've been a CB radio. It was unclear if they'd seen us.

"Floor it," said Enoch. "Run them over."

"Don't," said Paul. "They've got rifles, and they're good shots. There's too much ground to cover to get clear of them."

"Then back up," said Emma. "It's not worth the risk."

I decided she was right. Like all loops, there was a front way out and a back way out, through the day that was looped. The trouble with going out the back way was that you then had to travel through the past, and the trouble with the past (at least the last hundred years or so) was that it was full of hollows. But that was a problem I was uniquely equipped to handle. So I put the Aston in reverse and rolled us backward through the loop entrance. In a moment we returned to the daylit world of Miss Billie's motel.

"Back so soon?" she said, walking her dogs toward us. They had already begun to shrink. In a few hours, I guessed, they would be nipping at her heels again.

"There are more highwaymen out there," Paul said, leaning through his open window. "They must've put out a call for reinforcements."

"I wish we could take you all with us," I told Miss Billie.

Miss Billie shrugged. "As long as my dog treats hold out, we'll be all right."

"We'll ask H to send you more as soon as he can," Emma said.

"I'd appreciate that."

"Can you show us the back way out of here?" I said.

"Sure," said Miss Billie. "Though by taking it you're risking your lives. There were shadow creatures everywhere back in sixty-five, even down here in Florida."

"We'll be okay," I said. "I've got a nose for hollows."

Miss Billie stood a little straighter. "You're like H?"

"He's like *Abe*," Emma said proudly.

"Don't know him. But if H trusts you enough to hire you, I guess you know what you're doin'. And, of course, them boys outside wouldn't dare follow you into hollow territory. They'd soil their damn undies rather than face those creatures."

She gave us quick directions: past the garage, down Main Street, right at the courthouse, "And when you feel the pop in your ears, you know you've passed through the membrane."

We thanked her again, but there was no time for long goodbyes. Anyway, most of the Flamingo's residents were in hiding after the terrifying events of that morning, though a few shouted good luck to us as we curved around the highwaymen's patrol car and drove out of the forecourt. I couldn't help thinking that they were the ones who needed luck, and a good deal more, stuck here at the mercy of thugs.

We drove down Main Street. I kept one eye on my mirrors as we went, half expecting to see another old squad car pull into view. When we turned right at the courthouse, I felt my stomach drop and there was a ripple in the air like a heat wave. But nothing had changed—at least, nothing we could see.

"We're out," said Paul, his tone an odd mix of relief and dread.

We had passed through the membrane and out of the protective boundaries of the loop. Now time would march forward day by day, and hollows, if there were any to be found, would be coming for us. I had to remind myself that they were no less deadly for being historical, and my hand drifted involuntarily to my stomach as I surveyed it for any unusual twinges. For now, there was nothing.

We passed in and out of small towns, riding mostly in silence, just processing the crazy events of the past day. We were tired, too. Not only had what happened at the motel been emotionally and physically exhausting, but it was late—midday here, but nearly midnight back in the present. To think that we had discovered my grandfather's safe house that same day was unfathomable. It felt like a lifetime had passed since then.

"We should call home," Bronwyn said. "Tell everyone we're okay. They're probably worried."

"We can't," said Millard. "We're in 1965, so we'd be calling Jacob's house in 1965."

"Oh," replied Bronwyn. "Right."

I glanced at her in the rearview and caught a glimpse of Emma. She wore an intense but inscrutable expression, like she was wrestling with an uncomfortable thought. Then she saw me and her face went blank.

There was a brief silence that I'm sure felt normal to everyone except me and Emma, and then Emma said, "Paul, how far is your loop?"

"Should get there before sundown," he said.

"Can you point out the town it's in on our map?"

With some effort, she pulled out the road atlas and found the page for Georgia. (There was hardly room to move in the back, with four people crammed into three seats.) Emma passed the map to Paul.

"It's right . . . here," Paul said, tapping a mostly blank space halfway between Atlanta and Savannah.

Enoch shifted his legs and leaned over to look, then laughed. "You're kidding. Someone hid a time loop in a town called *Portal*?"

"Actually, the town's named after the loop," Paul said. "Or so the story goes."

"Are there peculiar thugs and highwaymen in Portal, Georgia?" asked Millard.

"Surely aren't," he said. "That's why the ymbryne who started our loop made it move around from day to day; so nobody mal-intentioned could find it."

"Which ymbryne made it?" asked Millard.

"Her name was Miss Honeythrush, but I never met her. We use a loop-keeper now, just like most folks do."

"Do you know what happened to her?"

He shook his head. "I don't, but Miss Annie might. We can ask her. I hope you'll be able to stay and rest awhile."

"I doubt we'll be able to stay long," Emma said. "We're getting an important mission."

Rest. The very word sounded so delicious that I started day-dreaming about beds and pillows and soft sheets. I realized that, if I was going to get us all the way to Portal, Georgia, without driving us into a tree, I needed coffee, and I needed it soon. But first, I wanted to put some distance between us and Starke, so I waited until we were near the Georgia border before I started scanning for coffee shops. They were fairly plentiful, this being a time before commer-cial coffee chains had colonized every street corner. That said, these towns seemed more populated and prosperous here in 1965. They all had a bank, a hardware store, a doctor's office, a couple of restaurants, a movie theater, and a lot more, too; not just some shuttered stores and a big-box shopping center on the outskirts. It didn't take a genius to see the connection.

When I could no longer stop myself from nodding off at the wheel, I pulled over at the next likely-looking place. It was called Johnnie's Brite Spot.

"Who wants coffee?" I said. "I'm dying here."

Everyone raised a hand but Paul.

"I'm not a coffee drinker," he said.

"Have a sandwich, then," I said. "It's lunchtime."

"No, thanks. I'll just wait here."

"We should all stay close to Jacob," said Emma. "In case there are any hollows around."

Paul folded his hands in his lap and stared down at them. "I can't go in there," he said finally.

"Why is he being difficult?" said Enoch.

And then I realized why, and a shudder of revulsion went through me.

"They won't *let* him," I said.

"What do you mean?" said Enoch, irritated.

Paul looked angry and embarrassed. "Because I'm black," he said quietly.

"What the hell does that have to do with anything?" said Enoch.

Millard sighed. "Enoch isn't a great student of history."

"It's 1965," I said. "We're in the Deep South." I felt awful that this hadn't occurred to me sooner.

"That's terrible!" said Bronwyn.

"It makes me sick," said Emma. "How can you treat people like that?"

"Are you sure they won't let you in?" said Enoch, peering at the diner's window. "I don't see a sign or anything."

"They don't need one," said Paul. "This is a white town."

"How can you tell?" said Enoch.

Paul's head snapped up. "Because it's *nice*."

"Oh," said Enoch, chastened.

"Hollowgast aren't the only reason I don't like traveling through the past," said Paul. "They're not even the biggest reason." He drew in a deep breath and looked down again, and when he looked up a moment later, he'd stuffed his feelings away somewhere deep. He waved his hand. "You all just go on in. I'll wait here."

"Forget it," Emma said. "I wouldn't eat here if I was dying of starvation."

"Me, neither," I said. I wasn't tired anymore, just pissed off and deeply unsettled. I had grown up in the American South—a weird, tropical version of it, filled with transplants from other parts of the country; but still, the South. But I'd never really confronted its ugly past. I'd never been forced to; I was a wealthy white kid in a mostly white town. I felt ashamed that I had never really reckoned with it, never imagined what a simple road trip through my own state might've been like for anyone who didn't look like me. And not just in the past. Just because Jim Crow was dead didn't mean racism was. Hell, in some parts of the country, those laws were still officially on the books.

"What if we burned the place down?" Enoch suggested. "It would only take a minute."

"That would accomplish nothing," said Millard. "The past—"

"I know, I know, the past heals itself."

"The past?" Paul shook his head. "Is nothing but an open wound."

"What he meant was you can't *change* the past," said Bronwyn.

"I know what he meant," Paul said, then went quiet again.

There was a sudden, sharp knock on my window. I turned to see a man in an apron and a paper hat staring at us, one hand on the car's roof.

I rolled my window down a few inches.

"He'p you?" he said. No trace of a smile.

"We were just leaving," I said.

"Mm-hmm." His eyes slid to the back seat, then to the passenger seat. "You kids old enough to drive?"

"Yeah," I said.

"This your car?"

"Of course."

"Are you a cop or something?" asked Emma.

He ignored her. "What model vee-hicle is this?"

"1979 Aston Martin Vantage," Enoch said quickly. Then his eyes widened as he realized his mistake.

The man stared at us for a moment, expressionless. "You a comedian?" He straightened and waved someone down. "Carl!"

A police officer had just turned a corner at the end of the block. He pivoted and started heading toward us.

"*Start the car*," Emma hissed.

I turned the key. The engine made a noise loud enough to wake the dead, and the man stumbled back.

When he regained his balance, he tried to reach through my window, but the gap was too small to get his arm through. I put the car in reverse and started to roll, and he swore and yanked his arm out before it could get ripped off.

◆   ◆   ◆

The downside of the Aston's fat, growly engine note was how thirsty it was, and in the seven hours it took to reach Portal, we had to stop twice to fill the tank. In those days you didn't pump your own gas, so we had to endure nosy questions from both station attendants while they did it for us. This being the South, they were *slow* about it, too. They pumped slowly and talked slowly and made change slowly and offered to check the oil and tires and wash the windshield and twenty other unnecessary things, all just an excuse to walk around the car and study it, and us, from every angle. It could've been a good opportunity to get out and stretch our legs and pee, but we didn't have clothes for 1965, and besides, I had no interest in using a bathroom that Paul couldn't use, and I knew the others felt the same. Instead, we stopped to relieve ourselves in an orange grove along the Georgia border, scattering among the trees and coming back with handfuls of ripe fruit, which we ate as we drove, juice running down our chins and peels flying out the windows. The only ones who got out were Emma and Enoch; they went into the second filling station and returned after a few minutes with three coffees in Styrofoam cups to share among us. After we pulled away, there was an awkward, sullen mood in the car, most of it emanating from Emma. Bronwyn, who was sitting beside her in the back, asked if she was okay, and she said yes in a way that sounded like no, but didn't elaborate.

The oranges and coffee were enough to sustain me through the rest of the drive, and the drive was tedious. The interstate highway system was not yet complete in 1965, which meant we had to wend our way down bad country roads, through stoplight-infested towns. And because our car attracted a lot of attention to begin with (exotic-looking in 1979, the Aston was positively futuristic in 1965), I had to be careful to drive under the speed limit, despite a constant temptation to stomp my foot down on the gas just to hear that thirsty V8 engine purr. We were stuck in 1965 until we found a loop that could connect us back to the present—preferably, it would be Paul's loop—and getting to Portal a little faster was definitely not worth the *Dukes of Hazzard*–style car chase it was likely to provoke.

We finally reached Portal as evening was approaching. It was a nowhere within a nowhere: low hills stippled with cornfields encircled by deep woods; a strangely named town hidden among towns with names nearly as strange—Needmore, Thrift, Hopeulikit, Santa Claus (no kidding)—the weird names acting, I suppose, as a sort of camouflage. The town boundary was marked with a bullet-pocked sign that read WELCOME TO PORTAL, though I didn't see any town beyond it, just more cornfields.

Millard cleared his throat and turned to Paul. "You said the entrance point . . . *changes*?"

"It does," he said. "Now, could you stop here?" Paul said. "I'll need to fetch my rod."

I braked and pulled onto the shoulder. Paul got out and walked to the PORTAL sign. He took a small key out of his coat, knelt down and fit it into the base of the wooden signpost, and unlocked a hidden door. From a narrow compartment inside it, he removed what looked like a wooden orb and an armload of oddly shaped sticks.

"What on earth is he up to?" Emma muttered.

Paul attached the larger stick to the orb, connected two smaller sticks, then screwed them both into the top of it. It looked like some bizarre root vegetable that had sprouted a pair of antennae. He started walking back toward the car with the thing held aloft. But before he'd reached us, the rod jerked to the right. He stopped and gripped it with both hands. It began to vibrate, and then it looked like the rod nearly flew away from him. He planted his feet and leaned back, and the rod pointed its antennae somewhere behind us. After a moment the rod stopped vibrating, and he lowered it and walked back to the car.

"It's juiced up today!" Paul said, laughing. He got in, hung the rod and the upper half of his body out the window, and let the rod point the way as I drove. When it jerked suddenly to the right, Paul cried, "That way!" and I hung a quick right down a dirt road. After about a half mile it pulled sharply to the left, pointing into a field of corn.

"Left!" Paul cried.

I looked at him doubtfully. "Through the field?"

The crop had been harvested and bundled, and what was left were rows of stubble and little pyramids of corn that stretched away over a low hill and out of sight.

"Loop entrance is somewhere over that way," Paul said, the rod pulling his arm so hard I worried it might dislocate his shoulder.

I gazed across the rough, uneven ground. "I don't want to mess the car up."

"Yes, don't," said Enoch. "You'll throw the wheels out of alignment. Or worse."

"Couldn't we just walk into the loop?" asked Millard.

"You can't leave this car outside the loop," said Paul. "If someone finds it, they'll know just where to look for the entrance."

"You said there were no highwaymen around here," I said.

"There aren't, usually. But one could be following us."

"Well, then." I put the car into gear. "I'll try to be gentle."

"Actually," Paul said, "don't be. Our loop is such that such a big, heavy thing needs a lot of momentum to get inside. You'd better go as fast as you can."

I felt a smile forming on my face.

"Well. If I *have* so."

"If you break the car, *you're* fixing it this time," Enoch grumbled.

"Oh, *fun*," said Bronwyn, rubbing her hands together.

"Everybody hang on," I said. "Ready?"

Paul leaned back out the window with the divining rod gripped in both hands, his back pressed against the doorjamb and his feet planted against the inside of the windshield. He looked at me and nodded.

"Ready."

I revved the engine twice, let off the brake, jammed my foot down on the gas. We took off through the field. Suddenly everything was vibrating—the car, the steering wheel, my teeth.

"To the right!" Paul shouted, and I veered right, around a corn pyramid.

"Left!" he said, leaning way out the window.

The tires sprayed jets of dirt behind us. Stands of unharvested

corn drummed the car's undercarriage and slapped against Paul's body.

"Now stay straight!" he yelled.

We were aimed directly at one of the corn pyramids, which was fast approaching.

"I have to turn!" I shouted.

"Straight, I said! Straight!"

I fought an overwhelming instinct to cut the wheel. The corn pyramid came rushing toward us, and everyone but Paul screamed. There was an instant of blackness, like a missing frame in a movie, then a moment of weightlessness, and a pressure change. Then the corn pyramid was gone, and the field we were hurtling through was nothing but dirt.

Paul pulled himself back inside the car and shouted, "Okay, okay, *brake, brake*, YOU SHOULD BRAKE," and I hit the brake as we crested a rise. All four wheels of the car left the ground for a second, and when we landed again I felt the car bottom out before we skidded to a stop.

"Ughhhhh," Millard groaned from the back seat.

Dust swirled in the air. The engine ticked. We had come to rest by an old red barn at the edge of a little town.

Paul opened his door and stepped out. "Welcome to Portal!"

"Oh, thank Hades," said Millard. He shoved his way out of the car, and a moment later I heard him throwing up.

Everyone got out, grateful to have solid ground beneath their feet. The car's windows had been open as we barreled through the field, and now everyone was covered in a film of dust and sweat. I raked a hand down my face and my fingers came away gritty.

"Now you've got stripes," Emma said, using her sleeve to wipe my cheek.

"You can clean up at my house," said Paul, and he waved us after him.

◆　　◆　　◆

We followed him into town. It was all of three blocks from end to end and looked as if had been made entirely, but expertly, by hand, from the houses to the packed-dirt streets to the wooden sidewalks. It was 1935 here, Paul explained, and the loop at Portal had been made in the worst depths of the Great Depression. Despite all that, it was neat as a pin, and everywhere someone could've planted flowers or painted a happy color it had been done, and the dozen or so people I saw walking were all dressed to the nines. It was a cheerful, homey place, and I already wished we didn't have to leave in such a hurry.

"Paul Hemsley!" someone shouted.

"Uh-oh," I heard Paul mutter.

A teenage girl came running toward him. She wore a crisp white dress and a fashionable floppy hat, and there was fire in her eyes. "You don't call, you don't write—"

"Sorry I'm late, Alene."

"Late!" She took off the hat and swatted him with it. "You've been gone two years!"

"I got hung up."

"I'm 'bout to hang *you* up," she said, and he leapt off the sidewalk as she swatted at him again. She huffed, then turned to us and nodded. "Alene Norcross. Pleased to meet you."

Before any of us could reply, two other girls who looked about Alene's age ran up. Paul introduced them as June and Fern, his sisters. They wrapped Paul in fierce embraces, berated him for being gone so long, then turned to us.

"Thank you for bringing him back," said Fern. "I hope he didn't cause you too much trouble."

"Not at all," I said. "He did us a huge favor."

"Yeah!" said Bronwyn. "We needed to find this place, but we thought we were looking for an actual portal, not a *town* called Portal, because we have this—*oww!*"

Emma had pinched her on the arm, and now she walked on tiptoes to whisper something in Bronwyn's ear. Even Paul didn't know

about H, or about the package we were here to deliver. We had agreed to follow H's advice and keep that information to ourselves until we knew where to deliver it. Bronwyn scowled at Emma, and Emma scowled back at her.

"We have an important meeting here," I said.

Fern perked up. "Oh yes? With who?"

"With *whom*," said June.

"With wh*ooooooo*m," said Fern, sounding like an owl.

"With *whom*ever is in charge," said Emma. "I guess you don't have an ymbryne, but is there someone close to that?"

"Miss Annie," said June.

Fern and Alene nodded in agreement. "Miss Annie's been here longer than anyone. You got a question, you need advice, you go to her."

"Can we meet her now?" said Emma.

The girls looked at one another, and something passed silently between them. "I think she's sleeping," Alene said.

"But stay for supper," said Fern. "Elmer's serving up his famous seventy-two-hour lamb, and Miss Annie hates to miss it."

"Spit-roasted," said June. "Falls right off the bone."

I looked at Emma. She shrugged. It looked like we were staying for supper.

We followed Paul through town. He slowed as we approached a young man kneeling by a seriously cute puppy.

"Brother Reggie!" Paul called out. "You teach him to roll over yet?"

"Hey, look who's back!" the boy said, looking up and giving Paul a salute. "Not yet. He's a good pup, but I think his brain's too small."

"Aww, that's cruel," said Bronwyn.

"I don't mean to be," said Reggie. "I just have to let him out of this loop for a while so he can get bigger. He won't grow here."

"I didn't think of that," said Bronwyn.

"That's why you almost never see babies in loops," Emma explained. "It's considered immoral to keep them that young for an unnaturally long time."

A minute later we passed a little white boy standing at an open window in a clapboard house. He wore antiquated headphones and seemed deep in concentration. Paul raised a hand and the boy leaned out the window and waved.

"What are they saying today, Hawley?" Paul called out.

The boy slipped his headphones off. "Nothing interesting," he replied glumly. "Talking about money again."

"Better luck tomorrow, then. You coming to supper?"

He nodded forcefully. "Yep!"

As we walked away, Paul explained. "That's my brother Hawley. His peculiarity lets him eavesdrop on the dead over the radio."

"I'm confused," said Emma, turning to look back at Hawley. "*He's* your brother?"

"Oh, we're none of us *blood* family," Paul said. "Most of us are diviners, though, and that's close enough."

"And diviners can all do the same thing?"

"Well, there's differences. No two diviners are gifted in *exactly* the same way. Alene can find water in a desert. Fern and June specialize in finding lost people. Hawley dials into spiritual frequencies. There are even those of us who can read hearts—tell if someone loves you or not."

Paul nodded to an old woman sitting in a rocking chair in the alley between two close-set houses. She wore glasses over an eyepatch, but she seemed to see us well enough despite it, and raised her hand in a silent hello. Something kept my gaze locked on her, and I turned to keep her in my sights as we passed.

"What about you?" Millard said to Paul.

"I divine doors. That's why I can always find my way home. Ah, speaking of which!" We had arrived at a house with flowers in its postage-stamp yard and curtains in the windows.

"We kept it nice for you," said June. "Like the curtains?"

"They're lovely."

"Figured you'd come back eventually," said Fern.

"I wasn't so sure," Alene muttered.

Paul stepped onto his porch, then turned back to face us. He looked delighted. "Well, don't just stand there. Come on in and get washed up for supper!"

CHAPTER ELEVEN

*W*e washed the dust and dirt off ourselves, grateful to be in a comfortable home after so many hours on the road, and then Paul led us out to a long table that had been set up in a big backyard that was common to several houses. It was a fine day to eat outside, and the smell coming from that table was divine. For seven hundred miles we had had only Al Potts's stale crullers and some immortal snacks to eat, and I think none of us realized how hungry we were until plates of steaming lamb and potatoes were set before us. We tore hunks from loaves of homemade bread and gulped down mint iced tea, and it was maybe the best food I'd ever tasted. It seemed like half the town had come by for supper, and we were surrounded by all the people we'd met since we'd arrived: June and Fern and Alene; Reggie and his puppy, who scampered around under the table; Hawley, who kept his headphones over one ear the whole meal; and some new faces, as well. Directly across from me was Elmer, a man whose black suit and tie clashed with the apron he wore over it, which was decorated with puckered lips and read KISS THE COOK! Beside him sat a younger man who introduced himself as Joseph.

"This is absolutely delectable," said Millard, dabbing his mouth with a napkin. No one thought him strange or even stared at his floating napkin; either they were polite, or Millard was not the first invisible person they had shared their table with. "One question, though. How do you cook a seventy-two-hour lamb in a twenty-four-hour loop?"

"They made the loop after the lamb had already been roasting two days," said Elmer. "That way we can have three-day lamb *every* day."

"What a brilliant use of loop-time," said Millard.

"That was way before *I* arrived," he said. "Wish I could take credit for it, but all I do is take it off the spit and carve it up!"

"So, tell us about yourselves," said Alene. "Who are you people?"

"Don't be rude," said June. "They're Paul's guests."

"What? We have a right to know."

"It's okay," said Emma, "I would want to know, too."

"We're Miss Peregrine's wards," Enoch said through a mouthful of potatoes. "From Wales. You've heard of us?"

He said it as if they had, naturally.

"Doesn't ring a bell," said Joseph.

"Really?" said Enoch. He looked around the table. "Anybody?"

Everyone shook their heads.

"Hm. Well, we're kind of a big deal."

"Don't be conceited, Enoch," Millard said. "What he means is that we enjoy some small prominence in our own peculiar community, thanks to the role we played in the victory over the wights at the Battle of Devil's Acre. Especially crucial to our success was Jacob here—"

"*Cut it out,*" I hissed at him.

"—but you Americans may be more familiar with his grandfather, Abraham Portman?"

More head shakes.

"Sorry," said Reggie, leaning down to feed his puppy under the table. "Don't know him."

"That's odd," said Millard. "I thought for certain . . ."

"He probably traveled under a false name," said Emma. "He could see hollowgast? And . . . influence them?"

"Oh!" Alene said. "Could they mean Mr. Gandy?"

That name rang a bell, but I couldn't place it immediately.

"Did your grandfather have an unusual accent?" asked a younger man sitting beside Elmer.

"Polish," I said.

"Mm." He nodded. "And did he sometimes travel with another man or a young lady?"

"A young lady?" said Enoch, raising his eyebrows at Emma.

"That couldn't have been him," Emma said, suddenly tense.

June sped away from the table and returned a minute later with a photo album. "I believe we have a picture of him in here." She flipped through the album's pages. "We keep this to remember the folks who come and go, and so we know who to trust when someone comes back after a long time gone. We've had enemies come posing as friends."

"The wights are masters of disguise, you know," said Elmer.

"Oh, we know," I said.

"Then you should double-check Paul's photo," said Alene. "Make sure he is who he says he is."

Paul looked hurt. "I don't look the same as I used to?"

"I think he looks better," said Fern.

"Here." June wedged between my seat and Emma's and leaned over the table with the album. "This is Gandy." She tapped a small black-and-white photo of a man relaxing under a tree. He was speaking to someone out of frame, and I wondered who it was, and what he'd been saying. His face was unlined, his hair black, and he had a sweet-looking dog with him. The dog was wearing a cap. It was my grandfather as I had rarely seen him: approaching middle age but still young, still in his prime. I wished I could have known him then.

Our friends got up from their seats and crowded around to look. Emma's face was paper-white, haunted. "That's him," she said, her voice barely above a whisper. "That's Abe."

"You're Gandy's grandson?" Paul said, surprised. "Why didn't you say so earlier?"

Partly it was because I hadn't known Abe used a false identity

while working, not just on his car registration (which I now realized was where I'd seen the name Gandy before). But mostly it was H's rule. "Someone I trust told me not to talk about the hollow-hunters," I said.

"Not even with other peculiars?" said June.

"Nobody."

"Can't imagine why," said Elmer. "They're heroes to all of us."

Now that I saw how people reacted to his name, I thought maybe I'd loosen up on that rule a bit.

"How can we be sure they're telling the truth about who they are?" said Alene. "I don't mean offense, but we don't know these people."

"I can vouch for them," said Paul.

"And you've known them for, what, a day?"

"They killed two highwaymen and ran another one off!" said Paul. "Helped out the Flamingo Manor peculiars down in Starke."

Elmer pointed again at my grandfather's photo. "Can't you see the resemblance?" he said. "This boy's the spitting image of Gandy."

Alene's eyes darted from me to the photo and back, and by the look on her face, I could tell she agreed. "You say his real name was Abraham?"

I nodded.

"How's he doing?" said Elmer. "He must be getting on in years. We haven't seen him in quite a while now."

"Ah," said Millard. "He passed away several months ago, unfortunately."

There was a collective murmur of sorrow.

"I'm sorry for your loss," said Joseph.

"What got him?" asked Reggie.

Fern scowled at him. "What a thing to ask!"

"It's okay," I said. "It was a hollowgast."

"A fighter to the end," Elmer said, and raised his glass of tea. "To Abraham."

The table raised their glasses and chorused, "To Abraham!"

Emma did not join in. "What about the people he traveled with?" she said.

June began to flip pages in the album again. "The fellow with the suits and cigars, that was his associate. He'd been coming through here and helping us for nearly as long as Gandy." She turned another page and slid her finger across until it came to rest on a portrait of a young H from many years ago. "It's an old picture," she said. "But that's him."

June was right. The photo was quite old, but it was unmistakably H—he had the same face, the same eyes that seemed to digest you in an instant. He was holding an unlit cigar between his lips. He was a man who had more important things to do than stop for a photo, and was impatient to get back to doing them.

"He was Gandy's partner," said Joseph. "Real funny guy. You know what he said to me one time? I had just gotten back from Vietnam, and he came through driving this big old car—"

"What about the girl?" Emma said flatly.

Joseph stopped mid-sentence and suppressed a laugh.

"Uh-oh," Enoch said, grinning wickedly. "Someone's on the warpath."

"The girl," said Alene. "I remember they called her V. She was a might strange."

"Real quiet," said Elmer. "Always watching. At first it seemed like she might've been Abe's protégé, like he meant for her to take over from him one day. But sometimes I got the feeling maybe she was the one really in charge."

"I heard her say once that she used to be in the circus," said Joseph.

"I heard she was in the national ballet of Russia," said Fern.

"I heard she went out west to be a cowgirl," said Reggie.

"I heard she killed seven people in a bar fight in a loop in Texas and had to run away to South America," said June.

"She sounds like a con artist," said Emma.

"Come to think of it," said Joseph, studying her, "she looked a bit a like you. In fact, first moment I saw you today I thought maybe you were her."

I half expected fumes to start coming out of Emma's ears. I leaned over to her and whispered, "*I'm sure it's not what you think.*"

She ignored me. "Got a picture of her?"

"Here," said June, turning to a page she'd marked with her finger.

In her photo, V looked like someone who ate nails for breakfast. Or rode grizzly bears for a living, and had finished doing so just before the photo was taken. She stood with her arms crossed and her chin raised, defiant. And I couldn't help but agree with Joseph—she did look a bit like Emma. Not that I ever would've admitted it out loud.

Emma stared at the photo like she was committing the girl's face to memory. She said nothing for a moment, then just, "Okay." I saw her make a conscious effort to swallow whatever she was feeling; I could almost trace the progress of the bile as it descended her throat down into her belly. And then her face cleared, and she smiled a bit too sweetly at June and said, "Thank you very much."

June clapped the album shut. "Good," she said, and started back to her seat. "My food's about to get cold."

Reggie leaned across the table toward me. "So, Jacob. Did Gandy teach you everything he knew? About hunting hollows and such? You must have stories!"

"Not exactly," I said. "I grew up thinking I was normal."

"He didn't realize he was peculiar until earlier this year," Millard explained.

"Good gravy," said Elmer. "You're getting a real crash course, then."

"That's for sure."

"It's definitely more crash than course," said Enoch.

"Did you know your grandfather was one of the first two peculiars I ever met?" said Joseph. He had cleaned his plate and was leaned back in his chair, rocking slightly on its rear legs. "I was uncontacted at the time, living in Clarksville, Mississippi, 1930. Thirteen years old, my parents dead from Spanish flu. I didn't know the first thing about peculiarness. But I knew something was changing inside me—that was my divining coming in—and soon after that I could feel something *hunting* me. But before it could get to me, your grandfather and H did. And they brought me here."

"Gandy and H brought more than one child here, over the years," said Elmer.

"But why come so far?" Millard asked. "Weren't there loops closer to where you grew up?"

"Not for diviners," said Joseph.

I scanned my friends' faces, and they all seemed to have the same question in mind.

"So, only diviners can live here?" I asked.

"Oh no, no, no, we're not like that," said Fern. "We allow any type of peculiar in our loop." She pointed at a house across the yard. "Smith over there is a wind-shaper. Moss Parker next door to him is a telekinetic, but only for foodstuffs. Which does help when it comes to setting a table."

"For quite a few years we had a boy who could turn gold into aluminum," said June, "though it wasn't a skill much called for."

"There *are* some loops that don't allow outsiders, though," said Elmer. "They'll chase you right out."

"They don't trust anybody but peculiars like themselves," said Alene.

"But we're all peculiar," said Bronwyn. "Isn't that alike enough?"

"Seems not," Reggie said. He tossed a scrap of gristle into the grass, and his puppy went bounding after it.

"Isn't it against the ymbrynic codes for only one type of peculiar to live together?" said Bronwyn.

"Of course not," said Enoch. "Remember the sheep-speakers in that Mongolian loop and the town of floaters in North Africa?"

"There are lots of reasons peculiars of one ability might band together," said Millard. "I know of several invisible communities, for instance."

"Oh," said Bronwyn. "I thought it was illegal."

"Partitionment according to ability is *discouraged* under the ymbrynic codes, because it can promote clannish thinking and unnecessary conflict," said Millard. "What's expressly forbidden are closed loops, in which only one type of peculiar is allowed to live and all others are banned."

"All due respect," said Elmer, "but there aren't many ymbrynes around anymore. Their codes don't hold much water."

"But why *aren't* there ymbrynes around?" asked Bronwyn. "No one's been able to explain what happened to them, and it's really starting to wind me up."

"It's just how it's always been, for as long as any of us can remember," Reggie said.

"Some of us remember," said a voice from behind us.

I turned to see the old lady with the eyepatch hobbling toward the table. "You all started without me, I see."

"Sorry, Miss Annie," said Fern.

"No respect for your elders," Miss Annie muttered, but it was clear, as the diviners all stood up from the table to greet her, that she commanded a great deal of respect. We followed their example and stood up, too. Fern darted out and helped Miss Annie to the table, where a seat right at the head had been reserved, and when she reached it she gripped the edge and lowered herself slowly into the chair. Only then did the rest of us sit down again.

"You want to know how things got the way they are." Her voice had such grit and gravitas, it sounded like it was bubbling up from the depths of a muddy river. "What happened to our ymbrynes." Miss Annie folded her hands on the table. A hush fell over the group. "They used to be the heart of our society, just like they are yours. The seeds of their downfall were planted a long time back. Back when the British and French and Spanish and native peoples were still fighting over who owned this country. Before it had occurred to anybody to fight over whether or not people should own one another."

"*Miss Annie's old as the hills*," Fern whispered. "*She was probably there.*"

"I'm one hundred and sixty-three, give or take," Miss Annie said, "and still got ears that work, Fern Mayo."

Fern stared into her potatoes. "Yes, Miss Annie."

"Some of you aren't from here"—Miss Annie was looking at my friends—"so maybe you don't know. But this nation was built with the stolen labor of black people and on the stolen land of native people. A century and a half ago, the southern part of this country was, by itself, one of the richest places in the whole world, and the vast bulk of that wealth was held not in cotton nor gold nor oil, but in the form of enslaved human beings."

She paused to let her words sink in. Emma looked ill. Bronwyn and Enoch were silent, eyes downcast. I tried to wrap my mind around it. This vast, institutionalized evil, unfathomable in scale, swallowing up one generation after the next. Grandparents and parents and children and children and children. It was unimaginable, overwhelming.

After a moment, Miss Annie went on. "All that money and all that wealth depended on one thing: the ability of one kind of people to subdue and control another kind. So think about what happens when you introduce peculiarness into a system like that."

"It raises hell," said Elmer.

"And scares the life out of the people in control," said Miss Annie. "Imagine. A person slaves all day chopping cotton. That is their life, and their life sentence. Then, one afternoon, from out of nowhere, this person—a young girl—manifests a *peculiarness*. And now, she can *fly*." As she said it, Miss Annie's eyes rose above the table and her hands spread out wide, and the image was suddenly so clear in my head that I had to wonder if she was describing her own experience. Miss Annie's gaze fell to Bronwyn. "What do you do if you're that girl?"

"I fly away," said Bronwyn. "No—I wait until nighttime, then use my power to help everyone else escape, and *then* fly away."

"And what if there was one who could turn day into night? Or a man into a donkey?"

"I'd make it midnight at noon," said June. "And turn the overseer into an ass."

"So you see why they were frightened of us," said Miss Annie, her hands settling back onto the table, her voice lowering. "Our numbers were always small. Peculiarness has always been rare. But they were so terrified of even those few that they paid fortune-tellers and quack doctors and exorcists to try and tell us apart from the normals. They invented lies and folk stories about how peculiars were the spawn of Satan himself. Tried to get us to turn one another in. They'd kill you if you even *knew* a peculiar. If you even *said* the word peculiar! And the ones they were most frightened of?"

"Our ymbrynes," said Paul.

"That's right," said Miss Annie. "Our ymbrynes. The ones who made our places of refuge. The places no normal could find, or get into. That made it possible for us to survive. They hated the ymbrynes worse than anything."

"So these normals knew about ymbrynes?" Emma said. "They knew what they were?"

"They made it their business to know," said Miss Annie. "Because it *was* their business. Peculiarness threatened their economy, their way of life, the bottom line of the whole wicked establishment, so the slaveowners plotted against us in ways that may not have occurred to normals in other parts of the world. They formed a secret organization devoted to rooting us out, destroying our loops, but especially to killing our ymbrynes. They were ruthless, tireless, obsessed. So much so that their organization continued to exist even after the Confederacy died, even after Reconstruction ended. And it took a toll on us. When I was growing up in the 1860s, we never had enough ymbrynes. They were always spread thin. Always in danger. We'd have one ymbryne to maintain four or five loops, and you'd hardly ever see her. And then one day it seemed like there were none. Instead, we had demi-ymbrynes and loop-keepers—functionaries and mercenaries, not leaders—and in the absence of ymbrynely in-fluence, peculiars in this country gradually became divided and dis-trustful of one another."

Something occurred to me, a flash memory of the diner we'd stopped at in 1965, and I asked, "Were loops segregated back then? By race?"

"Of course they were," said Miss Annie. "Just because folks were peculiar didn't mean they weren't racist. Our loops weren't some kind of utopia. In a lot of ways they were just a reflection of the society outside them."

"But they're not segregated anymore," said Bronwyn, her eyes flicking to Hawley, the white boy wearing headphones down at the other end of the table, and the older white girl across from him.

"It took a good long time to integrate," said Miss Annie. "But slowly, we did."

"Hollowgast don't care what color you are," said Elmer. "They just want your soul. That helped bring us all together."

"What about loops in other parts of the country?" said Enoch. "Do they have ymbrynes?"

"Ymbrynes down south got the first of it and the worst of it," said Elmer. "But gradually, ymbrynes all over the nation disap-peared."

"Every single one?" said Bronwyn. "There are none left at all?"

"I've heard there are still a few," said Miss Annie. "Some who managed to hide. But they don't have anything like the power or influence they used to."

"What about Native Americans?" Millard asked. "Did they have loops?"

"They did. But not many, because by and large they weren't afraid of peculiarness, and their peculiars weren't persecuted. Not by their own people, anyway."

"That brings us to the twentieth century, which I can speak to," Elmer said. "The Organization started fading away, mainly because there weren't many ymbrynes left to kill. Normals began to forget us. Instead the loops began fighting one another. For territory, influence, resources."

"It's something the ymbrynes would never have allowed to happen," said Alene.

"We heard a bit about what you folks were going through in Europe with the hollowgast," said Elmer, "but the monsters mostly kept to your side of the pond. That all changed in the late fifties, when the wights and hollows came in with a vengeance. That put a stop to most of the inter-clan battles, but we could hardly leave our loops for fear of being eaten by these damned shadow monsters."

"That's when my grandfather and H started fighting them," I said.

"Right," said Elmer.

"So the normals in America," said Bronwyn. "Do they *still* know about us?"

"No," said June. "They haven't for a long time. And it wasn't many people who knew about us, even back in the 1800s."

"No, no, no, Junie, that's wrong," Miss Annie said, shaking her head vigorously. "That's just what they *want* you to think. Mark my words, there are those who still know. There are still normals who understand our power, who are frightened of us, who seek to control us."

"What on earth are they frightened of?" asked June.

"Of an *idea*," said Miss Annie. "The idea of us peculiars as anything other than divided up and scared of one another. The power that a united peculiardom could wield. It's as frightening to them today as it was *back* in the day." She nodded with a sharp finality, let out a breath, and picked up her fork. "Now if you'll excuse me. You all have finished eating, but I haven't taken a single bite."

◆　　◆　　◆

Everyone waited for Miss Annie to clear her plate before leaving the table, and then we began to clean up. It was obvious to me that Miss Annie was the one I was supposed to give the package to, so when she got up to leave I offered to help her get to wherever she was heading.

She told me she was going back to her house. I offered her my arm. After the short walk to her house, I gave her the package, which was just big enough to fit in my pocket. She seemed to be expecting it.

"You're not going to open it?" I asked.

"I know what it is and who it's from," she said. "Help me up the stairs."

We climbed the three steps to her porch, her back at nearly a ninety-degree angle, and when we reached the top she said, "Hold on a moment," and disappeared into her house.

A few seconds later she returned and put something in my hand.

"He asked me to give you this."

In my palm she'd placed an old, worn matchbook.

"What's this?"

"Read it and see."

On one side was an address—a town in North Carolina—and as if that weren't straightforward enough, the other side read, *It's SMART to stop here . . . you get MORE for your money!*

I tucked it into my pocket.

"When you see him, tell him thank you," she said. "And then tell him to come here his damn self next time, so I can see his handsome face again. He is missed."

"Thank you," I said.

"Don't give up on him. He can be frustrating and pigheaded and a pain in the rear end. But don't let him convince you he doesn't need help. He's been carrying a lot of weight for a lot of years, and he needs you. He needs you all."

I nodded solemnly and raised my hand to her, and she went inside and shut the door.

I went back to gather my friends. I saw Emma talking close with June and strode across the grass toward them. Before they noticed me, June seemed to be explaining something that didn't please Emma, and Emma was standing with her arms crossed. Her face was drawn and serious. When she saw me, her expression blanked, and she said a quick goodbye to June and ran to meet me.

"What was that about?" I asked.

"Just trading darkroom tips. Did you know she printed most of the photos in that album herself?"

It was clearly a lie, and it had come to her so quickly that I was taken by surprise.

"Then why do you look upset?" I asked.

"I'm not."

"You were asking her about the girl. The one Abe traveled with sometimes."

"No," said Emma. "I don't care about that."

"Could've fooled me."

Her eyes cut away. "Quit giving me the third degree, will you? Here come Bronwyn and Enoch."

Millard was with them, too—he had put on clothes and was easy to spot—and June and Fern and Paul, with whom they'd all made fast friends.

"We'll talk about this later," I said.

It's SMART to stop here......
You get MORE for your money!

FOR YOUR OWN SAFETY
PLEASE DON'T
SMOKE IN BED

Emma shrugged. "There's nothing to talk about."

I nearly lost my temper, but managed to tamp it down. I told myself I would never understand what Emma was feeling, and if I wanted to be with her, I needed to respect that she was going through something and give her space to feel it.

That made sense. But it didn't make me feel less hurt.

We made plans to leave. Paul arrived carrying a metal thermos.

"Coffee for your trip. So you don't have to stop."

Elmer came by and shook our hands. "If any of you ever need a diviner, you know where to find us."

"What an interesting man," said Millard as he walked away. "Did you know he fought in three wars over seventy years? During the Great War he slept in a loop at the trenches in Verdun so he wouldn't age forward."

Bronwyn and Fern hugged.

"You'll write?" said Fern.

"Even better, we'll visit," said Bronwyn.

"We'd like that."

They said goodbye, and Paul walked us back to the edge of town, and our car. Along the way, I showed everyone the pack of matches Miss Annie had given me.

"An address!" said Millard. "H made it easy on us this time."

"I think the tests are over," I said. "It's time for the real mission."

"We'll see," said Emma. "H never seems to get tired of testing us."

"You all be careful out there," Paul said. "And watch yourselves up north. I hear it's every bit as dangerous."

He explained how to get back to the present. There was no returning to 1965—not that we would've wanted to—because exiting the back way out of this loop would get us to a spring day in 1930, when the Portal loop was made. Leaving the front way was simple: We had to go out the same way we'd come in—through the fields, and fast.

We said goodbye to Paul. I made sure everyone was belted in, started the car, and punched the gas. The car shook as I followed my tire tracks back across the bare field, speeding faster and faster even as the terrain grew rougher. Halfway across, just as we reached the spot where we had entered the loop and my tire tracks disappeared, there was a gut-wrenching lurch. Day turned to night. The flat dirt before me turned into a wall of green cornstalks. We crashed through them, flattening row after row as the stalks and green cobs hammered the car. I was about to slam on the brakes when I heard Millard yell, "*Keep going or we'll get stuck!*" so I pushed even harder on the gas, and the engine bellowed and somehow the tires found traction, and a few seconds later we broke through the corn and onto a road.

I stopped. We caught our breaths. I turned on the headlights. The dirt road was paved now, but otherwise the outskirts of Portal looked much the same as in 1965.

I got out to inspect the damage, and Millard got out to throw up. There was a crack at the top edge of the windshield and shredded cornstalks stuck in the grille and the wheel wells, which I was able to pull out. Other than that, we had made it in one piece.

"Everyone okay?" I said, poking my head through the window.

"Millard's not," said Emma, and then I heard a retching sound and looked up just in time to see an air-burst of vomit splatter the pavement. I had never seen an invisible person throw up before, and it was something I won't soon forget.

As he was voiding his guts, I felt my phone—alive again here in the present—buzz madly in my pocket. *24 missed calls*, the screen read. *23 voicemails.*

I knew who they were from without even looking.

I walked around to the rear of the car and pretended to check something while I surreptitiously listened. The first few messages were mildly concerned. But they got more alarmed and more angry as they went on. The thirteenth went like this: "Mr. Portman, this is your ymbryne speaking. Again. I want you to listen to me very carefully. I am disappointed that you would embark on a journey without informing me. Exceedingly so. But you *have no right* to take the children with you without my say-so. Return to this house *at once*. Thank you. All the best."

I stopped listening after that. I thought about telling the others, then decided against it. They had all known Miss Peregrine wouldn't approve; there was no reason to agitate them with the voicemails and risk having them decide to turn back.

"All right," said Millard, stumbling back toward the car. "I have finished."

I slipped the phone into my pocket. "Sorry you're not feeling good."

"I don't suppose there's a train we could catch," he said weakly. "I'm growing a bit weary of automobiles."

"The rest of the way will be smooth sailing," I said. "I promise."

He sighed. "I wish you wouldn't make promises you can't keep."

CHAPTER TWELVE

*I*t was the present day once more, and the modern highway system made for a quick ride, in the middle of the night, anyway. Fueled by Paul's thermos of coffee and an 8-track of *Dark Side of the Moon* I found in the back of the glove box, the miles peeled away fast. Before I knew it, we'd made it through the rest of Georgia and the whole of South Carolina, and we were within striking distance of the town in northern North Carolina written on the matchbook. After the brief flare-up between Emma and me back in Portal, things had cooled to what felt like subzero temperatures. She had chosen to sit in the back, despite how cramped it was, and Enoch was up front next to me.

I looked up at Emma in the mirror now and then, and when she wasn't sleeping or staring moodily out the window, she was flipping through Abe's operations log, reading it by the flickering light of a single pinkie flame. Again, I tried to tell myself that she was going through something. Processing something she'd never been forced to face quite so head-on, because she'd always been far away from Abe, across time, across the sea. But it felt like she was icing me out, punishing me for questioning her. And I didn't know how much longer I could take it.

It was three thirty in the morning and my butt was almost completely numb when we finally reached the exit. I followed directions from my phone to the address printed on H's matchbook. We had no idea what we'd find there. A gas station? A café? Another motel?

None of the above. It was a fast-food place called 24-HR OK BURGER. It shone palely in the middle of an empty, black parking lot in a deserted shopping center, and true to its name, it was open, and it looked okay. All the chairs were turned upside down on the tables, and a sign on the door read DRIVE-THRU OPEN.

I parked right in front, the only car in the lot. H was not here. *No one* was here except for one unlucky employee who'd gotten stuck with the graveyard shift. I could see him inside, reading his phone behind the counter.

"Did the matchbook say what time to meet H?" asked Bronwyn.

"No," I said. "But I don't think he expected us to come at three thirty a.m."

"So we're supposed to just wait here until morning?" said Enoch. "This is idiotic."

"Just be patient," said Millard. "He could arrive at any moment. The middle of the night seems like the best time to meet, if you mean to do it in secret."

So we waited. The minutes ticked by. The kid inside put down his phone and started sweeping the floor.

A loud grumbling noise came from the passenger seat, and everyone looked at Enoch.

"Was that a truck engine?" Millard said.

"I'm hungry," said Enoch, looking down at his stomach.

"Can't you wait?" said Bronwyn. "What if H comes by but doesn't see us because we're in the drive-through, and we miss him?"

"No, Enoch's got the right idea," said Millard. "May I see the matchbook again?"

I handed it back to him. Millard turned it over in his hands. "It's more than just an address," he said. "It's a clue. Look what's written."

He gave the matchbook to Bronwyn, who read it aloud. "It's

smart to stop here . . . you get *more* for your money." She looked up. "So?"

"So," said Millard, "I think we're supposed to buy something."

I started the car and pulled around into the drive-through lane. We rolled up to the ordering speaker and its glowing, backlit menu. A very loud, tinny voice crackled, "WELCOME TO TWENTY-FOUR-HOUR OKAY BURGER WHAT CAN I—"

Bronwyn screamed, and with a lightning-quick reaction, she flung her long arm through the open window and punched the speaker so hard that it unbolted from the ground and fell over, dented and silent.

"Bronwyn, what the hell!" I shouted. "He was just taking our order!"

"Sorry." Bronwyn shrunk down into her seat. "I got scared."

"We can't take you anywhere, can we?" said Enoch.

Under any normal circumstances I would've peeled out and left the scene, but this wasn't a normal circumstance, so I eased my foot off the brake and rolled slowly around to the pickup window, where the kid in the orange apron was still talking into his headset.

"Hello? Can you hear me?"

He spoke very slowly, and his eyes were red and puffy. He looked high.

"Hey," I said. "The speaker, uh, isn't working."

He blew out through his mouth, his lips flapping. "Ooooo-kay," he said, opening his window. "What'll you have?"

Millard spoke up. "What's good here?"

"What are you *doing*?" Emma hissed at him.

The kid scrunched his brow together and peered into the back seat. "Who said that?"

"I did," said Millard. "I'm invisible. Sorry, should've mentioned that."

"Millard!" Bronwyn exclaimed. "You are so daft!"

But the kid didn't seem freaked out. "Oh, okay," he said, nodding highly. "If I were you? Combo two, for sure."

"Then please prepare us a *combo two*," said Millard.

"And five hamburgers, please!" Enoch shouted from the back seat. "With everything. And chips."

"We don't have chips," the guy said.

"He means french fries," I said.

The kid charged me, I paid, and then he went into the kitchen to prepare the food. He came back a few minutes later and handed me a heavy paper bag that was already turning clear from grease stains. I unrolled the top and looked inside. There were a lot of burgers, a huge order of fries, and a wad of napkins. I distributed the food to my friends, and at the bottom of the bag I noticed a small white envelope. It was fancy-looking and sealed with red wax.

"What's this?" I said, holding it up to show the others.

Emma shrugged. "Part of the combo?"

I drove into the lot, parked, and opened the envelope. I turned on the dome light to read by, and everyone leaned over to look. Inside the envelope was another napkin, but this one had been typed on. With a typewriter. The greasy napkin read:

Uncontacted subject being hunted, highly threatened.
Mission: protect and extract.
Suggest delivery to loop 10044.
Extreme caution advised.

That was it. The uncontacted peculiar wasn't named. It didn't specify where loop 10044 was. But on the back of the napkin was a set of coordinates.

"I can read coordinates," Millard said excitedly. "The line of longitude number is negative, which means it's well west of the prime meridian—"

"It's a high school in Brooklyn, New York," I said, holding up my phone. "I typed them into the Maps app."

Uncontacted subject being hunted,
  highly threatened.
Mission: protect and extract.
Suggest delivery to loop 10044.
Extreme caution advised.

Millard harrumphed. "No piece of technology can replace a real cartographer."

"We've got a mission, and we've got a location," Emma said. "The only thing we don't have is the name of the peculiar we're looking for."

"Maybe H doesn't know the name, either," said Bronwyn, "and finding it out is part of the mission."

"Or it's for security," said Enoch. "You wouldn't want to go around naming uncontacted peculiars on napkins that could fall into the hands of, say, a hamburger chef."

"I think he's more than simply a chef," said Millard. "Say, Jacob, would you mind pulling round to his window again?"

I started the car, rounded the small building, and drove back into the drive-through lane. When he slid the window open this time, he looked annoyed. "Uhhh. Hi."

Millard leaned out the window. "Sorry to trouble you, old boy. If we could just have one of your combo number *threes*."

The kid typed the order onto a greasy keyboard and charged me $10.50. As I was paying, Bronwyn leaned toward the open window and said, "Do you know H? Are you a hollow-hunter? What is this place?"

He gave me my change, acting as if he hadn't heard her.

"Hey!" said Bronwyn.

He turned and went into the kitchen.

"I don't think he's allowed to answer questions like that," I said.

After a minute he came back and dropped a greasy paper bag onto the window ledge. It made a solid *thud* as it landed.

"You have a great night, now," he said, and shut the window.

I picked up the bag, which was unusually heavy, and unrolled the top. Nothing but french fries and onion rings. Not much of a combo, I thought, handing it to Millard as I pulled out of the lot and headed back toward the highway. It was a long way to Brooklyn, and I wanted to get going before the morning rush hour turned the major arteries into parking lots.

Ten minutes later, as we were flying up I-95, Millard had eaten his way to the bottom of the bag. I heard him laugh and turned my head to look. He pulled out something heavy and egg-shaped.

"What's that?" I said.

"Combo number three, it would seem. French fries and a hand grenade." Bronwyn yelped and ducked behind my seat.

It seemed OK Burger was more than just a message relay station. It was a peculiar weapons depot. I wondered how many of my grandfather's secret way stations were like this, hiding in plain sight. (I also wondered what prize came with a combo number one.)

Millard chuckled, rolling the grease-covered grenade from one hand to another. "My, they really do give you *more* for your money!"

◆　　◆　　◆

I drove, nibbling at my meal with one hand while my friends scarfed theirs. Their teenage bodies, now aging forward for the first time in many years, were sometimes insatiably hungry. After they finished they all fell into a deep sleep—all but Emma, next to me in the passenger seat. She said she didn't want to sleep if I couldn't.

For an hour we hardly spoke. I scanned through radio stations at a low volume while she watched the dark world slide by outside the window. We were halfway through Virginia when a pale gray dawn began to smear the sky. The silence between us felt like a stone forming in my chest. I'd been talking to Emma in my head for the last fifty miles, and finally I couldn't take it anymore.

"We have to—"

"Jacob, I—"

Neither of us had said a word in a long time, and then we'd

both spoken at once. We snapped our heads to look at each other, surprised at our odd synchronicity.

"You first," I said.

She shook her head. "You."

I glanced up at the rearview. Bronwyn and Enoch were fast asleep. Enoch was snoring lightly.

"You're not over him." I hadn't meant to be so blunt, but I'd held back the words for so long that they'd gotten stuck in my mouth, and I just had to spit them out. "You're not over him. And it's not fair to me."

She stared at me, shocked, her lips a tight line. Like there was something she was afraid to say.

"Whenever someone mentions his name," I said, "you flinch. Ever since we found out one of his hollow-hunter comrades was a girl, your head's been somewhere else. You're acting like he cheated on you. And not years and years ago, either."

"You don't understand," she said quietly. "You couldn't possibly."

My face went hot. All I'd really wanted was an acknowledgment that she'd been acting weird and an apology, but this was going somewhere else. Somewhere worse.

"I've been trying," I said. "I've been telling myself to ignore it, to not be so sensitive, to give you space, that you're going through this hard, strange thing. But we've got to talk about it."

"I don't think you really want to hear what I'm thinking," she said.

"If we can't talk about it, we're not going to make it."

She glanced down briefly. We were passing a factory, twin smokestacks belching smoke into the air. Then she said, "Have you ever loved someone so much it made you sick?"

"I love you," I said. "But it doesn't make me *sick*."

She nodded. "I'm glad. I hope you never feel like that, because it's terrible."

"Have you ever felt like that?" I asked.

She nodded. "About Abe. After he left, especially."

"Hm." I tried to keep my expression neutral, but I was hurt.

"It was bad. I was really obsessed for a few years. I think he was, too, in the beginning. But for him, it wore off. For me, it only got worse."

"Why do you think that was?"

"Because I was trapped in our loop, and he wasn't. It makes the world feel very small to be cooped up like that for years and years. It isn't good for the mind or the soul. It makes small problems seem very large. And a longing for someone that might otherwise have subsided after a few months became . . . consuming. For a while I was actually considering trying to run away and join him in America—even though it would have been extremely dangerous for me."

I tried to imagine Emma as she was then. Lonely and pining, living on the letters he sent less and less frequently, the outside world a distant dream.

The factory gave way to rolling fields. Horses grazed in the morning mist.

"Why didn't you try?" I said. Emma wasn't the type of person to shrink from a challenge, especially for someone she loved.

"Because I was afraid he wouldn't have been as happy to see me as I would've been to see him," she said. "And that would've killed me. But also, it would just have been trading one loop for another, one prison for another. Abe wasn't loop-bound. I would've had to find some nearby loop to live in, like a bird in a cage, and then wait for him to come visit me when he had time. I'm not cut out for that—to be a ship captain's wife, watching the sea every day, worried and waiting—I'm meant to be the one out there, journeying."

"But now you are," I said. "And now you're with me. So why are you still hung up on my grandfather?"

She shook her head. "You make it sound so simple. But it's

not easy to switch off something I felt for fifty years. Fifty years of longing and hurt and anger."

"You're right, I can't imagine. But I thought this was behind us. I thought we'd talked it all through."

"We did," she said. "I thought I was over it, too. I wouldn't have said all the things I said to you if I didn't. I just . . . I didn't know how much coming here would affect me. Everything we've been doing, all the places we go—it's like his ghost is around every corner. And that old wound I thought had healed keeps getting sliced open, over and over again."

"For pity's sake," said Enoch from the back seat, "can you two finish breaking up so I can go back to sleep?"

"You're supposed to be asleep already!" Emma said.

"Who can sleep with all this heartbroken yammering?"

"We're not *breaking up*," I said.

"Oh? Could've fooled me."

Emma tossed a wadded-up potato chip bag at Enoch. "Go crawl in a hole."

He snickered and closed his eyes again. He may have gone to sleep, or he may not have. Either way, we no longer felt free to talk. So we just rode, and in lieu of words I reached out my hand, and Emma took it, our hands clasped awkwardly below the gearshift, fingers interlaced and gripping tight, as if we were both afraid to let go.

Emma's words circled in my head. Part of me was grateful for what she'd said, but a bigger part of me wished she hadn't said it at all. There had always been a small, quiet voice inside me that whispered, in dark moments, *She loved him more.* But I had always been able to shut it up, to drown it out. Now Emma had handed it a megaphone. And I would never be able admit it to her, because then she would know I had already been nurturing this little fear, that I was insecure, and that would only make the little voice louder. So I just squeezed her hand and kept driving.

Driving the cool car your grandfather owned, the little voice nagged. *To go on a mission you inherited from him. To prove . . . what?*

That I was as capable and necessary and deserving of respect as he had been.

I had said I didn't want my grandfather's life, and that was true enough. I wanted my own. But I wanted people to *feel* about me the way they did about him. Having named it, I could see how pathetic it was. But giving up and turning back now would be more pathetic still. The only choice, as I saw it, was to succeed at this so much that I broke the mold, won everybody's respect, escaped my grandfather's shadow once and for all, and got the girl—not an echo of the affection she'd felt for Abe, but every last bit of her.

It was a tall order. But at least this time the fate of all peculiardom didn't hang in the balance. Just my relationship and my sense of self-worth.

Ha.

Then Enoch, who had, again, only been pretending to be asleep, said, "After you break up with Emma, can I ride up front? Bronwyn's massive legs are crushing me."

"I'm going to kill him," Emma said. "Actual murder."

Enoch sat forward. Put a hand to his heart, feigning shock. "Oh my God. You're not going to do it, are you, Jacob?"

"Mind your own damn business," I said.

"Grow a spine, man. The girl's still in love with your grandfather."

"You don't know what you're talking about," Emma said loudly enough to wake up Bronwyn and Millard.

"Then who were you saying *I love you* to on the phone yesterday, if not Abe?"

"What?" I said, swiveling in my seat to look at Emma. "What phone?"

She was staring a hole through her lap.

"The one around the back of that filling station in 1965," said Enoch. "Uh-oh! You didn't tell him, did you?"

"That was a private conversation," Emma muttered.

We were about to pass an exit, and I swung the car off the highway at the last possible moment.

"Whoa!" said Bronwyn. "Don't kill us!"

I pulled off the side of the road, parked, got out, and walked away from the car without looking back. There was a freeway overpass nearby and I stalked into the shadows beneath it, shuffling through a tide of trash thrown from passing cars. It sounded like an ocean under there.

"I should've told you." It was Emma, coming up behind me.

I kept walking. She followed.

"I'm sorry, Jacob. I'm sorry. I had to hear his voice one last time."

She had talked to his past self, some long-ago looped version of him from the days when he was merely middle-aged.

"You don't think I wish *I* could talk to him? Every day?"

"You know it's not the same."

"You're right, it's not. He was your boyfriend. You loved him. But that man *raised* me. He meant more to me than my own father. And I loved him more than you did." I was shouting to be heard above the echoing roar of traffic. "So you don't get to do this. You don't get to make secret phone calls to past-Abe when I've been *dying* to talk to him again. You don't get to tell me I don't understand what it's like to miss someone or to be angry he left you behind and kept secrets from you. Because I do know what that's like."

"Jacob, I—"

"And you don't get to tell me you love me, and tell me we're going to be together, and flirt with me and be cute and sweet and strong and amazing and all the wonderful things that you are and then be heartsick about him and tell him you love him behind my back!"

"I was saying goodbye. That's all."

"But you kept it a secret. That's the worst part."

"I was going to talk to you about it," she said "but we're always surrounded by other people."

"How can I believe you?"

"I wanted to. I did. It was eating a hole in me. But I didn't know how."

"You just say it: I still love him! I can't get him out of my mind! You're just a pale imitation of him, but you'll do in a pinch!"

Her eyes got wide. "No, no, no. Don't say that. That's not what you are at all. At *all*."

"That's how it feels. Isn't that why you came along on this mission with me?"

"What," she said, voice rising to a shout, "are you *talking* about?"

"Aren't you just living out some old fantasy? Trying to make up for feeling left behind all those years? Here's your chance to finally go on a mission with Abe—or the next best thing."

"Now *you're* not being fair!"

"Oh no?"

"NO!" she shouted, spinning away from me just as a little ball of flame escaped from her clenched fists and sprayed across the ground, catching a few fast-food wrappers and a filthy old sweater on fire.

She turned slowly back to face me. "That isn't why," she said, speaking slowly, deliberately. "I came along because this meant a lot to *you*. Because I wanted to help *you*. It had nothing whatsoever to do with him."

"The grass is catching on fire."

We ran to stomp it out, and when we had—our ankles and shoes covered with kicked dirt—she said, "I should've listened to my instincts. They said never to come to Florida. Never go to the place where Abe lived. It would feel too much like I was chasing his ghost."

"And is that what you're doing?"

She took a second and really seemed to think it over. "No," she said finally.

"Sometimes it feels like that's what *I'm* doing."

Her face changed. She looked at me with a new openness, and for the first time in minutes she showed a glimmer of vulnerability. "You're not chasing his ghost," she said. "You're standing on his shoulders."

I started to smile, then stopped myself. I wanted to reach for her, but kept my hands in my pockets. Something still felt wrong, and I didn't want to pretend it wasn't there. A moment of shared understanding couldn't fix this.

"If you want me to leave, just say it," she said. "I'll go back to the Acre. There's plenty for me to do there."

I shook my head. "No. I just don't want us to lie to each other. About what we are, or what we're doing."

"Okay." She crossed her arms tightly across her chest. "Then what are we?"

"We're friends."

My body went cold as I said it. But it felt true and right. We were unequal in our feelings for each other, and my only choice was to pull back. We stood there for a long moment, the sound of traffic washing over us in waves, not knowing quite what to do next. And then she put her arms around me and hugged me, and said she was sorry.

I didn't return the hug.

She let go and started back toward the car without me.

◆　　◆　　◆

The others were hungry, so we bought coffee and breakfast sandwiches at a drive-through and then got back on the road. Emma stayed up front next to me, but for a long time we didn't speak to each other. The others didn't know what had happened between us, but they knew *something* had gone down, and even Enoch was smart enough not to mention it again.

Emma and I seemed to agree, without needing to discuss it, that we wouldn't talk about our personal issues in front of the others. We wouldn't argue. We would be professional. We would finish the mission. And when it was over, maybe we wouldn't see each other for a while.

I tried not to think about it. I tried to lose myself in the rhythm of the road. But the hurt was always there, throbbing just above the threshold of ignorability, painful enough to distract me a little at all times.

We began to hit the big cities of the East Coast, Washington, DC, first among them. One of the maps Abe and I had made when I was younger covered this part of the Northeast Corridor and his obscure markings were scribbled all over it. Some roads on the map were crosshatched, others reinforced with parallel lines. Surrounding each city were clusters of symbols: dotted lines in a pyramid, a spiral inside a triangle. It was clear that each corresponded to a location of importance to Abe and H and the other hunters, but whether they indicated something helpful or dangerous, we didn't know.

As we were driving around the DC Beltway, we came very close to one such oddly marked place, and we debated stopping to check it out.

"Could be a safe house," said Millard. "Or a murder den. No way of knowing."

"All these marks could be different loops," said Bronwyn.

"Or different girlfriends," said Enoch.

Emma gave him a bloodthirsty stare.

And then my phone rang. It took me a moment to excavate it from beneath a layer of napkins and cold french fries on the center console.

On the screen it said ME, which meant someone was calling from my house's landline.

"Answer it!" said Bronwyn.

"No, no, no, not a good idea," I said, thinking it must be Miss Peregrine again, and I tried to hit MUTE but fumbled and accidentally answered the call.

"Crap!"

"Hello? Jacob?"

It was Horace, not Miss Peregrine. I put the call on speaker.

"Horace?"

"We're all here," said Millard.

"Oh, thank God," Horace said. "I was afraid you were all dead!"

"What?" said Emma. "Why?"

"I, uh . . . never mind."

He'd had a dream, clearly, but didn't want to freak us out by describing it.

"Is that them?" I heard Olive say. "When are they coming back?"

"Never!" said Enoch, yelling into the phone.

"Don't listen to him," said Millard. "We're driving now. We'll be back as soon as we can. A few more days, at the most."

It was a guess, but it would've been mine, too. How long could it take to find a peculiar at a high school, take her somewhere else, then drive home? A few days sounded reasonable.

"Listen," said Horace. "Miss P is hopping mad. We tried to cover for you as long as we could, but Claire slipped up and told her the truth, and now she's gunning for you. Absolutely livid."

"Is that why you're calling?" I said. "We knew she'd be mad."

"Do me a favor," said Horace. "If she asks, tell her we all told you *not* to do it, and you didn't listen."

"You better come home right away," said Olive.

"We can't," said Bronwyn. "We're on a mission."

"When she finds out what we've been up to, I'm certain she'll understand," said Millard.

"I'm not so sure," said Olive. "She turns a funny color whenever your names come up."

"Where is she now?" I asked.

"Out looking for you," said another voice. "This is Hugh, incidentally."

Now I was imagining them all crowded around the receiver in my parents' room, listening with their heads together.

"Hi, Hugh," said Emma. "Where's Miss P looking for us?"

"She didn't say. She just told us not to leave the house or we'd be grounded forever, then flew off."

"Grounded, my buttock!" said Enoch. "You can't let her treat you like babies."

"Easy for you to say," said Hugh. "You're out there having adventures while we're here with a steaming-mad headmistress. We got a four-hour lecture last night—which was meant for *you*—about responsibility and honor and trust and on and on until I thought my head would fall off."

"It's not all fun and games, you know," said Bronwyn. "Adventuring is a real pain. We haven't slept or showered or eaten properly since we left, and we nearly got shot in Florida and Enoch is starting to smell like a wet dog."

Enoch sneered. "At least I don't *look* like one."

"That still sounds better than being stuck here," said Horace. "Anyway, please be safe and come back alive. And I realize this will sound strange, but in the process of your adventuring, please remember—Chinese restaurants *good*, Continental cuisine *bad*."

"What is that supposed to mean?" asked Emma.

"What is 'Continental cuisine,' even?" I said.

"It was part of a dream I had," said Horace. "All I know is, it's important."

We said we would remember, and then Horace and Olive said goodbye. Before he hung up, Hugh asked us if we had heard anything about Fiona during our travels.

I looked at Emma, who looked as ashamed as I suddenly felt.

"Not yet," Emma said. "But we'll keep asking, Hugh. Everywhere we go."

"Okay," he said softly. "Thanks." And he hung up.

I put the phone down. Emma turned and grimaced at the back seat.

"Don't look at me that way," said Enoch. "Fiona was a wonderful, sweet girl. But she is dead, and if Hugh can't accept that, it isn't our fault."

"We should still have asked," said Bronwyn. "We could have asked at the Flamingo hotel, and in Portal . . ."

"We'll ask from now on," I said. "And if it turns out she really is dead, at least we can say we did right by Hugh."

"Agreed," said Emma.

"Agreed," said Bronwyn.

"Eh," said Enoch.

"Shall we discuss our plan?" said Millard, who excelled at changing the subject when things got too emotional.

"Jolly good idea," said Enoch. "I didn't realize we had one."

"We're going to the school," Bronwyn said. "To find a peculiar person who's in danger, and help them."

"That's right. I forgot, we already have an excellent, detailed plan. What was I thinking?"

"I can tell now when you're using sarcasm," said Bronwyn. "And you are. Right?"

"Not at all!" Enoch said sarcastically. "It'll be dead simple. We walk into this school we've never been to and ask everyone we meet, 'Say, do you children know any peculiar people? Anyone around here manifest any peculiar abilities lately?' And, sooner or later, we'll find them."

Bronwyn was shaking her head. "Enoch, that sounds like a *bad* plan."

"He's being sarcastic," said Millard.

"You said you weren't!" said Bronwyn, looking hurt.

Morning rush hour was beginning to congest the highway. A semi truck merged in front of me and I had to slow down suddenly, and then it belched a cloud of black fumes all over us. Millard and I started coughing. I rolled up my window.

"And where are we supposed to take this peculiar, exactly?" asked Enoch.

Emma unfolded the mission report. "Loop ten thousand forty-four," she read.

"And where is that?" said Bronwyn.

"We don't know yet," Emma replied.

Bronwyn buried her face in her hands. "Oh, this isn't going to work, is it? And Miss Peregrine's never going to forgive us, and it will have all been for nothing!"

A moment ago she had been convinced it would be easy, and now she had lost all hope.

"You're getting overwhelmed," said Emma. "Big tasks always seem that way if you try and figure out every little piece of them beforehand. We have to take it bit by bit."

"It's like that old saying," said Millard. "About eating a grimbear?"

"That's *revolting*," Bronwyn said into her hands.

"It's just a metaphor. Nobody actually eats grimbears."

"I bet someone does," said Enoch. "Do you think they grill them or just eat them raw?"

"Shut up," Emma said. "You do it one bite at a time, that's how. So let's concentrate on the next bite, and then we'll worry about the one after that. We'll find the peculiar. *Then* we'll worry about finding the loop. Okay?"

Bronwyn raised her head and peeked at Emma through her fingers. "Can we use a different metaphor?"

Emma laughed. "Sure."

After a while rush hour began to ease its grip on us. Then we were free of traffic and hurtling toward Philadelphia, and after that New York, and all the unknowns waiting for us there. We sank into silence, contemplating the next bite.

CHAPTER THIRTEEN

$\mathscr{I}$ had done and been through a lot of crazy things that summer, but driving into New York City for the first time ranked among the most intense. It was a stressful blur of honking cars and changing lanes and suffocating tunnels and vertiginous bridges. My friends were shouting at me to watch out for this or that hazard while I white-knuckled the wheel and sweat pooled in the small of my back. Somehow, after countless near-collisions and missed turns, the directions provided by the unflappably bland robot voice from my phone got us to within a block of our destination: J. Edgar Hoover High School. I didn't know New York geography well at all—I had only been there once, as a young kid, on a trip with my parents—but Hoover High wasn't near any landmarks I recognized from TV or the movies. This was Brooklyn, not Manhattan, and not even one of the "hipster" neighborhoods of Brooklyn I'd heard about. This was like a dingier, more crowded version of suburbia, with smaller, older houses packed tight together and cars jamming the sides of the streets.

We found the school easily enough. It was an imposing, block-long edifice of brick punctuated now and then by windows, the kind of place that could have been a minimum-security prison or a wastewater treatment plant or any number of institutions, but in this case housed a few thousand impressionable young minds. In other words, it looked a lot like the high school I attended in Florida, and the thought of going in gave me pit sweats.

It was the middle of the afternoon. We parked across the

street and sat watching the building from the car, debating our first move.

"So, how's that detailed plan of ours shaping up?" asked Enoch.

"Perhaps we just go inside and have a look round," said Millard. "See if anyone catches our eye."

"Thousands of kids go to this school," I said. "I don't think we're going to find the peculiar one just by looking."

"We don't know until we've tired," Millard said, and then he yawned. "I mean, tried."

"I'm tired, too," said Bronwyn. "My brain feels like mush."

"Mine too," I said.

Bronwyn offered me the thermos of coffee Paul had given us—still half full but long since cold—but I couldn't stomach it. I was both wired and tired, and coffee was just making me jittery. We'd been going nonstop for over twenty-four hours, and I was starting to come apart at the seams.

We heard the school bell ring. Thirty seconds later its front doors flung open and students began to flood outside. In seconds the courtyard was filled with teenagers.

"Here's our chance," said Bronwyn. "Any of them look peculiar?"

A boy with a purple mohawk walked by us on the sidewalk, followed by a girl in drop-crotch pants and paisley combat boots and a hundred other kids with their own quirks of style and dress.

"Yeah," Emma said. "All of them."

"It's useless anyway," said Enoch. "If the person we're looking for is in danger, then they're scared, and if they're scared, they're going to try and blend in, not stand out."

"Ah, so we're looking for someone who seems *suspiciously* normal," said Bronwyn. "*Too* normal."

"No, you idiot, I meant we're not going to find them by looking *at all*. Any other ideas?"

We scanned the masses as they streamed past for another minute, but it was clear that Enoch was right. It would be like finding a needle in a haystack.

"Maybe we should, I don't know, *ask* people," said Emma.

Enoch laughed. "Yes, excuse me, we were looking for someone with strange powers or abilities? Or perhaps an extra mouth in the back of their head?"

"You know who would know?" I said. "Abe."

Enoch rolled his eyes. "He's dead, remember?"

"But he left us a how-to guide. Or the closest thing we're going to get to one." I reached under Emma's legs and pulled Abe's operations log from the footwell.

"Perhaps you're onto something," said Millard. "That's every mission he and H ran for thirty-five years. They had to have been in situations like this. We'll just find out what *they* did."

"And we'll come back tomorrow, when we've had some rest," I said. Forget the needle—at that moment I wouldn't have been able to find the haystack.

"Excellent plan," said Emma. "If I don't get some sleep soon, I may start hallucinating."

"Someone's coming!" hissed Bronwyn.

I looked out my window to see a trim white man walking toward the car. He wore a black polo shirt tucked into khaki pants, plastic mirrored sunglasses, and held a walkie-talkie in one hand. He was a classic vice-principal type.

"Names!" he barked.

"Hi there," I said, calm and friendly.

"What are your names?" he repeated, humorless. "Let me see your driver's license."

"We don't go to school here, so we don't have to tell you," said Bronwyn.

Enoch's face fell into his hands. "You *idiot*."

The man bent to peer inside the car and raised his walkie-talkie.

"Base, this is perimeter, I've got some unknown youths here," and then he walked around the back of the car and started reading off the license plate number.

I started the car and gave it a little gas at the same time, which made the engine bark loudly enough that the man jumped and stumbled backward. (It was a trick I was coming to depend on.) Before he could regain his footing, I pulled away from the curb.

"He gave me a bad feeling," said Emma.

"Most vice principals do," I said.

But then I got a sudden, sharp pain in my stomach. As I turned the corner and drove down the long side of the school, I clenched my jaw and hunched forward, trying to hide it from the others.

I wondered, could it have been a hollowgast? Was that the danger this uncontacted peculiar was in?

Then the pain subsided, vanishing just as quickly as it had come, and I decided, for the time being, to keep those thoughts to myself.

*　　*　　*

We found a place to rest our heads by looking through the stack of postcards I'd brought from home—the ones Abe had sent me during his later-life travels. I remembered having seen one from the New York area, and when we'd put a few miles between us and the school, I parked the car and looked through the stack to find it. On the picture side was a very dated, exceedingly bland photo of a hotel room, and on the back was the hotel's name, address, and a short note from Abe to me, postmarked nine years ago.

> *Looks like I'll be staying here a few days, just*
> *Outside of NYC. Nice, quiet place, great amenities. I'm seeing*
> *Old friends. If you ever come to New York, I recommend this*
> *Particular hotel. Ask for room 203. Much love, Grandpa*

"Notice anything about his note?" Millard said.

"It's a bit random," said Emma. "Why did he bother saying what room he stayed in?"

"It's the simplest code there is. An acrostic."

"A what?" I said.

"Read the first letter of each line. What does it spell?"

I squinted at it. "L-O-O-P."

"Oh my wow *goodness*," Bronwyn said, leaning forward to look.

"He was leaving you coded messages," said Millard. "Good old Abe, looking out for you even beyond the grave."

I shook my head, amazed, turning the postcard over in my hands. "*Thanks, Grandpa,*" I said quietly.

"But we don't need to stay in loops," said Emma. "We're not running from hollows, we're not in danger of aging forward, and it could be more trouble than it's worth."

"Yes, you do meet some strange people in loops," said Bronwyn, "and I don't mean to be antisocial, but I just want to sleep."

"I think we should give it a try," said Millard. "We need to find out where loop ten thousand forty-four is, and perhaps someone there will know."

Enoch sighed. "As long as it's got a bed. My neck is half broken from trying to sleep in this car."

I wanted to go, and so I cast the deciding vote. It was mostly out of curiosity, and I liked the feeling that I was following in Abe's footsteps. So we drove through Brooklyn and crossed a giant, double-decked suspension bridge to Staten Island. Within twenty minutes we had arrived at the place, a motel called The Falls. It was a shabby two-level building with rooms that opened onto a busy street and a sign that boasted TV IN EVERY ROOM.

We went into the office and asked for room 203. The clerk was tall and gangly and had his legs propped up on his desk. He wore a heavy wool sweater even though it was hot outside. He put down the magazine he'd been reading and studied us.

"Why do you want that room?"

"It was highly recommended," I said.

He took his feet off the desk. "What clan you with?"

"Miss Peregrine's," said Bronwyn.

"Never heard of it."

"Then, none."

"You must not be from around here."

"Isn't that the point of a hotel?" said Emma. "To accommodate people who don't live nearby?"

"Look, usually we only rent to people who are clan-affiliated, but we're almost empty, so I'll make an exception. I'll just have to see some proof of identification first."

"Sure," I said, starting to get out my wallet.

"Not like that," he said. "I mean, *proof*."

"I think he means proof that we're peculiar," said Millard. He lifted a business card holder on the front desk, twirled it in the air, and set it down again. "Invisible here, hello!"

"That'll do," the clerk said. "What type of room you want?"

"We don't care," Enoch said, "we just want to sleep." But the clerk was already pulling a laminated binder out from under the desk. He set it down, opened it, and began to list the options.

"Now, of course there's your standard room—nice, but nothing fancy—but what we're famous for are the special accommodations we offer our peculiar guests. We have a room for the gravitationally challenged." He flipped to a picture of a smiling family posing in a room that had all its furniture bolted to the ceiling. "The floaters love it. They can relax, dine, even sleep in total comfort without need of weighted garments or belts."

He turned to a picture of a girl in bed with a wolf, both of them in nightclothes. "There's pet-friendly rooms where peculiar animals of most persuasions are welcome, so long as they're house-trained, under a hundred pounds, and are certified nonlethal."

He flipped another page to a photo of what looked like a nicely furnished underground bunker. "And we have a special room for our, eh, *combustible* guests." He flicked his eyes to Emma. "So they don't burn down the rest of the property in their sleep."

Emma looked offended. "I never combust spontaneously. And we don't have pets, and we don't float."

The clerk wasn't done. "We also have a room filled with nice, loamy soil for guests with roots, or the partially dead—"

"We don't need any weird rooms!" Enoch snapped. "A regular one is fine!"

"Suit yourself." The clerk slapped the book shut. "Regular room. Just a few more questions."

Enoch groaned as the clerk began filling out a form.

"Smoking or nonsmoking?"

"None of us smoke cigarettes," Bronwyn said.

"I didn't ask about cigarettes. Do you emit smoke from any part of your body?"

"No."

"Nonsmoking." He checked a box on the form. "Singles or doubles?"

"We'd all like to be together in the same room," said Millard.

"I didn't ask that," the clerk said. "Do any of you *have* doubles? Doppelgängers, replicants, mirror brothers. We'll need an extra deposit and photo ID for each one."

"None," I said.

He marked the form. "How many years will you be staying?"

"How many *years*?"

". . . will you be staying?"

"Just one night," said Emma.

"Extra charge for that," he muttered, marking the form, then looked up. "Right this way."

He slouched out of the office. We followed him down a dingy exterior hall polluted with traffic noise and into a dim utility room. It was a loop entrance. I realized that going in, this time, so I was

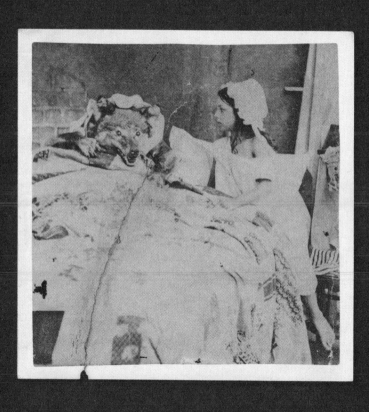

ready for the jolt. When we came out, it was nighttime and cold and very quiet. The clerk walked us back down the hall, which was much tidier in this past version of itself. "It's always nighttime here. Makes it easier for our guests to sleep any time they want."

He stopped at a room and opened the door for us. "Anything you need, I'm just through the loop closet, at the desk where you found me. Ice is down the hall."

He walked away and we went inside. The room looked just like the picture in the postcard my grandfather had sent me. There was a large bed, some terrible curtains, a fat orange TV on a stand, and fake knotted-pine wall panels, the patterns all clashing to create a disharmony that felt almost like noise, a constant undertone buzz that was vaguely unsettling. The room had a fold-out sofa and a double-wide cot, too, so everyone had a place to sleep. We settled in, got comfortable, and then Millard and I climbed onto the fold-out sofa to pore over Abe's logbook.

"Abe and H went on a number of missions which bore some resemblance to ours," said Millard. "It might be instructive to see how they dealt with their challenges."

Luckily, Millard had read the entire thing twice during the long road trip, and his memory for details was so sharp that he had an almost instant recall of vast portions of the log. He turned to a mission report from the early 1960s. Abe and H had been tasked with extracting an endangered peculiar child from a county in the Texas Panhandle, but they didn't know which town the child was in. "And how did they begin their search?" Millard asked, scanning the report. "By blending in with the local populace and talking to people. Before long they heard a traveling carnival was in the area, which, as you know, is just the sort of place peculiars feel comfortable blending in. They caught up with it outside of Amarillo, and found the peculiar child hiding inside a giant cardboard elephant on wheels that traveled with the carnival." The report included a picture of the elephant, and it was indeed enormous, taller than a house. "Can you believe it?" Millard said, laughing. "A Trojan elephant!"

"So they just *asked* people?" said Enoch, who had been listening in. "That was their brilliant detective work?"

"Simple, straightforward detective work," said Millard. "The best kind."

"Okay," I said, "what else did they do?"

"Periodical searches!" he said, weirdly excited. "Here, here." He turned a lot of pages, then landed on the report he was looking for. "There was a young woman rapidly turning invisible. She was uncontacted and, if my own experiences can be brought to bear, almost certainly terrified. Abe's goal was to find her before she could disappear altogether, and bring her into the fold of some benevolent peculiar clan—preferably other invisibles. But it would be difficult; the young woman had fled from every prior attempt at contact."

"And they found her using the newspaper?" I said. "How?"

"They were able to pinpoint her location via headlines in a tabloid. Tabloids can't always be taken seriously, but once in a while they do contain nuggets of truth. See?" He turned the page, and clipped to the backside of the mission log was a photo of a couple of kids on a beach and a newspaper crumpled in the sand. The headline was blurred but partially readable—something about a nude mystery girl.

"Thanks to this ridiculous article," Millard continued, "they were able to track her to a beach town in California, and then to a particular beach. Beaches are terrible places to be invisible, because the sand gives your footsteps away, so they were able to corner her long enough to introduce themselves and explain what was happening to her, and she accepted their offer of help."

"What if there are no newspaper headlines about our subject?" asked Emma. "And nothing so obvious as a carnival in town?"

"What if they're in a school of three thousand kids who *all* look peculiar?" said Enoch.

nk, and left a supernatural stink
e that could only have been a pecul
ll, which nearly overcame us . . .

"In such cases, where there's a known location but no other lead, they would go to the area, blend in, and simply wait for the peculiar to give themselves away somehow."

"A stakeout," I said. "Like in the movies."

"How long do stakeouts take?" Bronwyn asked.

"Weeks, sometimes longer."

"Weeks!" said Enoch. "Longer!"

"We won't need weeks," I said. "We'll go in the school. Talk to people. Ask around. You guys will just have to blend in."

"That'll be a snap, thanks to the extensive and thorough normalling lessons you've given us," said Enoch.

"That was sarcasm!" said Bronwyn.

Enoch pointed at her. "Now you're catching on."

◆　　◆　　◆

If I hadn't been so tired, I'm sure the weirdness of sleeping on the pull-out sofa while Emma lay across the room would've kept me awake half the night. The distance between us felt unnatural, and in the rare moments of quiet we enjoyed, it preoccupied my mind completely. But the instant my head hit the pillow I was unconscious, and it seemed like only minutes had passed when I opened my eyes again to see Bronwyn bending over me, shaking my shoulder. Eight hours had disappeared in a dreamless blip, and though I hardly felt rested, it was already time to get moving again.

School would be starting in a couple of hours, and I wanted us to have the whole day to search. The one time-suck we allowed ourselves to indulge in was showers. Our hair was greasy and we had road dirt in our ears and under our nails. We would be representing all of peculiardom when we introduced ourselves to this person, whoever they were. At the very least, we agreed, we shouldn't look like we'd all been sleeping in a car.

I showered first, then had some time to kill. I decided to do a newspaper search, like Abe and H had done in the case of the invisible girl. Such things were easier now, in the internet age, though I did have to leave the room and go back out of the loop so that my phone would function.

Standing by the ice machine in the hot, noisy present, I conducted a quick search for recent articles that mentioned the school. Within a short time, I found an article in the Brooklyn *Eagle*, dated a few weeks earlier, with the headline BIZARRE POWER OUTAGES MYSTIFY CON EDISON, FRAY NERVES AT HOOVER HIGH. The gist of the story was that, in the middle of a school day, during a presentation in the auditorium, all the lights had gone out. Eight hundred kids had been plunged into sudden blackness, and it had caused such chaos that there was a stampede, which led to injuries.

I thought that seemed strange. What was so terrifying about a blackout? It happened at our school, in lightning-storm-prone Florida, all the time. So I scrolled down to the comments, where actual students had posted, and learned that it was more than just a blackout. The generator-powered emergency lights failed, too. Strangest of all, one commenter wrote: "The flashlight on my cell didn't work, and neither did anyone else's." The lights came on again a few minutes later, but by then the damage had been done.

To me, it sounded like an EMP—an electromagnetic pulse—that had knocked out devices, both electric and battery-powered. But there was another part of the story that didn't fit that theory. Later that same day, there had been an explosion in the girls' bathroom. Except it wasn't exactly an explosion, according to the commenters.

"It looked like a flash bomb had gone off," one person wrote. "The walls were burned and stuff, but nothing was broken."

In other words, there was no blast damage. That meant it wasn't a bomb, or a traditional explosion, or a fire. So what had happened?

Two men were reported injured, both school employees. The suspect in the blast was a female student, whose name wasn't given because she was a minor. She had fled the scene and was being sought for questioning. What had two male employees of the school been doing in the girls' bathroom? The article didn't speculate, but one commenter did:

"PERRRRRRVS!!!!"

I returned to the loop, went back to our room, and told the others what I'd learned.

"Sounds like a peculiar event to me," said Bronwyn.

Emma leaned out of the bathroom door, vigorously drying her hair. "If it is," she said, her voice vibrating as she dried, "then I reckon we're looking for someone who can manipulate electricity."

"Or light," said Millard.

"So we should start by talking to people about that day," I said. "Ask them what they remember and who was involved. High schools are gossip factories. All we have to do is make some fast friends, and tap into people's natural inclination to talk crap about one another."

As I heard myself saying it, it sounded slightly absurd. Fast friends? In two years of high school, I'd had *one*.

"Maybe someone will know who the suspect girl was," said Bronwyn. "The one who ran from the bathroom fire."

"Maybe we can get our hands on the security camera footage," said Enoch.

"Sounds like they're powerful, whoever they are," said Emma.

"Unquestionably," said Millard. He was fully clothed in dress pants, a collared shirt, and a newsboy cap. "If someone is hunting them, they must be worth hunting. So, yes, I'd say they're powerful. And possibly dangerous. If you suspect you've found them, do not engage. Alert the rest of us, and we'll determine the best course of action."

"Why'd you bother getting dressed?" I asked. "We're going back out there in a minute."

"I miss wearing clothes sometimes. Also, chafing becomes an issue."

"Say we've found this person," said Enoch. "Then what? We say, 'Come with us. We need to take you to a time loop.'?"

"Why not?" said Bronwyn.

"Because it sounds *mad*!"

"They're uncontacted, remember," I said. "They won't know what a time loop is, what a peculiar is, that there are other people like them in the world—nothing."

Enoch had just pulled on his creeper sneakers and was rolling his feet around in them. "Ugh, they're so *springy*."

"Jacob didn't know anything when we first met him, and that worked out okay," Bronwyn said.

"I thought I had gone insane," I said, "and then Emma attacked me and nearly cut my throat!"

"I thought you were a wight!" she called from the bathroom.

"So you had a rocky start," Bronwyn said, shrugging. "But now you're in love!"

I pretended to be busy packing my bag. Enoch and Millard ignored her.

Bronwyn looked baffled. "What'd I say?"

Emma came out of the bathroom. Her sandy hair was tied into a loose ponytail. She wore a light green sweater that matched her eyes and dark jeans that fit her, well, perfectly, and contrasted with her Reeboks. The pang of longing I felt in that moment was so deep and sustained that I had to look away.

In a passable American accent, she said, "You guys ready to blend in?"

Bronwyn gave a big thumbs-up. "Flipping *totally*." Her accent was sharp and weird. "Coooooooool, dudes."

Just listening to her set my teeth on edge.

"Maybe you should stick to your regular accent. And no slang."

She pooched out her bottom lip and flipped her thumb downward. "Bummer."

CHAPTER FOURTEEN

*W*e arrived at the school just before first bell. I parked several blocks away to avoid being spotted by an overzealous vice principal. As we walked, I paid close attention to my gut, on alert for any telltale twinges, but there were none.

We joined a mass of students climbing the main steps, then entered a long, bright hallway lined with classrooms and jammed with bodies. We flattened ourselves against a wall to keep from getting trampled and stood there, overwhelmed, as teenagers flowed around us like schools of fish.

We ducked into an empty classroom to talk. There were posters of Shakespeare and James Joyce on the wall and the desks were arranged in rows. I remembered what Emma said about never having attended a real school, and she looked a bit wistful as she took it in.

"I would never normally suggest this," said Millard, "but I think we should split up. We'll attract less attention than we would walking around in a big, baffled clump."

"And we'll cover more area, too," said Emma.

"Then it's decided."

I wasn't sure they were ready to be on their own in a modern American high school, but Millard was right; there was no choice but to dive in. Bronwyn paired off with Enoch and volunteered to observe the PE fields and outdoor areas. They would talk to people (but not in Bronwyn's weird pseudo-American accent) and learn what they could. Being invisible, Millard couldn't talk to anyone, so he would sneak into the main office. "If there was an incident dramatic enough to rate mention in a local newspaper," he said, "then there are certainly records of other, smaller incidents somewhere in their files."

"There might be a disciplinary write-up on this person, too," said Emma.

"Or a psychiatric one," I said. "If they ever tried to tell the truth about what was happening, they at least got sent to the school nurse for a mental health screening."

"Good thinking," said Millard.

That left Emma and me alone together, reluctantly paired. I suggested we go to the cafeteria, always a hotbed of gossip, and she agreed.

"Are you guys sure you'll be okay?" I said before we all split up. "You'll remember not to talk about the 1940s or use your abilities?"

"Yeah, Portman, we've got it," Enoch said, waving his hand at me. "You just worry about you."

"Everyone meet outside this room in one hour," I said. "Anything goes wrong, pull a fire alarm and run for the front entrance. Got it?"

"Got it," said everyone but Millard.

"Millard?" Emma said. "Where are you?"

The classroom door swung shut. He was already gone.

◆　◆　◆

School cafeterias had long ranked among my least favorite places on the planet. They were loud, ugly, they stank, and they were filled— as this one was—with cliques of anxious teenagers swirling around in a complex social dance I could never quite figure out the steps to. And yet here I was, standing against a scuffed linoleum wall with Emma, having volunteered to spend an hour in one. I imagined myself, like I often did in school, as an anthropologist observing the rituals of some alien culture. Emma looked much more at home, even though the room was filled with people eight decades her junior. Her posture was loose. Her eyes coolly scanned the room.

She suggested we join the line for breakfast and sit down to eat.

"To blend in," I said. "Smart."

"Because I'm hungry."

"Right."

We got in line, shuffled past hair-netted cafeteria ladies, and were handed trays piled with rubbery scrambled eggs, scoops of greasy brown sausage-stuff, and boxes of chocolate milk. Emma recoiled a little, but accepted it without complaint. We took our trays and began to circle the room, looking for a place to sit, and at that point my just-talk-to-people plan, which had sounded reasonable in theory, began to seem absurd. What were we supposed to do, introduce ourselves to someone at random? *So, have you noticed anybody strange lately?* Everyone in the room was doing their own thing, talking to other people, locked into long-established friend groups—

"Hi, mind if we sit down? I'm Emma; this is Jacob."

Emma had stopped at a table. Four dumbstruck faces looked up at us—a blond girl whose tray had only an apple on it, a girl with pink-dyed hair poking out from under a beanie, and two sporty-looking guys in baseball hats whose trays were overflowing.

Pink Hair shrugged and said, "Sure."

"*Karen*," the apple girl said under her breath, but then she moved over so I could sit.

We put our trays down and sat. Three of them were looking at us like we were freaks, but Emma didn't even seem to notice. She just dove right in.

"We're new here, and we heard this school was, like, weird."

She sounded practically American, but not quite—and they noticed.

"Where are you from?" Pink Hair said.

"England and Wales, thereabouts."

"That's cool," said one of the hat guys. "I'm from seals. And he's from dolphin."

"It's a country, dumbass," said Pink Hair. "Near England."

"Pss." Hat Guy #1 rolled his neck. "*Duh*."

"We're exchange students," I said.

Apple Girl raised an eyebrow. "*You* don't sound foreign."

"Canada." I was about to dip my plastic spork into the greasy brown stuff, then thought better of it.

"This school is definitely weird," said Pink Hair. "Especially lately."

"What happened with your auditorium?" I asked. "Power outage, or something?"

"Nah." The quieter hat guy was shaking his head. "That's just what the school told our parents."

Apple Girl nodded at him. "Jon was there. He thinks this place is, like, haunted now."

"I do not. I just don't buy this 'power outage' thing. They're covering something up."

"Like what?" I said.

He looked down at his tray. Stirred his brown stuff.

"*He doesn't like talking about it*," Pink Hair whispered. "*He thinks it makes him sound nuts.*"

"Shut *up*, Karen," said Apple Girl. She turned to Jon. "You didn't tell me."

"Come on, man," said the other hat guy. "You tell Karen, but you won't tell us?"

Jon held up his hands. "Fine, fine. And, like, it's not even that this is what *happened*, okay? It's just how it *seemed*."

Everyone was looking at him expectantly. He drew in a deep breath.

"It was super dark. Nobody's phones or flashlights were working. They say it was some kind of electrical thing. But there's one door in the auditorium that leads straight outside, to the faculty parking lot?" He leaned forward slightly, his voice dropping. "Someone opened it. But it barely gave off any light. And it was sunny that day."

"What?" said Apple Girl. "I don't get it."

"It was like"—his voice dropped even more—"the dark was *eating* the light."

I was about to bring up the not-quite explosion in the bathroom that had happened later that same day when I felt a hard tap on my shoulder. I turned to see the vice-principal-ish man from yesterday and a frowning woman with short hair and cold blue eyes.

"Excuse me," said the man. "I need you both to come with us."

Emma held up one hand and turned away. "Go away, we're in the middle of a conversation."

The kids at our table looked impressed. "*Damn*," whispered Pink Hair.

"That wasn't a request." The cold-eyed lady grabbed Emma's shoulder.

Emma shrugged her hand off. "Don't touch me!"

Then things got ugly. It seemed like everyone in the cafeteria had stopped talking to stare at us. The lady went for Emma with both hands, and the man grabbed my arm. I flipped my tray of food at the man, who let me go long enough for me to jump up from the table, and Emma must have burned the lady because she shouted and leapt backward. And then we were running, together, toward the closest exit. The lady was down for the count, but the man was chasing us and shouting for other people to help stop us. A few tried, but we dodged them. Then, up ahead, a half-dozen athletes in basketball shirts blocked the exit we were running toward.

We stopped short of them and faced off.

"What now?" I said.

"We burn our way through," Emma said, but I caught her hands before she could raise them.

"*Don't*," I hissed. I could see people aiming their phones at us, recording everything. "Not while everyone's looking."

I resigned myself to getting caught and started thinking of ways to talk our way out of this, but then the exit doors burst open behind the athletes. A throng of girls ran in screaming bloody murder. And I mean *screaming*—their faces contorted with horror and streaked with tears—and the focus of the athletes and the vice principal-ish man and the whole room shifted immediately to them. I didn't even think about what might have made them scream like that; I just thanked the angels that it had happened. Emma and I plowed through the distracted jocks and out the open doors.

We skidded to a stop in the hallway, looking around and trying to remember which way the main entrance was, when I caught sight of something bizarre running down the hall toward us.

A pack of cats.

They were dripping wet and lurching in a stiff, very un-catlike way, and then I heard Enoch cackling and Bronwyn yelling as she chased him out of a science lab across the hall. He was doubled over laughing.

"I'm sorry! I couldn't resist!"

As the cats wobbled around our legs, a bitter smell hit my nose—formaldehyde.

"Enoch, you *idiot*!" Bronwyn was shouting. "You've ruined everything!"

He had created perhaps the only distraction powerful enough to save us: a herd of zombie cats.

"I never thought I'd say this," Emma said, "but thank the birds for that little weirdo."

The yelling in the cafeteria seemed to be dying down. It wouldn't be long before all those people remembered to chase us.

"We'll thank him later," I said, and I ran to the wall and pulled the fire alarm.

✦   ◆   ✦

"You turned them into *zombies*?"

Emma was trying to seem angry, but was closer to laughing. We were in the courtyard, hidden for the moment among a surge of evacuating high school students.

"It was such a waste of dead cats!" said Enoch. "They were just going to slice them up."

"For *science*," Bronwyn said.

"Sure." Enoch made air quotes with his fingers. "*Science*."

"You were supposed to be in the PE fields," I said.

"Nobody would talk to us," said Enoch.

"To *you*, you mean," said Bronwyn. "And he got bored and wandered off."

"I smelled sweet, sweet embalming fluid wafting through an open window, and I couldn't help myself . . ."

I nearly gagged.

"Lucky for you, I actually accomplished something while he was playing with dead animals," said Bronwyn. "I spoke to a very helpful young man who was in the school when the bathroom fire happened. He said there was a loud sound and a bright light, and he saw a girl running through the hall afterward, chased by a couple of adults."

"What did they look like?" I said.

"The girl had brown skin and long dark hair, and the adults had red skin from burns and their clothes were smoking, and they were *really* mad."

"Did they get her?" I asked.

"No. She got away."

"What was her name?" I asked.

Bronwyn shook her head. "I don't know."

I felt a hard tug at my sleeve. "*There you are!*" It was Millard, whispering because we were among so many normals. "I've been looking all over for you. Damn difficult. Some dolt pulled the fire alarm!"

"That was us," Emma said. "We needed to get out of there."

"We still do," I said. At several points around the courtyard and the front steps were administrator types in polo shirts scanning the crowd, looking for us.

The fire alarm stopped ringing, and a voice came over the PA system telling everyone to go back to class.

"Let's go, *now*," I said. "While we still have all these people for cover."

"Split up," Emma said. She pointed across the street. "Meet over there, behind those cars."

We divided, walked quickly out of the courtyard and across the street, and reconvened behind the row of parked cars Emma had indicated. The others crouched while I kept watch for adults in polo shirts.

"Now, listen," Emma said. "Jacob and I found something out, too."

"So did I," said Millard. "I didn't have any luck with the files and records, but I got to talking with a sweet young woman in the school office—"

"You *talked* to someone?" I said. "Do *none* of you care if we're exposed as peculiar?"

"I'm a great deal more suave than anyone gives me credit for being," Millard said. "Really, there's no need for hysterics."

"So you talked to someone," Bronwyn said.

"Yes! A rather lovely young lady who I believe knows our subject—and where to find her."

"Okay, where?" Emma said.

"I didn't want to push too hard. The subject is a friend of hers. She knows the subject is in danger, and she's understandably protective. I was gradually earning her trust when the blasted fire alarm sounded."

"So go back in there and finish earning her trust," Enoch said.

"We made arrangements to meet later. She wasn't entirely comfortable discussing the matter on school grounds, anyway."

"I can't *believe* you talked to someone," said Emma, shaking her head.

"I wasn't seen, I assure you," Millard huffed. "Does no one have any faith in old Nullings?"

The girl had agreed to meet Millard at a café after school ended. We had a few hours to kill, so we hiked back to the car, got in, and discussed what to do next. Bronwyn wanted to see the sights.

"We're in New York! We should see the Liberty Statue! And other touristical things!"

"We're on a mission," I said. "No way."

"So? Hollow-hunters never had fun on a mission?"

"If they did," said Millard, "they never mentioned it in the operations log."

Bronwyn crossed her arms and sulked. I didn't care. Even if we'd had time to go to the Statue of Liberty, I wouldn't have had the bandwidth to enjoy it. Bronwyn had this way of compartmentalizing experiences and setting stressful things aside, but I was too preoccupied with finding the girl and persuading her to accept our help. But even if we managed to do both, we still didn't know where this loop ten thousand forty-four was. I understood why so many things had to be veiled in secrets and written in code, but I wished, just this once, that H could have just told me what to do and where to go in plain English.

"What do we think this loop number means?" I said.

We were sitting in the car, trying to figure out our next move.

"Are all loops in America numbered?" Enoch asked. "If they are, we just need a directory of the numbers."

"That would be nice, but we don't have one," I said. "What we have are the documents I brought from home."

I fished them out of my duffel bag, and the others helped me look through them for anything I might've missed. We searched for the number 10044 on the handmade maps, the postcards from Abe, and on every page of the operations log. After an hour, my eyes were starting to cross and some of us were yawning. Even though we'd gotten eight hours of sleep the night before, it had barely made a dent in our exhaustion. I fell asleep with the operations log in my lap and my head on the steering wheel.

I woke with a crick my neck to Bronwyn yelling at Enoch.

"Now I'll have to launder my clothes!" she was saying. "It's *disgusting*!"

Before I could ask what she meant, I smelled it for myself—formaldehyde. Earlier I'd been too exhausted to notice, but Enoch stank of it, and now that we'd been shut in the car with him for a few hours, we did, too.

"We must find a restroom where we can wash and you all can change clothes," Millard said. He sounded panicked.

We'd been asleep for a couple of hours, and there wasn't much time left before we were supposed to meet Millard's contact. He gave me the name of the café. I typed it into my phone.

"It's only a mile away," I said. "We'll be there in plenty of time."

"I hope so," he said. "First impressions are everything!"

"Wow, you must really fancy her," Enoch said. "Caring how you smell? That's almost love."

I started the engine and pulled away from the curb. Only then, as I was about to merge onto a busy road, did Millard say, very casually, "By the way, while you were sleeping I deduced the location of loop ten thousand forty-four."

"What?" I said. "Really?"

He held up one of Abe's postcards. I could only glance at it, but on the front was an illustration of an enormous bridge that spanned a river and a long, skinny island, which looked even narrower than

Needle Key. I came to a stoplight, which gave me a chance to look a little closer. Written across the top was *Queensboro Bridge and Blackwell's Island, New York City.*

"Blackwell's Island," I said. "Never heard of it."

"Read the back." Millard flipped the postcard over.

I started to read aloud the note from my grandfather, but Millard said, "No, here. The postmark, Jacob."

The postmark was a bit smudged and incompletely stamped, but you could just make out the date—twelve years ago—and at the bottom of the little black circle, a number.

10044.

"I'll be damned," I said.

I passed the card to my friends in the back, who were clamoring to have a look. With one hand on the wheel and the other gripping my phone, I thumb-typed a search for the number 10044. Right away, a map popped up: a red line drawn around a long, skinny island in the middle of the East River, between Manhattan and Queens.

The loop number wasn't a secret code at all. It was a zip code.

◆   ◆   ◆

We drove the rest of the way to the café with the windows down to air the formaldehyde smell out the car, then freshened up in the bathroom of a fast-food restaurant. Millard cleaned himself from head to toe with faucet water and soap from the hand dispenser, and when he was feeling sufficiently presentable—which I found funny, considering his condition—we walked to the café. It was a dark, cozy place that felt like someone's living room, with old couches and Christmas lights strung between rafters and a bar at one end where a big coffee grinder was whirring away. The room was half empty, and I noticed the girl immediately, sitting at a table in the corner. She had wavy brown hair and wore a black beret and army pants. An

QUEENSBORO BRIDGE AND BLACKWELL'S ISLAND, NEW YORK CITY.

arty type, I thought. She was nursing a giant coffee and listening to something on her phone with one earbud. When we came through the door, her head cocked in our direction.

Millard led us over to the table.

"Lilly?"

"Millard," she said, and looked up—but not quite *at*—Millard.

"These are my friends," Millard said. "The ones I was telling you about."

We traded hellos and sat down. I was trying to figure out why she didn't seem perturbed that a voice was emanating from thin air.

"What are you listening to?" Millard asked her.

"See for yourself."

The second earbud, which had been lying on the table, began to float as Millard inserted it into his ear. While he listened, two things came to my attention: the thin white cane that was leaning against her chair, and Lilly's eyes, which never came to rest on any of our faces.

Emma nudged me and we traded surprised looks.

"He did say he hadn't been seen," she murmured.

"Ahh!" Millard said, with what must have been a look of rapture. "I haven't heard this piece in years. Segovia, yes?"

"Very good!" said Lilly.

"That," Millard said, "is one of the greatest pieces of music ever written."

"It's not every day that I meet another classical guitar geek. Nobody my age knows anything about real music."

"Me, neither. And I'm ninety-seven."

Emma scowled at Millard and mouthed, *WHY?*

Lilly chuckled and ran her fingers along Millard's forearm. "Pretty smooth skin for a nonagenarian."

"The body is young, but the soul . . ."

"I know *exactly* what you mean," she said.

It was starting to feel like we were intruding on a date.

"Hey," Enoch more or less shouted, "you're *blind*!"

At which Lilly burst out laughing. "Uh, yeah."

"Oh, shut *up*, Enoch," said Bronwyn.

"Millard, you old dog!" said Enoch, laughing.

"I must apologize," said Millard. "There's something the matter with Enoch's brain. Whatever enters it slips out instantly through his mouth."

"You okay, Lil?" the barista called over.

Lilly flashed him an okay sign. "All good, Ricko."

"They know you here," I said.

"It's practically my second home," Lilly said. "I have a standing gig every Thursday night. Pop and jazz, though. No Segovia." She nodded to a guitar case propped nearby, then shrugged. "I guess the world isn't ready." Her expression changed suddenly. Hardened a bit, as if she had remembered something unpleasant. "Millard says you're looking for someone."

"We're looking for the girl who . . . who burned those two men," said Bronwyn.

Lilly's face soured. "They attacked *her*. She was just defending herself."

"I didn't mean to say otherwise."

"Hell of a defense," said Enoch.

"They deserved worse," Lilly answered.

"Can you tell us where she is?" Emma asked.

Our questions were making Lilly tense. "Why do you care about Noor? You don't even know her."

Noor. Her name was Noor.

"We can help her," said Bronwyn.

"I'm not sure I believe you, and that doesn't answer my question."

"We understand a little about what she's going through," I said, hoping I could approach the truth without going all the way to it.

"Okay." Lilly took a sip of her coffee. Swirled it a little. "What's she going through?"

I traded a glance with Emma. How much could we say? Even if we could trust Lilly, what would she believe?

"Something's happening to her that she doesn't know how to make sense of," said Bronwyn.

"And she can't go to her parents about it," I added.

"Foster parents," Lilly said.

"It might be affecting her body," said Emma. "Changing it."

"There could be people watching her," said Millard. "People she doesn't know. And it's frightening."

"You're describing the experience of almost every teenage girl," said Lilly.

"And," I said, leaning toward her and lowering my voice, "she can do things other people can't. Things that don't seem possible."

"Powerful, dangerous things," Millard added.

Lilly was still for a moment. Then she said very quietly, "Yes."

"We know what she's going through because we've all been through it ourselves," Emma said. "Each of us in our own way."

And then we told her, one by one, the peculiar things we could do. She listened quietly, nodding, saying very little. She did not seem frightened. She did not run away.

Millard was the last to speak. I could sense his reluctance. That he liked this girl was obvious, and he didn't want to let go of the fantasy he'd been entertaining for the last few hours, in which he was just a normal guy who maybe, maybe had a chance with her.

"And I, my dear—this is Millard speaking—I regret to inform you that, well, like my friends here, I, too, am not *completely* normal . . ."

Enoch shook his head. "Ugh, this is painful."

"It's all right, Millard," said Lilly. "I know."

"You do?"

"You're invisible."

I couldn't see Millard's expression, but I could guess at it—eyes wide, mouth hanging open.

"How—how did you—"

"I'm not *completely* blind," she said. "A lot of blind people have a little bit of vision. I have about ten percent. Not enough to get by without this cane, but more than enough to tell when a voice is talking to me out of thin air! I gotta say, at first I thought I was losing it, but when you started asking me about Noor, it all began to make sense."

"I hardly know what to say," said Millard.

"I knew Noor couldn't be the only one."

"My dear, why didn't you say something?" Millard said.

"I wanted to see if you'd admit it." Lilly smiled. "I'm glad you did."

"I feel so silly," said Millard. "I hope you don't think me a cad."

"Not at all," said Lilly. "You've got to be careful, I'm sure. But so do I." She lowered her voice. "You're not the only people looking for her, you know."

"Who else is?" I asked. "Police?"

"No. I'm not sure who they are. They came to her house, and to school, asking questions."

"What do they look like?" I said.

"She's *blind*," said Enoch.

"Yes, you keep pointing that out," said Lilly. "They're the people who came after Noor at school, after what happened with the lights in the auditorium. They cornered her in the bathroom, and she was forced to defend herself."

My mind went right to the vice principal-ish man and his cold-eyed companion. Could they have been peculiar? Or wights, even?

"Noor says they drive SUVs with the windows blacked out," Lilly went on. "They pose as authority figures. Cops, social workers, school faculty. She can't trust adults at all anymore." Lilly looked pained. "She's the strongest person I know. And I've never seen her so scared of anything."

"We were sent here to help her," Emma said. "I think we're supposed to protect her from those people."

"So, you told me what you can do," she said, "but who *are* you?"

"We're Miss Peregrine's peculiar children," said Bronwyn.

"You know what," said Enoch. "That doesn't sound quite right anymore."

"We don't know what we're called yet," I said. "But my grandfather was in . . . sort of like the FBI, for people like us? And we're taking over."

"Oddfellows," said Lilly. "The Oddfellows . . . League of . . . Defense."

"It spells O-L-D," said Bronwyn.

"Did she just make up a name for us?" said Bronwyn. "On the spot?"

"I like it," said Millard.

"Of course you do," said Enoch.

"If we can't find your friend and help her, we won't need a fancy name," said Emma. "We'll be back in the Acre getting punished for the rest of our natural lives."

"Can you take us to her?" I asked.

"She's in hiding," said Lilly. "But I can send her a message to ask if she'll meet you."

Just then, through the café's front window, I saw a black-tinted SUV roll by very slowly. The passenger window was rolled down a few inches, and inside I could see someone in mirrored glasses, scanning the neighborhood.

"We'd better make a move," I said. "Is there a back way out of here?"

"I'll show you, but first I need to text Noor," said Lilly. "Which means talking loudly into my phone's speech-to-text app. Considering the subject matter, I think I'd better do it in private."

"May I be of help?" asked Millard, scooting his chair back.

Someone at another table looked over sharply.

"Millard, cool it," I whispered. "People are noticing."

Lilly stood up. "Thanks, but I'm good." She began walking, a bit slowly but with confidence, toward the restrooms at the back of the café.

When she was out of earshot, Millard let out a long, wistful sigh.

"Fellows," he announced, "I think I'm in love."

CHAPTER FIFTEEN

*W*hen Lilly emerged from the restroom after a few minutes, Millard ran to offer her his arm. She took it—subtly, so it wouldn't look strange to the other patrons—and when they'd made it back to the table, she said, "Okay. She's agreed to meet you."

"That's great," I said. "Where?"

"I'll have to show you the way. Where she is, I'm the only one who can reach her."

I couldn't imagine what she meant, but I was intrigued nonetheless. We followed Lilly out a back door into an alley behind the café. As stealthily as I could, I walked around front to our parked car—there were no black SUVs in sight—then drove to the alley to pick everyone up. They piled in. Millard insisted Lilly ride up front. She gave us an address that wasn't far away.

As we drove, the character of the neighborhood changed. The houses got older, uglier, then disappeared altogether, replaced by warehouses and industrial buildings, old and rusted. I noticed in my mirror that a certain gray sedan had been following us for a while. I took a sudden right turn, then three more in quick succession. After that, it was gone.

The address Lilly had given us led to a row of brick warehouses. At the end of the block was a building, five or six stories tall, that was still under construction. The bottom story was ringed by chain-link fences, the top half windowless and skeletal. I drove past it and parked down a side street.

Before we left the car, I grabbed my duffel bag and tossed in a few essentials. A flashlight. Abe's operations log—heavy, but I was paranoid about leaving it. And a certain pear-shaped fast-food combo item from the glove box. (One never knew when such a thing could come in handy on a mission.) I slung the duffel crosswise over my back, shut the trunk, and turned to face the group.

"Ready."

"How do we get in?" Emma said.

"There's a hidden entrance," Lilly said. "Follow me."

And then we were off, actually struggling to keep up with Lilly at times as she strode down the street, tapping her cane before her.

"You really seem to know where you're going," Millard said.

"Yeah," Lilly replied. "We've hung out here a few times, Noor and me. When we need to get away from people?"

"Like who?" I said.

"You know. Parents. Noor's foster parents, especially." She muttered something about them under her breath that I didn't quite catch, and then she turned and tap-walked down an alley that ran between a warehouse and the under-construction building. Halfway down the alley she slowed and started feeling along the wooden fence with her hand. When she reached a particular board, she stopped.

"Here." She pushed the board and it tipped upward, revealing an entrance to the site. "After you."

"You guys hang out *here*?" said Bronwyn.

"It's pretty safe," said Lilly. "Not even the bums know how to get in."

The place looked like a project some shady developer had started a decade ago, then abandoned when the money had run out. It had been left in a state of unfinished decay, both old and new at once.

Lilly got out her phone, pushed a button, and said, "Coming up," into it, which was translated into a text message and sent.

A moment later the reply came, which her phone read out for us all to hear in an automated voice.

"Stop at the atrium and wait. I want to get a look at them."

It was Noor. Our peculiar. We were close now.

We were following Lilly through the scaffolding when my phone began buzzing in my pocket. I pulled it out and looked.

Unknown number. Normally I would've ignored it, but something told me not to.

"Just a minute," I said to the group.

I turned back, ducked out into the construction yard, and answered it.

"It's H."

My whole body tensed.

"Where have you been? I thought we were going to see you after Portal."

"No time to explain. Look, I need you to abort the mission."

I thought I'd misheard. "You what?"

"Abort. Cancel. You heard me."

"Why? Everything's going according to—"

"Circumstances have changed. It's not important that you know the details. Just go home, now. All of you."

I could feel my temper starting to rise. After all we'd done. I couldn't believe it.

"Was it something we did? Did we screw something up?"

"No, no. Look, son, it's getting too dangerous. Just do what I say. Abort. Go home."

I was gripping the phone so tight my hand was starting to shake. We'd come too far to quit now.

"You're breaking up," I said. "I can't hear you."

"I said GO HOME."

"Sorry, Boss. Bad connection."

"Who's that?" I heard Emma say, and I turned to see her coming out to retrieve me.

I ended the call, then tucked the phone into the duffel bag on my back, where I wouldn't feel it vibrating.

"Wrong number."

◆　　◆　　◆

We followed Lilly into the building through a doorway with no door, then down a hallway from which the copper wiring had been torn, long gashes striping the walls like black veins. Grit and plaster crunched beneath our feet. Ripped insulation lay everywhere like puffs of pink cotton candy. When Lilly moved she put her feet in almost the exact spots where there were already prints, as if she'd memorized the route step by step. Every so often, I noticed, there was an object that didn't belong—an old coffee can or a cardboard box turned upside down—that her cane would knock against, and I realized they had been put there as way markers, so she would know how much of the hall she'd walked down, and how much was left to go.

Turning a corner, we entered a stairwell.

"I can do this on my own, but it's safer if you help me," she said, and we all knew that *you* meant Millard.

He was more than happy to give her his arm. We climbed six flights of stairs, then were all a bit winded.

"Now it's going to get a little weird," Lilly warned.

We left the stairwell and walked into a hallway that was absolutely pitch-black. By which I mean there was no light at all, not even a minor glow from the stairwell. Rather than soft, gradual falloff of illumination, there was a hard line, like the light had hit some unseen barrier, and once we crossed it we could see the stairwell behind us but absolutely nothing in the other direction.

"Like the auditorium door," I said, and I heard Emma say, "Mm-hmm."

I took out my flashlight and shone it into the dark, but the beam was swallowed up. Emma lit a flame in her upturned hand. The glow petered out after only a few inches.

"Noor took the light," Lilly explained. "So no one can find her but me."

"Brilliant," said Enoch.

"Link arms and form a human chain behind me," said Lilly. "I'll guide us."

We followed her down the hall, slow and stumbling in the dark. Two times we passed rooms lit by windows, but the light from outside didn't pass even an inch beyond the rooms' doorways. It felt a bit like we were underwater, or in outer space. We made a few turns, and though I tried to make a mental map of our progress, I was soon confused, unsure I'd be able to get out again without Lilly's help.

The sound of our footsteps changed. The hallway had ended at a large room.

"We're here!" Lilly called out.

A searing beam of light shone down from above. We shielded our eyes, blinded now by light rather than dark.

"Let me see your faces!" a girl's voice called down. "And tell me your names!"

I moved my hand away and blinked up into the light, then shouted my name. The others did the same.

"Who are you?" the girl called. "What do you want?"

"Can we talk face-to-face?" I said.

"Not yet," came the echoing reply.

I wondered how often my grandfather had been in situations like this, and I wished I'd had a little of his vast experience to lean on. All that we'd been through came down to this. If this girl didn't like what I said next, or if she didn't believe me, all our efforts would have been for nothing.

"We traveled a long way to find you," I said. "We came to tell you you're not alone, that there are others like you. *We're* like you."

"You don't know the first thing about me," the girl called back.

"We know you're not like most people," Emma said.

"And there are people who are after you," I said.

"And you're scared," said Bronwyn. "I was scared, too, when I first realized how different I was from most people."

"Yeah?" said the girl. "Different how?"

We decided the best thing would be to show her. Since there wasn't much I could do that was visibly peculiar, Emma lit a flame in her hands, Bronwyn lifted a heavy block of concrete above her head, and Millard picked up some random objects to demonstrate that he was there, but invisible.

"He's the one I was telling you about," Lilly said, and I could practically hear Millard beaming.

"So, can we talk?" I said.

"Wait there," the girl said, and then the light she had made winked out.

◆   ◆   ◆

We waited in the dark while the sound of her footsteps approached. I heard them above us, then coming down stairs, and then I saw her. I drew a sharp, involuntary breath. She was, quite literally, glowing. At first, she looked like a moving ball of light, but as she got closer, and my eyes adjusted, I could see she was a teenager—a tall Indian girl with sharp features, jet-black hair that framed her face, and wide-set eyes flashing with intensity. Every pore of her brown skin was emanating light. Even the hooded windbreaker and jeans she wore glowed slightly from the light that shone beneath.

She went to Lilly and hugged her, hard. The top of Lilly's head only reached Noor's cheek, and with Noor's arms encircling her, it looked for a moment like Lilly was wrapped in light.

"Are you okay?" Lilly asked.

"Bored, mostly," Noor said, and Lilly laughed a little and turned to introduce her friend.

"This is Noor."

"Hi," Noor said evenly, still assessing us.

"Noor, this is . . . uh, what do you call yourselves?"

Lilly happened to be looking at Emma.

"I'm Emma," she said.

"I mean, what *are* you, again?" said Lilly.

Emma frowned. "Emma's good enough for now, I think."

"I'm Jacob," I said. I stepped toward Noor and offered my hand, but she just looked at it. I lowered it, feeling awkward. "Is there somewhere we can talk?"

"Sure," said Noor. "Let me show you to the grand salon."

Taking Lilly's arm, she turned and began to walk down a hall. She didn't seem to mind having her back to us, so it seemed she'd decided we weren't a threat. I noticed that the light emanating from her had gradually begun to dim, shrinking down into her core so that soon only her torso was glowing, and I caught glimpses of her shine only through her unzipped windbreaker and a rip in her jeans. She had been on guard when we first met but was starting to relax, and the light inside her corresponded somehow to her emotions.

We followed her from a large room with bare concrete walls into a smaller, windowless room with bare concrete walls. A couple of chairs and an old couch had been dragged in and draped with blankets, and there were some paperback books and comics and empty pizza boxes scattered around, evidence of long days and nights spent here. There were no lamps that I could see, but light shone from the room's four corners, an apparently sourceless glow that was warm and yellow and breathed like firelight.

We sat. We talked. Actually, *I* did most of the talking—since it was only a few months ago that I was making these same life-altering discoveries myself—while Noor listened, watchful and guarded. I told her how I had grown up knowing nothing about my true nature. How my grandfather's death had sparked this quest for truth that had led to me finding a time loop and meeting the peculiar children.

She put up a hand to stop me. "I was with you until *time loop*."

"Oh, right," I said. "I'm so used to this stuff now, I forget how bizarre it must sound."

"It's a day that repeats over and over again, every twenty-four hours," Emma explained. "They have sheltered our kind from danger for centuries."

"Normal people can't enter them," Millard said. "Nor could the monsters who used to hunt us."

"What monsters?" Noor asked.

We explained, as best we could, what a hollowgast looked like, smelled like, sounded like. When we'd finished, Noor seemed puzzled.

"What's wrong?" I asked. "Have you been attacked by one?"

"I'm trying to figure you out," she said. "You talk like crazy people. Time loops. Monsters nobody can see. Shape-shifting." She went to the couch, picked up a dog-eared comic book, and waved it in the air. "You talk like you've read too many of these. And I would one hundred percent have kicked your asses out of here already if not for Lilly, who really seems to like you, and that—well—"

"This." Emma lit a ball of fire in her hand, then poured it from her right palm into her left, the flames dancing hypnotically.

"Yeah." Noor dropped the comic book. "That." She crossed her arms and leaned against the arm of the couch. "And it's not monsters who've been chasing me. At least, I don't think they are."

"Why don't you tell them about it?" said Lilly. "They want to help."

"You know how many times I've heard that in my life? 'They only want to help. Trust them. What could it hurt?' Always the same lines." She drew in a deep breath and let it out sharply. "But I guess, in this case, I'm out of options."

"You're hiding in an abandoned building," Enoch said. "Relying on a blind girl to bring you food."

Noor leveled a withering stare at him. "So what makes *you* peculiar, little man?"

"Oh, nothing too interesting," Emma said quickly, stepping in front of Enoch.

"*Excuse* me?" Enoch peeked around her. "What, are you embarrassed?"

"Of course not," Emma said, "I just thought it might be a little . . . *soon*."

"If anything, it's late," Noor said. "It's cards-on-the-table time. No secrets."

Enoch shoved Emma aside. "You heard the lady. No secrets."

"Fine," Emma said. "Just don't go overboard."

Enoch stood and fished a plastic bag out of his pocket. It swung with the weight of something wet and dark. "Luckily, I saved a cat heart from the school." He began to search around the room. "Has anyone got a doll or a stuffed animal? Or . . . a *dead* animal?"

Noor recoiled slightly, but seemed intrigued. "There's a room full of mummified pigeons down the hall."

She went out and showed him where it was. A minute later she came running back into the room, laughing and swatting at the air, and then a pigeon missing one wing and both its eyes flew into the room and fluttered around madly. The rest of us covered our heads and dove out of the way. The pigeon flung itself against the wall, dropped to the floor in a cloud of feathers, and stopped moving.

Enoch ran in. "I've never controlled a bird before! Wicked!"

"That was *nuts*," Noor said, smiling while she caught her breath. "What the hell?!"

"What can I say?" said Enoch. "I'm extremely talented."

"You're a freak!" she said, laughing again. "But I think it's cool. Really."

Enoch beamed.

"Now you know everything," said Emma, picking herself up from the floor.

"Your turn," I said.

"Okay, okay." Noor went to the couch and sat. "It'll be a relief to tell you, actually. The only person who knows any of this is Lilly."

We sat around her in a loose circle. The lights dimmed a bit. In a soft but unhesitating voice, Noor began to tell her story.

"The first time I noticed something weird was last spring." She sighed, then looked around at us. "It's so strange to be saying any of this out loud."

"Take your time," Emma said. "We're not in a rush."

Noor nodded appreciatively, and began again. "June second, a Tuesday, early afternoon. I had just gotten home from school, and Fartface—that's my not-father—had been waiting around for me all day."

The actual name she called her foster dad didn't begin with *Fart*, but it did start with an *F*.

"We had a super-long talk about how I was wasting my time with clubs after school and instead I should get a crappy minimum-wage job at Ices Queen down the street. I told him my after-school things were for college applications and I didn't need extra money, and anyway the state was paying him and Teena to take care of me. He didn't like that. He started yelling. And I did what I always do when he yells, which is to run into the kids' room, where my two not-siblings and I live, and which has a door with a lock. Greg and Amber weren't home, so I was the only one in there, and Fartface wouldn't leave me alone. He kept yelling through the door, and I was getting more and more upset, and I didn't know what to do, and finally I opened my mouth to scream back at him, but instead of my voice coming out? All the lights in the room got brighter for a second—like *much* brighter—and then *broke*."

"And that's when you knew?" said Emma. "That you were different?"

"No, no, I thought there was a ghost in the room with me or something." A quick and vanishing smile glanced across her face, and then she shook her head. "I didn't realize anything until a few days later. At El Taco Junior."

"Oh my God, *right*," said Lilly. "That was the day?"

"Mm-hmm. I had just gotten accepted into this accelerated student arts program at Bard. I never thought I had a chance, but you made me apply."

"You were always going to get in," said Lilly. "Come on."

Noor shrugged. "It was for college credit and everything, but it cost three thousand dollars, which was exactly two thousand and six hundred dollars more than I had. So I was going to quit the after-school stuff and get that job at Ices Queen to pay for it. Fartface said 'damn right' I was getting that job, but the money I made was going to their household bills, not to pay for some college before I was even out of high school. So I reminded him that I had the legal right to an emancipation bank account, and he started yelling again, and anyway that's when I ran away and met you at El Taco Junior."

"He followed her," said Lilly, "and screamed at her right there in the restaurant. And then I started yelling at *him*, and I guess he couldn't bring himself to scream at a blind girl in public, so he stormed off into the street to wait for us to finish."

"So we had the longest taco meal in history."

"We actually had time to finish the Macho Meal together," said Lilly, "which we'd never done before because it's forty-six hundred calories, but we sat there so long and I was just stress-eating . . ."

"While he was standing in the street just staring at us. Finally, I got really upset and couldn't take it anymore, and to keep from losing my shit with Fartface watching, I ran into the bathroom. And that's where it happened. I could feel it building up in me, and I was about to scream, but this time I held it in. And the lights in the bathroom started to flicker and get weird, and I—I don't know how to explain it, I just knew what to do. Knew I *could*. I reached out, reached above me, and scooped the light out of the air. And the whole room went dark, but the little space inside my hands was glowing like I had caught the world's brightest firefly."

"That," Enoch said, "is *so* wickedly cool."

"You'd think so," said Noor. "But it was scary as hell. I thought my brain had broken. It started happening all the time, and at first I didn't know how to control it. Whenever I'd get really upset—sad or pissed off about something—it would start to happen. And because school is so awful, it happened a lot at school. I could feel it coming, though, and I always managed to run away just in time, into some room where I could be alone and no one would see. I think a few people did notice something, though they couldn't exactly connect it to me—they'd just see me looking upset and some lights flickering. But it was about then that they started coming around school. The new people."

"Who were they?"

"I still don't know. They looked like faculty, and the faculty seemed to treat them like they belonged on campus, but no one recognized them. At first they seemed to be watching everyone, but after a while I got the feeling they were looking for me. Then that thing in the auditorium happened, and then I knew for sure."

"What happened, exactly?"

"We read about it in a newspaper," said Millard, "but we'd love to hear your version of events."

"That was the worst day of my life. Well, maybe the second or third worst. I had an episode in the middle of a school assembly. It started out as one of those awful, mandatory things where they drone at you about school spirit, but then it turned into an assembly about *me*. Except they didn't know it was me. They said someone had been vandalizing school property, breaking lightbulbs and burning things, and they said if the person was in the room they should stand up and apologize, and they wouldn't be expelled. Otherwise, they would. And I started feeling sick, like I was sure they knew it was me but they were just messing with my head to see if I would confess. And then this girl in the row behind me—this total witch, Suze Grant—starts whispering that it was probably me since I came from a broken home, la la la, orphan girl from the wrong side of the tracks or whatever, vandalizing the school, and I could feel myself getting angry. Really, really angry."

"And that's when it happened?" I said.

"The auditorium has all these theater lights on the ceiling, and they all lit up at once, and then broke, and a *ton* of broken glass came down on everyone."

"Damn," said Lilly. "I didn't know it was like *that*."

"It was bad," said Noor. "I knew I needed to get out there. So I made it dark, and I ran. And a couple of the fake faculty people started chasing me, and I could tell they were sure it was me, now. They chased me into the bathroom, and I had no choice but to let all the light I had taken out of that big auditorium go, all at once, right in their faces."

"What did they look like?" I asked, though I was pretty sure I knew already.

"They're so normal-looking they're almost hard to describe," said Noor.

"Age? Height? Build? Race?"

"Middle-aged. Middle height. Middle build. Mostly men, one or two ladies. A couple white, a couple brown."

"And how were they dressed?" asked Millard.

"Polo shits. Button-downs. A coat. Navy-blue or black, always. Like out of a catalog for average people with average jobs and no particular background."

"After you burned them, what did you do?" I asked.

"I tried running back to my house, but they were waiting for me there, too. So I came here. Lucky for me, I've got a lot of experience hiding from people."

"The more I hear about these people," said Bronwyn, "the less they sound like peculiars."

"They don't sound at *all* like peculiars," said Millard. "They sound like wights to me."

"Like *whites*?" said Noor, looking confused. "I just told you, some of them were brown."

"No, no, *wights*," said Emma. "W-i-g-h-t. They used to be peculiar, turned themselves into monsters by accident, and have been our enemies for more than a century."

"Oh," said Noor. "Well, that's confusing."

"They couldn't be wights," I said. "There are too many of them. Wights work in small groups, or alone."

"And there aren't even that many of them left anymore," said Emma.

"That we know of," said Enoch.

"I might have felt a hollow at the school yesterday," I admitted.

"What?" Emma shouted. "Why didn't you say anything?"

"The feeling only lasted a few seconds," I said. "I wasn't sure what it was. But if they were wights, they probably would've had at least one hollowgast traveling with them."

"Fellows, *who* they are isn't the most important thing," Millard said. "Getting Noor to safety is. Once that's completed, we can argue till we're blue about who the people in the polo shirts are."

"Safety?" said Noor. "Where's that, exactly?"

I looked at her. "A time loop."

She looked away and passed a hand across her forehead. The light in the corner flickered. "I guess after everything you've shown me, I should be ready to believe that, too. But—"

"I know," I said. "It's a lot. And it comes at you fast."

"It's not just a lot. It's insane. I'd have to be out of my mind to go with you."

"You'll just have to trust us," Emma said.

Noor looked at us for a few seconds. She started nodding. Then she said, "But I don't." She stood up and took a few steps toward the door. "I'm sorry. You seem nice enough, but I'm done trusting people I barely know. Even if they can resurrect dead birds and make fire in their hands."

I looked at Emma and Bronwyn and Enoch. We were all quiet. I genuinely didn't know what to say, didn't know how to argue with her, but I knew I had to say something. I couldn't fail this way. I couldn't fail her, couldn't fail my grandfather, couldn't fail my friends. Couldn't fail myself. But as soon as I opened my mouth to speak, the building began to shake.

The sensation was accompanied by the sound of a churning engine. There was a helicopter hovering above the building.

◆　　◆　　◆

We traded anxious looks, waiting for the roar of the helicopter to pass. Seconds ticked by, but it only grew louder. We knew what it meant without anyone having to say it. But I said it anyway.

"They tracked us here."

Noor's eyes flashed at me, angry and frightened. "Or did you *lead* them here?"

Noor grasped Lilly by the arm and speed-walked her out of the room. We followed, pleading with them.

"We didn't lead them anywhere!" Millard said. "Not purposely, anyway—I'd swear on an ymbryne's life!"

We came into a larger room and stood looking up through an unglassed atrium that was open to the sky. Suddenly the helicopter lurched into view, blocking the sky and filling the room with noise and whipping downdraft from its rotors.

A spotlight blasted down, blanching everything and casting stark shadows onto the floor. Noor stared straight up into it, her eyes fierce, seemingly ready to make a stand against these people, whoever they were, rather than follow us.

"You've got to come with us!" I shouted. "There's no other choice!"

"Sure there is," she shouted back, and she reached up with both hands and tore the light out of the air. The room around us and the space overhead went black, so that the only illumination came from a pinhole of sky above us and a glowing orb in Noor's hands.

Something dropped down from above, a small hissing object that tumbled through the blackness before bouncing with a sharp metal *ting* against the concrete floor. It began spraying a cloud of white smoke—tear gas or something similar.

"Hold your breath!" Emma shouted.

Lilly started to cough. Bronwyn scooped her up. "This is Bronwyn! I'm going to carry you!"

Noor nodded her thanks to Bronwyn. "This way," she said, and started at a run down one of the blacked-out hallways.

We practically rode the back of her heels. Nobody wanted to be left behind in that unnatural dark. Sprinting to the end of the hall, we arrived at a T where we could go either left or right. Noor headed right and we followed her, but a second later we heard voices and heavy footsteps and two men wielding a bright light came around a corner up ahead.

They shouted at us to stop. We heard an echoing *pop* and another canister came flying down the hall, landed near us, and sprayed gas everywhere.

We all started to cough, then ran in the opposite direction. They weren't trying to kill us, that much was clear. They wanted Noor alive. Maybe, at this point, they wanted all of us.

"We need to get out of the building," I shouted as we ran. "The stairs. Where are the stairs?"

We rounded a corner and came to a dead end. Noor spun around and looked behind us.

"Past those men," she said, pointing in the direction of the footsteps.

"We're screwed," I said. "I'll have to use our Happy Meal prize . . ."

I slung the duffel bag around to my front and started to reach inside for the grenade, but Noor didn't seem at all fazed by our lack of escape options. "In here!" she shouted, ducking through a doorway and into a small room.

We followed her in. There were no windows, no doors—no other exits.

"We're trapped in here!" I said, my hand inside the bag, gripping the grenade. I didn't want to use it—what if it brought the building down on our heads?—but if given no other choice, I'd take the risk.

"You asked me to trust you," said Noor. "First, trust me."

The footsteps were growing louder and louder. I slipped my empty hand out of the bag. Noor pushed us into the corner, then stood in the center of the room and began to rake her hands through the air. With each pass of her hands the room around us grew darker by degrees, the little natural light that shone in from the hallway dimming and then disappearing altogether—into her hands. And then she took all that glowing concentrated light, stuffed it into her mouth, and swallowed it.

I can only tell you what I saw, and it was one of the most peculiar things I'd ever witnessed. I watched that ball of light glow through her cheeks and travel down her throat and into her stomach, where her body seemed to absorb and dampen it, until finally, just as the footsteps were reaching the doorway, it disappeared completely. We were left standing in a blackness so total that when two men filled the doorway and aimed their blinding flashlights into the room, the dark seemed to reach out and wrap itself around them. Their lights were reduced to pinpricks, and they stumbled into the room half blind, one whacking the light against his hand while the other spoke into a crackling walkie-talkie.

"Subjects are on level six. Repeat, level six."

We pressed our backs to the wall, silent, hardly daring to breathe. We were so hidden by the enveloping dark that I really thought they might not find us. And they might not have, except for one thing.

My phone. It was set to vibrate, but even muffled inside my bag, it made noise—a tiny humming sound that gave us away instantly.

Everything that happened after that unfolded with incredible speed. The men both dropped to one knee. The words *firing position* flitted through my head just as Noor made a sudden guttural growl, and the light she'd been holding in her stomach shot up into her throat and burst forth from her mouth toward the two men in a blast that looked—even with my face turned and my eyes shut—like a thousand flashbulbs going off at once. I felt a wave of heat. I heard the men scream and fall. When I opened my eyes again, every inch of the room was alive with bright white light, and the men were on the ground clutching their faces.

We were about to run past them, out of the room, when more footsteps came. Another man rounded in from the hallway. He had a gun and looked about to use it, but Bronwyn lunged at him, grabbed him by the shoulders, and, as his gun went off, flung him toward the back wall. He crashed right through it, pulverized concrete dust mixing in the air with a pink puff of blood. There was just enough time for Noor to turn from the hole to Bronwyn, her mouth forming a perfect O, before we all came to our senses and climbed through it.

On the other side of the hole in the wall, beyond the man's crumpled body, was a room flooded with daylight, and beyond that a stairway. We barreled down it, Bronwyn carrying Lilly over her shoulder, rounding corners at a dizzying pace until we'd descended six stories to the ground floor. We ran outside then through a hole in the fence into some back alley, then through the parking lot of a warehouse and into another alley, not even looking behind us, just listening for the helicopter, which faded a little more and then a little more still, until we were forced to stop and catch our breath.

"I think—I think you might have *killed* that guy," Noor said to Bronwyn, her eyes wide.

"He had a gun," Bronwyn said, and set Lilly down on her feet. "If you point a gun at my friends, I get to kill you. That's—" She wiped her glistening forehead and let out a sighing breath. "That's the rule."

"Good rule," said Noor. She turned to me. "Sorry for what I said. About you maybe being one of them."

"It's okay," I said. "If I were you, I might not have believed us either."

Noor went to Lilly and took her hand. "You all right, Lil?"

"Little shaken up," said Lilly. "I'll live."

"We have to get far away from here, and quickly," Emma said. "What's the fastest way?"

"The train," said Noor. "Station's a block away."

"What about the *car*?" said Enoch.

"They know the car by now," I said. "We'll have to come back for it later."

"If we live that long," said Millard.

❖   ❖   ❖

Minutes later we were riding a cramped subway car toward Manhattan. Was that the right way to go? We had jumped onto the first train that came, just to get away from the people hunting us. While my friends talked in hushed voices about who those people might have been—wights? Some hostile peculiar clan we knew nothing about?—I stood up and looked at the map on the wall of the subway car, routes branching out everywhere. We were supposed to take

Noor to that island in the middle of a river—10044. Blackwell's Island, it had said on the postcard. I asked Noor and Lilly if they knew where it was. Neither had heard of it. I had no phone reception to do a map search. And once we found the island, how would we find the loop? Loop entrances were rarely obvious.

But the more I thought about it, the less certain I felt about the plan. It was the mission we'd been given, but H's sudden order to abort had thrown everything into doubt. What circumstances had changed? What had he been calling to warn me about, exactly? Was it the people who were hunting us that he'd been worried about, or was loop 10044 no longer safe?

What's more, the subject of the mission was more than just *the subject* now. She was Noor, and she had a name and a story and a face (a very pretty one, at that); it was hard for me to imagine delivering her into the hands of strangers. Was I really supposed to dump her into some loop I knew nothing about, wash my hands of her, and head home?

I glanced over at her now, her scuffed Vans on the plastic bench seat and knees hugged to her chest, staring at the floor with a weariness the depth of which I could hardly fathom.

"Would you miss New York, if you had to leave?" I asked her.

It took five full seconds to draw herself out of whatever thought she'd been sunk in and look at me.

"Miss New York? Why?"

"Because I think you should come home with us, instead."

Emma looked at me sharply, but it was Millard who objected aloud.

"That's not the mission!"

"Forget the mission," I said. "She'll be safer with us than in any loop in this crazy city. Or on this side of the ocean."

"We live in London, most of the time," Emma explained. "In Devil's Acre."

Noor recoiled a bit.

"It's not as bad as it sounds," Millard said. "Once you get past the smell, anyway."

"We're nearly finished with this mission from hell," said Enoch. "Let's not muck it up now. Let's just take her where she's supposed to go and be *done* with it already."

"We don't know who's in this loop we're going to," I said, "or how capable they are. Or anything."

"Is that any of our concern?" said Enoch.

"I agree with Jacob," said Millard. "There are almost no ymbrynes left in America, and it's an ymbryne's job to protect and shape uncontacted peculiars. Who's going to teach her how to be peculiar?"

Noor raised her hand. "Is anyone going to fill me in here?"

"An ymbryne—they're like teachers," I said. "And protectors."

"And government leaders," said Millard, and then he added, under his breath, "though unelected . . ."

"And overbearing know-it-alls who are always minding other people's business," said Enoch.

"Essentially, the backbone of our whole society," said Emma.

"We don't need an ymbryne," I said, "we just need someplace safe. Anyway, Miss Peregrine probably wants to kill us right now."

"She'll get over it," Enoch said.

"So, would you come with us?" I asked Noor.

She sighed, then chuckled. "What the hell. I could use a vacation."

"Hey, what about me?" Lilly said.

"You'd be more than welcome to come," Millard said, a bit too eagerly. "Though normal people cannot enter loops, I'm afraid."

"I can't leave anyway!" Lilly said. "School just started." Then she laughed and said, "God, listen to me. As if none of this insanity even happened. That's how badly school has messed up my brain."

"Well, education *is* important," said Millard.

"But I have parents. Pretty good ones, actually. And they would worry about me a lot."

"I'll be back," said Noor. "But getting out of town until this stuff blows over sounds like an excellent idea."

"So you trust us now?" I said.

She shrugged. "Enough."

"How do you feel about road trips?"

Out of nowhere, Bronwyn slumped forward in her seat and crumpled to the floor.

"Bronwyn!" Emma cried, and leapt down next to her.

If any of the other people in the subway car had seen, they pretended they hadn't.

"Is she okay?" Enoch said.

"I don't know," said Emma. She slapped Bronwyn's cheek lightly and repeated her name until her eyes blinked open again.

"Fellows, I think—Rats, I should have mentioned this earlier." Bronwyn winced. Raised the hem of her shirt. She was bleeding from her torso.

"Bronwyn!" said Emma. "My God!"

"The man with the gun . . . I think he shot me. Don't worry, though. Not with a bullet." Bronwyn opened her palm to show us a small dart, tipped now with her own blood.

"Why didn't you *say* something?" I said.

"We needed to get out of there quickly. And I thought I was strong enough to overcome whatever he'd shot me with. But apparently . . ."

Her head lolled to the side and she passed out.

CHAPTER SIXTEEN

*W*e weren't looking for a loop. At that moment, we wanted anything *but* to find a loop. All that was in our minds was getting Bronwyn to a hospital. We jumped out of the train at the next stop, hardly even looking to see where we were, and climbed the steps out of the subway station. Lilly held on to Millard's arm, and Emma, Noor, and I helped prop up Bronwyn, who was weak but still conscious, as she shuffled heavily up the steps and along the sidewalk. We were in Manhattan now, and the buildings were taller, the sidewalks bustling.

I dug out my phone to call 911. Enoch approached people on the street shouting, "Hospital! Where's a hospital?" This turned out to be an effective strategy. We were pointed down a particular street by a kind, concerned lady who hustled us in the right direction, asking after Bronwyn. Of course, we didn't want to tell her anything, didn't want her following us into the emergency room or asking our names (I was already imagining having to bring in an ymbryne to memory-wipe her . . . and the doctors and nurses), so we pretended we'd been joking about the injury and after a block she stormed off, understandably angry.

The hospital was just ahead; I could see the sign hanging from a building a block away. And then the sweetest, richest smell of cooking food hit my nose, and my steps began to slow.

"Do you smell that?" said Enoch. "That's rosemary toast and goose liver pâté!"

"No way," said Emma. "It's shepherd's pie."

Our momentum was waning.

"I'd know that smell anywhere," said Noor. "Dosas. Paneer masala dosas."

"What are you guys talking about?" said Lilly. "And why are you *stopping*?"

"She's right, we have to get Bronwyn to a doctor," said Millard. "Although that might be the most aromatic coq au vin I've ever laid nostrils on . . ."

Our progress had been completely arrested. We were standing in front of a storefront with drawn shades that might have been a restaurant, though there was no sign for one—just a placard that read OPEN ALWAYS and ALL ARE WELCOME.

"You know, I feel okay," Bronwyn said. "A bit peckish, though, now that you mention it."

She didn't seem particularly okay—her speech was slurred, and she was still leaning heavily on our arms—but the part of my brain that registered this seemed to be wrapped in cotton.

"She's bleeding!" Emma said. "And the hospital is right there."

Bronwyn looked down at her shirt. "Not bleeding *much*," she said, though the patch of red appeared to be spreading.

There were two desires at war inside me. One was a voice shouting, *Go to the hospital, dumbass!* but I could barely hear it over the other voice, which sounded weirdly like my dad's. It was insisting, in this peppy, dorky way, that *it was getting near dinnertime and shouldn't we try New York food while we're here, and gosh-darnit, why don't we just stop in for dinner real quick?*

We all seemed to agree except Lilly and Emma, but even their objections were starting to fade.

I pushed the door open and ushered everyone inside. It was indeed a restaurant: a small old place with checkered tablecloths and cane-backed chairs and a soda fountain along one wall. Behind the counter stood a waitress in an apron and a paper hat, and she was smiling like she'd been waiting for us all day. We were the only ones there.

"You kids look hungry!" she said, bouncing on her heels.

"Oh, we *are*," said Bronwyn.

The waitress didn't seem to notice the blood on Bronwyn's shirt. "In fact, you look like you're downright starving."

"Yes," said Enoch, his voice a bit robotic. "Starving."

"What kind of restaurant is this?" asked Noor. "I thought I smelled paneer."

"Oh, we've got everything," said Bernice with a small wave of her hand. "Everything you could ever want."

Had she said her name? How did I know it? My brain felt like mush.

The little voice that wondered if this was a good idea had faded to a whisper. Lilly's objections, too, had quieted. The last thing I'd heard her say was, "You guys can stay here if you want, but I'm taking your friend to the hospital!" But her efforts to drag Bronwyn out by the elbow hadn't been very effective. (You can't drag Bronwyn anywhere she doesn't want to go.)

"We don't have money," I said, and the disappointment I felt as I realized I had left our cash in the trunk of the car was so total it felt like I was suddenly in mourning.

"It just so happens we're having a special promotion today," said Bernice. "Everything's on the house."

"Really?" said Bronwyn.

"That's right. Your money's no good here."

We bellied up to the counter and sat on the fixed, plastic stools, all in a row. There was no menu. We simply told Bernice what we wanted, and she shouted the orders to an unseen line cook in the back. A remarkably short time later, a bell dinged and she began to bring out plate after plate of food. A rooster cooked in wine for Millard. Paneer masala dosas and a mango lassi for Noor. A lamb roast trimmed with mint jelly for Emma. A double cheeseburger and fries and strawberry shake for me. A lobster for Bronwyn, complete with a shell-cracker and a bib with a picture of a lobster on it. A steaming

Korean bibimbap with an egg cracked over it for Lilly. It was a more eclectic array than I'd thought possible in any restaurant—much less a greasy old diner with only one person working the kitchen—but the part of my brain that was objecting to all this had gotten very quiet:

> *Don't eat that.*
>
> *You should leave.*
>
> *This is a bad idea.*
>
> *Stop now before it's*
>
> *too late.*

I don't remember eating my double cheeseburger and fries and strawberry shake. But the next thing I knew, the shake was drained, there were only greasy crumbs left on my plate, and my head was heavy, so heavy.

"Oh, honey!" Bernice trotted out from behind the counter, a hand to her chest. "You look beat!"

And I was. I really was.

"I'm so, so, *so* tired," I heard Emma say, and a murmur of agreement rippled through my friends.

"Why don't you head on upstairs and catch a little sleep?"

"We have to go," said Noor. She was trying to get up from her counter stool, but couldn't seem to work up the momentum.

"Do you?" said Bernice. "I don't think you do."

"*Jacob,*" Emma whispered in my ear.

She sounded drunk.

"*We gotta go.*"

"*I know.*"

We had been hypnotized somehow. I knew it. It was like what the Mermaid Fantasyland peculiars had tried to do to us—but this time we had taken the bait.

"We've got rooms upstairs with beds all made for you. Just through here . . ."

Now that she'd said it, I found that I could make myself stand.

In fact, we were all standing. And Bernice was pushing us toward the exit—a strange tunnel of hallway painted with red and white candy stripes.

We let ourselves be pushed. The hallway seemed to elongate as we approached it. I heard a scuffle and turned to see Bernice barring Lilly's way with her arm.

"Hey," I said vaguely. "Be nice to her."

Lilly was speaking. I saw her mouth moving, her throat constricting with the effort, but her voice did not (or could not) reach my ears.

"We'll be back soon, Lil, just wait here," Noor said.

Of course, Lilly wouldn't have been able to join us even if she had been allowed to walk down the hall. Around the halfway point I felt the rush in my head and the drop in my stomach, and *whump*, the loop took us.

Lilly was no longer behind us, and up ahead the candy-striped hallway now had an endpoint: a staircase.

"It's just upstairs!" Bernice's voice echoed, though she was nowhere to be seen.

We dragged ourselves slowly up, one step at a time, and as we mounted the landing I felt the last of my willpower dissipate. We were at the mercy of whatever siren was luring us along, and all we could seem to do, for now, was obey.

◆　◆　◆

On the landing were two young girls on their hands and knees, engaged in what seemed to be a thorough, inch-by-inch examination of the floorboards. When we came into the hall, they stopped what they were doing and looked up at us.

"Have you seen a doll?" the older girl asked. "Frankie lost one of her dolls."

She seemed to be telling a joke, but she didn't crack a smile.

"Sorry," said Noor.

"We ordered a . . . sleep?" said Millard, sounding confused.

"Through there," said the older girl, nodding to the door behind her.

We stepped past them. "*Run*," I thought I heard one hiss, "*run while you can.*" But when I turned back to look again, they were staring at the floor, having returned to their methodical search. I felt like I was moving through a dream.

Through the door was a small, neat kitchen area. A young boy sat at a table and a man in a bow tie stood over him. There were puzzles and a little tower of stacking blocks on the table, as if the man were giving the boy some kind of examination. When he heard us come in, the man lifted his arm and pointed to the next room. "Through there." He didn't even look at us. His attention was locked on the boy. "*Sanguis bebimus*," he said. "*Corpus edimus.*"

"*Mater semper certa est*," the boy replied, while staring at nothing. "*Mater semper certa est.*"

" 'The mother is always certain,' " Millard translated.

The teacher straightened, then banged on the wall. "Keep it down in there!" he shouted—not at us. I couldn't tell what had upset him until we were nearly out of the room and into the next one, and I heard the singing.

A woozy, tuneless voice moaned, "Happy biiiiiirthday, dear Frankieeeeee . . . haaaaaapy biiiirthday to *youuuuuuu* . . ."

I couldn't make my feet move any faster, though I would have run if they'd have let me. The singer was a man in clown makeup and a bone-white wig. He was seated on a daybed, bellied up to a small cocktail table, and was pouring himself a drink from a bottle. He seemed to be stuck: He would sip from the glass in his hand, splash a bit more from the bottle into the glass, sing a few words, then sip again. When he saw us he raised his glass and said, "Chin-chin! Happy birthday, Frankie!"

"Happy birthday," I said involuntarily.

The clown seemed to freeze like that, with his glass raised and his mouth open, and from the back of his throat there came a sound like something unwinding, barely intelligible as words:

Let

me

sleeeeeep

"Come in here!" called a shrill voice from the next room.

We came, all in a bunch, into a bedroom crowded with dolls. Every available space was crammed with them. There were dolls on the floor, dolls on the shelves on the walls, dolls overflowing from a big armchair in the corner and from an iron-railed bed. There were so many that I didn't notice the girl among them—on the bed, half buried in an avalanche of little porcelain faces—until she spoke a second time.

"Siddown!" she barked, and began flinging the dolls off her.

We sat down on the floor, the action automatic. I heard Bron-wyn groan; her pain must have been getting worse.

"I didn't say you could make noise!" the girl said. She wore a cotton nightshirt and yellow corduroy pants that looked like they were from the 1970s or 80s, and when she spoke her upper lip curled into a sneer. "Well? Who are you?"

I felt my tongue unlock and started to answer. "My name is Jacob, and I come from a town in Florida—"

"Bored, bored, *bored*!" she shouted. She pointed to Emma. "You!"

A jolt went through Emma and she began to speak. "My name is Emma Bloom. I was born in Cornwall and came of age in a loop in Wales and—"

"BORING!" the girl screamed, and pointed at Enoch.

"I'm Enoch O'Connor," he said, "and we have something in common."

The girl seemed intrigued. As he spoke she stood up from the bed, where she'd been lying among her dolls, and walked over to him.

"I can make dead things move using the hearts of living things," Enoch said. "I have to take them apart first, but—"

The girl snapped her fingers, and Enoch's mouth clapped shut. "You're nice-looking," she said, tracing a finger along the line of Enoch's jaw, "but when you talk it gets ruined." She smooshed the tip of his nose with her finger. "*Boop*. More for you later."

She turned to Bronwyn. "You."

"My name is Bronwyn Bruntley and I'm quite strong and my brother, Victor, was also—"

"BORING!" the girl screamed. "*POOP!*"

Feet scurried toward us. The bow-tied teacher appeared in the doorway.

"Yes?"

"I don't want any more dolls like these, Poop. Just *look* at them. Do they seem like they would be fun to play Monopoly with? DO THEY?"

"Er . . . no?"

"THAT'S RIGHT. THEY DO NOT."

She kicked a pile of dolls and they flew everywhere.

"Well, *him* I like." She pointed at Enoch. "But the rest are HORRIBLE and BORING."

"I'm very sorry, Frankie."

"What should we do with them, Poop?" She turned to offer us a quick aside. "His name isn't really *Poop*. I just call him that because I can call anyone anything I like."

"Perhaps we should eat them," Poop suggested.

Frankie sneered. "You always want to eat them. It's weird, Poop. And anyway, that gave me a stomachache last time."

"Or we could sell them."

"Sell them? To who?"

"To *whom*," the teacher said, and then he put a hand over his mouth and turned pale.

The girl flew into a rage. She pointed at him, then drew a quick, invisible line downward. The teacher fell to his knees as if pulled by strings. "YOU. DO NOT. TELL ME THINGS."

"Yes, Frankie. Yes, ma'am." His voice was quivering. "*Mater semper certa est.*"

"That's right. That is extremely correct." A small line of dolls was marching toward him across the room. "Because you're so obedient, Poop, I'm only going to have them chew off *one* of your legs."

The teacher repeated the phrase over and over, faster and faster—"*Mater semper certa est, mater semper certa est!*"—until the words were slurring together. The dolls swarmed him, grasping and champing their porcelain teeth. The man was crying, sobbing, but he didn't struggle. When he seemed about to pass out, the girl spread her arms and then brought her hands together, and the clap made all the dolls go limp and fall over.

"Oh, Poop. You're so funny."

The man gathered himself, wiped his face, and wobbled to his feet. "Where was I?" He cleared his throat. "You could sell them to the Animists, the Mentats, the Weathermen . . ." He pressed a trembling hand to his neck, quickly checking his pulse, then tucked it behind his back. "But, as always, the Untouchables are paying the highest rate."

"Blecch. I *hate* them. But as long as none set foot here . . ."

"I'll call them and arrange a sales meeting."

"I'm not selling *him*, though." She pointed at Enoch, then traced a U in the air with two fingers. Enoch's lips curled into an exaggerated, grotesque smile.

"That's fine, Frankie. That's very good."

"I *know* it's good. The rest of them, I don't care. I just have one condition. If whoever buys them does something nasty to them? I get to watch."

After a long and dreamless blank, I woke up tied to a chair. We were spaced out all in a row, our feet bound to the chair legs and our hands strapped behind us: Emma, Bronwyn, Noor, and even Millard, the ropes hovering around what looked like an empty seat. All but Enoch. He was nowhere to be seen.

We were on the stage of an old theater, arranged behind a tattered yellow curtain. If I craned my neck, I could see ropes and pulleys behind us and lights along a catwalk above. We weren't gagged, and yet I couldn't speak. I couldn't even persuade my mouth to open. Then I heard voices on the other side of the curtain. They seemed to be talking about us.

"They were trespassing on my property! Trying to steal from me!" It was the psychotic little girl, Frankie. "I had every right to hang them, but I'm showing mercy instead. *And* doing you all a favor."

"That's funny, usually it's you who's tryin' to steal from us," said a gravelly male voice. "The last specimen I bought from you turned to corpse-dust after only two days."

"S'not my fault if you don't take care of 'em right," said Frankie.

"The seller isn't responsible for user error." An oily-sounding voice I recognized—Poop, the tutor.

"You sold me junk! I'm owed a free one!"

It sounded like a scuffle was about to break out, but then a lady shouted, "Stop it! No brawling allowed on neutral ground!"

Things settled down. The gravelly voice said, "You've wasted too much of my day already, Frankie. Let's get your dog and pony show started."

"Fine. POOP!"

With a loud squeak and a puff of dust, the curtain began to rise. Beyond it was an empty and decaying theater. The seats were torn, the balcony level was teetering at a precarious angle and looked as if it might collapse at any moment.

On the stage were six people. Their gazes were trained on us but they seemed to be watching one another just as closely, each maintaining a wary distance from the rest. Frankie and Poop stood closest to us, Frankie wearing a coat with tails and holding a baton, as if she were the ringleader of a circus.

It seems amazing to me now, but I had no way of knowing then who the others were. That was probably for the best, because if I'd known their reputations, I might've been too intimidated to think straight. Frankie had reached out to the most notorious peculiar gangs in New York, and the leaders of three had made an appearance. Front and center was a young fellow with hair like a cresting wave. He wore an immaculate suit, shoes caked in red mud, and a thin, threatening smile. His name was Wreck Donovan. Standing behind him were his two flunkies, a demure girl who was casually reading a newspaper and a boy who didn't strike me as someone who could read at all, his mouth hanging open in dim amazement.

Wreck was staring at me while having an argument with someone else: a young-looking girl in an immaculate white dress tied with a huge silk bow. Her hair was coiffed in complicated, ironed curls that cascaded down her back. Her face was milky-white and smooth and very cold, the mouth an inverse of Wreck's, turned down at the corners and always moving, as if she were chewing something, or talking to herself silently. The strangest thing about her was the cloud of black smoke that hovered around her head and shoulders, churning slowly but never dissipating. It narrowed to a funnel shape that seemed to emanate from her right ear. Her name was Angelica, and she was alone.

Wreck hated to be photographed, but one day I would see a blurred snapshot of him posing much as he sat before me now. Angelica, on the other hand, loved the camera, and one portrait of her in particular—moping on a swing, smoke cloud wafting to one side—would become famous among American peculiars, framed and hung with pride by some, used as target practice or a wanted poster by others.

Wreck and Angelica were arguing about someone who hadn't shown up yet—the representative for the Untouchables—and Frankie was refusing to start without him.

"There's no chance he's gonna show his hairy mug here," Wreck said. "Or anywhere else in the city, for that matter." He had a melodious voice tinged with a light Irish accent.

"I hope he does," said his gape-mouthed flunkie. "I'll tie him up and turn him in for the bounty."

"That, I'd pay to see," said Angelica. "None of you are getting that bounty, anyhow. Dogface and his clan aren't afraid of you. Leo and his goons, yes, but not you." She spoke in a kind of lilting sigh, the sentences starting high and chirpy before fluttering down to the floor.

Wreck glanced at his pocket watch, uncrossed his legs, and stood. "One more minute, Frankie. Then I take my associates and blow."

"Poop, make him sit!" Frankie shouted.

"Please sit down, Mr. Donovan," said the tutor.

"I'll never take orders from someone who lets a child call him names," said Wreck.

"You're gonna regret talking about me like that," Frankie said. "One day, you're gonna beg for my forgiveness."

Before their argument could escalate, there was a loud slam from the rear of the theater, a set of double doors swung wide, and a small figure rushed in.

"There he is!" said Frankie. "Told you he'd show."

He charged down the aisle, peeling off a hat and high-collared coat that had obscured his face. "Sorry I'm late," he said in a high, sharp New York accent. "Traffic was a nightmare!"

He bounded up the steps and into the stage lights, and I was shocked to see that his face—every square inch but his eyeballs and lips—was covered in long, thick fur. This was Dogface, the leader of the Eldritch Street Untouchables, the most despised peculiar clan in New York.

"Dogface!" Wreck shouted. "I truly didn't think you'd have the stones to show yourself, after the beating we gave you last week."

"Is *that* what you're calling it?" Dogface replied, licking two fingers and brushing a lock of fur from his eyes. "Funny, I remember three of yours getting carted off to the healer, and only two of mine."

"I think you forgot how to count," said Wreck. "Just stay out of my territory, or it won't be the healer they take you to, it'll be the deadhouse."

"Wahh, waah, waah," the furry boy said, mocking him. " '*Stay out of my territory!*' Someone needs to have his diaper changed."

Wreck, who had sat down again, jumped out of his chair, but one of his flunkies held him back. Dogface didn't flinch, chuckling to himself as Wreck made a show of needing to be dragged back to his seat to prevent a brawl.

"I wouldn't try it," said Dogface. "I got three boyos waiting with their ears to the door, and if they so much as hear me bark, you're a dead man."

"Enough of this tiresome peacocking," said Angelica, her face placid but her smoke cloud dense and swirling.

"Yes, may we *please* begin," said the tutor.

Everyone took a seat. Though the tension between the clan leaders was palpable, their focus gradually returned to my friends and me.

"What have you got for us today, Frankie?" Dogface said. "More rubes from the sticks?"

"I don't need any more parlor-trick peculiars," said Wreck. "I want genuine talent this time."

"Yeah," said Dogface. "He's got enough deadweight morons in his crew as it is."

Wreck shot him a nasty look.

"No, no, these here are the real deal," said Frankie. "And they're gonna be *real* expensive."

"We'll see," said Angelica.

"Only thing I care about is, can they rob?" said Wreck. "I need muscle. I need lookouts."

"I need chameleons," said Dogface. "My crew have been getting noticed by normals lately, and we've had some close shaves."

"You could surely use one," Wreck said, laughing.

"This one's invisible!" said Frankie. She spun around and poked Millard with her baton, and he squeaked.

We still couldn't talk.

"Hmm," said Wreck, drumming his fingers together. "I could be interested . . ."

"They ain't ugly enough for your crew," said Dogface. "Better leave 'em to me."

"I need weatherfolk, as ever," Angelica said with a sigh. "Wind-shifters, cloud-seeders. *Competent* ones."

"All right, talk," said Frankie, waving her baton in our direction. "Tell 'em what you can do."

I felt my jaw slacken and my tongue, which had nearly gone numb, suddenly go all pins and needles as the feeling flooded back. It was hard to talk at first. Bronwyn tried to speak, too, but it sounded like we had forgotten how to form consonants.

Dogface tossed up his hands. "What are they, idiots?"

"Of course they are, why d'you think Frankie was able to catch 'em in the first place?" said Wreck.

"Lose my telegraph number," Angelica said, and stood up from her chair.

"Their tongues are just tired!" Frankie pleaded. "Don't leave!"

Frankie started to beat Bronwyn with her baton and scream, "TALK RIGHT!"

Seeing that made me so furious that something jarred loose in my head, and I found my voice again and shouted, "STOP IT!"

Frankie turned, enraged, and came at me with the baton. She had to pass Emma to reach me, though, and Emma had burned through her wrist restraints without anyone noticing. Though her feet were still tied to the chair, she was able to lunge at the girl with the top half of her body and tackle Frankie to the floor.

Emma got Frankie in a choke hold, one arm around her neck and a flaming hand held beside her face.

"Stop, stop, *stop*!" Frankie screamed, wriggling and writhing. She seemed to have lost her telekinetic grip on Emma, and though she was trying mightily, she couldn't get it back.

"Let us go or I'll melt her face off!" Emma yelled. "I mean it! I'll really do it!"

"Oh, *please* do," said Angelica. "She's such a pain."

The others laughed. They seemed surprised, but not particularly upset, by the sudden turn of events.

"Why are you just standing there?" Frankie shouted. "Murder them!"

Dogface crossed his ankles and laced his fingers behind his head. "I don't know, Frankie. This just got interesting."

"I agree," said Angelica. "For once, I'm glad I got out of bed today."

Emma looked annoyed. "None of you cares if she dies?"

"I do," the tutor said halfheartedly.

"You can't do this to me!" Frankie shouted. "You're mine! I caught you!"

I was starting to feel control returning to my arms and legs as well as my tongue. The girl's spell had been broken. I looked at my friends, and I could see them beginning to move their limbs as well.

"I say we split them evenly," said Wreck, and he drew a fat-barreled pistol from his waist belt and cocked it. "One each for you, two for me."

"I've got a better idea," said Dogface. He dropped onto all fours and snarled ferociously. "I get all of them."

"That won't work out so well for you," Angelica warned him. Her cloud flashed bright white, then rumbled. What I had thought was smoke was really a storm cloud. "And don't even think about using that fire on us," she said to Emma.

"Nobody's taking us," I said. "Nobody's buying us, either."

"When the Ymbryne Council finds out what you're doing, you're all in serious, serious trouble," said Millard.

That comment prompted a few raised eyebrows. Wreck stepped forward, his tone suddenly a bit more respectful, and he said, "You've misunderstood us. We don't *buy* people. That sort of trade has been illegal for a long time. But we will occasionally make monetary bids to post bail for peculiars guilty of criminal offenses. *If we like said peculiars.*"

"What criminal offenses?" Millard said. "*You're* the criminals."

"Trespassing on Frankie's turf," said Dogface, and Frankie, who was too scared to talk, nodded vigorously.

"She trapped us!" Bronwyn said. "Drugged us with food!"

"*Ignorantia legis neminem excusat,*" said the tutor. "'Ignorance of the law excuses no one.'"

"We post your bail," Wreck continued. "You skip jail, then repay us with your service for a period of three months. After that, many people decide to stay on with us."

"Those who are still alive," said Dogface with a sly grin. "Our initiations ain't for the faint of heart."

"You, miss, are very talented," said Angelica, taking a cautious step toward Emma and bowing slightly. "I think you'd feel right at home with my clan. We're elementals, like you."

"Let's get one thing straight," Emma said. "I'm not going anywhere with you, and neither are my friends."

"I think you are," Dogface said.

There was a loud snap as Bronwyn's ropes broke and she stood up from her chair.

"Don't you move!" Wreck shouted. "I'll shoot!"

"You shoot, I burn," said Emma.

"Do what she says!" Frankie whimpered.

Wreck hesitated, then lowered his gun a little. Despite their tough talk, they really didn't want Frankie to die. Or they didn't really want to kill us.

Bronwyn went to Noor's chair and snapped the ropes binding her.

"Thanks," Noor said, standing and rubbing her wrists. Then she swatted her hand through the air and scooped away the blinding spotlight. It was still on, shining up in the catwalk, but now its cone of light stopped high above our heads. "There. That's better." She pushed her hands together, compressing the handful of light she'd collected, then tucked it into her cheek, where it bulged like a glowing lump of chewing gum.

"Mother Mary," Wreck muttered under his breath.

"Who *are* you people?" said Dogface.

Bronwyn had just snapped Millard's ropes, and now she was coming over to free me.

"They can't be from around here," said Angelica. "With peculiarities like that, everybody would know their names."

"Remember the wights?" said Millard.

"You must be joking," said Wreck.

"They're dead or in jail now because of us."

"Because of *him*, mostly," said Bronwyn. She snapped the rope that held my wrists and then held up my arm like the winner in a footrace. "We're Miss Peregrine's wards. And when she hears about what you people are doing, she and the other ymbrynes are gonna bring such hell down on your heads, you won't know what hit you."

"That's the craziest thing I ever heard," said Wreck.

"Then I think they'll fit in just fine," said Dogface.

The dynamic in the room had changed. We had earned some grudging respect from them, and the balance of power had evened. But the clan leaders were still wary of us—and of one another—and no one had let their guard down. Wreck was still aiming his gun, Emma was still holding her flame to Frankie's face, Dogface was crouched on all fours, ready to pounce, and Angelica's cloud was now quietly storming, pellets of rain wetting her head and shoulders. It felt like we were dancing around a stick of lit dynamite.

"I got one question to ask you, and you'd best answer it true," said Wreck. "People like you don't come through town without a good reason. So what are you doing here?"

I suppose I thought I could talk to them like equals, but thinking back, I don't know why I said it. I was feeling proud and reckless, and the truth just came tumbling out. "We came to help her," I said, nodding at Noor. "She's a brand-new peculiar who's in danger, and we're taking her home with us."

There was a moment of tense quiet as the clan leaders digested this, then looked at one another.

"You say she's new?" said Dogface. "You mean . . . uncontacted?" He leaned back on his heels, his voice rising from a snarl back to normal.

"That's right," said Emma. "What's it matter?

Angelica was shaking her head, rainwater dripping off her chin. "That's bad."

"Damn it!" said Wreck. He punched the air. "Damn it, I really wanted the fiery one on my crew."

"What are you talking about?" said Bronwyn.

"Yeah, what just happened?" said Noor.

Frankie started laughing. "Oh, you're in *trouble*," she said.

"You shut up," said Emma.

"Kidnapping an uncontacted peculiar is a serious crime," said the tutor. "A very grave offense."

"No one's *kidnapping* me," said Noor.

"You're outsiders," said Wreck, "and you're transporting an uncontacted across territory lines. And that means—" He let out a loud breath and stamped his foot. "I *hate* this!"

Dogface stood up and brushed off his hands. "We've got to turn you in," he said. "Or we'll be accessories to the crime."

"*Must* we?" said Angelica. "I like them more and more."

"You must be joking." Dogface started pacing nervously. "If we don't report this and Leo hears about it? Our lives are worth nothing. *Less* than nothing."

"I thought you weren't afraid of 'nobody, no man, no nothing,'" Angelica said.

Dogface spun toward her and yelled, "Only an idiot wouldn't be afraid of Leo!"

Wreck turned away, and when he turned back he was holding something that looked like a small cell phone. "I hate to do this. I really do. I was looking forward to working with you. But I'm afraid I have no choice."

He punched a few buttons on the device. A moment later, a siren began to blare. It seemed to come from everywhere at once—the walls, ceiling, the air itself. My friends and I looked at one another, then at the Americans, who had lowered their weapons and were no longer making threatening moves toward us at all anymore. They just seemed disappointed.

Emma let go of Frankie. She fell to the floor. "Where's our friend?" she shouted at the girl. "What did you do with Enoch?"

Frankie scurried away toward the Americans. "He's part of my collection now!" She peeked out between Wreck's knees. "You're not getting him back, either!"

With that, there seemed no reason left to stay, and nothing compelling us to. The siren blared. My friends and I looked around.

"I think we'd better go," I said.

"You don't have to tell me twice," said Emma.

Emma, Noor, and I helped Bronwyn, who seemed almost her old self again but was still a little woozy, and we ran down the stairs and up the aisle toward the back exit as fast as we could—which wasn't very. Neither the Americans nor their flunkies made the slightest attempt to stop us. We burst through the doors and out into the fading day.

Running toward us were a half-dozen men in 1920s-era suits

carrying antique machine guns. They raised them and shouted for us to stop. A spray of bullets ricocheted off the concrete behind us.

One of the men kicked my legs out from under me, and then I was lying facedown on the pavement with a shoe grinding into the back of my neck.

A gruff order was given. "*Wink 'em.*" A hood was pulled over my head.

Everything went black.

CHAPTER SEVENTEEN

I was hauled onto my feet and pulled along roughly, then lifted by my arms and thrown onto a metal floor. A door slammed. I seemed to be in the back of a vehicle. I couldn't see anything through the hood they'd pulled over my head; I could hardly breathe through it. My chin ached where it had been ground into the concrete, and my wrists, bound again, chafed in their tight restraints. A big, many-cylindered engine chugged to life. I heard Emma say something, and one of the goons barked, "*Shaddap!*" and there was a slap, then quiet, as rage coiled in my chest.

The vehicle juddered and shook. No one spoke. Two things occurred to me as we waited for our fate to reveal itself: that these goons must work for Leo, the only person in New York everyone seemed to be afraid of, and that I'd lost my duffel bag. My duffel bag with Abe's operations log in it. The only thing he'd bothered to keep locked in his secret underground bunker. Full of sensitive information. A near-full accounting of his years as a hollow-hunter. And I had lost track of it.

I'd last had possession of the duffel going into Frankie's. The tutor must have taken it off me between there and the abandoned theater. Had he looked inside it? Did he know what he had? What was worse: if he threw it away, or if he read it?

Not that any of that mattered now. If these really were Leo's guys, and he was as terrible as everyone seemed to think he was, I might not live out the day anyway.

The driver hit the brakes hard. I started to slide across the metal floor when a goon grabbed me by the neck. The vehicle stopped and I heard the doors open. We were dragged out, hustled into some kind of building, down a hall, and through a loop entrance so gentle I almost didn't realize what had happened. Then we were taken outside again, but now our environment felt and sounded different. It was cold, and the street was bustling. We had passed into an older era. The sound of people's shoes on the pavement was different—harder, because no one wore sneakers. There were cars all around us, and their engines were rougher-sounding, their horns throatier, their exhaust smokier.

When I stumbled twice on uneven pavement, the man who had my arm warned me not to try anything stupid, then tore off the hood before marching me on again. I blinked against the sudden bright daylight, trying to take in the scene and figure out where I was. I knew that my life might depend on a quick escape later.

It was New York, sometime in the first half of the twentieth century—1930s or '40s, I guessed. The old cars and buses were unmistakable, and every man wore a suit and hat. My captors blended in perfectly here. They'd felt comfortable taking off my hood because they no longer had to worry about me seeing where I was. They probably controlled the whole place. Shouting for help in this loop would've done me no good—the goons would've killed any normals who gave them trouble. The only things they bothered to hide, so as not to make a scene, were their machine guns, tucked inside newspapers under their arms.

We walked down the street. Nobody seemed to notice us, and I wasn't sure if that was just the way of New Yorkers, or if people here were trained to ignore Leo's men because it was better for their health. I tried to look behind me, to see if my friends were there, but that earned me a slap on the back of the head. I could see my captors in front of me and to each side, and I could hear, somewhere to the rear, Dogface and Wreck, talking low.

We turned down an alley, then walked up a loading ramp, past several men in work coveralls, and into a dark warehouse.

"Leo's waiting," one of the workers growled.

We were marched through a kitchen buzzing with chefs and waiters who pressed themselves against the walls to let us pass, careful never to make eye contact. We walked through a ballroom, through a plush bar that was gloomy at midday but nearly half full with patrons, then up a gilded staircase, to an office.

The office was big and fancy, with fine carved wood and touches of gold. At the far end, behind a hulking, mirror-polished desk, a man sat waiting for us. He wore a black pinstriped suit with a loud purple tie and a cream-colored felt homburg that didn't quite match the rest of his outfit. A tall man stood next to him, looking like an undertaker, all dressed in black.

As I was walked toward him, the man at the desk stared at me. My skin prickled like it was being probed with icicles. He was playing with a letter opener, pushing the point into the green felt of his desk, leaving little divots. His eyes shifted, and in short order Emma, Millard, and Bronwyn were hauled up beside me.

Noor was not among them. I wondered what they'd done with her, a chill of dread going through me. Then Wreck, Angelica, and Wreck's two flunkies were rushed in, a goon attached to each of them. Dogface was nowhere to be seen; clearly, he'd made his escape.

"Leo, good to see you, been too long," said Wreck, making a hat-tip gesture though he didn't wear a hat. His flunkies were silent.

Angelica bowed. "Hello, Leo," she said, her cloud a polite size and hugged close to her body, as if it, too, were intimidated.

Leo pointed the letter opener at her. "You better not rain in here, angel face. I just had this carpet steamed."

"I won't, sir."

"So." Leo aimed the opener at us. "This them?"

"That's them," said Wreck.

"Where's the dog boy?"

"He got away," said the tall man, his voice a snaky slither.

Leo gripped the letter opener a little tighter. "That ain't good, Bill. People are gonna get the idea that we're soft on crime."

"We'll get him, Leo."

"You better." He looked to Wreck and Angelica. "Now, as for you. I heard you were attending an illegal auction."

"Oh no, nothing like that," said Wreck. "These peculiars here?" He gestured to my friends and me. "We were trying to hire them. It was a . . . job fair."

"Job fair!" Leo chuckled. "That's a new one. You sure you weren't trading them under the table? Inducing them via threats or intimidation to render services to you free of charge?"

"No, no, no," Wreck was saying.

"We'd never do that," said Angelica.

"And what are you supposed to do with outsiders?" said Leo.

"Bring them to you," said Wreck.

"That's right."

"Frankie thought they were nobody special, that's why—"

"Frankie's a mental midget!" Leo shouted. "Sorting out who's nobody and who's an infiltrator ain't her department. You bring outsiders to me and *I* sort 'em out! Got it?"

"Yes, Leo," they said in unison.

"Now, where's the light-eater?"

"Cooling her heels in the lounge," said Leo's man, Bill. "I got Jimmy and Walker with her."

"Good. Don't be rough on her. We want to try and make friends first, remember."

"Got it, Leo."

Leo turned to us. Took his feet off the desk and sat forward. "Where you from?" he said. "You're *Californios*, ain't ya? Meese's people?"

"I'm from Florida," I said.

"We're from the UK," said Bronwyn. Her voice sounded raw.

"We don't know who Meese is or understand any of what you're talking about," said Emma.

Leo nodded. Looked down at his desk. Was quiet for a strangely long moment. When he looked up again, his face had gone ruddy with anger.

"My name's Leo Burnham, and I run this town."

"Whole East Coast," said Bill.

"Here's how this is gonna work. I ask you questions and you answer straight. I'm not a guy you lie to. I'm not a guy whose time you waste." Leo raised his hand above his head and brought it down hard, stabbing the letter opener deep into the top of his desk. Everyone in the room jumped.

"Read the charges, Bill," said Leo.

Bill flipped open a pad of paper. "Trespassing. Resisting arrest. Kidnapping an uncontacted peculiar."

"Add lying about their identity," said Leo.

"Got it, Leo," said Bill, scribbling.

Leo stood up from his tall chair, walked around behind it, and rested his forearms on its golden trim. "After the wights and shadow beasts skipped town and things started to open up," he said, "I knew it was only a matter of time before somebody tried to make a move on our territory. I figured they'd start by trying to pick off one of the podunk loops on the outskirts. Missy Fineman's outfit out in the Pine Barrens. Juice Barrow's joint in the Poconos. But to come after one of the most powerful ferals we've seen in I don't know how long, and to do it *right in our backyard* in broad daylight—" He straightened as he said it, spittle flying in a flash of anger. "That's not only brazen, it's an insult. That's the Californios saying, 'Leo's weak. Leo's sleeping. Let's just waltz into his house and steal his piggy bank, because we *can get away with it*.'"

"You're clearly quite upset," said Millard, "and while I

certainly don't want to upset you further by disagreeing with you, we simply aren't who you seem to think we are."

Leo came out from behind his chair and stood in front of Millard, who had been forced to wear a striped gown that made it harder for him to slip away unnoticed.

"Are you from here?" Leo asked, his tone even.

"No," replied Millard.

"Were you trying to remove that feral?"

"What's a feral, exactly?"

Leo punched Millard in the stomach. Millard doubled over and groaned.

"Stop it!" Emma shouted.

"Bill, tell 'em what a feral is."

"A peculiar who don't know they're peculiar and ain't yet allied with any particular clan or crew," Bill said, as if reciting from memory.

"Feral" seemed to be another word for uncontacted—but more derogatory.

"She was in danger," I said. "We were trying to help her."

"By taking her out of the five boroughs." Leo sounded incredulous.

"To our loop in London," said Bronwyn. "Where she'd be safe from people like you."

Leo's eyebrows went up. "London. See, Bill, it's worse than I thought. Now we got limey peculiars coming after us, not just Los Californios."

"She's not one of you, and she's not yours," I said. "It was her choice to come with us."

Leo straightened his collar and came right up to me. His goon's grip on my arm tightened. "I don't know if you're really ignorant or just pretending to be," he said quietly, "but it don't matter. The law is the law, and it's the same law all over this country. That light-eater's a local, and inducing her to leave is a crime—one you've

admitted to. I got no choice but to make an example out of you."
He raised his hand and slapped me, and it happened so fast I didn't
have time to prepare myself for the blow. The shock and force of it
almost knocked me over.

"Bill, get these punks out of my office. Find out who they are,
and don't be afraid to put the screws on. We're done looking soft."

"You got it, Leo."

I saw Emma's face as we were being dragged out, and she saw
mine. I mouthed, *We'll be okay.* But for the first time since we'd left
my house in Florida days ago, I really wasn't sure.

That was the first time I met Leo, but it would not be the last.

◆   ◆   ◆

I couldn't tell you how long I spent in that cell. It felt like days, but
it was probably less than twenty-four hours. There was no window,
no sun, no furniture other than a cot and a toilet. The only light was
a bare bulb that never stopped burning, and under those conditions
the passage of time becomes harder to gauge, especially when you're
suffering from loop lag and your body hardly knows what time it is
in the first place.

They brought me food in a tin bowl, water in a tin cup. Every
few hours someone came to interrogate me. Usually a different person each time. At first all they wanted to know was where I was
from and who I worked with. They really seemed to believe I was
from California but lying about it. That I was a "Californio"—that
was the word they kept using. Though I denied it in every possible
way, the truth—that I was part of this band of peculiars from Great
Britain—sounded so unlikely, given my obvious Americanness and
the fact that I came from the modern day and my friends did not. It
was very difficult to convince them. My story made no sense. They
talked with cruel ease about killing me, and the various terrible pen-
alties for the "crimes" my friends and I had committed. But they

didn't beat me. They didn't torture me. I think it had something to do with the man down the hall. Every few hours they would take me out of the cell and walk me down to another windowless room, where I would sit across from an owlish man with tight-cropped hair and little round glasses. He would stare at me for long minutes without speaking, leaned way back in his chair, nibbling on pickles.

My theory is that he was trying to read my mind. I don't know if the pickles were part of his technique or if he just had an addiction to them. Eventually he must have found out whatever it was he wanted to find out—or perhaps they got through to one of my friends' brains—because my other interrogators suddenly changed their tune. Now they seemed to believe me when I insisted I wasn't from California, and that I was part of this group of peculiars from across the ocean.

After that they wanted to know all about the European peculiars, about the ymbrynes, about Miss Peregrine. They were convinced the ymbrynes were planning some sort of invasion or attack. They wanted to know how many other peculiars we'd kidnapped from America. How many ferals we'd lured away. I told them none, and that we had acted alone and without the ymbrynes' knowledge. And I repeated what I'd said to Leo: We'd answered a call to help an uncontacted peculiar who was in danger. We wanted to help her, and that was all.

"In danger from *what*," my interrogator asked. He was a big guy with unshaven jowls and chalk-white hair.

I figured there was no harm in telling them, so I described the people who'd been stalking her. The SUVs with blacked-out windows. The helicopter above the building site and the men who'd chased us and shot Bronwyn with some kind of tranquilizer dart.

"I ain't an educated man," said my interrogator. "But one thing I know back to front is our enemies. I know what they look like, how they dress, what they eat for breakfast, their mothers' names. And these people don't fit none of their descriptions."

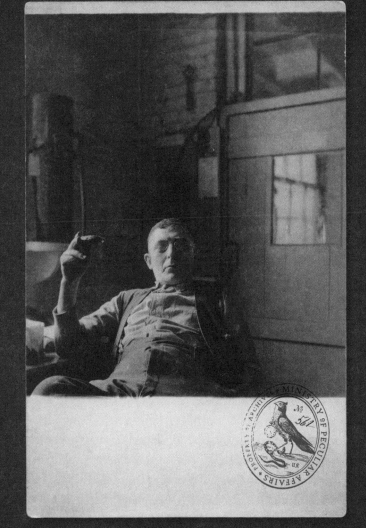

"I swear it's true," I said. "The ymbrynes had nothing to do with it. Miss Peregrine had nothing to do with it. This girl was in danger and we just wanted to help."

My interrogator burst out laughing. "Just wanted to help." He leaned in so close I could smell his skin, sour like menthol and night sweats. "I seen an ymbryne once. In Schenectady. Old lady, lived in the woods with about twenty kids. They followed her around like little ducks. Slept in the same bed. Followed her to the *john*." He shook his head. "Nobody in this world *just wants to help*. And no wards of no ymbryne ever acted on their own."

I felt a swell of bitterness and wounded pride.

"My grandfather did." Why keep it a secret? I couldn't let them think the ymbrynes were making moves against them. Who knew what sort of consequences that could have. "He ran a crew that fought hollowgast and helped peculiars who were in danger. People knew him as Gandy."

My interrogator wasn't laughing anymore. He was writing down everything I said on a little pad.

"He died earlier this year," I continued, "and he wanted me to take over for him. At least, I think he did. We got this mission from an associate of his."

The interrogator looked up from his pad. "You say one of Gandy's associates is still alive?"

The way he was staring at me gave me a chill. I knew then I had made an error.

"No—" I acted like I was confused. "I meant, we got the mission from a machine," I lied. "One of those teletype printers? The orders just printed out while I was standing near it, like it knew I was there. But I *assumed* it was from an old associate of my grandfather's." I wanted to bury what I'd said about H, but it was too late.

The interrogator closed his pad. "You've been very helpful," he said, and he winked and scraped back his chair.

"We didn't mean to step on any toes," I said quickly. "We didn't know about your territory or laws or anything like that."

Keys rattled in the door and it opened. The interrogator smiled. "You have a nice day."

◆   ◆   ◆

Twenty minutes later they dragged me in to see Leo. The room was empty but for him, the man holding me, and Leo's funereal right-hand man, Bill. Leo came at me as soon as I got through the door. Got right up into my face.

"Your grandfather was a murderer. You knew that, right?"

I didn't know what to say, so I didn't say anything. He was clearly unhinged.

"Gandy. Or whatever you call him."

"His name was Abraham Portman," I said quietly.

"Kidnapping. Murder. Man was sick in the head. *Look* at me."

I raised my eyes to meet his. "You don't know what you're talking about."

"Oh yeah?" he said. "Bill, get me the file on Gandy."

Bill went over to a filing cabinet and starting rifling through it.

"He was a good man," I said. "He fought monsters. He saved people."

"Yeah, we thought so, too," said Leo. "Until we found out *he* was the monster."

"Got it right here, Leo," said Bill.

Bill walked over with a brown folder in his hand. Leo took it and flipped it open. He turned a page, and something cracked behind his stony expression. "Here," he said, and then I saw him wince.

He slapped me hard across the cheek. I stumbled. The man holding me yanked me up again. My head tingled.

"She was my goddaughter," said Leo. "Sweet as sugarcane. Eight years old. Agatha."

He turned the file so I could see it. Clipped to the page was a photo of a little girl astride a tricycle. A black knot of dread began to well in my stomach.

"They took her in the night. Gandy and his men. They even had a shadow creature with them. *Working* for them. It broke the window to her bedroom and pulled her right out—from the second floor. There was a trail of black muck leading right to her bed."

"He wouldn't," I said. "He would never kidnap a child."

"He was *seen*!" he shouted. "But she wasn't. Not ever again. And we looked, don't you know we looked. He either fed her to that thing or killed her himself. If he'd sold her to some other clan, I woulda heard. She woulda got free, reached out."

"I'm sorry that happened," I said. "But I can promise you it wasn't him."

He slapped me again, on the other cheek this time, and the room blurred and my ear started to ring. When my vision cleared, he was staring out the window at a gray afternoon.

"That's just one of about ten kidnappings we can pin on him. Ten kids who were taken and never seen again. Blood on his hands. But he's dead, you say. So I say that's blood on *your* hands."

He went over to a cart stocked with bottles and poured himself a shot of brown liquor. Downed it in one swallow.

"Now, where is this associate you say is still alive?"

"I don't know. I don't know."

I decided to come clean about H; I had let the cat out of the bag already, and it's not as if I had information that would lead them to him. I didn't even know where he lived.

Leo's goon had me by the neck, and I felt his grip tighten.

"You *know*. You were taking the girl to him!"

"No, to a loop. Not to him."

"What loop?"

"I don't know," I lied. "He hadn't told me yet."

Bill cracked his knuckles. "He's playing dumb, Leo. He thinks you're a sucker."

"It's fine," said Leo. "We'll find him. Nobody hides from me in my city. What I really want to know is, what do you *do* with them? Your victims?"

"Nothing," I said. "We don't have victims."

He grabbed the file off the table where he dropped it, flipped the page, and shoved it in my face. "Here's one of the kids your grandpa saved. We found him two weeks later. Does he look saved to you? Huh?"

It was a photo of a dead person. A little boy. Maimed. Horrible.

He punched me in the stomach. I doubled over, groaning.

"Is it some kind of sick family business? Is that it?"

He kicked me and I fell to the floor.

"Where is she? Where's Agatha?"

I was saying, "I don't know, I don't know," or trying to, while he kicked me twice more, until I could hardly breathe, and my nose was leaking blood all over the floor.

"Get him up," Leo said, disgusted. "Goddamn it, now I gotta get the carpet steamed again."

I was hauled up by my arms, but my legs wouldn't take my weight, so I knelt.

"I was gonna kill Gandy," said Leo. "I was gonna kill that sick son of a bitch with my own hands."

"Gandy's dead, Leo," said Bill.

"Gandy's dead," Leo repeated. "Then I guess you'll have to do, junior. What time is it?"

"Almost six," said Bill.

"We'll kill him in the morning. Make a thing of it. Invite the troops."

"*You're wrong*," I whispered, voice trembling. "*You're wrong about him.*"

"How do you want it, kid? Drowning or shooting?"

"*I can prove it.*"

"How about both?" said Bill.

"Nice idea, Bill. One time for him, one time for dear old Grand-pop. Now get him out of here."

❖   ❖   ❖

That night they turned off the light in my cell for the first time. I lay aching in the thin dark, wishing my body would disappear, wrestling with my thoughts. I worried for my friends. Were they being beaten, tortured, threatened? I worried for Noor, and what they were planning to do with her. Would she have been better off if I hadn't tried to help her at all? If I had listened to H and aborted the mission when he told me to?

Yes. Almost certainly yes.

I admit, I worried for myself, too. Leo's goons had been threatening me since I arrived, but for the first time their promise to kill me felt genuine. Leo didn't need anything from me anymore. He wasn't trying to get information out of me. He seemed only to want to watch me die.

And what was all this madness about my grandfather? I didn't think for a second that any of it could be true—but how could anyone? My one thought was that wights had framed him, staging kidnappings and killings to look as if Abe had committed them, in hopes that Leo's clan might have killed him and done the wights' work for them. As for my grandfather being identified at the scenes of some of these crimes (a point Leo had emphasized), the wights were masters of disguise. Maybe one of them had dressed like him, or made a lifelike mask.

There was a sudden, loud banging at my cell door.

This was it. They had come for me. They hadn't even waited until morning.

The hatch in the door slid open.

"Portman."

It was Leo. I was surprised, but then it made sense—he wanted to pull the trigger himself.

"Get over here."

I got up from the cot and stood before the hatch.

"The wights framed my grandfather," I said, not because I thought he'd believe me, but because I needed to say it.

"Shut your goddamn trap." He paused to collect himself. "You know this lady?"

He held a photo up to the hatch. I was so thrown off by this unexpected pivot that it took me a moment to react. It was a snapshot of a dyed-blond diva in white gloves and a feathered hat. She was holding a can of Drano, and she was, it seemed, singing to it.

"That's the baroness," I said, grateful my memory hadn't gone blank.

Leo lowered the picture. He observed me for a moment with his brow furrowed. I couldn't read him at all. Had I passed a test? Or had I said the wrong thing?

"We made some calls," he said finally. "Your associates told us you stopped through the Flamingo. Naturally, we were concerned, so we put in a call to our friends down there, to see if you'd left anyone alive. Much to my surprise, not only did you comport yourselves as gentlemen and ladies, you also took care of some business I'd been meaning to handle."

I was floored. "Business?"

"Those idiot road warriors who act like they run things? I've been meaning to go to Florida and stomp them. You saved me the trouble."

"It was, uh, no problem." I was trying to sound calm and collected, not like someone who was still half expecting to be killed.

Leo chuckled and looked at the floor, as if embarrassed. "You might be wondering why a big shot like me cares about some tourist loop. Well, I wouldn't, except my sister lives there."

"The baroness?"

"Her real name's Donna. She likes the weather down there."
He shook his head and muttered to himself, "She takes a *couple*
opera lessons . . ."

"Are you letting me go?"

"Normally, a good word from my sister would only be enough
to get your death sentence commuted. But you got friends in interesting places."

"I do?"

He slapped shut the view-hatch. A key turned in the lock and
the door opened. We were standing a few feet apart, nothing now
between us. Then he stepped aside, and there, striding down the hall
toward me, was Miss Peregrine.

For a moment I thought I was dreaming. And then she spoke.

"Jacob. Come out of there at once."

She was angry with me, but her face was so etched with the pain
of worry and her eyes so wide with relief that I knew she would open
her arms when I ran to her—and she did, and I hugged her tight.

"Miss Peregrine. Miss Peregrine. I'm so sorry."

She patted my back and kissed me on the forehead.

"Save it for later, Mr. Portman."

I turned to Leo. "What about my friends?"

"Waiting in the loading dock."

"And Noor?"

His expression soured instantly. "Don't push it, kid. And don't
ever come back here. Helping my sister was your get-out-of-jail-free
card. But you only get one."

◆   ◆   ◆

Leo's men escorted us down the hallways, through Leo's club and
the kitchen, and out to the loading dock. In the weak light of dawn
I saw Emma and Bronwyn waiting, and beside them the white shirt

and gray slacks that I knew belonged to Millard. When I saw them whole and standing and unhurt, the shudder of relief I felt was almost like a chill. I hadn't realized until that moment how dimmed my hopes had become.

"Oh my bird, thank the birds," Bronwyn sang, clasping her hands as Miss Peregrine and I approached them.

"I told you he'd be fine," Millard said. "Jacob can take care of himself."

"*Fine?*" Emma said, going pale as she looked me over. "What did they do to you?"

I hadn't seen a mirror in a while, but between my busted nose and other injuries, I must've looked fearful.

Emma hugged me. For a moment it didn't matter what had happened between us, it just felt good to have her in my arms again. Then she hugged a little too tight, and pain ricocheted across my cracked ribs. I sucked in my breath and pulled away.

I assured her I was okay, though my head felt like a balloon that was about to pop. "Where's Enoch?" I said.

"In the Acre," said Millard.

"Thank God."

"He escaped that horrible diner," said Emma, "then called your house and told Miss P everything that had happened, and they tracked us here."

"We owe him our lives," said Millard. "That's something I never thought I'd say."

"You can catch up on the way back to the Acre," said someone with a French accent, and I turned to see Miss Cuckoo standing near the exit with another ymbryne. She wore an electric-blue dress with a tall silver collar, and her expression was flat. Neither she nor the other ymbryne betrayed any trace of happiness at seeing us.

"Come, there is a car waiting."

Leo's men watched as we walked out, their eyes and guns trained on us. I thought again of Noor, and the fact that we were leaving her here, in some form of captivity. I felt awful about it. Not only had we failed the mission, I had probably consigned her to a worse fate than if I'd left her alone entirely.

The ymbrynes bundled us out of the loading dock and into a big car. It lurched away from the curb before the doors had even closed.

"Miss Peregrine?" I said.

She turned slightly, her face in profile. "It would be better," she said, "if you didn't speak."

CHAPTER EIGHTEEN

*W*e were brought back to Devil's Acre via a Manhattan loop entrance that connected to the Panloopticon—a route that would have saved my friends and me days of driving and untold trouble if only we'd known about it. I was spared an immediate tongue-lashing because I was injured. Instead, the ymbrynes brought me to a bone-mender named Rafael, who worked out of a tumbledown house on Little Stabbing Street. For the rest of the day and all that night, I lay in a room filled with apothecary bottles while he applied stinging powders and pungent poultices to my wounds. He was no Mother Dust, but I could feel myself beginning to heal.

I was confined to the bed, mostly sleepless, haunted by failures and doubts and guilt. (If only I had listened to H. If only I had aborted the mission when he'd begged me to.) Haunted by the things Leo had said about my grandfather. Not that I thought they could be true—of course he had been framed by wights, it's the only explanation that made any sense—but the simple fact that anyone would fabricate such lies about him made me deeply uncomfortable. I would have to set that right, if I could ever get H to talk to me again. But I was haunted primarily by guilt about Noor. If she had never met me at all, she'd be safer than she was now. Hunted, yes, but at least she'd be free.

My friends came to see me in the morning. Emma, Millard, Bronwyn. And Enoch, too, who recounted how he had come out of Frankie's odd trance to find himself dressed in doll's clothes, which he took off as fast as he could before running away.

"We think he woke up when I tackled Frankie," said Emma. "She let go of us all, and that must have broken her hold on Enoch, too."

"She's quite powerful, to be able to influence people remotely that way," said Millard. "I'll have to include her in my new book, *Who's Who in Peculiar America*."

"I can control people remotely, too," said Enoch. "Provided they're dead."

"It's too bad, you would have made a cute couple," I said.

Enoch leaned over my bed and flicked a bruise on my arm, and I yelped.

They told me Miss Peregrine hadn't talked to them yet—not even to reprimand them. She'd hardly said a word to any of us since we'd returned, other than to warn us not to leave the Acre.

"She's still too angry," said Emma. "I've never seen her like this."

"Me, neither," said Bronwyn. "Not even the time my brother sank the Cairnholm ferry with all of us aboard."

"What if they excommunicate us from peculiardom?" said Emma.

"You *can't* be excommunicated from peculiardom," Enoch said. "Can you?"

"This whole thing was such an awful idea," Bronwyn said miserably.

"We were doing fine until you got shot with that sleep dart, or whatever it was," said Enoch.

"So it's *my* fault?"

"We never would've gotten stuck in Frankie's loop-trap if we hadn't had to go looking for a hospital!"

"It's nobody's fault," I said. "We just had some bad luck."

"If it weren't that, something else would've gotten us," said Emma. "I'm amazed we made it as far as we did, considering the vastness of our ignorance. We were fools to think we could do a mission in America with so little preparation and training." She glanced at me briefly, then looked away. "There was only one Abe Portman."

It was a cheap shot, but it stung. With painful effort, I sat up in bed. "His partner thought we were prepared. He gave us the mission."

"And I would very much like to know why," came a voice from the doorway.

We turned to see Miss Peregrine, leaning against the jamb holding an unlit pipe. How long had she been there?

Everyone tensed, ready for a dressing-down. Miss Peregrine walked in, surveying the room and all its equipment. "I don't suppose you children know how much trouble you've caused." She stopped in the middle of the floor.

"You must have been very worried," said Millard.

She turned her head sharply toward him and narrowed her eyes. It was clear we were not yet welcome to speak. "I was, yes, but not only about you people." She spoke with uncharacteristic coldness. "We have been engaged for some months—even before the hollowgast menace subsided—in an effort to negotiate peace between the American clans. Your actions have thrown those efforts into dire jeopardy."

"We didn't know," I said quietly. "You and Miss Cuckoo said the ymbrynes were busy with the reconstruction effort."

"It was top-secret ymbryne business," she said. "It would never have occurred to me that I would need to caution my own wards against striking out on their own into dangerous and poorly charted territory—not only without permission, but without even *telling* me—in order to conduct some ill-conceived rescue mission assigned to you by an unknown and *utterly* untrustworthy source . . ." Her tone rose shrilly, and then she paused, rubbing a knuckle into her eye. "Excuse me. I haven't slept in days."

She took a match from her dress pocket, lifted her foot and

struck it deftly against the sole, and lit her pipe. When she'd taken a few meditative puffs, she continued.

"The other ymbrynes and I worked around the clock to negotiate your release from Leo Burnham's Five Boroughs clan. It's quite a complex thing when the very people who are trying to broker a peace treaty are accused of committing high crimes." Miss Peregrine let that sink in for a moment before she went on. "America is badly divided. Here's the gist of it, which I share now only because I want to impress upon you how difficult you've made things. There are three major factions: the Five Boroughs clan, whose influence extends through much of the East Coast; the Invisible Hand, with power concentrated in Detroit; and the Californios in the West, with Los Angeles as its capital. Texas and the South are autonomous, semi-lawless zones, which have resisted efforts to centralize control in any one loop, an unfortunate situation that has only worsened societal rifts. But tensions among the big three are the primary concern. They have long-standing boundary disputes, old grudges, and the like, but for a hundred years the threat of hollowgast attacks seriously reduced their mobility and prevented occasional skirmishes from escalating into war. Now that the hollows are mostly gone, however, the skirmishes are worsening."

"In other words, we couldn't have picked a worse time to go blundering in," said Millard.

"You could not have," Miss Peregrine agreed. "Especially given the delicate work we ymbrynes have taken on."

I had heard some of this before, but my friends had not. They looked deflated and horrified.

"I get why the situation is delicate," I said. "I just don't understand why trying to help one peculiar in need was such a terrible thing."

"It wouldn't have been, in Europe," said Miss Peregrine. "But in America it's a serious offense."

"But my grandfather spent his whole career finding and helping uncontacted peculiars."

"Years ago!" she said, nearly shouting. "Conventions change, Mr. Portman! Laws are rewritten! And if you had simply *asked* me, or any ymbryne, we would have told you that the Americans are territorial, and what was an act of heroism twenty-five years ago is now considered a capital offense."

"But *why*?"

"Because the most valuable resource in peculiardom is us. Peculiars. If two loops are in conflict with each other, they need as many peculiars in their ranks as they can find—to be fighters, bone-menders, runners, invisible spies, and so on. An *army*. But we peculiars have a very limited population from which to recruit. And thanks to the evil hunger of the hollows, new peculiars were hard to find for a very long time. They got snapped up—quite literally. Starved of new blood, peculiar populations grew older and became loop-bound. An army that can't stray far from its loop for fear of aging forward isn't very effective. So there is really nothing more valuable in peculiardom than a never-contacted peculiar. Especially a powerfully talented one."

"Why didn't H tell us that?" I said. "He must've known helping Noor would make the local clans angry."

"I'd like to ask him that same question," Miss Peregrine said angrily. "And several more, as well."

"I'm sure his motives were virtuous," said Millard. "She was being hunted by some very nasty people."

"Helping her might've been virtuous," said Miss Peregrine. "Involving my wards in the matter was not."

"We're so sorry," said Emma. "I hope you can believe that."

Miss Peregrine ignored her, as she had ignored all our attempts to apologize. She went to the window and blew a cloud of pipe-smoke out toward the humming street. "We were making progress in our peace talks, but this episode has seriously damaged the clans' trust in us. The neutral party cannot be suspected of having any agenda other than peace. It's a bad setback."

"Do you think they'll go to war?" asked Millard. "Because of us?"

"We may yet have an opportunity to mend things. But the clans are quite far apart on a number of key issues. They must agree on territorial boundaries, elect a peacekeeping council . . . these are no small matters, and the stakes are considerable. If war should break out between them, it would be a disaster not only for American peculiars, but for all of us. War is a germ that can rarely be contained. It would surely spread."

Judging from our slumped shoulders and downcast expressions, all of us were feeling intense shame. I was starting to regret everything—even reaching out to H in the first place.

After what felt like a long time, Miss Peregrine turned to look at us. "Worse than any of that," she said, sighing, "worse than the clans not trusting us, is that I feel I can no longer trust *you*."

"Don't say that, miss, don't say that," pleaded Bronwyn.

"I think I'm perhaps most disappointed in you, Miss Bruntley. This sort of behavior isn't so surprising from Miss Bloom or Mr. O'Connor. But you have always been so loyal and kind."

"I'll make it up to you," Bronwyn said. "I promise."

"You'll start by working on the kitchen cleanup crew here in the Acre for one month."

"Yes, yes, of course," said Bronwyn, nodding eagerly. She seemed relieved to have a punishment, which meant forgiveness was possible.

"Miss Bloom, I'm reassigning you to the Smoking Street garbage incinerator." I saw Emma wince, but she said nothing. "Mr. O'Connor, you'll be sweeping chimneys. Mr. Nullings—"

"Miss Peregrine?" I interrupted her.

She stopped mid-sentence. My friends looked at me with various shades of disbelief.

"What is it?" said Miss Peregrine.

I knew that what I was about to ask would be met with a barrage of resistance. But I had to say it anyway.

"What about Noor?"

"What about her?" said Miss Peregrine. I knew her patience was wearing thin. But I couldn't let this go.

"We just . . . *left* her there," I said.

"I'm aware of what happened," Miss Peregrine said. "And if it had been possible to bring her back to the Acre with us, I would have done it. But it took all the leverage I had to secure *your* release. To then insist upon taking her, too, would have made it seem as if it were her we'd wanted all along. That we really *were* after their un-contacted peculiars. And that would have derailed the peace talks."

Miss Peregrine had a point, but she was talking about politics, and I was talking about a person. Couldn't we avoid war *and* save Noor? And so I persisted.

"Leo's crazy and dangerous," I said. "I know it would look bad, so maybe there's a way we can *sneak* her out, so they wouldn't know it was us . . ."

Emma was shooting me daggers with her eyes. *Stop*, she mouthed.

Miss Peregrine was about to lose it, I could tell.

"Mr. Portman," she said, "if that girl's in danger, it's your fault. I cannot believe, after all I just told you, that you're still insisting we attempt to remove her from that loop. I simply can't believe it."

"I know it's my fault, and I admit that." I was talking fast, trying to make my point without pushing Miss Peregrine too far. "But you should've seen the people who were after her; they had helicopters and, like, special-ops tactical gear."

"Obviously, that was one of the other clans."

"It wasn't, though," I said, talking over her now, "Leo's guys didn't know *who* they were—"

"Mr. Portman."

"There's something special about her, something important, I have this feeling—

"Mr. Portman!"

"Jacob, *desist*," Millard hissed at me.

"I just don't think H would've sent us after her if she *weren't* important, you know? He's not an idiot."

"Mr. Portman, she is none of your *concern*!" Miss Peregrine yelled.

I had never heard her shout like that. The room went quiet. Even the street noise coming through the window seemed to hush.

She was trembling with anger.

"Sometimes imperfect situations must be tolerated in order to achieve a greater good," she said, struggling to control her tone. "The safety of one cannot outweigh the safety of thousands."

I was angry, too. Which is why I couldn't come up with anything more articulate to say than "Well, that sucks."

Bronwyn gasped. No one spoke to Miss Peregrine that way.

Miss Peregrine took a step forward. Leaned over me in my bed. "Yes, Mr. Portman, it *sucks*. But deciding between choices that *suck* is precisely why being a leader can *suck*. Which is precisely the reason we don't, and will never, involve children in high-level leadership decisions." She said the word *children* so pointedly, it felt like she was throwing it in our faces.

I saw Emma's brow furrow. "Miss Peregrine?" she said.

Miss Peregrine turned sharply to face her, as if daring her to speak. "What *is* it, Miss Bloom?"

"We aren't children anymore."

"Yes," she said, "you are. You have proven that today." And she turned on her heel and stalked out of the room.

Miss Peregrine left a stunned silence in her wake. When the sound of her footfalls leaving the house had faded, my friends found their voices.

"You're such an ass, Portman," said Enoch. "You made her even madder. Rambling on about that girl!"

"If one of you were still in that loop, *we'd* all be worried," I said. "Why shouldn't we worry about her?"

"It's none of our concern," Bronwyn mumbled. "Like Miss P said."

"They're not going to *kill* her or anything," said Enoch. "She's got to be safer with Leo's people than she was hiding from helicopters in some abandoned building."

"We don't know that!" I said. "The mission was to get her to a safe loop, not just drop her off wherever—"

"Forget the bloody *mission*!" Emma exploded. "There is no mission anymore! Mission over! Mission stupid to begin with!"

"Agreed, agreed, agreed," said Bronwyn. "We should just forget it ever happened and hope the ymbrynes forgive us."

"It was partly their fault!" I said. "None of this would have happened if they had just told us what was going on. I didn't know they were forging some peace accord . . ."

"Don't try and pin this on the ymbrynes," Bronwyn said.

"They treat us like idiots!" I said. "You all said it yourselves!"

"I don't know about you," said Bronwyn, "but after seeing how the Americans live, I'm *glad* we have ymbrynes, and I'm never going to complain about them again. So if that's what we're doing right now, please count me out."

"I'm not complaining, I'm just saying—"

"We're not their equals, Jacob. And you aren't, either. I mean, it's really great what you did for everybody in the Library of Souls, but just because you're a famous hero and people want your autograph doesn't mean you're as important as an ymbryne."

"I never said I was."

"Well, you're acting like you are. So if Miss Peregrine wants to keep a secret from you, I'm sure there's a good reason, and that's the end of it."

Bronwyn turned and went out, leaving another silence behind her.

"What about the rest of you?" I said.

"What about us, *what*?" Emma said sourly.

"What happened to being independent? Making our own decisions? Is that all out the window now that Miss P is pissed at us?"

"Don't be purposely thick," said Enoch. "We could have started a *war*."

"Miss Peregrine has every right to be furious with us," said Emma.

"I agree that we are often treated like children," said Millard. "But we picked a bad time to assert our independence."

"We couldn't have known that," I said. "But just because we made one mistake doesn't mean we should give up completely."

"Yes, it does," said Enoch. "In this case, it does. I'm going to put my head down, sweep some chimneys, and hope things go back to normal soon."

"What a heroic sentiment," I said.

Enoch laughed, but I could tell I'd hurt him. He came up to my bed, pulled some wilted daisies from his pocket, and tossed them onto my blanket. "You're no hero, either," he said. "You're not Abe Portman and you're never going to be. So why don't you just stop trying." And he walked out.

I felt frozen. I didn't know what to say.

"I'd better be going, too," Millard mumbled. "I don't want the headmistress to think we're . . ."

I couldn't hear the rest of what he said.

"What? Conspiring?"

"Something like that," he said.

"What about the others? Are they coming to see me?" I hadn't seen Horace, Hugh, Olive, or Claire since we'd left on the mission, which felt like a lifetime ago.

"I don't think so," said Millard. "See you later, Jacob."

I didn't like how this was ending. I could feel a line being drawn, with me on one side, and everyone else on the other.

Millard left, his coat and pants floating out the door. And now I was alone with Emma—and she was moving toward the exit, too.

"Don't leave," I said, a sudden, shameful desperation coming over me.

"I really should. I'm sorry, Jacob."

"It doesn't have to be over. This is just a setback."

"Stop. Please." Her eyes were brimming with tears, and so, I realized, were mine. "It does. It does have to be over."

"We'll get H on the phone somehow, talk about what happened, what to do next—"

"Listen, Jacob. Please listen." She pressed her palms together and touched the tips of her fingers to her lips—prayerful, pleading. "You're not Abe," she said. "You're not Abe, and I'm afraid if you keep trying to be, it will kill you." She turned away slowly, the doorway framing her, and walked out.

◆　　◆　　◆

I lay in bed listening to noise from the street, thinking, dreaming, talking with Rafael when he came in to sprinkle me with strange dusts. I drifted in and out of an uneasy sleep. My emotions swung between anger and regret. Yes, I felt abandoned by my friends— could I even call them that anymore?—but part of me understood why they'd refused to take my side. They had risked a lot for me and nearly lost it all. I didn't know if you could be excommunicated from peculiardom, but I imagine we'd all come close.

I was angry at Emma, too, for what she'd done, for what she'd said, for walking away. But I also wondered if the breakdown of our relationship had been my fault. Had I pushed her toward old feelings she'd purposely avoided for years? If I had never gone into Abe's bunker, never called H, never involved Emma in any of this, would we still be together?

And Miss Peregrine. Miss P could be suffocating and frustrating and condescending, but she did have reason to be angry with me. So did my friends. The whole undertaking had been motivated to an uncomfortable degree by my own frustration with the ymbrynes and anger at my parents. The problem, really, was that I had been trying to navigate a world for which I had not been prepared. The peculiar universe was deeply complex, with rules and traditions and taxonomies and histories that even my friends, who had been studying it for nearly all of their long lives, had not yet wrapped their minds around. Newcomers should be required to train and study as hard as astronauts preparing for space. But when Miss Peregrine's loop collapsed, I was thrown into it with no choice but to swim for my life. Miraculously, through some combination of dumb luck, peculiar talent, and the bravery of my friends, I had survived—emerged victorious, even.

But luck isn't something you can depend upon, and my mistake was thinking I could dive in again and everything would work out somehow. In a fit of pique, and completely of my own accord, I had jumped back into that dark water, and had lashed several of my friends to me in the bargain, which was not only unwise, ultimately, but unkind. And I had very nearly died.

I was underprepared and overconfident. I couldn't blame Miss Peregrine for that. So I couldn't even be mad at her, really, or at my friends. The more I mulled it over, the more my anger homed in on someone else. A person who hadn't even been present. A person who wasn't even alive: my grandfather. He had known, my whole life, who I was. He had known, as a peculiar, what I would have to face one day. But he had not prepared me for it at all.

Why? Because I'd been rude to him in the fourth grade? Because I'd hurt his feelings? It was hard to believe he could've been so petty. Or was it, as Miss Peregrine had once suggested, because he was trying to spare me pain? Because he wanted me to grow up feeling normal?

It was a sweet idea, on its face. But not if I interrogated it a little bit. Because he *knew*. He had lived here, in this complicated and bloody and divided peculiar America. If he was really withholding the truth in order to spare me pain, he knew it was putting me at risk. Even if the hollows never got me, some gang of peculiar Americans would have sniffed me out eventually. Imagine my surprise, had I found out I was peculiar *that* way, as some heartless highwayman's feral prize.

Abe left me without a map, without a key, without a clue. Without a single hint about how to navigate this strange new reality. It had been his duty to tell me, and he had not.

How could he have been so careless?

Because he didn't care.

That nasty little voice in my head, back again.

I couldn't believe he hadn't cared. There had to be some other answer.

And then I realized there was someone still living who might know it.

"Rafael?"

The bone-mender stirred. He'd been sleeping in a chair by the window, the blue light of early morning washing over him.

"Yes, Master Portman?"

"I need to get out of this bed."

❖   ❖   ❖

Three hours later, I was up and moving again. I had a purple bruise under one eye and my ribs still ached, but otherwise Rafael had worked miracles and I was feeling pretty good. I made my way back toward Bentham's Panloopticon as stealthily as I could, but there were people everywhere—the morning rush was in full swing—and I got stopped a few times for autographs. (It still surprised me every time I was recognized. I had spent so much of my life as an unremarkable nobody, that whenever I was approached my first thought was that they had confused me for someone else.)

I knew I wasn't supposed to leave the Acre. I was risking being seen by someone who would report me to Miss Peregrine. But that wasn't at the top of my list of concerns. I managed to make it through the front door, down the main hall, and upstairs to the

Panloopticon hallways without being recognized. When the clerk at the Panloopticon entrance did, I told him I was going home and he waved me through. I ran down the hall, past busy travelers and officials at checkpoint desks and Sharon's voice booming from an open door. I rounded a corner into the shorter hall, where my door was, found the broom closet marked A. PEREGRINE AND WARDS ONLY, and dove inside.

I walked out of the potting shed into the slanting sun and muggy heat of a Florida afternoon.

My friends were in Devil's Acre. My parents were traveling in Asia.

The house was empty.

I went inside, settled onto a sofa in the living room, and took my phone out of my pocket. It still had a little battery left. I dialed H's number. After three rings, a man answered.

"Hong's."

"I'm calling for H," I said.

"Hold on."

In the background I could hear voices, the noise of clattering plates. Then H came on the line.

"Hello?" he said warily.

"It's Jacob."

"I figured the ymbrynes would have had you under lock and key by now."

"Not quite," I said, "but they're pretty angry. I'm sure they wouldn't be happy if they knew I was calling you, either."

He chuckled. "I'm sure they wouldn't." I knew he was angry with me, too. I could hear it in his voice. But he seemed to have forgiven me already, probably even before we'd talked. "Hey, I'm glad you're all right. You had me worried."

"Yeah. I had me worried, too."

"Why the hell didn't you listen to me? Now things are all fouled up."

"I know. I'm sorry. Let me help fix it."

"No, thank you. You've done quite enough."

"I should've aborted the mission when you told me to," I said. "But—" I hesitated, worried this would sound like an accusation. "Why didn't you tell me we were doing something illegal?"

"*Illegal?* Where'd you get that?"

"It's the clans' law. You can't take an uncontacted peculiar—"

"We should all be free to go where we like," he interrupted. "Any law that takes your freedom away should be ignored."

"Well, I agree. But the ymbrynes are trying to negotiate a peace treaty between the clans, and—"

"You think I don't know that?" he said, getting frustrated. "The clans will go to war if that's what they want to do, and don't let anyone fool you into thinking it's got anything to do with you or me. Anyway, there's bigger things at stake than whether the damned clans want to fight with one another."

"Really? Like what?"

"Like the girl."

"You mean Noor."

"Of course I mean her. And don't say her name out loud again."

"Why is she so important?"

"I'm not going to tell you over an unsecured telephone line. And, anyhow, you don't need to know. Truth is, I should never have gotten you involved in the first place. I went against my better judgment. I broke a promise, too, and I'm sick about it. You nearly got killed because of it."

"What promise? To who?"

There was a pause. I might've thought the line had gone dead, but I could hear dishes rattling in the background. Finally, he said, "To your grandfather."

Which reminded me of the reason I'd called H in the first place.

"Why?" I said. "Why did he never tell me anything? Why would he ask you to keep secrets from me?"

"Because he wanted to protect you, son."

"That was never going to be possible. All it did was leave me totally unprepared."

"He always meant to tell you who you were. But he died too soon to do it himself."

"Then what was he protecting me from?"

"From our work. He didn't want you involved."

"Then why did he send me postcards from your missions? Or make maps for me? Or make my nickname the passcode to the bunker under his house?"

I heard H take a deep breath and let it out slowly. "He was leaving you tools in case of emergency. But that's it. Now, I'm afraid you caught me on my way out."

"To do what?"

"One last job," he replied. "Then I'm retired for good."

"You're going to try to get her back, aren't you?"

"That's no business of yours."

"Wait for me. I'll come to you. I want to help. *Please*."

"No, thank you. Like I said, you've done quite enough—and you don't take orders."

"I will. I promise."

"Okay, then take this order. Go back to your life. Go back to your ymbrynes and your safe little world, because you aren't ready for this one yet. Maybe we'll meet again, someday, when you are."

And then he hung up.

CHAPTER NINETEEN

I stood in my living room, phone in hand, still listening to the silence on the dead line. My mind was racing. I had to get to H, and quickly. I had to help him. I was green and inexperienced, yes, but he was old and out of practice. He needed me, even if he wouldn't admit it. He was right about one thing, though—I was terrible at taking orders. Oh, well; it was a second chance at helping Noor. Maybe just a sliver of a chance, but at this point I would take what I could get.

First, I would have to find H. Luckily, I knew right where to start looking: on the book of matches where I'd first gotten his phone number. It was from a Chinese restaurant somewhere in Manhattan. When I'd called him this time, I'd heard what sounded like a restaurant in the background—a busy kitchen, maybe, or the dish prep area—and I was pretty sure someone who worked there had answered the phone. I figured H lived in the back, or above it. The name and address were on the matchbook, so it would be easy enough to find. I just had to get to New York.

This time I didn't pack a bag or bring anything special. I changed the clothes I'd been in for days, which were bloodstained and beginning to smell a bit ripe. And then I ran out the back door and into the potting shed. Once I'd come out the other side and I was in the Panloopticon's hallway, I knew just where to go. Miss Peregrine had brought us back from New York through a door half-way down the hall on the Panloopticon's upper level. All I had to do was retrace our steps from the day before. It would've attracted too much attention to run, so I walked quickly with my head down, hoping none of the travelers or transport agents or desk clerks would notice me. I had made it all the way to the stairwell and up the stairs into the upper hall without being stopped when I ran face-first into a giant black wall.

The wall spoke, and the booming basso voice that came out of it was unmistakably Sharon's. "Portman! Aren't you supposed to be in Miss Wren's new menagerie loop scraping out grimbear cages?"

Miss Peregrine had stormed out before she'd told me what my punishment was, but somehow Sharon knew. Embarrassing news travels fast.

"How did you hear about that?" I said.

"The walls have ears, my friend. I'll show you sometime; they need regular de-waxing."

I shuddered and tried to put the image out of my mind. "I was on my way there now."

"How strange. That loop is downstairs." He crossed his arms and leaned down. "You caused quite a stir around here, you know that? Ruffled a lot of feathers."

"My friends and I didn't mean to upset anyone. Really."

"I'm not saying you did a bad thing." He lowered his voice. "Sometimes feathers *need* to be ruffled. If you take my meaning."

"Uh-huh," I said, fidgeting nervously. At any moment an ymbryne could've walked by and seen me.

"Not everyone likes the way the ymbrynes have been running things. They're too used to making all the decisions by themselves. They don't consult anyone. They don't ask for opinions."

"I know what you mean," I said.

"Do you?"

I did. I just didn't want to talk about it right at that moment.

Sharon leaned closer and whispered in my ear. His breath was cold and smelled like the earth. *"There's a meeting next Saturday evening at the old abattoir. I'd like to see you there."*

"What kind of meeting?" I said.

"Just some like-minded people kicking around ideas. Your presence would be much appreciated."

I peered into his hood. There was a faint shine of white teeth, engulfed in darkness.

"I'll come," I said. "But don't expect me to go against the ymbrynes."

The gleam in his hood widened into a smile. "Isn't that where you're going now?"

"It's more complicated than that."

"I'm sure it is." Sharon stood up to his full height, then stepped out of my way. "Your secret's safe with me."

He extended his hand. "You'll need this." It was a ticket. On one side was printed MINISTRY OF TEMPORAL AFFAIRS, and on the other side, ANYWHERE. "The American loops are closely guarded. The situation there is tense. Can't let just anyone go."

I tried to take the ticket from him, but he didn't let it go at first.

"Saturday," he said, then opened his hand.

◆　　◆　　◆

Now that I was traveling alone, moving from place to place was easier. After having to worry over the whereabouts of three or four other people for most of the last week, it was freeing to be able to speed-walk down a crowded hall without checking over my shoulder, to slip effortlessly into a crowd, to hand the clerk just my own ticket. He was a big man perched on a tiny stool behind a desk, and he looked at my ANYWHERE ticket like he'd never seen one before.

"You've got modern clothes on," he said, looking me over. "Have you been checked for anachronisms by the costumers?"

"Yep," I said. "They said I'm fine."

"Did they give you a waiver?"

"Uh, yeah," I said, patting my pockets, "let me see where I put it . . ."

A line was stacking up behind me. The desk clerk was manning five doors at once, and he was losing patience. "Just cover up with one of the coats inside the door there," he said, and waved me on. "There's a map in the pocket, if you need one."

I thanked him and went to the door. The little gold plate on it read BULLOCK'S DEPARTMENT STORE, NEW YORK, FEBRUARY 8, 1937.

I stepped through, lifted an old-looking black coat from a hook inside the door—emergency wardrobe—and pulled it on over my clothes. I walked to the back of the tiny, featureless room, and after a quick blackout and the now-familiar temporal rush, I heard the noises beyond the door change. I walked out into a department store. It looked like it had recently closed: The floor was full of empty racks and dusty, naked mannequins, and a muted glow was cast over everything from windows that had been papered with newsprint. There was a sleepy guard by the front entrance, and I could tell by his uniform, which looked a lot like the desk clerk's, that he was one of ours. His job was to screen people entering Devil's Acre, not bother people leaving it, so as a solo traveler with no baggage it was easy to get past him with just a self-assured nod.

Then I was out on the street, speed-walking down Sixth Avenue on a dim winter day, past a laundry billowing steam onto the sidewalk, past mounds of black snow, past a line of shivering men in threadbare coats and a sign that read HOT MEALS ONE CENT. I reached into my coat's pocket to find a rudimentary map. It showed the loop's department store entrance, and a half mile ahead of me, its outer membrane, beyond which lay the present. The map was marked with an instruction to burn after reading, so I tossed it into a flaming barrel around which a group of ragged men were huddled. Starting to shiver myself, I ran.

After a few blocks I could feel the air begin to thin and tremble around me. A short distance later, I passed through the loop membrane, out of 1937 and back into the present. The air warmed and brightened instantly, and the buildings rose to towering heights.

I hailed a cab, gave the driver the address from the matchbook, and ten minutes later we pulled up outside a brick building wrapped in fire escapes. On the street level was a small Chinese restaurant—Hong's. There were ducks hanging in the window and a fringed red lantern above the door. I paid the cabbie, went inside, and asked a waiter for H. He looked confused, so I showed him the matchbook, and then he nodded and took me outside.

"Number four, around the back," he said, pointing to an alley. "Tell him rent is coming Wednesday."

There was a pay phone in the alley—a strangely old-fashioned thing in modern day New York, housed in a box with a door that folded open. The phone box stood between the back entrance to Hong's, where I could hear food frying and dishes clanking, and a door that led into a run-down apartment building lobby. I pushed it open and came into a room with mailboxes along one wall and two elevators on the other, one marked OUT OF ORDER.

Which floor? I pressed the elevator button, and as it dinged and the door slid open, I felt it—that prick in my gut when a hollow was close. The sensation could mean the hollow was in the building at that moment, or that it had come and gone so many times it had left a lasting trail. The hollow could only belong to H.

I got into the elevator and pressed the top floor button. The door creaked shut. The car began to rise.

As it climbed, I could feel the compass-point pain in my belly shifting—180 degrees straight up at first, then lower the higher I went. When I passed the fourteenth floor, it was nearly a level 90 degrees, so I hit the button for 15.

The car stopped. The door opened. Right away I noticed two things that seemed very wrong. The first was a trail of blood running down the middle of the hall. When I saw it, I looked down at my feet; the trail led to the rear corner of the elevator car, and a rapidly congealing puddle.

My chest began to pound. Someone was hurt, and hurt badly.

The second thing was that halfway down the long hall, there was no light. None at all. It wasn't simply dim. I couldn't see the walls, the floor, the ceiling. And my compass was pointing directly into the dark.

It meant Noor was here. Noor was here and something terrible had happened. I was too late.

I sprinted down the hall, following the trail of blood into the darkness. When I could no longer see my feet hitting the floor, I slowed a little and stuck out my arms, letting the pain in my stomach be my guide. I rounded a corner, stumbled over a box someone had left in the hall. After a few more strides into the dark, the compass swung sharply left, toward an apartment door.

It had been left open a crack, and through it I could see, finally, a sliver of light. I shouldered the door open. It was unexpectedly heavy, as if made from reinforced steel. I followed the light down a short hall, through a cramped kitchen piled up with dirty pots, into a den. A dingy warren festooned with potted plants and pervaded by a cloying-sweet smell.

Curled on a sofa in the corner was Noor. Her body filled the room with a soft orange glow. She wasn't moving.

I ran to her. Her hair was covering her face. I rolled her gently onto her back, squinting against the light that shone from inside her. I pressed two fingers to her neck. Her skin was hot to the touch. After a moment, I found an artery—and a pulse—and I breathed a sigh of relief.

A strange, keening wail sounded from across the room. I spun to look. H lay splayed on his back on an old Persian rug. His hollowgast sat astride him, one muscled tongue lashed around H's waist and the other two around his wrists. The thing looked like it was about to crack open his skull and eat his brain.

"Get away!" I shouted, and the wailing stopped as the hollow hissed at me.

It was not about to kill him, I realized. Its friend was dying.

It was *crying*.

I summoned a few words of hollowspeak to shoo the creature away. It hissed at me again, unwound its tongues reluctantly from H's wrists, and scuttled into the kitchen.

I crouched beside the old man. Blood had soaked through his shirt, his pants, and the carpet beneath him.

"H. It's Jacob Portman. Can you hear me?"

He sharpened. His eyes fixed on me.

"Damn it, son," he said, scowling, "you really don't follow orders for shit."

"We've got to get you to a hospital."

I began to slide my arms underneath him. He groaned in pain, and the hollowgast let out a howl from the kitchen.

"Forget it. I've lost too much blood already."

"You can make it. We just have to—"

He wrenched away from me. "*No!*" His voice and his arms were so strong that it shocked me, but then he collapsed back to the floor. "Don't make me sic Horatio on you. The whole neighborhood is crawling with Leo's guys. If I go out there again, it'll rain bullets."

Noor moaned from the corner. I looked over to see her shift on the couch, eyes still closed.

"She'll be okay," said H. "She got sleep-dusted pretty good, but she'll come out of it."

He winced, and his eyes went a little glassy.

"Water."

I sprang up to run to the kitchen, but before I could take three steps, a hollowgast tongue was already sliding through the air past me, wrapped around a sloshing glass. I helped H sit up while the hollow's tongue tipped the glass to his lips, marveling at the strange tenderness of it.

H finished drinking, and the hollow's tongue ferried the glass away and set it down on the coffee table. On a coaster.

"You've got him trained pretty good," I said.

"Should have by now," H replied. "Been together forty years. We're like an old married couple." He tipped his head to look down at himself. "God, they made Swiss cheese out of me." He coughed a mist of blood into the air.

The hollow groaned and bounced on its haunches. It had crept out of the kitchen and was crouched nearby, and its black eyes wept oily tears down its cheeks and onto a stained handkerchief tied around its neck.

I looked at H, and suddenly I wanted to cry, too. *It's happening again*, I thought, a sob forming in my chest. *I'm losing another one.*

I swallowed back the sob and managed to say, "What happened?"

"Should've been a piece of cake," he croaked. "A simple extraction. If it weren't for Horatio, who carried us both out of there, we'd all be Leo's prisoners now." He sighed. "Guess I got old."

"Why didn't you let me help you?"

"Couldn't risk you getting hurt," he said. He looked past me at the ceiling, picturing something. "Abe's special boy. Baby Moses in the reeds."

"What do you mean?" I said.

His head turned to Noor. "You can help Miss Pradesh now. I'm dying, so there's nobody else."

"What do I do? Where do we go?"

"Out of New York, for starters."

"We could go to Devil's Acre."

"No. The ymbrynes would only send her back to Leo. They don't know how important she is." He was fading, starting to mumble. "Neither does she."

"Why is she important?"

"You know, before she got dusted, she saved my ass about three times today? Thought I was supposed to be saving hers." He laughed weakly. "Too bad her lightbulb trick can't stop bullets."

His thoughts were running away from him. His eyes beginning to close.

I put my hand on his cheek, his rough beard, and forced him look at me. "H, why is she important?"

"I made a vow to your grandfather. Not to involve you."

"We're way past that now."

He nodded sadly. "I guess we are." He drew a shaky breath. "She's one of the seven whose coming was foretold."

Of all the things I thought he might say to me, that was not among them.

"One of the seven. Seven what?"

"They will be the emancipators of peculiardom. So says the *Apocryphon*."

"What is that? Some kind of prophecy?"

"Writings from long ago. Her birth signals the arrival of a new age. A very dangerous one." He grimaced in pain and shut his eyes. "That's why those people are hunting her."

"The ones with the helicopter and the black cars."

"The same," he said.

"They're one of the clans?"

"No. Much worse. A very old, very secret society of normals. Who want to subvert and"—he winced, sucking air through his teeth—"control us." He was losing his breath now, gasping between words. "No time for history lessons. Take the girl to V. She's the last of us. The last of the hunters."

"V," I said, my mind starting to reel. "From Abe's mission log. The one he trained himself."

"Yes. She lives in the big wind. Doesn't want to be found, so be careful. Horatio, the map is in the safe . . ."

The hollowgast grunted, loped over to the wall, and moved a picture aside to reveal a small safe. While Horatio spun the number wheel, I focused on H. I could feel him slackening.

I squeezed his hand. "H, I have to know something." He was slipping away, and the idea that this last, best link to my grandfather's secrets was about to be severed shook something loose in me. Something I'd been trying to bury since I heard it.

"Why would someone call my grandfather a murderer?"

H looked at me with new intensity. "Who said that to you?"

I leaned in close. He was shaking. I told him, quickly, about the insane things Leo had accused Abe of. Stealing his goddaughter. Killing people. Not just people—*kids*.

H might have said, *The wights made it all up*. He might have said, simply, *It's a lie*. But he didn't say either of those things.

He said, "So you know."

My vision blurred for a moment. And doubt, like a virus, began to spread through me. "What do you mean? What are you *talking about*?"

I had H by the shoulders. I was shaking him. The hollowgast screamed, whipped a tongue around my waist, and pulled me away from H. I was flung halfway across the room, skidding across the floor into the leg of a table.

A terrible fear had invaded me—that there had been truth to Leo's accusations. That this was my grandfather's secret: He had not been trying to protect me from a loss of normalcy, or from the hollows, or from some mysterious band of enemies in black cars. He had been protecting me from *himself*.

I picked myself up off the floor. The hollow was hissing at me, bent over H, blocking him from view. I commanded it in hollow-speak to move, but it was fighting me. Or maybe H and the hollow were *both* fighting me now.

I ran toward the hollowgast, yelling, *Go, go, let him go*—and it did, leaping away from H and up to the ceiling, where it clung to a light fixture with its tongues. I fixed, for a split second, on an odd detail: A forest of tree-shaped air fresheners suspended from the ceiling. To combat the smell, of course. Because the hollow *lived* here.

I knelt down over H. "I'm sorry." This time I didn't touch him. "Please. Tell me what he did."

"They fooled us. Seven times, they fooled us."

"Who? What?"

"The Society."

I was half listening. I only wanted to know one thing. "Did my grandfather *kill children*?"

"No. No."

"Did he *kidnap* them?"

"No." His face swam with pain—and what seemed like regret. "We thought"—he gasped for breath—"that we were saving them."

I sank back on my heels, suddenly light-headed. *He wasn't a killer. He wasn't a bad man.* I hadn't realized how much it had been weighing on me. The very notion.

"We did a lot of good," he said. "We also made some mistakes. But Abe's heart was always in the right place. *And he loved you very, very much*." His voice had diminished to a whisper.

A rush of tears stung my eyes.

"I'm sorry."

"Don't. Don't be." With the last of his strength, he touched my arm. "The torch is yours now. I'm just sorry there aren't more people to help you carry it."

"Thank you," I said. "I'll try to do you both proud."

"I know you will." He smiled. "Now, it's time." He looked up to the ceiling. "Horatio, come down here."

The hollow strained against my control.

"Let him come down," said H. "A long time ago I made this poor creature a promise, and it's got to be done before I die. Let him come."

I stood up, backed away, and let go. The hollowgast dropped to the floor.

"Come here, Horatio. I can feel myself going. Come here."

The hollow crept toward H. The old man tried to turn away from me.

"Don't look. I don't want this to be your last memory of me."

The hollowgast straddled H and sat on his chest. When I realized what was about to happen I tried to command the hollowgast to move—I shouted at the thing—but H was blocking me.

I could hear him whispering to the creature.

"You've been a real good boy, Horatio. Remember what I taught you. Now, go on."

The hollowgast whimpered, trembling.

"It's okay," H said gently, stroking the creature's clawlike hand. "I'll be okay."

I looked away as it happened, though I'll never forget the sound it made. When I looked back, his eyes were gone. The sockets looked like ripe plums with bites taken out of them. The hollowgast was chewing, and its shoulders were shaking, and it was making a noise that seemed caught between agony and ecstasy. After a minute it stood and turned slowly away, as if filled with shame.

"I forgive you," H said. "I forgive you, brother."

He seemed not to be speaking to the hollow, but to the air. To a ghost.

And then he was gone.

◆   ◆   ◆

The hollowgast and I stared at each other across H's body. I tried to gain control of it.

Sit down.

I had thought, if anything, it would be easier to control now that its master was dead. But my command had no effect.

I tried a second time, and then a third, with no results. I started planning ways to kill the thing, before it got a mind to come after my eyeballs next, and then Noor's.

The hollowgast ratcheted its jaws open all the way, reeled out its three tongues, and made a terrifying sound—a squeal so high-pitched I thought the windows might crack. I grabbed a brass paper-weight from a nearby table and steeled myself for a nasty fight.

But the hollowgast wasn't coming for me. It was stumbling backward, and after a few steps its back hit the wall and came to a stop. And then the dull, directional pain that told me where the hollow was at all times began, very rapidly, to fade. At the same time, the creature's tongues began to shrink. They shriveled and curled up and turned a deathly brown, and then they fell off, having withered like dead flowers.

The hollow was leaning against the wall with its head bowed and chest rising and falling as if it had just run a marathon. Then it collapsed to the floor, and its body began to shiver in the grip of a violent seizure.

I began to cross the room slowly, approaching it with careful, measured steps in case this was a trick. Then, as suddenly as they'd begun, the seizures stopped. At that same instant, the pain in my gut vanished.

The hollow began to stir. It turned its head and looked up at me. Its eyes were no longer black, weeping pools; now they were gray and lightening more by the second, gradually turning a pupil-less blank.

The creature was transforming into something else: It was becoming a wight. I watched it for a minute, queasy but fascinated, ready to bash its head in with the paperweight if I needed to.

Its body began to squirm. The movement seemed involuntary, like its organs were metamorphosing inside its chest cavity. Its breathing, which had been wet and ragged like a hollowgast's, quieted and became regular. It was almost like witnessing a birth.

It sat up and looked at me.

I took a step backward, gripped by a sudden idea. This creature had been H's constant companion for years. It had seen and overheard all sorts of things. And now it was almost human. What might it remember, if it could remember anything at all? How much of its past life as a hollowgast did a wight retain? How quickly did its memories fade?

"Say something," I commanded it. "Speak."

It just stared at me. Didn't even grunt. Maybe wights were born like livestock animals, able to stand and even to run, but mute, knowing nothing.

It reached out its arm, steadied itself against the wall, and rose slowly to its feet. It shuffled a short distance to an end table and ripped the tablecloth away. I thought for a moment it was going to tie the cloth around its waist—as if the creature had suddenly realized it was naked, and felt shame—but instead it hobbled to H, knelt beside him, and settled the cloth over his face.

That meant it remembered something: H had been its master.

"Can you speak?" I said. "I want to hear your voice."

It turned to look at me, its face slack, swaying slightly on its feet. Its mouth fell open. A sound came out.

"Ehhhhhhhhh."

A moan, not a word. But it was better than nothing.

"Yes," I said. "What's your name?"

It rocked its head from side to side. It was trying mightily to form words, but there seemed to be a great fog clouding its brain.

It opened its mouth again. Sucked in a breath.

A scream shattered the silence. Noor was sitting up now and terrified, her eyes going from the wight to me to H, dead under his shroud.

"It's all right!" I shouted. "Everything's fine!"

But my strained tone and everything before her contradicted that. Now that the hollow was transforming, it could be seen by anyone. She had woken suddenly into a terrifying scene and the light inside her, which had been pulsing gently while she was asleep, was now a sharp and brightening star rising up the column of her throat. I moved toward her, repeating that she wasn't in danger, but she was shaking her head and couldn't seem to speak. She looked afraid. Not of me or the wight or the dead man—but of the thing inside her she didn't know how to stop. She was a brand-new peculiar and couldn't fully control her ability yet.

I flung myself to the floor and covered my head with my arms. Through split fingers I saw Noor grip the sofa and turn away from me. Like a sneeze made of light, an explosion came out of her nose and mouth: a cone-shaped jet-engine exhalation that roared through the air and blasted into the kitchen. The walls, the floor, the whole apartment shook. A hot pressure wave blew over me, singeing the fine hairs on the back of my neck. There was an all-encompassing din of tile cracking and dishes breaking and metal warping, and the sudden, dazzling glare of the blast forced my eyes shut.

When it had dimmed again, I raised my head. There was a new light in the room—not the reddish-orange glow that had emanated from Noor, but daylight streaming through an open window. Smoke was pouring out of the kitchen. The half hollow was nowhere to be seen. The blast's recoil had sent Noor flying over the couch and onto the floor, where I could hear her groaning.

"Noor?" I sat up slowly. "Are you hurt?"

"My head's killing me," I heard her say, and then her face appeared from behind the couch. "Otherwise . . ." She glanced down at herself. "No holes." Smoke wafted from her lips as she spoke. "You?"

"I'm okay," I said. "I don't know if you remember me, but—"

"Jacob." She stayed behind the couch, watching me. "What are you doing here?"

I sat up a little straighter. "I came to help you."

"That hasn't been working out so well." She looked at H and

winced. "For anyone." She let her face fall onto the couch. "I keep telling myself none of this is happening," she said into the cushions. "But I can't seem to wake up from the nightmare." She looked up at me. "Damn. You're still here."

"It's not a dream," I said. "I went through the same thing just a few months ago. I know exactly what you're feeling."

"I'm sure you don't," she said. "Just tell me what the hell is happening."

"That would take hours, but the CliffsNotes version is: Bad people want to get their hands you; I'm one of the good guys; and we need to get you out of New York as quickly as possible."

"You don't even know me. Why are you helping me?"

"It's a little hard to explain, but it's kind of the family business." I glanced behind me at H. "Also, I made a promise."

"Does anything you say ever make sense?"

"It'll start to." I stood up and went to her. "Can you walk?"

She grabbed the arm of the couch and put her weight on it as she stood, then took a step.

"Looks like it," she said.

"How about run?" I asked.

She wobbled a little, then sat heavily on the cushions. "Still getting my strength back," she said. "And where are we running to, exactly?"

"To find someone named V. She used to work with H and my grandfather. That's all I know."

She laughed and shook her head. "This is crazy."

"It always is. You'll get used to it."

There was a noise from behind us, and we both turned to see the rounded, white back of the thing that had formerly been a hollowgast but was not yet quite a wight. It was crouched in the window like a gargoyle, gripping the frame with its hands. Its body was aimed toward the street, as if it were about to jump.

Noor recoiled into the cushions.

"His name is Horatio," I said. "You couldn't see him before, but he was always by the old man's side."

"Eeeeeee," the half hollow said, turning to look at us over its shoulder. It seemed to be trying to speak. "Sssssssss . . . iiiiiiicks."

"Six! Is that what you said?" I took an excited step toward it, and it gave a squeal of warning and started to let go.

I froze and raised both hands. "Don't!"

It looked both newborn and unfathomably old. And so, so tired.

It opened its mouth again.

"Deeeeeeee," said the half hollow.

Noor sat forward on the couch. "Was that a D?"

"Fie . . . vuh."

"Five," I said.

I looked at Noor, excited. "It's talking to us!"

"They sound like grid coordinates," said Noor. "E-six. D-five. Like on a map."

Like on a Map of Days.

"In the storm," said the half hollow in a high, tremulous voice. It could talk!

"In the heart . . . of the storm."

"What is?" I said. "What's in the heart of the storm?"

"The one you seek."

It lifted one hand from the window and pointed at the wall. The wall with the safe in it, which was now hanging open.

I got up and ran to it. The wind from Noor's blast had blown off the door, and the floor was strewn with papers: a money clip stuffed with bills; a single photograph; a book; and an old, worn-looking map. I bent down and picked up the photograph. It was a black-and-white snapshot of a little town with a threatening sky and the black funnel of a tornado bearing down in the distance.

The heart of the storm. In the big wind.

I held the photo up. "Is this where we're supposed to find V?"

I looked back to find the window empty, and where the half hollow had been a moment earlier there was just a curtain blowing in the breeze.

I turned to Noor. "What happened?"

She was on her feet, halfway to the window, eyes wide. "He just . . . *let go*."

Voices were shouting from the street below. Noor rushed over to look.

"Don't!" I hissed. "They could see you!"

She caught herself too late and ducked down below the window. "I think they just did."

"It's fine. We'll find a back way out."

I gathered the map, the money, and the photo, and met Noor under the window. We were both in a crouch, our knees touching, a breeze tousling our hair.

"Are you ready?" I said.

"No." But she looked unafraid, challenging me with her eyes.

"Do you trust me?"

"Hell, no."

I laughed. "We can work on that."

I offered her my hand.

She took it.

A MAP OF DAYS

PROLOGUE